TW

GUNS OF MONTANA

"We, the jury, find the defendent, the Crow Broken Leg, guilty of murder, as charged by the prosecution."

Those were the words that would have sent an innocent man to a hangman's rope if Judge Lemanuel Bates hadn't smelled a set-up. Together with his sidekick Tobacco Jones, Bates was determined to save Broken Leg.

But in the violent Old West, the only men who could see that justice was served were the ones who had a ready six-shooter and an appetite for blood — men like Judge Bates and Tobacco.

CALLAHAN RIDES ALONE

Callahan rode up to Montana with a belt full of gold, ready to buy a ranch and settle down. But there were people who didn't even want him to pass through, much less stay.

They wanted his gold, though, and they figured they could take it and then run him off the range.

But they hadn't counted on what it would be like to tangle with a Texan. Callahan wasn't ready to leave...and nobody was going to make him!

BY THE TWO-TIME WINNER OF *THE SPUR AWARD* LEE FLOREN

Other *Leisure Books* by Lee Floren:

Triple Western

**RENEGADE RIFLES/BUCKSKIN
CHALLENGE/GUN QUICK**

Double Westerns

**NORTH TO POWDER RIVER/THE GRINGO
SADDLES NORTH/GAMBLER WITH A GUN
GAMBLER'S GUNS/BOOTHILL BRAND
WYOMING GUN LAW/FIGHTING RAMROD
TRAIL TO HIGH PINE/
        WEST OF THE BARBWIRE
BROOMTAIL BASIN/TRAIL TO GUNSMOKE
THE BUSHWHACKERS/
        RIDE THE WILD COUNTRY
SCATTERGUN GRASS/DOUBLE CROSS RANCH**

GUNS OF MONTANA/
CALLAHAN RIDES ALONE
LEE FLOREN

LEISURE BOOKS　　**NEW YORK CITY**

A LEISURE BOOK®

September 1992

Published by

Dorchester Publishing Co., Inc.
276 Fifth Avenue
New York, NY 10001

GUNS OF MONTANA Copyright © MCMLXXX by Lee Floren

CALLAHAN RIDES ALONE Copyright © MCMLXXVII by Lee Floren

The name "Leisure Books" and the stylized "L" with design are trademarks of Dorchester Publishing Co., Inc.

Printed in the United States of America.

GUNS OF MONTANA

One

Although summer-time is short in Wyoming, in this particular year it seemed to die a premature death. By September first the wind was chilly; already cottonwoods and boxelders were ready to shed golden leaves. The wind made sounds in the eaves of Judge Lemanuel Bates' chambers that seemed to prophesy a cold winter.

"Take that pot if you can, Bates." Tobacco Jones spread his cards on the table.

"What have you got?"

The postmaster bit from his plug of Horseshoe. "That wind's enough to drive a man crazy, Bates. You've looked at them cards long enough. Cain't you read?"

"I can read, friend."

Tobacco Jones chewed, long jaw working. He was not looking at the stack of chips, but his gaze was seeking the outside through the window. Finally he said, "I wish to Christmas that jury'd come in with a verdict."

"Your pot, Tobacco."

The postmaster absently raked in the chips and sorted them as Judge Lemanuel Bates dealt another hand. The judge's black robe was draped across the back of a chair, where he had left it more than twenty-four hours ago. Judge Bates squinted at his cards.

"Bet five, Jones."

"Call you an' raise you ten."

"You're reckless, friend."

Sheriff Whiting, a lanky, string-bean type of individual, stuck his head in the door with, "How's the game, men?"

"Fair," Tobacco Jones grunted.

Judge Bates said, "Luck's running against me, sheriff. Any news from the jury room?"

"They still can't agree, I reckon. The bailiff looked in a minute ago an' them jurors is still arguin'."

The judge consulted his big watch. "Almost four o'clock. I was in hopes the verdict would come in before it was too late for today's session. I'll take that raise, friend, and check it to you."

Tobacco spread out his cards, looked at the judge's hand, said, "By golly, fer onct you take me, Bates. Wish there was some way to hurry up that danged jury. Why does juries take so long? A prisoner is either innercent or guilty, ain't he? Then why does they argue that-a-way?"

"An unanswerable question," Judge Bates replied, handing his postmaster the deck of cards. "A question that has been debated for years in legal circles, and as yet unanswered or solved."

Sheriff Whiting said, "See you later, men," and his lanky neck pulled his ugly head out of the door. Above the shrillness of the wind in the eaves they heard his boots go down the corridor. Then the wind and distance killed the rap of his heels.

Tobacco leaned back, looked at his cards, and

then at Judge Bates. "You figger this Injun is guilty, Bates, or is he not guilty?"

"What Indian do you mean?"

Tobacco snorted, nostrils dilated. "Now don't play that dumb stuff, Bates. You know danged well what Injun I mean. This Injun you just held trial on, the one the jury is debatin' about. Is Broken Leg guilty of murder, or ain't he? What'd you think?"

"Deal a hand of stud this time, huh?"

"Bates, I asked you a question, an' I expect an answer."

"Stud this time, instead of draw?"

"Stud it'll be, Bates. I'm still waitin' for an answer."

Judge Bates looked at his hole card. Sometimes his partner got too impetuous; this trait, though, seemed to be born in Tobacco Jones. He had hoped that the jury would bring in a verdict of not guilty against Broken Leg. For a week—sitting as a Federal judge—he and the jury had heard testimony. Now the case was in the hands of the jury and they were awaiting the verdict.

The Indian Agency up at Spotted Pony—north across the line in the Territory of Montana—had charged Broken Leg with the murder of a white man, one Charley Peterson. Because of the excitement, the case had been transferred from Spotted Pony to Cowtrail, and Judge Lemanuel Bates, acting in the capacity of a Federal judge, had presided over the case, transferred on a change of venue plea by the Federal judge in that section of Montana Territory.

Skilfully the Indian Agency office had presented evidence showing that Broken Leg, a Crow of about thirty summers, had killed one Charley Peterson, producing everything in evidence against the

Crow except the body of Peterson, who had, because of sanitary reasons, been buried already.

The Government attorney had presented a well-balanced, well-presented case. As for that matter, the attorneys appointed to represent Broken Leg had also conducted a good defense for their client. But, in Judge Bates's opinion, the prosecuting attorneys had done the better job.

The prosecuting attorneys had proven all but two points: had Broken Leg really murdered the white man, Charley Peterson? and why had the Crow murdered the white man?

To answer the first question would have required a full confession from Broken Leg, and to the second he said he had fought with Charley Peterson because Peterson had broken into his lodge and tried to steal his moccasins and other clothing, all of which made no sense.

Judge Lemanuel Bates had listened carefully, trying to find the real motivation behind the fight between Broken Leg and Peterson. According to Broken Leg, he and Peterson had fought that night, when he had caught the white man trying to rob his lodge. He had not killed Peterson, he maintained.

The prosecuting attorney had not pressed that point, but had pointed out that the next morning Peterson had been found dead in the back door of a saloon, dead from a knife wound. Where else had he received that knife slash except in the fight in the lodge with Broken Leg?

And it didn't make sense, the attorneys declared: What man in his right mind would try to rob an Indian of his clothing? What did an Indian's clothes consist of, anyway? Moccasins, buckskin pants, buckskin shirt. Yes, and maybe a beaded band, for

8

around his head?

Now who, in his right mind, would try to steal such junk? And Charley Peterson had been in full possession of his mental faculties, hadn't he? Anyway, witnesses to that effect had testified long and faithfully, so long, in fact, that Judge Bates had found himself dozing on the judicial bench.

"Me no kill him. Me fight him, he break loose— him run like I chase him. He no git my moccasins."

"Your moccasins?"

Judge Bates had interposed at this point. Moccasins, he emphasized, meant clothes to the Crow Indians. All Broken Leg meant was that, "He no get my clothes." Or, as the jurist pointed out, Peterson never got a chance to rob Broken Leg's lodge.

"Thank ye, judge."

"No comments from the prisoner, please."

The trial had been more or less a puzzle to Broken Leg, from beginning to end. Why go to all this just because a white man died? Did thousands of redskins fight Custer and kill him and his men and why no trial after that? Yes, and many a redskin got killed by white man, and still no trial? Why try a red for killing a white, when it meant defense of his wigwam?

Those were points Broken Leg could not understand, and their perplexity had been written across his dusky, long-nosed face all during the trial. And Judge Bates, for lack of something to do, sat on the judicial bench and pondered on why Charley Peterson had tried to rob an Indian as poor as Broken Leg.

That didn't make sense.

Unknown to the Government attorneys, Judge Lemanuel Bates and Tobacco Jones knew Broken

9

Leg's old father, the Crow Red Beaver. They also knew Red Beaver as a notorious evader of the truth, a rather sly old gentleman of about eighty summers, maybe more. According to Red Beaver, he had thrown his counting-stick away, sometime before Custer got his on the Little Bighorn, north of here in Montana Territory.

Neither of the partners had known Broken Leg as well as they knew Red Beaver. But both of them had known Charley Peterson. When they had run into that mess of trouble on their Double Cross Ranch, up to the northeast, Judge Bates had run into Charley Peterson, on the trip he had made into Deadwood, in the Black Hills of Dakota Territory.

The Deadwood judge, Jurist Mark Hannock, had told Judge Bates he had given Charley Peterson a floater out of Deadwood, at that time a tough mining-town. Later Tobacco Jones had met Peterson in Sundance, the trading-post where the Double Cross outfit bought supplies. Peterson had drifted into the cowtown from Deadwood, immediately had got into trouble, and the Sundance marshal had put the run on him. From there Peterson had evidently gone into Buffalo or Sheridan, then headed north into Montana.

"Maybe they're givin' him a floater outa heaven, Bates?"

Judge Bates played a card. "Charley Peterson never got to the Good Land, friend. He had a black record, so the judge of Deadwood told me: robbery, maybe a murder that had never been proved."

"Wish that jury'd come in."

"It'll report in time."

"Yeah, lotsa time, Bates. I hope they turn that Indian lose, I do. Me, I don't figger that Injun did nothin' much wrong."

"My pot, Jones."

"My luck has turned, Bates."

"Don't step on your jaw." Judge Bates took a nip from his jug which sat beside him.

"Some judge you are," Tobacco scoffed. "Sittin' on the bench of justice with whiskey on your breath."

"You never have seen me under the influence of whiskey, have you?"

"No. . . ."

"Then, sir—"

Sheriff Whiting looked in. "The jury's filin' in, your honor. The bailiff says they've got a verdict at last."

Whiting's ugly face left the door, and Tobacco helped Judge Bates don his judicial robe. The judge grumbled and said, "Terrible a learned man has to wear one of these things just because years ago— centuries ago, in fact—some Englishman decided a judge should wear black. Small wonder they don't still cram wigs on our heads!"

"You'd look good in a wig, Bates. Turn aroun', so I kin button it— You in a wig— That'd be really somethin'."

"Your laugh is worse than a jackass' snarl, Jones."

They got the robe settled around the jurist's thick shoulders, and the judge got his jug under the flowing garment with the remark that a judge got a break in one way—his robe was so loose he could hide his whiskey-jug under it. To this, Tobacco scowled: he was an ardent foe of strong drink. But, for once, he held his tongue.

"You're all set, Bates. Wait a minute, did I strap up your corset?"

"No remarks, sir."

The judge went down the hall, followed by

11

Tobacco. The bailiff met His Honor at the door to the court-room and went ahead, proclaiming the audience to rise. With the people standing, Judge Bates crossed the platform, took his seat and his gavel.

"Hear ye, hear ye! The first Federal Court of the Territory of Wyoming is now in order, Judge Lemanuel Bates presiding. Sit ye down, people."

There was the creaking of chairs, and then the sounds died out before the wave of interest. By this time the jury was seated, the bony foreman holding his slip of paper.

"Sheriff Whiting, bring in the prisoner, please."

"Yes, Your Honor."

Necks turned as Broken Leg hobbled in, followed by Sheriff Whiting and three deputies sworn in for the court-term. Judge Bates sighed, realized that this was the last case on his docket, and then looked at Broken Leg, who now stood before his Bench.

Pity was a human trait that Time had almost pulled away from Judge Lemanuel Bates. He had sat on his Bench—and on other Benches—and he had heard the sordidness of life and seen that sordidness parade past in front of him. But he had to feel pity for the Crow Indian, Broken Leg.

Broken Leg's thin, sun-bleached face showed only one element: puzzlement. With his limited knowledge, he did not fully comprehend this environment. He had fought a man to protect his lodge, and that man had died from the fight—and now, for some reason, the Great Father in Washington wanted his life.

That didn't make sense, and Broken Leg's face showed this.

Judge Bates intoned the charge against the

Crow. He summed up the case briefly, then asked, "Do you, sir, think you had a fair trial?"

"What you say?"

The judge repeated the question.

Suddenly Broken Leg smiled. "Me, I free now? I go back to my lodge an' squaw?"

Judge Bates saw his words were getting nowhere. Sheriff Whiting scowled, went to spit tobacco-juice, then realized his position and swallowed it, instead. Tobacco Jones, sitting in the front row, shook his head gently, and Judge Bates caught the gesture.

"Bailiff, receive the verdict from the jury, please. Foreman of the jury, you have reached a verdict, I understand."

"We have, Your Honor."

"One moment before you take the verdict, Bailiff. Jury men, you understand the instructions, I believe. If you have found the prisoner innocent of this charge, he shall be instantly dismissed and transported to his reservation. But if he is found guilty, you have two verdicts to reach, gentlemen."

"We understand that, Your Honor," the foreman said.

Judge Bates said, "Elaborate, sir?"

The foreman repeated the Court's instructions. If a verdict of guilty were reached the jury could recommend mercy and this would forestall the death penalty. But if the jury did not recommend mercy the Court, by law, was required to sentence the prisoner to death on the gallows.

"That is right, sir," Judge Bates said.

"Then, sir, we have the verdict."

Judge Bates said, "Bailiff, take it and hand it to me."

Somewhere, out in the audience, a woman

13

screamed, and then was silent. Wooden-faced, Judge Bates watched two men carry her outside. This was the part of judgeship he did not like. This was the suspense, the terror, the horror of it all.

The slip met his hand, folded four times; the hand of the bailiff withdrew. Judge Bates couldn't help but look down at Broken Leg's childish, red face. Then, he saw the terror—the naked, deadly terror—in the Crow's dark eyes. He had to take his gaze away.

He thought, I wish I had a drink.

He found his fingers opening the verdict. Only the jury seemed composed, and even there one man had his head down on his arms on the railing. Sheriff Whiting watched the judge, so did the bailiff, and beyond them Tobacco Jones sat and watched, still chewing.

And Judge Bates thought, He'll chew tobacco when they check him through the Pearly Gates.

He had the paper open, and the words made reality. He read the verdict silently, then handed it to the bailiff, who cleared his throat.

"We, the jury, find the defendant, the Crow Broken Leg, guilty of murder, as charged by the prosecution."

For the first time in his life, Judge Lemanuel Bates saw an Indian buck faint.

Two

When you leave Cowtrail, Wyoming, and head for Spotted Pony, Montana, you head northwest out of Cowtrail. You cross the Powder River near the site of old Fort Reno and you head northwest still toward Crazy Woman Creek.

"You'd be an easy man to trail, Bates."

"And what, sir, brought on that sudden summation?"

"What'd you mean? Talk American."

"You know full well what I mean, Tobacco. You're just playing dumb. What brought on that question—or rather, that surmise?"

"All a man would have to do to trail you, Bates, is to check at the saloons. Sooner or later some bartender would tell him about a stocky, heavy-set gent that had come in an' bought not a bottle of hard-stuff, but had bought a jug of whiskey. An' the gink'd say, 'A jug of likker, eh? That's the hairpin I'm trailin'.'"

"Thanks, Jones."

Tobacco spat. Over in the distance a buck antelope stood on a small hill and watched them.

Finally Tobacco asked, "What are you going to

do with that jug when you hit the Crow Reservation? They won't let even a federal judge tote whiskey on that Injun ground."

"You ask too many questions."

"Reckon that's a habit I got," Tobacco had to admit.

They forded Crazy Woman Creek at the point where the Indians tangled with the whites in 1866. They both rode mules and they had a pack-mule along. The judge fished the creek for a while and caught a catfish. They had him for supper and Tobacco said, "Never cut no Injun sign all day, I didn't." He was using a small fire though, one that didn't smoke.

Judge Bates doubted if any redskins were off their reservations. "Custer took a heck of a beating a few years ago, but it showed the redskins they weren't as big as they figured, because General Miles sure put the Sioux on the run."

"Custer sure did it the hard way," Tobacco muttered.

From Cowtrail to Buffalo, across country, is about seventy-five miles, and after two days on the trail, Judge Bates got his jug filled in Buffalo. He rode out to Fort McKinney, gave his greetings to the commandant—they had fought side by side in the Civil War—and then he and Tobacco headed due north, past the site of the Fetterman Massacre, and noon of the second day found them north of what is now Sheridan, Wyoming, and inside the territorial line of Montana.

"One more day of travel, Bates?"

"One more day, and then Spotted Pony."

Tobacco turned the trout in the frying pan. Down in the Little Big Horn, trout leaped for flies in the cool

16

of the evening. Judge Bates sat with his back against a rock, jug beside him. He was in a leisurely mood.

"Look at this beautiful valley, Tobacco. Cottonwoods and boxelders, and choke-cherry trees laden with ripe berries, and yet man fights and kills. Yonder stream is filled with trout waiting for the hook and pan."

"I've thought that over too, friend. You're still behind me."

"Them redskins didn't cause this trouble, Bates; you kin lay it at the door of the greedy whites. How would you like to be Sittin' Bull an' how'd you like to have the Black Hills stole from you because of gold in 'em? You'd holler an' go on the warpath, too. Mind them buffaler in the Black Hills? That's buffaler country an' them Siouxs had to have buffaler for tepees, for buckskin, for chuck."

"I'd fight for it," the judge conceded.

"Uh-huh, an' so would I, if'n I was a Sioux. Wonder how Broken Leg is gettin' along in his cell about now? Nice you gave his lawyers an appeal, Bates. How come they ask you for one?"

"Very simple. Off the record I asked them to appeal. I assured them that regardless how much of a howl the opposing Government attorneys would make I would give them an appeal."

"You figure Broken Leg is innercent?"

"I don't know for sure whether he is innocent or guilty. But I still believe that jury—had it had a nickel's worth of brains—could not have returned a death penalty on such flimsy evidence."

"Flimsy?"

"Never at any time did the prosecuting attorneys prove conclusively that Broken Leg killed Charley

17

Peterson."

"Broken Leg admits he knifed Peterson."

"Knifing a man, sir, is not killing him."

Tobacco put two trout on each tin plate, put some spuds on each plate also, then handed one to Judge Lemanuel Bates, who fell to with his fork.

Tobacco said, "I ain't so sure about this Injun bein' innercent, Bates. Knifin' a man is a serious offense, in itself."

"But one not great enough to send a man plummeting through a trapdoor on a gallows, friend. Once a noose breaks a man's neck you can't keep him alive, even if later evidence proves him innocent of his charged crime."

Tobacco chewed thoughtfully. "Well, look at it this way, Bates. We've rid three days on bumpy mules. That pack-mule has danged near pulled the kak off my mount, he's that hard to lead. An' what does this Injun mean to me an' you, anyway?"

"I've been expecting that, Tobacco. He's a fellow human and to him the most precious thing he has is his life. You and I have some spare time on our hands. We needed to go fishing, anyway."

"I'd hate to see an innercent man hung, too."

"Yes, and we both know his sire, ol' Red Beaver."

Tobacco had to chuckle, despite his mouth being full of fish and potatoes. "Bates, that's a joke, fella! Ol' Red Beaver ain't nobody's friend, an' you know it."

"He's a man's friend if he figures he can work a man out of something," the jurist corrected.

Tobacco was full of trout and spuds, he had plenty of chewing tobacco, he had a good partner and fish jumped in the Little Big Horn. He leaned back on the dried grass.

"I'm glad I come along, Bates."

Judge Bates laid down his plate and knife. "Remember, sir, we came to this section not to **help** the Indian Broken Leg, but to find out whether or not he really killed Charley Peterson, and if he did kill him—why he killed him?"

"In other words, Bates, if Broken Leg is guilty, to the gallow he goes; if innocent, he will have evidence granting him a new trial?"

"Well said, sir."

Tobacco laced his hands behind his head and watched the clouds move lazily along. "Where will we start, Bates?"

"In Spotted Pony, of course."

Tobacco sat up, mouth opened a little, head cocked. "Mebbeso I'm wrong again, Bates, but it seems to me I heard hoofs in the distance. You hear them?"

The jurist listened. He heard the splash of rippling water, the scolding of a jay, and the crackle of the dying fire.

"No hoofs, Tobacco."

"They stopped, Bates."

They were both on their feet. Both knew that there still were a few "reservation jumpers" in the Crows that were not against lifting an occasional patch of hair from a white man, if they could get that white-man unawares with their battle-axes.

Some of the Crows still smarted under the fact they were penned in on a reservation. And Judge Bates hardly blamed them. Once they had ridden this wide country, their borders only limited by the power of the Blackfeet and Sioux and Cheyennes. But now they were penned in on Spotted Pony Reservation. . . .

"You sure of your ears, Jones?" The judge's

breathing was coarse.

"I'm sure, Bates."

The judge said, "You swing to the left, partner. I'll take to the right. Mind that lightning-struck cotton-wood tree back up along the river?"

"About a half-mile?"

"That's the one. We meet there. Careful, Jones."

"Same to you, judge."

They left their mules picketed in the clearing. They were a good decoy. Maybe the person was a trapper, aiming to steal some mules. Some of these buckskin men, the judge knew, were more thieving then the most thieving Indians.

But the judge, through past experience, had built a great faith in his partner's ability to hear. His ears, he knew, did not have the keenness that the ears of Tobacco Jones possessed. If Tobacco had heard a horse, he had heard one—if he had heard that bronc stop, then a rider had dismounted. For a loose horse, grazing through the brush, did not stop for long: he nibbled on grass a while, then sauntered on. The judge went along a path made by deer going down to water, and he had his rifle over his arm.

He stopped, listened. And he thought, "Wish that danged bluejay would stop that yowling." The bluejay was down along the creek. Maybe he was scolding the intruder. Bluejays had that habit.

The judge worked that way.

Once he got entangled in a wild roseberry bush. Patiently he worked his coat loose of the sharp thorns, once severely sticking his thumb. This drew a light oath from him and he pulled his thumb into his mouth.

Standing there, he listened. Maybe Tobacco was

wrong, at that. But still— Then he heard a movement to his right. Evidently somebody was circling their camp looking it over.

He followed the sound, trying to make no noise himself. And, despite his bulk and weight, he succeeded. He moved his rifle ahead of him, so he and it would take less space in the brush; he would stop and listen, and now the sounds of the intruder were clearer and closer.

Then, he found the intruder's bronc. He was a bay and brush almost hid him; he had no saddle but a rawhide thong ran around his jaw for a bridle. That thong told the judge one thing, "A Crow." The horse did not snort, but looked at him with no interest.

Common sense told Judge Lemanuel Bates that if he stuck around close to the bronc its rider would eventually return to him. But he decided he would keep between the intruder and his horse, thereby shutting off the Crow from his mount and possible flight.

Buckbrush was high, but he came to a small clearing. Ahead of him he saw the Crow: the buck's back was to him and the redskin carried a rifle. His back was broad and he squatted in the brush, and the judge could only see his back. The Indian wore a buckskin jacket.

The judge came in, then. The Indian heard him just as he closed in, and the Indian whirled, raising the rifle. The broad, dead-pan face showed nothing, and they crashed to the ground.

"Tobacco, over here!"

"Comin', pard!"

Tobacco came on the run, threshing through buckbrush. When he hit the clearing Judge Bates sat on the Indian, who lay on his back. The judge had a queer, lopsided grin.

"What's so funny, Bates?"

"Look at this Indian, Jones."

Tobacco stared down. Then he started to chew again, and with the motions of his jaws a smile began to form on the corners of his tobacco-stained mouth. And the smile widened.

Tobacco said, "Get up, Bates. Don't you know it ain't perlite to sit on a woman's back, even if that woman is a **Crow squaw**!"

Three

The Crow squaw was mad. Her broad, almost homely face broke at the mouth, and she cursed them in Crow, Gros Ventres, and a smattering of the Sioux tongue. Judge Bates laughed until tears came to his eyes. Tobacco Jones grinned and giggled.

"He—hurt your—spine, squaw?"

"You shut big mouth, jackass white man."

Tobacco spat out his chew. "She kin talk U.S., anyway," he said. "Who are you, lady, an' what's your name?"

"Yes," the judge cut in. "Who in hades are you?"

"Me Running Deer. Me squaw to Broken Leg."

The Cowtrail pair exchanged glances.

"You two—you know Broken Leg, my husband?"

"We've heard of him," the judge admitted. There was a lot here he did not understand. Therefore he aimed to play ignorant for a spell to see which way the wind blew.

"What'd you mean by jumpin' two white men?" Tobacco asked, winking at Judge Bates.

The squaw said she had been heading for Cowtrail to see her husband, who was in jail there. Evidently she did not know that Broken Leg had been sentenced to die on the gallows and that was logical, for word had no way of getting to her. The Government attorneys, instead of reporting back to Spotted Pony after the trial, had headed for Leavenworth, Kansas, there to get ready to protest the chance of a new trial for Broken Leg.

"You hear about my husband?"

Judge Bates said, "Yes, we heard about the trial when we were in Buffalo, at Fort McKinney."

"What the trial, he say?"

The judge, lying magnificently, told her that her husband had been acquitted, but had had to go with the Government attorneys to Leavenworth, Kansas, and, after his business with the Government had been finished at that point, he would return to Spotted Pony.

"No need I go to Cowtrail, then. He come back, me glad. Papooses, they glad, too."

"How many papooses?"

"Me got four." She held up four fingers. "Where you men, you go, huh?"

The judge said, "Spotted Pony."

"I maybe see you there. Thanks for the words—the good words."

Judge Bates asked, "Why did you try to sneak up on us, squaw?"

She regarded them with dark, bland eyes. "I know but you bad white mens. I think maybe you take Broken Leg back to home. Still, me afraid. So I try to—what you say—sneak in?"

The judge allowed that was a reasonable precaution. Some whites, he knew, had not been very considerate in the way they treated a lone squaw away from the protection of her men.

"You sure—Broken Leg, he come soon?"

"Yes."

"How you know, Heavy Man?"

The judge almost winced. His weight, to him, was a matter of some touchiness. The less he ate, the thicker became his waist. Tobacco blamed it on the whiskey the judge consumed but the judge blamed it only on middle-age.

"Can you keep a secret, Running Deer?"

"What him—a secret?"

The judge used a little sign language. He pointed to his ear, opened his mouth, and that meant somebody was going to tell her something. She nodded with great concern. The judge then drew his forefinger vertically across his lips and sealed them.

Running Deer broke into a wide smile. "Me, I keep my mouth sealed, mister white man."

The judge then introduced himself and Tobacco Jones. She was so happy to hear who they were that she got down on her knees. She took the judge's hand and rubbed it across her lips and said, "My mouth, he sealed now. You two come to help me?"

Tobacco Jones couldn't help it, but his throat got a little tight. He looked at the judge, then down at Running Deer. "Yeah, we come t'help you, Squaw. Now git up on your pins, 'cause you embarrass me."

"Nothing could embarrass you," Judge Bates breathed.

Tobacco glared at him, then spat.

Running Deer got on her feet. She held back her sobs. Judge Bates' voice took on a stern note.

"Did your husband knife Charley Peterson?"

"He knife him, yes."

"Did he kill Peterson?"

"That—me no know. Peterson, he run. He come at

25

night to rob lodge. He try to get off with moccasins."

"Did he?"

"No."

"Why did he try to rob you?"

This made her look away. "Peterson, he run away. Moonlight, me see him—me know him. Maybe he die later from Broken Leg's knife."

"You think so?"

A shake of the thick head. "No, me no think that. Peterson, he not hurt bad. Knife only cut on shoulder."

The judge knew the rest, and did not press her for details. For one solid week he had heard the details at the trial. The Crow marshal had found Peterson dead the next morning. He had died of knife wounds, so the reservation doctor had testified. Naturally, all signs pointed to Broken Leg, for Broken Leg dutifully had reported to the marshal his fight with Charley Peterson.

The judge repeated, "Why did Peterson try to rob you?"

Again he got no answer to this. This was the part that had puzzled him throughout the week of trial. Broken Leg had been very secretive on this point, too. All in all, why should Charley Peterson try to rob a few Crow Indians?

That was the weak point—the illogical point—of the whole thing. And this squaw did not seem to be able to put any light on this matter, either. And, for that matter, she did not want to disclose anything. Or did she know anything?

Judge Bates figured, just from her lack of desire to talk, that she knew the reason why Charley Peterson had tried to rob her lodge. For Running Deer seemed suddenly tongue-tied.

Tobacco said, "Squaw, tell us."

26

The brown, deep eyes went from the postmaster to Judge Lemanuel Bates, then swept across the timber, then to the ground.

"Me no know."

"I think you do," the judge corrected.

Tobacco had withdrawn from the field, leaving the questioning to his partner. He watched Running Deer like a weasel watches a rabbit.

The squaw turned and started away, then stopped. She looked at them again as if apprising them, trying to guess through their honesty.

"Maybe I tell you when you come to Spotted Pony."

The partners exchanged glances. The judge murmured, "Guess we'll have to let it rest at that, Jones," and Tobacco Jones nodded. The judge spoke to Running Deer. "All right, you may go."

"Me thank you again."

"You've thanked us enough."

She went to her horse.

Tobacco said, "Maybe I oughta help her git on that plug."

"She can mount that horse faster than you can," the judge grunted.

The squaw got on her pony, turned him, and rode north, down the river. Suddenly Tobacco sat down and laughed. The judge knew what prompted this mirth, and he shook his jug to verify its contents, scowling a little.

Tobacco said, "Dang it, Bates, that was funny. Here I round the corner an' you're settin' on this squaw. Couldn't you see she's got a dress on?"

"The bottom part of her," said the judge, "was hidden by brush. Laugh loud and long, you rude Rocky Mountain canary."

27

Tobacco realized he was not nettling the jurist. There is no point in teasing a person—or making fun of him—if he doesn't respond with anger. Therefore the Cowtrail postmaster sobered and scowled in deep thought.

"That deal about Peterson robbin' their tepee— That sure seems funny to me, Bates. I sure cain't see through thet a-tall."

The judge had to admit he was also in the dark. One thing was certain: evidently Broken Leg's tepee had contained something that Charley Peterson would give his life to get. But what was it?

"I sure ain't got no idea, Bates."

The judge was tired. He stretched out on the ground. "Maybe we are putting too much attention onto an irrelevant point, Jones. These Indians like to play mysterious and silent."

"Yeah, thet's a habit with them, 'specially these Crows."

The judge admired the sky. One thing about the sky: it was never the same. It was always changing, clouds moving here, then moving back. He wanted to take a nap, but fought off the lassitude and took his mind back to the present.

"You get around a Crow camp when those redskins like you or don't know you're around and you'll find them joking and laughing. This old saw about the wooden-faced warriors and dumb squaws belong to those boys who write this wild west stuff. But one thing is certain, Jones."

"Yeah. . . . An' thet, Bates?"

"Running Deer is evidently holding back some vital information. I can see her point, too: she's bossed by Broken Leg. She can add, that girl can: her mind works this way—'These men don't know

28

why Peterson tried to rob our lodge. That means that Broken Leg kept that a secret at his trial. That means he doesn't want anybody to know, so I'm not going to tell.'"

"That's the way it 'pears to me, Bates."

They decided to camp the night away on this spot. Water was close, their mules had grass, and if they did ride on they would get into Spotted Pony about midnight. "Better we head in tomorrow, Jones."

"Fer onct I agree with you."

The night was marked by brilliant moonlight. Dawn found them up and saw the lift of their campfire against the coolness of this high altitude. Tobacco squatted by the fire and said, "Feels like snow soon, Bates."

"You can't tell about Montana weather."

This prophecy completed, Judge Bates gave himself to his breakfast trout, his hotcakes, and his coffee. Usually he drank coffee without adding a snort of whiskey but this morning he spiked his java good.

"Want a snort, Jones?"

"Never," Tobacco retorted.

The judge drank, yawned. "Still sleepy from my trick at watch. That was a good idea you had for one of us to stand watch. But I'd still like to know why that fellow came snooping, knife in hand."

"They sure cotton to usin' knives aroun' here, don't they though? Me, I never did cotton to cold steel. Them bayonets in the war was enough for me. Lord, Bates, can a man ever fergit a war?"

"Never."

They killed their fire with water and the judge, using his hand as a funnel, poured the contents of his

29

whiskey-jug into half-point flasks he had obtained down at Fort McKenzie. This way he could transport his whiskey in on the reservation. Had he tried to tote in his jug it would have been spotted immediately but these flasks could be hidden in his saddlebags.

"Hope the marshal picks you up, Bates. Sure would look good for a federal judge to be arrested for smuggling whiskey in on a Federal Injun reservation."

"Crude, ugly humor, Jones. Try some other tactic, please?"

Neither was in a very good humor. They got saddles and Tobacco led the pack mule. After they had gone a mile the postmaster looked back at the mule with, "His load ridin' all right, Bates?"

Judge Bates rode over and inspected the mule's new burden. The man was thrown belly-down across the mule's back, hands tied to the off-rings of the pack-saddle's cinch, his feet tied to the near rings.

"He's ridin' all right."

The man didn't know he was on a mule, for the man was dead.

Four

The cockroach crawled across the rough plank floor. He crawled across the whiskery cheek of the dead man. He halted by the lobe of the man's right ear, then crawled on. The cockroach came back on the floor again.

A big boot came out, and the cockroach scooted to safety under the mopboard.

The marshal said, "Danged things. Must be a million of 'em here. Danged neart as many as at the resturaw."

Judge Bates said, "So this gent's name is Skunk Ferguson, eh? How come they call him Skunk? Surely he must have had a given name."

The marshal was a thick, short man. Smallpox had made craters in his red, ugly face.

"Done heard somebody onct call him Virgil," the marshal said.

Tobacco looked at Judge Bates. "I'd rather be called Skunk," the postmaster said.

The marshal said, "Gimme another bite off'n your chew, Jones," and then, to Judge Lemanuel Bates, "Tell me ag'in about findin' Skunk's body, will you. I want t'git it clear for my report."

31

The judge repeated his story. According to him they had been riding along the Little Big Horn and had come upon the body of Skunk Ferguson lying beside the trail.

"He was dead then, huh?"

"Very dead, marshal."

"Okay, Your Honor, continue."

"Well, Marshal Smith, it was this way—" Judge Bates continued with his lying. He and Tobacco had talked it over and had decided to not claim the dubious honor of killing Skunk Ferguson. The judge had not wanted to kill the man. But Ferguson had been caught sneaking up on their camp. The jurist had called to him and Skunk Ferguson, a total stranger to them, had turned with his gun talking. Luckily, his shots had missed, and Judge Bates had been forced to use his rifle.

"So, we took him into your office, marshal."

"You did the right thing." Marshal Smith scowled deeply. He was at least a quarterbreed, or else he could not have held down the job of marshal on the Spotted Pony Reservation. Evidently he had had a brush or two with schooling, for he did not speak a bad brand of English.

Tobacco chewed, leaving the discussion to Judge Bates.

"Wonder who killed him?" the marshal pondered.

"Perhaps he accidentally shot himself. We found a spent cartridge beside him on the ground, alongside his rifle."

"He was a friend of Charley Peterson's," the marshal said. "So Broken Leg was cleared. I'm glad to hear that."

"How did you find that out, marshal?"

The marshal said that Running Deer had told about her meeting with the judge and postmaster, and how she had ridden back to Spotted Pony to inform all within hearing distance that her husband had been freed.

Judge Bates gave this a moment of thought. He wondered if he had done right by lying in this manner to Running Deer. Sooner or later she would find out her husband was still in jail, waiting to see if his appeal to a higher court was successful. Or would she find that out?

Judge Bates' methodical, legally-trained mind gave this matter deep thought. Then he decided the squaw would probably not hear the truth. Three witnesses had been brought to Cowtrail to give testimony. But, right after testifying, they had returned to Spotted Pony.

They had not waited for the verdict.

The prosecuting attorneys had come out from Leavenworth, and would return there—they had no reason for going to Spotted Pony. One by one, the judge eliminated persons who might come to Spotted Pony and reveal that, instead of being acquitted, Broken Leg had drawn the death penalty.

By rights, nobody should come, and his fabrication was safe.

"Skunk Ferguson stuck around town all day yesterday," the marshal explained. "Onct I saw him talkin' with Runnin' Deer."

That gave the judge his clue. Skunk Ferguson had been a friend—a good friend, according to Marshal Smith—of the dead Charley Peterson. Had Skunk Ferguson, after talking with Running Deer, decided to ride out and ambush him and Tobacco, thereby hoping to make Charley Peterson sleep more soundly in his grave?

That was possible and probable.

It was simple. Ferguson and Peterson had been close friends. He, Judge Lemanuel Bates, had, according to Running Deer, turned loose Broken Leg. Ferguson, on hearing this, had ridden out to kill the judge who had turned loose the slayer of his best friend.

It had been done before, and undoubtedly it would be done again. And this thought drew Judge Bates' thick jowls into thick thought. For the first time he fully realized the danger he and Tobacco Jones faced on this Spotted Pony Reservation. And the maddening thing was this: Why were they in danger? What was behind all this?

"You have heard our story, Marshal Smith. Are you satisfied and are we free to go to breakfast?"

"I'm satisfied."

The Cowtrail partners went outside. Already word had got around Spotted Pony that they had packed in the body of Skunk Ferguson. Judge Bates looked at the blanket-bucks, sitting in front of the Trading Post. At the end of the street was the Agency buildings. These were brown-stained one-storey buildings, set in a square, and with lawns and trees around them. Over them flew the Stars and Stripes.

"Who is agent here?" Tobacco asked.

"John Miller, I believe."

Tobacco chewed. "Wasn't he agent over on Wind River, too? When they had thet trouble with the Shoshones a year or so ago?"

"The same man."

"You ever meet him?"

The judge said he had met John Miller once.

34

Traveling federal circuit judge, he had held court at Fort Washakie, the agency point for the Wind River Reservation.

"What kind of a gent is he, Bates?"

"He's a glad-hander," the judge replied. "Holds his job on political pull, and when the brains was dished out his bowl was awful small."

"Seems to me they's quite a bit of white men in this place, Bates. An' what are they doin' on a squaw reservation?"

"I've noticed two or three white men, too."

There were no sidewalks. Just paths, winding along on each side of the road, ground smooth by moccasins and boots. Tepees were outside of the town proper, and the camping-space beyond the agency buildings were thick with lodges—one behind the other.

"Guess about time the beef ration is comin' in," Tobacco grunted. "That's why all them bucks is in town."

The judge looked at the pine-pole corrals to the right of the agency buildings. "No cattle in them yet. But they must be waitin' for their beef consignment. Somebody told me there isn't a buffalo left on this reservation."

"When they got the buffaler off the grass, they whupped the Injuns without firin' a shot."

"How about something to eat, friend?"

"My belly," said Tobacco, "thinks my throat is cut."

They turned into a log building that had the sign: Spotted Pony Cafe. They were the only customers and the cook—a half-breed—stuck his big head over the swinging doors that shut the kitchen from the dining room. He pulled his head down as the partners found stools.

The waitress was a white girl, and not too pretty. She took their orders and Tobacco said, "What's wrong with that squaw that's makin' that terrible noise? She settin' on a red hot rock er sumpin'?"

"She's kept that up for days," the girl said. She went into the kitchen. She explained their orders in Crow and a mixture of English. The keening wail of the squaw almost drowned out her words.

They heard the waitress holler out the back door. "Hungry Dog, for the love of mui, stop that screeching. I've got customers."

The wailing did not waiver for a moment. It was the same level pitch, and it reminded the judge of a file running across quavering steel. It kept on and on and on.

The waitress came back, brushing aside a wisp of hair. "I can't make her stop. She's driving away what little trade I do have."

"Somebody dead in her family?" Tobacco asked. "Her husband."

"She'll git a new one directly," Tobacco said, spearing a hunk of steak. "Them high-bawlin' ones always git another man pronto. Dunno why, either, but the harder they take it, the sooner they seems to forgit."

"What happened to her husband?" Judge Bates wanted to know.

The girl looked at them. She had a queer touch of a smile. "You two just brought him into town, I understand. You found him dead along the river, didn't you?"

"Oh."

The partners attacked their steaks in silence. The girl seemed to want to talk. "I get tired of looking at these ugly redskins, day after day. They had a

36

cavalry post here but they moved it over to Fort Keogh. Now all the men are married. And there are only three reservation workers, including Mr. Miller."

"Honey," Tobacco said, "I'm too old for you. Let me introduce Judge Lemanuel Bates, my partner. He's a judge, has a good home in Cowtrail, makes a good salary, loafs a lot between terms of court, is honest and kind and—"

"That's enough," the judge said. He looked at the girl. "Emma, I didn't know I was that good a man."

"You're both too old for me," Emma said. "And how did you know my name, Judge Bates?"

"Heard the cook call you Emma, young lady."

"Emma Dalberg's my full name."

All the time, Hungry Dog was screeching. Occasionally the screech would die down and hit a plateau and then it would slowly rise in tempo and pitch. To Tobacco it sounded like a violin bow hitting a wet string.

"How long was her an' Skunk Ferguson man an' wife?" Tobacco asked.

Emma frowned, held her fingers to her ears, and said, "About six months, no more. I'm glad you said man and wife, too."

Tobacco and the jurist understood. Skunk Ferguson had been a squaw man. But the noise was getting tiresome.

"She's cut her face all up with her knife," Emma said. "We've told Mr. Miller, but he doesn't seem worried. But I guess they'll come soon and lock her up until her crazy spell is over with."

The judge had a hunch that Hungry Dog was not weeping so much out of love for Skunk Ferguson as she was wailing out of pure disgust. Here she, a Crow, had snagged a white man, and now that

37

white-man was a corpse. And the topmost desire of every squaw, he knew, was to get a white man.

And besides, it was the habit of Crow women to wail and disfigure themselves after their bucks had been killed or died. This was a sign to the rest of the redskins that she had loved her husband very much. The louder the wailing, the greater the love.

"She sure must've thought the world of him," Tobacco said.

Suddenly the squaw's wailing stopped. It stopped so suddenly that it sounded like somebody had closed both hands over her throat. There was a commotion—somewhere behind the cafe a timber fell, hitting the cafe. The judge heard moccasins rustle, heard more timber falling.

"Sounds like a tepee's fallin' down." Tobacco paused, steak suspended on fork. "Maybe the vibration of her yowlin' shook down her lodge."

Emma had run out the back door and the cook had left, too. The partners heard people talking out in the alley.

Somebody said, "Git that beaver pelt off'n her head, or she'll choke."

"Leave it on," a buck said in Sioux. "Let 'er choke."

"Get it off her."

Tobacco sucked his coffee.

Judge Bates said, "Somebody must've throttled her. Judgin' from the talk, I'd say he tied a beaver pelt over her head."

"My nerves has already settled, Bates."

There was more commotion. Emma came back and said, "The kid did it. Her kid, too. He's fourteen. He come up behind her with a pelt—a beaver pelt— and he shut her up quick."

"Her boy?" the judge asked, wanting to make

sure.

"Yes, Jimmy. She had a buck for a husband, but he got killed against the Piegans. Jimmy's her boy."

The judge said, "Oh."

Emma gathered up some dishes. "The agency police is taking her to a cell in the jail. That's best. She can't have her knife there and if she gets too wild, they'll tie her. It's all show to her. She never cared about Skunk Ferguson. He hooked up with her just to get her agency money."

"They do that," Tobacco said.

"More coffee, gentlemen?"

The judge wished he had a drink of something stronger than coffee. Emma returned to the kitchen with their cups. The cook was struggling with somebody, grunting and cursing, and Emma said, "Enough of that, cook."

A boy came running through the swinging doors. He was a skinny young Crow, with black braids hanging down his back. Evidently he had had a bit of schooling for he said, in English, "You're Judge Bates, ain't you?"

"I am he, young man."

"I'm Jimmy. I want to thank you two for one thing. You found that skunk of a father-in-law of mine dead, that was good."

The dark, wan face was savage. So savage that neither of the partners said anything.

"But you should've left the rat out here for the c'yoties, men. He ain't worth a plantin'."

"Hush, son," the judge said gently.

Emma said, "Jimmy, get out of here."

"I'm not going. I'm with Judge Bates."

The boy's hand was a claw gripping Judge Bates' arm.

"You git goin'."

"I'm not goin'." Judge Bates helped Broken Leg. These white man ain't here for no good. Judge Bates'll help me, too."

Emma looked rather mystified. Then she asked, "Have you met him before, Your Honor?"

"He's a stranger to me."

Emma said, "The marshal is coming after you. He wants you for almost stranglin' your mother to death. That's no way for a boy to do to his mother."

"No woman that'd hook up with Skunk Ferguson is much of a mother," Jimmy corrected. He had both arms on the Judge's stool, squatting and hanging on. "You gotta pull this stool out to git me, Emma. I'm stickin' with Judge Bates, I tell you."

Emma looked at the judge in despair. The big cook was standing in the kitchen doorway, apparently waiting for Emma to give him orders to throw Jimmy out.

Judge Bates said, "Let the boy stay, miss."

"Well, if you say so, Judge Bates."

The judge said, "Stand up, Jimmy." Then to Emma, "He's just frightened, Miss Emma."

"I don't want him to disturb you, sir."

"He's not disturbin' us," Tobacco said.

Emma went back to the kitchen. Jimmy stood beside the judge. His young face was very serious as he said, "Thank you for your help, sir. I knew you would help me, because you helped Broken Leg."

"What is the matter?"

Jimmy smiled. "That marshal'll be comin' for me soon. I had to shut my mother off. The noise was drivin' me loco. I didn't want to kill her. But my father—my stepfather, I guess Skunk was—used to choke her."

The judge gave the boy a brief lecture on behavior. "You should never have hurt your mother, son. You should have gone to Mr. Miller up at the Agency and reported the case and acted like a gentleman, instead of a rowdy. Surely your teacher in school would not recommend such behavior?"

"No, she wouldn't."

"I want you to apologize to your mother."

Jimmy scowled. He eyed the judge's empty plate. His tongue wet his dark lips. "All right. But not today. Tomorrow."

"That's all right."

Tobacco asked, "You hungry, younker?"

"No."

Tobacco said, "Spuds an' steak for Jimmy, Miss Emma."

Jimmy was eating when Marshal Smith came in. He gave the youth a severe dressing-down and Judge Bates said nothing. The kid had earned a bawling-out. Smith really laid it on, too.

"I should lock you up over night. What do you say, Mr. Bates?" Jimmy didn't see the marshal wink at the judge.

The judge appeared very serious. "I think it is a good idea, Marshal Smith. He has to be taught to respect the law."

Jimmy looked up from his steak, alarm in his eyes. He looked at the judge and then Tobacco.

"Do you mean that, sir?"

The judge nodded.

Jimmy said, "Well, if you think I need a day in jail, I'll go." He gulped a little bit. "But they won't beat me like Skunk Ferguson used to beat my mother, will they?"

"They won't beat you."

Jimmy said, "Wait till I finish, eh?" He was very hungry and he ate rapidly. "But I shore hate to go."

The marshal realized the boy had been scared enough. He extracted the promise from Jimmy that he would not harm his mother again, and that if he felt the desire to do wrong he'd come and talk with him first in his office.

"Could I talk to Judge Bates, Mr. Smith?"

"Yes, either me or the judge."

Jimmy said, "Thanks a lot, men. I feel better now."

The marshal stood up, winked again at the judge and Tobacco, and left the restaurant. The judge looked down on the blackhaired boy who ate as if his life depended on each bite. Life was a complicated affair, he realized. He found himself thinking, "I'd hate to be his age. He's got a lot to go through before the final curtain comes down."

But Jimmy didn't know that. No more than a boy named Lem Bates had known when he'd been Jimmy's age, over in Kentucky. Maybe that was the fun of life—meeting obstacles, conquering them. That put variety in life and made it worthwhile.

The judge sighed and wished he had a drink.

Five

The partners put their mules in the livery-stable and got rooms at the Willow House. Jimmy followed them with the reverence a cur shows when he follows a new master. The clerk took them down the hall and showed them their rooms and Jimmy sat in the lobby of the log building and waited for their return.

They got adjoining rooms at the end of the hall. Judge Bates' room was the last room and was next to the backdoor. The clerk assured them that he would not place any drunken Indians in any of the rooms and therefore they would be undisturbed.

"Drunken Indians?" Judge Bates repeated. "Where do they get whiskey?"

"Make it, I reckon."

"Whiskey," Tobacco said. "The bane of mankind."

"I agree with you completely," the clerk said. He had the thin blue-nose of a transplanted New Englander.

The judge did not rise for the bait. Too often had he and Tobacco discussed the evils of drink. According to Tobacco, even beer was injurious to the human system. The judge would point out the evils of tobacco. According to Tobacco Jones, the weed had no evils. Tobacco could see black but he couldn't see any other color when alcohol was mentioned.

They went back to the lobby, signed the register, and Jimmy got out of his chair. He started to follow them outside.

Judge Bates said, "You'd best go to your tepee, young man."

"I wanna foller you."

"You heard me, didn't you?"

Jimmy stopped. "All right."

The partners went down the street. Tobacco glanced back and said, "He's still standin' there, Bates. But we sure don't want him taggin' along. Mind what he said about the white men when he come runnin' into the cafe?"

Judge Bates nodded.

"Wonder what he meant?" Tobacco asked.

"He said something about the white men not being here for anybody's good, if I recollect rightly. Well, that's a natural statement for a redskin to make isn't it? They hate the whites. Do you blame them?"

Tobacco looked at two bucks squatting in the sun, blankets around them. How in heaven's name did they keep from boiling under that sun and with those heavy blankets around them? They claimed blankets kept the heat out.

They looked at him with dark eyes. One thing about an Indian, the postmaster thought, and that is that you never can read his eyes. He looked away, a feeling of almost fear permeating him. A few miles to the east was the scene of Custer's last stand. There were graves there—new graves—but most of them

44

contained whites, not redskins.

"Where we headin' for, Bates?"

"Over to see Agent John Miller."

Tobacco spat. "You're headin' for the livery-barn, not the Agency buildings. How come?"

The judge had no answer.

They went a hundred yards or so and Tobacco said, "You craves a drink. Your likker is on the mule."

"Not on the mule now," the jurist corrected. "In the pack, for I unsaddled the pack mule."

"Why be so technical?"

The judge grunted, "You're as sociable as an ulcerated tooth, friend."

The hostler was gone. The judge got out a flask and drank eagerly. Then he sighed and wiped his mouth with the back of his chubby hand. He put the flask under his belt and it was hidden by his shirt.

"Agent Miller'll smell likker on your breath, Bates."

"I don't think so."

"Why not? I can smell it away over here, I can."

"But you have no whiskey on your breath," the judge pointed out.

Jimmy came into the barn. "I come over here to watch your mules," the Crow said. "I ain't got nothin' to do so I might jus' as well keep an eye on your outerfits."

"Why?" the judge wanted to know. "Aren't they safe?"

Jimmy shrugged mysteriously. "A man never knows what to expect next in this town."

"Like what?" Tobacco asked.

"Well, now—"

Tobacco and the judge went toward the Agency. Spotted Pony was anything but a quiet town. Squaws haggled and gabbled, kids ran around

45

almost naked, dogs barked and a mule brayed somewhere.

The brown Montana hills stretched away. To the east you could see the cottonwoods and willows that grew along the Little Big Horn river. Then the narrow valley lifted, and the hills ran on again, rising until they became mountains in the distance, blue and serene, holding their endless snows.

"Yonder is the Big Horn River," Judge Bates said. "There's a canyon over there, where the Big Horn goes through those mountains."

"How'd you know about it? You ain't never been over there, have you?"

The judge had grubstaked a prospector some years before and the prospector had explored the Big Horn Canyon country. As usual, he had returned with no sign of gold—a habit the judge's grubstaked prospectors had.

"He told me about that country."

Tobacco bit off a chew. "You've spent a few hundred dollars, Bates, outfittin' them ol' prospectors, an' not a one has showed you a grain of gold, has he?"

One of them—Tim Keeburn—had brought back a small poke of dust, the judge allowed. But Tim had been the only one that ever found color.

"What about ol' Jack Minor," Tobacco pointed out. "He claimed he'd found no ore, then went back east to live, you notice. I still think that gent was lyin' to you, Bates."

"Jack Minor was the fellow that prospected the Big Horn Canyon."

"You're a sucker for them ol' goats, Bates. Every prospector in the country finally comes to you fer money. Word travels aroun' you're soft an' in they

46

come, like bums come to a housewife that feeds them all."

"Which tooth is it that hurts?" the judge asked.

Tobacco said, "T'hades with you, Bates."

Agent John Miller was not in his office. His aide said he was in his home. When the judge and Tobacco entered, Miller got out of his chair and came forward, hand extended.

"Heard you were in town, Your Honor. Very glad to have you visit this oasis of pleasure."

The judge remembered the howl of the squaws, the smell of their camps, and barking of the curs. He shook the agent's hand, introduced Tobacco Jones. Tobacco looked at Judge Bates and only the judge caught his sour smile. Agent Miller had whisky on his breath.

The judge knew that Miller would not offer him a drink. Miller was agent of Spotted Pony Reservation and, in having whiskey in his house, was violating war department rules. And Judge Bates was a federal judge.

"Sit down, sirs, and tell me why you came to this town?"

They took seats. The judge caught Tobacco looking for a spittoon, but the postmaster was not successful. Mrs. Miller, a gray-haired woman, came in and was introduced, and she left immediately to make tea.

The judge said, "We came in on a fishing trip. Broken Leg said fishing was very good along the river, sir."

"Indeed it is." Agent Miller, though, was frowning a little. Fishing was also good in the Crazy Woman, the Powder, and other creeks and rivers, all much closer to Cowtrail than was this section of the Little

Big Horn. "Very good fishing, Your Honor."

The judge noticed John Miller's frown and understood clearly the conjecture that motivated it. There was trouble here on Miller's reservation—and there had been the murder of Charley Peterson—but still Miller seemed calm and unconcerned.

Miller was a politician, the judge knew. If things got too bad here on Spotted Pony he would ask army officials to transfer him. Judge Bates understood that Miller's father—now retired—had been a major-general or some form of general. The old man still held power in Washington, D.C., though, and he had helped and would help his son along.

They talked about various things, none of them very interesting. Finally Miller said, "I understand Broken Leg was cleared of the murder charge."

"He drew a death penalty," the judge said.

Agent John Miller's thin eyebrows rose. "But his squaw, Running Deer, told me she had seen you down along the river, sir, and that you had told her that her husband had been acquitted, but had had to go to Fort Leavenworth."

"So I told her."

"But—"

"I couldn't tell her right out that her husband would be hanged," the judge said. "Broken Leg is appealing the case, and therefore he might get a new trial, with a different verdict."

"Oh, I see."

"I trust you'll keep this information secret, sir."

Agent John Miller swore himself to secrecy. Mrs. Miller came in with tea. She also had some small cookies she had baked. The judge hated tea and Tobacco claimed that tea was without any nourishment at all. But now he said, "Thank you, madam.

48

I'll enjoy this."

The judge also thanked her and held the cup by the handle, wondering if the cup were not so fragile the handle would fall off. He wished he could take out his bottle and spike his tea. He knew that Miller would have enjoyed a shot in his cup, too. But neither trusted the other so therefore they drank straight tea only.

Mrs. Miller sat down, and a painful silence followed. Judge Bates knew that Miller was still wondering why he and Tobacco had ridden into Spotted Pony. Agent Miller knew well they hadn't come to only fish.

A dark head came in the door, a smile showed flashing teeth, and a boy's voice said, "I'll wait for you out on the porch, Mr. Bates."

Mrs. Miller gasped. "Why, that was Jimmy Hungry Dog, wasn't it?"

Judge Bates said, "He adopted me."

"Oh."

The judge explained about the incident in the cafe. This led to talk of Hungry Dog, who was now in a cell in the agency jail. She was still whooping, Agent Miller said, but the jail was so far away nobody could hear her.

The judge then told about "finding" Skunk Ferguson's body. This occupied a few moments. The talk then shifted to Charley Peterson. Peterson and Ferguson had been friends. Peterson had had a squaw, too, but she had not mourned a bit. She had already married another buck.

"Got quite a few white men around," the judge offered. "Saw a couple of them sitting in the card room when I went by."

"There's no gambling there," Miller hastened to

say. He was a government official talking to a federal judge and he was all business. "I've checked and made sure no gambling goes on."

"Any whiskey get smuggled into the reservation?"

Miller assured the judge that none was coming in. But there was whiskey, though, and he was sure it was being manufactured by the redskins themselves, and not being smuggled in by white men.

"Marshal Smith and I are working to stamp it out, Your Honor. By the way, we have another bedroom or two, and we'd love to have you and Mr. Jones stay with us during your visit to Spotted Pony."

"Yes, do stay, gentlemen." Mrs. Miller showed a lifeless smile. She had one of those smiles she could turn off or on at will.

Sometimes, Judge Bates noticed, her timing was wrong, and she smiled at the wrong time.

The judge looked at Tobacco. He thought he read a touch of alarm in his partner's eyes. If they stayed here at Miller's home it would be the same as being under the agent's eyes all the time.

Tobacco said, "I'd like to stay, folks, but we got hotel rooms for four days, all paid for."

"Oh." Mrs. Miller sounded relieved.

The judge thanked them and they left. Miller shook hands again, offered to send a guide with them to show them the best fishing-holes; this was not successful either, for Jimmy Hungry Dog, said, "Me, I know where the fish are. I take them to lots of trout, Mr. Miller."

Miller said, "Don't bother these men," and he was stern.

"I pay no attention to you."

Miller started forward toward the boy, then stopped. For Judge Bates had throttled the young

Crow.

"Apologize to Mr. Miller, Jimmy."

Jimmy wriggled. "Why?"

"You know why. Apologize."

Jimmy looked at Miller. He looked at Tobacco, then at the Judge. Judge Bates' fingers tightened on the youth's neck.

"I'm sorry, Mr. Miller."

Miller said, "Apologies accepted, Jimmy."

Judge Bates released the youth. Jimmy rubbed his neck, eyes on the ground. The partners left, Jimmy trailing half a block behind.

"What'd we find out?" Tobacco asked.

"Just that Miller's either a fool or he's playing a tight hand. But we'll find out something soon, partner."

"Poor ol' Broken Leg," Tobacco grunted.

Six

Tobacco Jones sat on his bed and said, "Well, for two days we bin hangin' aroun' this burg, Bates. An so far we ain't found out nothin'. Fact is, I don't mind for sure jus' what we are lookin' for, at that."

"You mean to tell me, Jones, you see nothing wrong here?"

Tobacco chewed and scowled. "Well, things ain't good, if that's what you mean. But Broken Leg sure ain't no brother of mine; fer one thing, his skin is the wrong color."

"I'm going down to the pool room and get in a card game."

Tobacco speculatively eyed his partner. There was another thing he could not understand: Judge Bates seemed to have acquired a sudden love for playing poker in the pool room.

"Since when did you become such a poker fiend?"

"There is no poker playing on Spotted Pony Reservation."

Tobacco made the spittoon's contents splash. "Sure, they ain't ... accordin' to Agent Miller. Blind in one eye, he is, an' he cain't see outa the other. But

ou're a federal judge, Bates, an' legally you should
close thet game, instead of encouraging it by your
company."

The judge openly winced.

"Tobacco, you sure will get to the Next World."

"Sometimes I doubt about you," the postmaster
retorted.

The judge left his partner in the hotel room and
outside Jimmy Hungry Dog awaited him. He swung
down the street and Jimmy joined him.

"Going to the pool room, Your Honor?"

"How's your mother, young man?"

They were standing in front of the pool room.
Despite the fact that it was fall, the sun was still
warm, and an almost hot wind came in from the
Dakotas, moving across the endless sweep of hills
and buffalo-grass, now brown and bent beneath
heat and drought.

Two young bucks came into town on a wild lope,
a yell splitting from their leather-colored throats.
They roared down mainstreet, hoofs kicking dust,
and Judge Bates noticed they wore only buckskin
pants. Their torsos were brown and their ribs
showed.

One pulled his bay in close, made a motion with
his hand, and said clearly, "White man, bah," and
then loped out. They rounded a corner, broncs
almost skidding as they circled, and their hoofs ran
out.

The judge said, "Nice fellow, he was."

Jimmy accepted it more philosophically. "That's
Jack White Feather, Your Honor. He's a wild one, he
is. A few days ago he wouldn't've dared to talk to a
white man like that."

"Why not?"

53

"He done shot a buffaler the other day an' has meat for his lodge. Therefore he don't need to get c beef from the agency. He's—what's that word— indep—?"

"Independent?"

"Yeah, he's that, he is."

"You control the food that goes into a man's belly," the judge said, "and you control that man, body and soul. That goes for most men, I've found. Still, there are others who'll separate body and brain, and despite hunger and privation will still fight for their civil rights and liberties."

"My ol' lady won't eat," Jimmy said. "But she shore ain't fightin' fer nothing except the right to howl, is she?"

"We do not know."

"In what way, Mister Bates?"

"Maybe she loved Skunk Ferguson."

Jimmy considered this with the raptness a boy gives to a new thought. "Well, she might've been, at that. Though it shore seems odd she could cotton to that hunk of raw meat."

"What did Skunk do?"

"Do? What'd you mean?"

"What did he do for a living?"

"Nothing that I know of. He'd get ma's gover'ment allotment an' head down to the pool hall an' gamble. That's how come my belly got as flat as it did."

"He did nothing else?"

"Well, he'd git his mule an' head out, for Lord knows where, Your Honor. He'd claim he was out huntin' but I seen him shoot—he couldn't hit a antelope with a shotgun if the antelope was tied down ten feet away."

54

"Did he have any friends?"

"Only ones I seen him chummy with at all was this dead gent, Charley Peterson, an' them two you play cards with."

"You mean Mr. Frazier and Mr. Perrine?"

"Them's the two, only I'd not call them by mister."

The judge said, "I'm going to talk to your mother again." He had noticed neither Jack Frazier or Mike Perrine was in the pool room. "Yes, sir, I'm going to try to talk to her again."

"Try to is right," Jimmy corrected. "I'm not goin' with you, sir. I get around her an' she stops bawlin' jus' long enough to think of somethin' for me to do. I'll watch over your mules."

"All right."

Heat waves danced across the patio of the agency. Down by the corral squaws and bucks squatted in the shade, evidently waiting for the arrival of the beef allotment which, so John Miller said, was due in a week or so. According to the agent, the beef was being driven in from the Milk River country, up around Malta. Circle Diamond beef, he had said.

The wind met Judge Bates, lifted a fine sand, blew it against the jurist's face. He snorted and spat in disgust. Maybe Tobacco was right, at that. Maybe they were just wasting their time. Maybe Broken Leg had killed Charley Peterson, and therefore the verdict of hanging had been justified?

"Judge Bates."

The words were spoken brokenly. The judge stopped and saw an old buck who sat with his back against a building. He had a faded blanket over his shoulders, his hair was in gray braids, and an occasional gray whisker sprouted out of his leath-

55

ery chin, reminding the judge of a blade of gray grass trying to catch hold on brown rock.

"Red Beaver, how?"

"You come, judge? You sit beside me?"

The judge went over and squatted beside the father of Broken Leg. Red Beaver's tiny, wrinkle-enclosed eyes were on him, the sharp eyes of a gopher—they weighed and measured him.

"You came here to fish, judge?"

"Yes."

"That is all why you came?"

"That's right."

Red Beaver looked across the clearing at Agent Miller's house. Then he said, "White Man, he always poor with his mouth."

"He doesn't hide things like Red Man."

"This time, White Man he hide."

Judge Bates realized this conversation was getting nowhere. He had talked with Red Beaver before and the old man always seemed to be holding something back from him. Or was he using his imagination?

Judge Bates stood up, a sign the conversation had ended. But Red Beaver was not through. He looked up and the judge thought. He looks like an old walrus, minus the walrus' whiskers.

"My son, he come back to Spotted Pony?"

The judge couldn't honestly answer that question. But he found a way of evasion that was not a direct fabrication.

"I do not know, Red Beaver. I am not your son."

Red Beaver studied him, and the judge wondered just what the old buck's thoughts were. Red Beaver's aged, watery eyes were on him. Finally the old Crow looked away and he seemed under a heavy, unseen weight. A weight that was more than his years.

"A man has a son for the hope that son will be a better man than he is." He made the words also in sign language for his English was very broken. "Then the White Man comes with his sickness and soft hand and his knife behind his back. . . ." He bowed his head and apparently went into sleep.

The judge stood and looked across the clearing. Other Crows were watching them, but none met his gaze. He stood there and the wind came in and lifted a geyser of dust, and off in the distance riders toiled toward the reservation, their positions marked by the lift of prairie dust. Ten minutes from now, it would seem they were no closer; there was that much distance between them and Spotted Pony.

"Farewell, Red Beaver."

There was no answer, and the judge walked toward the agency jail. He looked at the squatting Crows again and heads went down or turned to one side to avoid seeing him, but he knew curiosity ate at the vitals of the bucks and squaws.

Agent John Miller came out of the barn. Suddenly and without warning he said, "I'm tired of these damn' redskins. They sit there and look at you and you can't read a thought they have, if any. They're like fenceposts."

The judge smiled, but not in amusement; he could see John Miller's position—day after day, day after day. And he knew Mrs. Miller was a sort of social bug and a woman can't do any social climbing among a bunch of Crow squaws.

"I can see your point, Mr. Miller."

"Judge Bates, there's some trouble here on this

57

reservation, and I cannot lay my hands on it, although I try hard. I question an Indian and all I get is grunts."

"Are you sure there is trouble?"

"Peterson got knifed. He was no good—just another squaw-man hanging around for his squaw's allotment check. Then Ferguson was found dead. But what's behind it all?"

"Broken Leg claimed Peterson tried to steal his moccasins. By that, I'd judge he meant his clothing."

"I heard that, too. That doesn't make sense! Who in his right mind would want to steal a redskin's dirty buckskins? They stink too much!"

The judge nodded. There was wisdom in those words, too. He had questioned Red Beaver and Running Deer, and had found out nothing.

"I'm as mystified as you are, Mr. Miller."

Miller said, "I hope you find something substantial, sir, if that is what you search for."

"I came to fish," the jurist reminded.

Miller said, "Oh, I see," and showed a big smile. "You going to question—I mean, talk—to Hungry Dog?"

"With your kind permission, Mr. Miller."

"You have my permission, Your Honor. She hasn't howled for a few minutes. And a welcome relief that is, sir."

The judge noticed that Agent John Miller did not have the same stiffness he had shown when the judge and Tobacco Jone had visited him in his home. Maybe it was because Mrs. Miller was absent. From what the judge had heard, Mrs. Miller was somewhat domineering. She wanted to steer her husband up in politics but Miller lacked the integrity to climb. The judge, being himself a politician, realized Miller, although not possessing too much brains, still had brains enough to climb the political ladder, had he the desire.

They went into the jailer's office, but the jailer was not around. "Guess he went down town for a chew," John Miller said. "He told me he was running out of tobacco."

The judge nodded. Miller seemed anxious to talk. That could be a method of drawing information out of him, Judge Bates realized. He didn't know which side of the fence Miller stood. In fact, he didn't even know where the fence was, or of what it was made—wood, brick, stone or what have you.

It was a little cooler in the jailer's office. The judge took a drink from the stone crock, wishing Miller were not along so he could take a nip out of his bottle. Miller scowled.

"Usually, when that squaw hears a newcomer out here, she starts bawlin' again. She must've have fallen asleep out of sheer exhaustion, Judge Bates."

They went down the cell corridor. The place had eight cells and Judge Bates knew, from Miller's talk, that Hungry Dog was the only prisoner.

"If she stops bawling, I'll free her," Miller said. "I hate to see a woman kept in—"

Something chopped Miller's words short. They were looking into Hungry Dog's cell. Judge Bates could not conceal his surprise, either.

They stood there a moment in front of the cell, both of them apparently speechless. Then Judge Bates walked to the rear door and opened it and then closed it and returned to Agent John Miller, who still stood in front of the cell.

"Back door was unlocked."

The jurist opened the cell door without a key.

"Jailer must have left his keys behind when he went out," the judge said. "Or has a duplicate set of keys?"

"Duplicate. In his desk." Miller's tongue wet his lips.

The judge said, "Heck of a jailer, that gent." He went into the cell and Miller followed on wooden legs. "Where'd she get the rope?"

"No rope in here—I made sure myself that the cell was empty."

Hungry Dog's slashed face had healed a little, with scabs over the scars. Her eyes were closed, but she was not asleep. She was hanging by her neck, the rope tied to the ceiling beam.

And Hungry Dog, the Crow squaw, was as dead as she would ever be. . . .

Seven

Judge Bates walked around the hanged squaw, taking in every detail. The rope even had a hangman's knot, he noticed.

Miller said, hollowly, "This will cost me my job!"

Judge Bates had a smile that hid his irritation. Here a woman had been hanged, and Miller thought not of her loss of life—rather, he thought of his job. Well, it showed how his thoughts ran, anyway.

Miller said, "Hell, she ain't hung herself, Judge Bates."

The judge asked, "What makes you say that?"

"Well, first thing, she never had no rope. Second thing, the cell was unlocked—my jailer never left it that way. For the third thing, there's no box under her feet to kick away, no chair."

"She could have jumped off her bunk."

"Rope would have been too long then. No, somebody's hung her, Your Honor—but why?"

That was a question the judge could not answer. The squaw's buckskins, he noticed, were disarranged—her blouse was crammed loosely into the waist of her buckskin skirt, and her moccasins were off. He got the impression that somebody had searched her body as she hung at the end of the rope.

But he did not mention this to Agent Miller. Instead he said, "Better get the marshal, Mr. Miller."

"I'm sure glad you were here to see her first, Judge Bates."

Miller went down the corridor and Judge Bates heard him slam the door. While he was gone the judge inspected the corpse closely. He found nothing on the dead squaw's person except her clothing. He was looking at one of her moccasins when Tobacco Jones said, "So somebody strung her up, huh?"

The judge nodded.

Tobacco said, "An' they took off her moccasins, eh? Now what were they looking for, Bates?"

"I'll be darned if I know."

Tobacco said, "Miller's comin' with the marshal an' jailer. You know, Bates, I never knew this until a minute ago, but Jimmy done tol' me his mother an' Runnin' Deer are sisters."

"**Were**," the judge said.

The jurist took a quick drink, restored his flask to its hiding place.

Tobacco said, "Don't get technical." He chewed and thought. "Somethin's rotten in this town."

The marshal and agent returned, the jailer right behind them. Word had got out about Hungry Dog and the squaws wailed with knife-like sharpness. Bucks tried to get into the jail but they locked the door.

The jailer stared, eyes popping, and then found his second set of keys. "My keys is here, men. So is the key to the back door."

Judge Bates had nothing to say. He wished word had not got out to the other Crows, for the din was terrible. They were at both the doors, pounding and keening; he decided to get out.

Tobacco followed him outside. Red Beaver and another old buck had not joined in the festivities. Red Beaver beckoned to the partners.

"She dead?"

"Yes."

"Good riddance."

The old buck made the sign of dismissal and the judge and Tobacco continued down toward town. Mrs. Miller and a young squaw, evidently her maid, stood on the porch of the Miller home, and she called to the partners, "What happened?"

The judge told her.

"Oh, my husband's job! Oh, why did it have to happen to us!"

The judge and Tobacco continued on their way. At the corner they met Jimmy. Jimmy said, "So my ol' lady is dead, huh?"

"Come with us," the judge said.

Jimmy said, "I—I can't, judge." He was weeping then, weeping as only a heartsick boy can weep. The tears knocked the pretence of maturity, the cockiness, out of him. Judge Bates picked him up and carried him to the hotel room and laid him on his bed. Tobacco bit off a fresh chew and said, "Dang it, anyway." That was about the closest he'd ever come to swearing.

"Let's go to your room," the judge said.

They left the weeping boy on the bed and went to Tobacco's room where the jurist sat on the bed and took a long pull out of his flask.

"Who hung her, an' why?"

63

"That," said the judge, "is the question."

"Some of them Indians must've have been in a position to see that back door, Bates. But none of them seen anybody leave it."

"They were playing mumble-peg and a man could have ridden a bronc in that door, and they'd not have seen him."

"They must have come in the front door first," Tobacco said, "or else how would they get the key to the back-door? It was in the jailer's desk. I sure can't savvy it. In broad daylight, too."

The judge said, "I'm going to talk to Red Beaver."

"That'll get you nothing."

Red Beaver had moved a little to get in the shade. The other Indians had, for the most part, left the jail and were in groups talking and gesturing.

"You see back door of jail, Red Beaver?"

"Me no see. Me no set right."

"Anybody see?"

"Nobody see."

Tobacco murmured, "We're gettin' everywhere in an awful hurry, Bates."

Judge Bates said, "You see anybody go in front door?"

"Nobody see."

Another buck said, "I see. Only jailer, he go in."

The judge and Tobacco went back to the hotel and sat on the porch. Tobacco chewed thoughtfully.

"In broad daylight, Bates, they sneak into jail an' string up a squaw. Nobody sees 'em. They're not only smart, they're invisible. Maybe they came through the roof?"

Judge Bates studied his partner. "Partner, you really said something. There's a skylight in that jail."

"But why leave the back door unlocked?"

"Maybe the jailer left it unlocked. He's that ignorant. He's got no memory—not in a case like this, anyway.

"Wonder if that roof can tell us anything?"

"Might," the judge admitted. "Evidently the roof is tarred. The tar is hot in this sun. They must've dropped down from the skylight. They could come up the other side of the jail and nobody would see them there."

Tobacco grunted, "Let's move."

They went back to the jail. When they carried out the body of Hungry Dog the keening rose in a new wave. They had the dead squaw on an improvised stretcher and the four white men turned the handles over to four bucks who carried her to the Indian village, the squaws screaming and jumping behind them.

The north side of the jail showed a sandy area unmarked by tepees or Crow dwellings. Buffalo grass grew high and was now brown and crisp. No ladder leaned against the jail wall.

"Footsteps," the judge intoned. "See where the grass has been trampled." He looked up at the roof, about nine feet above him. "They wouldn't need a ladder, if there were two of them. One could boost the other up, then he could help up the man on the ground."

"These ain't moccasin tracks," Tobacco said. "They look like shoes to me, Bates."

The judge went to one knee. "Hard to tell," he said. "But some of these Crows wear shoes, I've noticed."

"Not many."

"You get on my shoulders."

The judge got against the wall, with his back to

65

the siding—he helped Tobacco on his shoulders. Tobacco could look over the eaves and see the roof. He looked for some time—in fact, he stood on the judge's shoulders so long his weight got heavy.

"See anything, Jones?"

"Lemme down."

The judge got rid of the postmaster's weight and then brushed the imprints of Tobacco's boots off his shoulders. "Next time," he said, "I'll stand on you."

"You'd flatten me."

"Well, what did you see? Don't play the detective all the time, friend. Talk?"

Tobacco said, "Two men, both wearing shoes."

The Crows were still making a din. Dogs barked and kids hollered and squaws wailed. The sound moved across the prairie in waves, registering in the ears of Judge Lemanuel Bates and Tobacco Jones.

"You sure it was only two men, Tobacco?"

"Two men. One gink's feet is a little bigger than the other's."

"That sure is something to bank on," the judge murmured. "Maybe you and I did it? Your feet are bigger than mine."

"Shut up, Bates."

They went around to the front of the jail. Judge Bates looked at the compound with eyes that were heavy with thought. He seemed to be speaking to himself; Tobacco looked at him, chewed, and was silent.

"They came in from the skylight. They tried to make her talk, I think—did you notice the fresh bruise on her right wrist."

"I noticed that, Bates. Black already, it was. But maybe they didn't try to make her talk— Heck,

Bates, I dunno. Now they went in that skylight, we'll say. They're in her cell. She couldn't have got out the skylight 'cause it was too high an' it was bolted on he outside."

"Yes, they're in that cell. But there we're stuck, Jones."

Tobacco nodded, spat on a grasshopper climbing a stem of buffalo grass. The grasshopper ran into a miniature Niagara and landed on the ground. He started to prune himself free of the brown tobacco-juice.

"Yep, stuck we are, Bates. They're in the cell an' he cell is locked, an' they ain't no way to git the key an' unlock it—'cause them gents is locked in. That proves we're wrong, don't it?"

"It looks like it."

They went to Agent Miller's house. Miller sat on the porch and drank from a glass of lemonade and had a worried look on his long, handsome face.

"Now who t'hell hung her?" the agent wanted to know. "Nobody could come in the skylight, could they?"

"Never noticed the skylight," Judge Bates fabricated. "But if somebody did get into her cell via the skylight, how would they get out of it to get the key to the backdoor and the cell? They'd be locked in."

"Had two men up on that roof the other day," the agent said. "They checked the turn-bolt on that skylight and said it was down hard. I also had them tar the roof a little more."

Agent John Miller did not notice the look Judge Bates sent toward Tobacco Jones. That explained the footprints on the roof, eh? The judge thought, reckon we aren't so smart after all, Tobacco.

"No, they've come in the front door, bold as life,

and still nobody's seen them—or so those Crows claim. They've doped everything up so it would look like that squaw had hanged herself. Or maybe we're both wrong, Bates. Maybe she did hang herself. Maybe she got a rope smuggled to her and she stood on the bed and jumped—"

The judge almost said, "But that rope even had a hangman's knot," but he held his words. He listened to Miller drone on and gave the man's words only one small part of his attention.

The wind moved across the compound and it had a chillness now. Somewhere to the north hung the cold clouds of winter; soon this range, these hills, would feel the soft, hungry kiss of wet snow. Then the wind would come with its blizzards, and wind and snow would become a living hell.

Mrs. Miller said, "How terrible, Judge Bates. I'm glad you were with John when he found her. It will be a terrible report we will have to send in to Washington."

The judge said, "We'd best get back to our hotel, Tobacco."

They took farewell of the Millers, who went into their house. The wind shoved the judge's coat against his back, made Tobacco's pant legs lie flat on the postmaster's skinny shanks.

"Them two sure is worried," Tobacco grunted.

"That Miller gent," the judge said, "hasn't got sense enough to drive nails into a snowbank."

Tobacco looked at his partner with a slanted glance. "Are we any better, Bates? Here we figured they'd sneaked in that skylight and Miller'd had two men up there doin' repairs."

"You bray like a jackass in a tin barn."

68

Eight

Here the land rose suddenly, twisting as if in pain under the cover of night, then it fell into a ravine that slanted down toward the Little Big Horn River. Here in this ravine grew red willows and cottonwoods, and the chokecherry trees were heavy with black berries that almost bent their branches. When the frost came, those berries would loosen and fall.

A black bear, disturbed in a berry patch, lumbered to his hind feet, sniffing the air and catching the scent of humans. He stood there, silent in the darkness, and listened to the man go by, his horse making small sounds when his shod hoofs hit gravel. Then, realizing there was no danger to him, the bear dropped again to all fours, and started eating again. He was fat and lazy and overfed; hibernation was near and welcome.

There was a trail here, dim and uncertain because of the night, but the horse followed it, as other horses and men had followed it, from the beginning of time. The horse descended the slope, his rider braced against fork; he came with the side-crabbing, lurching movement a horse uses when he resists gravity. Finally the land levelled, and he came to the cabin door.

The cabin was dark. A trapper had built it years before, when the Sioux and Piegan and Crow were untamed, and now the trapper was buried down the creek, his grave unmarked and now level with the ground and the grass. The Piegans had not buried him; two other buckskin men had found his mutilated corpse and given it burial.

This had happened only forty years before, but already no living man knew about, and such was the irony. The trappers had wondered why the Piegans had not burned down the trapper's cabin. But, for some reason, the Piegans had left it standing.

The rider leaned in his saddle, and his voice was low: "Who's there?"

No answer. The rider went down and led his bronc into the willows and tied him there and returned to the cabin. He did not light the tallow candle that had been melted against the wall. He waited and the moon heeled up and it turned the canyon bright with colors and shadows.

The brush made sounds, and a rider came out of it. He was bulky in his saddle, and he said, "You here yet, Jack?"

"Inside, Mike,"

"Where's your bronc?"

"In the willows. Behind you."

Mike grunted, "You take no precautions," and he rode his horse into the brush. The man named Jack listened to him and thought, "He makes more noise than a honey-sopped bear."

The brush broke and Mike came out. He came into the cabin and asked, "Hermando, he ain't here yet?"

"No."

"Wonder what's keepin' him?" Mike did not wait for an answer. "An' Pinto, he ain't here yet, either?"

Jack growled his answer. "Dang it, Mike Perrine, you got eyes, ain't you? Neither of 'em is here yet."

"No need to git ruffled, Jack."

They sat against the cabin and listened to the night and its sounds. Up in the rocks the wind made its endless noise but it did not reach into this ravine. A bluejay talked somewhere, his raucous cries a wedge that drove into a man's peace of mind.

"That jay," Jack said, "must be crazy. Here it is close to midnight an' he's makin' a racket like it was broad noon."

"They do that sometimes. I dunno why, but they do. A mockin' bird is the same way, 'specially in the spring when his mate is nestin'. I mind when I was a kid in Texas. One mockin' bird'd set right outside my window an' chirp all night. I wanted to shoot him but my mother'd not let me."

Jack shifted his weight. "Shucks, I never knowed you had a mother, Mike. I thought you jus' hatched er sumpin'."

Mike was silent for a moment. Evidently he was giving this thought: Was there insult in it, or did it contain a compliment? This man known as Jack Frazier was deep and of many currents. He could smile, but his eyes would be blank; he could laugh, and his laugh could be genuine.

Anc it could be false, too, when it sounded genuine.

He settled there in the night, and gave his thoughts to other things then besides nettling his companion. He and Mike Perrine had become friends not through choice, but through necessity. It had all been, and still was, a matter of simple

71

arithmetic; two guns were better than one, two men had more strength than one. And two brains were smarter than one brain.

He had been run out of Alder Gulch by the vigilantes, and he had been part of the Henry Plummer gang—in fact, he had worn the star of a deputy-sheriff. But that had been twenty years ago and he had been a mere youth then: just reaching his early twenties. But that had been the beginning.

He had got out with his neck unbroken by a noose, and that had been more than some of the boys had done. He had drifted to other scattered gold-fields—to Last Chance and some of the Idaho diggings—but he had not mined, he had robbed and killed. But they had played out and the Black Hills had seen him, and he knew Deadwood and Lead, and he knew where a miner had been buried, for he had buried him.

But the Black Hills boom steadied and lost its wildness, for the strength of the town marshals had stiffened. He had been driven from Deadwood, for rumor had it he knew Jack McCall too well, and McCall had murdered Wild Bill Hickock. He had met Mike Perrine at Belle Fourche, north of the Black Hills.

Two of a kind had met.

Where Jack Frazier was big, Mike Perrine was solid and tougher. Where Frazier had a bluff, angular face marked by planes, Perrine had a round, almost stupid-looking face, dark and with its stupidity as a cloak to mask savagery. Frazier's cunning was more direct; Perrine's cunning was a soft, smooth breeze, hardly detectable, yet holding in its touch a fierce burst of strength.

The Sioux were moving, and both had joined the

army at Fort Lincoln; both had started out with Terry for the Rosebud, and both had deserted when the battle of the Little Big Horn had become a certainty. But desertion was common, and nobody asked questions, and so no questions were answered. The Civil War ceased to exist in reality, but still it was an ever-present threat to this land, for Texas and Arkansas had sent its warriors north to escape carpet-bag rule, and Texas men, after the fall of Custer, had driven Texas cattle into the Montana Territory. The army men—men stationed at Fort Keogh, at Fort Lincoln—were Northern men. Thus the danger was always present.

There were other camps after that, and other thievery. Jack Frazier and Mike Perrine had been riding north, aiming to head into Canada for a spell, for south of them a Union Pacific train had been robbed, the baggage man killed—yet the loot had not amounted to much. And, in the Big Horn Canyon, they had run across the Crow, and he had had gold.

Not much gold—a small poke—but where that gold had come from there would be more, so the torture began. But the Indian had died without telling where the gold had come from.

That had happened almost a year previous. They had searched, and others had come in—the two men called Charley Peterson and the man known as Skunk Ferguson. The dead buck had been some relation to an Indian named Broken Leg, and they had seen Broken Leg in the Canyon, but he had lost them in the labyrinth of rock and cut-coulees.

Ferguson had said, "Them Injuns know where this gold is. Me, I'm goin' git me a squaw. I'm goin' set back an' let her work an' I'l lissen hard."

Then there had been six of them, for carrion attracts flies. But now there were only four, for Ferguson and Peterson were in the Happy Hunting grounds. So Jack Frazier said, "We're gettin' nowhere in a heck of a hurry, Mike. Almost a year we been in this section."

"We've had tough luck."

Jack Frazier lifted a handful of dust and pounded it through his clenched first. "Only a few Injuns know, I think. Broken Leg, he knows. He's got that map; we've got to get it."

"Peterson tried," Mike Perrine reminded. "Yeah, Charley tried. That buck is hell with that knife."

"He didn't kill Peterson."

"No," Perrine said, "he didn't kill Charley. But we had to get Charley out of the way, and we got Broken Leg out of the way, too. All in one blow. Charley would talk a lot when he got a little whisky under his belt."

"He won't talk no more."

Mike Perrine stood up, movements liquid. He had a pistol in his hand and he said, "I heard two horses."

Jack Frazier did not rise; he remained hunkered, and he looked up at Perrine. The moonlight showed the dark savagery of the man's face. Frazier heard the hoofs now, far down the canyon, and he kept watching Perrine's face. Perrine listened, and the savagery broke away, falling away in slow degrees, but yet the man's face was not pleasant.

"Not horses," Perrine corrected slowly. "Mules."

"Them?"

"It's them, Jack."

The two riders came into the brief clearing, and moonlight identified them. One said, "Hello the

74

cabin," and he had a broken tongue. The other was silent, watching, listening. They did not see Perrine and Jack Frazier in the dark shadow running along the base of the cabin.

"Come down," Frazier ordered.

They came out of saddles, leaving their mules ground-hitched with trailing reins. They were both lithe men, well into middle-age, and both were dark and Spanish. They were some distant relatives—maybe cousins—but that did not bind them together. They had run sluiceboxes on California's American River, they had known the strike at Last Chance and Alder, and they had seen the Black Hills. They had also helped rob a few trains, the last being one of the Union Pacific's. But above all they both knew gold, and the formations that would hold gold.

"Any luck?" Jack Frazier asked.

Hermando said, "No luck, sir."

Pinto settled and sighed and Frazier caught the smell of hot peppers and hot food. Pinto said, "We look for that gold. But it is in there. Some day we run across it, Frazier."

"We've been here almost a year," Frazier growled.

Hermando sighed, and again the stink of hot peppers. "A year is not long, my fran. But there is gold there. That redman you kill—he have gold. You got from him he got it in the Canyon?"

"No, we got nothing from him. But Broken Leg got gold, and he's got the map. Or anyway, he did have the map."

"Maybe his squaw have it?"

Jack Frazier stretched and went into one pocket and got a match. He chewed it and said, "Maybe

75

Running Deer has it. But she's too smart to keep it on her person, I think."

Mike Perrine had his head back against the rough building; moonlight showed on his swarthiness. "She's too smart for that," he said quietly. "She knows why Peterson tried to rob her lodge."

"The other squaw," Hermando said. "She have map?"

"Which squaw?" asked Frazier.

"The one Skunk, he join with. Seester to Runnin' Deer."

Frazier looked at Perrine, and the touch of a smile touched Frazier's lips. He seemed to be smiling at some secret, and this drew a fine hardness to the lips of the man known as Hermando, made Pinto move a little and then settle.

"Skunk," said Jack Frazier, "is dead."

"Dead? How it happen?"

Frazier told about Judge Lemanuel Bates and Tobacco Jones toting the body of Skunk Ferguson into Spotted Pony. "They found him dead."

"Dead? He no keel heemself."

Frazier shrugged. "They said they found him dead. Judge Bates is a federal judge: would a judge lie? And Jones is a postmaster. Both are responsible men, and their words should be good."

"Thees Bates—he sentences Broken Leg, no?"

"He's the same judge."

The two small men looked at each other. "We cannot understand why he is here, and why Meester Jones, he ees with heem?"

Frazier said, surlily, "There's no question why they're here. They smell somethin' rotten, an' they're followin' it. That jury made Bates give Broken Leg the death penalty, but Bates figures the sentence

76

was not just. Or so it seems to me."

"I'd say you're right," Perrine said.

"I cannot onderstand theese," Pinto said.

Frazier said, "There's some I can't savvy, either. Now Bates lies to Runnin' Deer: he tells her her husband is in Leavenworth, and was freed. Why did he do that?"

Perrine had his head back, still against the wall, and the two smaller men watched Jack Frazier, and Frazier looked at them. Perrine's lips were solid, the other two said nothing, and time ran out and Frazier knew he would get no answer. And so he continued: "Bates an' Jones are here to get to the bottom of this. We sent Skunk down to stop them; they stopped Skunk."

"Skunk, he tough."

"No longer is he tough. He's buzzard meat."

Hermando said, "Skunk's squaw, mebbe she know? Me, I did not trust Skunk; he might know and keep it secret, wantin' gold for himself."

"The squaw doesn't know. She never had the map."

"She no know? How you know that?"

"Hungry Dog," Perrine said, "is dead. You tell them, Frazier."

Frazier said, "We searched her. She was in a cell; the poor fool loved Skunk, and she was killin' herself. We tried to make her talk, but we didn't have much time; she went to the end of that rope and it broke her neck."

"You hung her?"

"We had to silence her. What if she told John Miller about us gettin' into her cell? We had to shut her mouth for good."

"Anybody see you get into jail?"

77

"Nobody that we know of. There's another angle though. Well, what have you found out?"

"Nothing," said Hermando.

Pinto said, "I find nothing. I find formation that tells of gold. I follow it. Maybe gold no in Canyon?"

"That gold came from that Canyon." Jack Frazier spoke evenly. "Lemme tell you somethin' for the last time. A prospector named Jack Minor came out of Big Horn Canyon a few years back with gold enough to last him the rest of his life. I know that, for sure. He'd hit a pocket, he said, and it had run out; I talked to him in Deadwood."

"Why he tell you that?" Pinto wanted to know. "When a man find gold, he keep its place to himself; he no tell everybody."

"The pocket had played out. What difference did it make then if I knew where it was?"

"You get—Minor?"

Jack Frazier said, "No, I didn't. But the Sioux lifted his hair, I think. Maybe he got to the Big Muddy; I don't know. But I know there's gold in the Canyon. There's a map to it. One of these Crows has got it."

"Try an' find it," Mike Perrine murmured.

Pinto unconsciously summed it up for them when he said, "Broken Leg, he not have map. Charley Peterson search his clothes, not find it. Ferguson, he get in with squaw, try to work from inside: he no find map. Now thees squaw of hees: this Hungry Dog Crow; she dead, no map."

Hermando said, "Runnin' Deer has it. I'm sure of that."

"How sure?" Perrine's tone had a scoffing note.

"Not too sure," Hermando said.

Jack Frazier had listened in silence. They seemed through advancing ideas so he said, "Runnin' Deer

78

is next. She's got that map or she knows where it is. We were pretty safe until Bates an' Jones showed up. Now, I dunno."

"They dangerous men," Pinto said. "They kill Ferguson."

"Ferguson," said Mike Perrine, "was a complete idiot."

Frazier said, "Bates is playin' poker with us. Why, I dunno; surely he cain't suspect us. I wonder if Broken Leg told him about this gold?"

"I no think so," Pinto said. He put his head to one side and gave himself to long thought. "No, Broken Leg, he no tell."

Perrine put in with, "Jack, if they'd known about the gold, they'd've ridden out to the Canyon by now, wouldn't they?"

"That's right."

"Where we all stand now?" asked Pinto.

Jack Frazier summed up their position. "We're still after that gold. To get it, we have to get the map first; unless one of you stumble across it. We watch Bates and Jones carefully."

"Maybe you scare them?" Hermando sounded hopeful.

"They won't scare easy," Perrine murmured.

"We could do that," Frazier said. "Well, let that point ride for the moment. Hungry Dog didn't have the map; neither did Broken Leg. I don't reckon Bates saw you at the trial, Pinto?"

"No, I no go to court-house. I wait over in town in Cowtrail; I listen to men's talk."

"Broken Leg is away until he gets his new trial. Then the sign points to Runnin' Deer."

"If she ain't got the map," Perrie said slowly, "she'll know where the gold is. If she's got the map we'll make her produce it."

"She next then?" asked Pinto.

"We visit her," Jack Frazier said.

They talked of other things. Frazier had packed out some grub on his saddle for the two prospectors. He also had brought them some cartridges for their rifles. They would meet again, at this same cabin, inside of a week. But maybe by that time they'd have the gold, or know its location.

"We meet here then," Pinto said.

The two left, leaving Mike Perrine and Jack Frazier sitting by the cabin. Perrine listened to their mules leave and he said, with his words almost a whisper, "Those two poor fools."

Frazier ran a forefinger through the dust. The wind was moving and the wind was cold; it touched them and it had come off snow. Frazier got to his feet, sullen and strong and driven, and looked down at Mike Perrine.

"Simple fools," Perrine continued. "The most they could get out of it is a grave."

Jack Frazier said, "Let's ride back to Spotted Pony."

Nine

Although he was only eleven years old, Jimmy Hungry Dog was wise beyond his years. When Skunk Ferguson had gone "squaw-man" and married Jimmy's mother, Jimmy had ceased to regard Hungry Dog's lodge as home. He slept wherever he could: some nights with young friends in their lodges; he slept in the haymow of the livery-barn, in the alleys, behind buildings, in doorways.

He had hated Skunk Ferguson. His mother had been glad to get a man again, especially a white man; to Jimmy, though, Skunk Ferguson had not been white—he had been just what his name had implied, a skunk. Jimmy had had a run-in with him the third day, and Jimmy had left his mother's lodge.

When Judge Bates and Tobacco Jones had brought Skunk Ferguson's body into Spotted Pony, Jimmy Hungry Dog had actually been glad. He didn't know whether Skunk had killed himself by accident or by purpose, or if somebody else had shot down his step-father—Skunk was dead and out of the picture and his mother was a fool to carry on like she had.

Now his mother was dead, also. Even though she had married Skunk Ferguson—and he knew they had been married, for the local Father had performed the ceremony—she had been his mother in blood. Some squaws just lived with white men, but his mother had made Skunk Ferguson go through the white-man's ceremony—but—but what difference did that make now? Both his mother and Ferguson were dead. And somebody had hanged his mother.

Who had done it, and why?

Who . . . and why?

These were the questions that tormented him as he sat on the back porch of the Willow House. Judge Bates and Tobacco Jones had retired for the night and the little buck would sleep under the judge's window. The ground was soft there for the owner of the Willow House had planted flowers there.

Jimmy knew something was wrong. His uncle, Broken Leg, had gone to jail, but first, Charley Peterson had tried to rob his uncle. Now Peterson was dead, and Ferguson was dead. Both had been friends.

Jimmy knew that, although neither Peterson or Ferguson had guessed that he knew. During daylight the two men had met and exchanged only greetings. But at night they had been friends, for Jimmy had trailed his step-father one night, and he had found his step-father and Ferguson talking in the hay-corral behind the livery-barn.

He had not got close enough to hear their conversation. But they had been friends by night and acquaintances by day, and in that was something amiss. But both were dead now, and his mother was dead, and his sister had gone to live in

he lodge of her grandmother, who would not take
her grandson.

"I wouldn't go anyway," Jimmy told himself. Then
he thought, I talked out loud, like old Red Beaver
talks. I'm not an old man yet. That was an odd
thought; it was even funny, and he chuckled.

Then he rememberd the noose that had broken
his mother's neck; it had had a knot tied in it like the
man ties when he hangs people; his mother had not
known how to tie such a knot. Yet nobody had seen
any man enter the jail; hadn't the Crow old men
been around? Wouldn't they have seen?

But they argued a lot, and came close to fights;
they were not good men to watch, he knew. But why
had somebody hung his mother? Had the ghost of
Skunk Ferguson come back and—?

No, there were no such things as ghosts; the white-
man's school and white-man's books said no ghosts
existed.

The hall door opened behind him, catching him
unawares, and he got to his feet too late. The Willow
House proprietor held a broom menacingly.

"I caught you, you dog-goned Injun. You been
sleepin' in my flower beds, you have, until you've
tromped them flat. Now git ye outa here, an' go to
your wigwam, or wherever you redskins sleep. I'm
not a-furnishin' you with a bed, 'cause the gover'
ment give you money an' beddin'."

"They robbed our land," Jimmy said. "They stole
our buffalo. They killed us and put us on reservations."

"No don't git no high-falutin' ideas, Injun."

Jimmy watched the broom. He wasn't afraid. The
man swing the broom and he'd grab it and jerk him
forward and— But he'd be in Agent Miller's office

83

then. No, none of that, Jimmy.

"Ten years ago, my father he'd get your hair."

"Your father's dead, an' you cain't lift my hair. Now beat it, fella, or I'll report ye come mornin' at the agency."

Jimmy formed a hard retort, then held it. He wandered up the alley, and when he looked back the proprietor was watching him, still holding his broom. Jimmy put his nose and thumb together and waggled his fingers. The white boy—the grocer's boy—had taught him that.

Old Red Beaver and another old buck were talking about scouting for Reno, or some other Army officer; Jimmy listened and gave the words small attention. Finally Red Beaver said, "Why not in your lodge in buffalo robes, son?"

Jimmy made no reply. He went away and Red Beaver looked at him and said, "That young Crow, he thinks too much."

"His mother, she dead."

"He sick," Red Beaver tapped his chest. He put his hands up to his gnarled, wrinkled head; he rocked at the hips. His head came down and touched the dust and came up. "My son."

"Your son, he come."

"How you know."

"White man, Bates, he say so."

Red Beaver made his sign-talk—his wrinkled claws moved, they crossed each other, he touched his lips, his chest, his ears. He said it in Crow and then said it in English. "White man, he lie to redskin, all time. All time, he lie."

There was no answer to that. He had not expected one, for the truth was self evident; he did not get one. He looked at Jimmy, who was almost out of sight, despite the moonlight.

"Sioux kill my mother. Long years ago, down on iver called Powder by white man. I know how he eels, friend."

"Sick at belly, Red Beaver."

Red Beaver's arm made a circular motion, taking n all the Spotted Pony. "Stink like dead buffalo. All tink. Soldiers, they come. Miller order them. Rotten ike dead buffalo."

"What rotten, friend?"

"All rotten."

Jimmy Hungry Dog knew that the owner of the Willow House would come again to see he did not leep on the flower beds. There was no use in going back there, unless he went through the window in Judge Bates' room. He could do that, too; the screen was loose.

He stood in the shadows, and finally Red Beaver got to his feet, aided by his old companion; they hobbled down the street, bent like dogs on the scent, and they went out of sight as they turned to their lodges. The Crow camp was quiet, the moonlight white and pale on the lodges. A boy is apt to notice things, and he thought. When I was a small boy, the lodges were made of buffalo hides; now they are from cows. He was going to school, when they caught him, but if things had gone right, he'd been out hunting his first buffalo, with other young braves. But the white man and his rifle had changed his life.

He stood with his back against a cottonwood and rolled a cigaret. He lit it and puffed, and he felt the deadly sickness enter his belly; he threw the cigaret away. He couldn't get used to them. White Cloud could smoke, and he was only nine; so could Half

85

Moon Face, but he was twelve. Judge Bates had told him smoking would keep him from growing that would be his last cigaret. He got out his tobacco sack and his cigaret papers and he tore the papers in two and let the wind have them. He stomped the sack into the earth and left it there.

He went among the lodges, with the dogs barking. One came close—that was White Hand's cur—and he said, "Come, dog," in Crow. The dog came and nipped and he kicked him and the dog yipped and ran to his lodge, snarling with anger. Somewhere a buck yelled, "Quiet, dogs," and the barking stopped for a moment, only to come out again

He pulled back the flap, feeling the stong hair of the hide, and inside the lodge was silence. The air was sticky with many lungs breathing it; he did not like its taste or odor. He kept the flap open. He heard a dog growl and a girlish voice asked, "Who is there?" in English.

"Me Jimmy."

"What do you want?" This time the girl spoke Crow. "There is a robe beyond you. My mother's robe."

"Your mother will need it, Broken Nose."

"My mother, she go."

He let the flap drop. He was on his knees, creeping down a narrow aisle, and a buffalo robe stirred. He said in Crow, "Sleep, Little Sister, sleep," and the girl-child moved and returned to deep sleep. He found Broken Nose lying on her robe, an agency-issue cotton blanket over her. She was eight, and she was the oldest of Running Deer's children.

"Your sisters they sleep. But still Running Deer is gone? She is at some lodge talking? No, they are all dark."

"She is gone."

"Where?"

Broken Nose had his hand, and her fingers were pushing into his flesh. He had not know his girl-cousin had such strength.

"She is afraid, cousin. So she go, telling us she has to hide."

"What she afraid of ?"

They talked in Crow, voices guttural with their native tongue. The teacher said they should always talk in the White Man's tongue, but their own words were shorter and easier. The White Man took too many movements to say so little.

"They kill your mother. My mother, she afraid the same as—"Broken Nose halted. "She afraid of something."

"You are crying," Jimmy accused.

"She is my mother. I want her."

"My mother is dead. But I do not cry." He remembered crying in Judge Bates' room; Judge Bates would never tell. Judge Bates respected the dignity of a man. He had read that in a book, only the sentence had not had Judge Bates' name in it. He had substituted that for the name in the book.

"A woman, she is made of horse-hair. Like a horsehair rope, she bends easy. Your mother will be back."

"I—I hope so."

"She will be back. My mother will never be back."

The second girl—Willow Root—was weeping too. Jimmy said, "I came to talk to your mother, but she is gone so I go." He loosed Broken Nose's hand and crept outside again.

The air was good, cool and strong; it filled his

87

lungs. He heard them crying, and that sound was not good; it drew his boyish face into a scowl that marked him with a mannish appearance. The days had rushed on him and pushed him into adulthood before his boyhood had waned.

He decided he would sleep in the livery-barn. The hour was late; he would not disturb Judge Lemanuel Bates. The owner of the barn was asleep in a sideroom; he came awake instantly when Jimmy entered, although Jimmy tried to sneak in.

"Git outa here, injun."

"I want to sleep in your hay."

"You ain't sleepin' in my hay, injun." The man rubbed his eyes with his knuckles. "I've heard you've took to smokin'; I shore aint cottonin' to burnin' down my buildin's jes' cause some injun wants to puff a cigaret."

"I don't smoke."

"Half Moon Face says you smoke."

"Half Moon Face, he lie."

"Whether he lies or not, git out."

Jimmy left, swearing that when he met Half Moon Face again, that worthy would be packing the scars of a battle when they split company. The mainstreet, which was the only street of Spotted Pony, was quiet; not even a horse on it—only a dog trotting across the dust. The wind was cold and it was close to frost; Jimmy pulled his jacket up closer, but it did not cut the wind.

The clouds had absorbed the moon; they swept across the sky in a high wind. Snow was close and a lodge got cold in below-zero weather. Maybe he'd best make up with the cook at Agent Miller's; he'd let him sleep in the kitchen behind the big stove.

There had been more excitement when the

soldiers had been stationed here; now a few of them, he'd heard, were coming back. He was walking in the shadows when he saw the two riders come into Spotted Pony.

They did not ride down the mainstreet as honest men ride; they came in from behind, heading toward the livery-barn behind the pool-hall. Jimmy moved in between that building and the next; hidden there he watched Jack Frazier and Mike Perrine come to the barn.

The two dismounted, led their broncs into the barn; later Jimmy saw them come out and go to the hotel. He was curious—why had these two been out this late; where had they been?—and he went into the barn. He felt of their horses; they were warm yet, and he found sweat on them—they had come a long distance. They were still breathing heavily.

He stood beside the roan, and the bronc put his velvet nose against the little buck's hand; the horse's nose was soft and inquisitive.

Jimmy said to the horse, "Wonder where you've been?"

The horse nuzzled him.

"Why don't you talk, horse?"

The horse, seeing he was going to get no sugar, stuck his head in the manger and went to feeding. Jimmy thought, I might bed down here, but Jack Frazier had once caught him loitering around the barn. Frazier had run him off. If Frazier found him sleeping in the barn—

He went to the hotel. He came in from the back, came to Judge Bates' window, and he heard the move of the jurist inside. He heard the squeak of the bed-springs, and he knew Judge Bates was aware of him.

"Jimmy, Your Honor."

Judge Bates said, "Come in, child."

Jimmy got the screen up and slid inside, and fastened the screen behind him when he was in the room. Judge Bates had gone back to bed; Jimmy heard his deep sigh and heavy breath.

"I sleep on floor."

"In the bed, beside me."

"No, floor."

Judge Bates said, "You ain't got lice or fleas. Come on in this bed, and make it pronto."

Jimmy liked the authority in Judge Lemanuel Bates' voice. Judge Bates had made him take a bath in the big tub in the barber-shop; the barber had put some strong smelling stuff in his hair—he liked the smell of it, though. And the barber had put some of the stuff in the water, too. When he'd been washed he'd felt clean and strong, more like a white man than an Indian.

"All right, if you want me."

He got next to the wall. Judge Bates had the window open and the window over the door—he searched for the name of the window in English and gave up—was open too. The room did not smell like the lodges of the Crows.

"Where you been?"

"First, I talk with Red Beaver. Or he talk with me, sir."

"About what?"

Judge Bates was always inquisitive. He had told him that a man learns by asking questions.

"About nothing."

"Not much of a talk then?"

"Well," Jimmy searched for words. "I do not like it, sir. Red Beaver sits and looks at jail yet my mother is hanged."

"Maybe your mother hanged herself."

"That I do not believe. For my mother many times say life was good and she would hate to leave."

"People change their minds when they lose a person they love."

"Yes, true."

"Where else were you?"

"To the lodge of Running Deer. She has four girls—bah; they are alone now. All alone."

He felt Judge Bates stiffen, the mattress telegraphing this information. "What do you mean by that, Jimmy."

"Runnin' Deer, she leave."

"Where did she go?"

Jimmy explained. Running Deer figured that her sister, Hungry Dog, had been hanged; she'd fled to save her own life. None of her daughters knew where she had gone, but she had left that evening.

"I don't savvy that, Jimmy."

"Neither do I."

He also told about seeing Jack Frazier and Mike Perrine ride into Spotted Pony. He told about visiting their horses and how it looked like they had been ridden hard for some distance.

"Wonder where they were, Your Honor."

The judge said, "I have no idea." He kept asking questions about Frazier and Perrine: how long had they been in Spotted Pony? what did they do for a living? did they always seem to have money? who were their friends?

"Charley Peterson, he friend to Skunk Ferguson." He told about the meeting he had witnessed when Peterson and Skunk had talked behind the barn. "Skunk, he friend of them, at night only."

"At night only, huh?"

"Daytime, they not friends; one night they meet in barn, too. They talk an' talk—I sleep there then, that before man run me away. I no hear what they say, though."

"But Skunk was their friend, huh?"

"I think so."

They lay in silence and listened to the wind. Jimmy heard the deep respirations of the jurist, but he could tell by Judge Bates' breathing that he was not asleep yet. Chill crept into the room—the chill of frost. Jimmy was thankful for the thick blankets and sougans.

"You think of something, judge? That why you no sleep?"

"Maybe you're right, Jimmy."

Ten

The first hard frost had crept in toward morning, cutting through the living fabric of leaves and vines, repeating its century-old warning of winter. Tobacco Jones said, "Soon snowballs'll be hittin' us on our under end, Bates. Time we got out of this stinkin' camp, ain't it?"

"Our job isn't through, partner."

Tobacco shook his hangdog head and rolled his cud in exasperation. "Bates, I swah, but you are a stubborn man. You hol' down a soft job that lets you set close to a hot stove, yet a strange sense of justice keeps drivin' you."

"Would you like to see an innocent man hanged?"

"No, but is Broken Leg innercent?"

"I think he is."

"But proof counts."

"We're after that proof."

They went to the Cafe, both braced against the cold wind. Icy fingers plucked at their clothing; stormclouds scuttled across the north; overhead a wide V of geese, barely discernible because of height, flew to the southeast, their honking sounding like the breaking of cold twigs in a vacuum.

Tobacco blew his nose and said, "Winter's here." They came into the Spotted Pony Cafe and its warmth. Emma said, "Good morning, men," and she was cheery. Her housedress accentuated her form in the right spots.

"The answer to a man's dream," Judge Bates murmured.

She flushed, but she was pleased; she was a woman. She said, "Ah, shaw now, Mr. Bates," and moved a salt-cellar aimlessly. Tobacco said, "Winter is here, miss." and he added, "I love summer and hate winter."

"Winter is good, Mr. Jones. There are bobsled rides, skating, and a warm, good fire."

"Just now," said the judge, "I'll settle for coffee, bacon, and a pile of hotcakes."

"Make mine the same," Tobacco said; he smiled at her and she smiled back. Bates was right, for once; the world was already better, just for seeing Emma. Maybe a man should have married, at that. By this time, had he married in his early twenties, he might have had a daughter as old as Emma.

Whoa, Tobacco Jones, whoa up.

Emma called back their orders and Jimmy Hungry Dog stuck his head under the swinging door, standing on his hands and knees in the kitchen so he would be low enough to see under.

"Mornin', men."

Emma said, "Our new helper, fellows. He came here about an hour ago and applied and he's washing dishes for an hour morning and evenings."

"I get my chuck," Jimmy said.

They heard the cook growl, "Git on them dirty dishes, son," and Jimmy's head disappeared. Judge Bates said, "If he needs a little nicknack or two—like

94

some candy—give him some in proportion—and I'll pay you for it."

"He's had a rough time," Emma said. "He's a tough kid, though. He's smilin' now, but I can tell he's sick underneath."

Their orders came and they fell to. Judge Bates found himself remembering what Jimmy had told him: how he had seen Mike Perrine and Jack Frazier ride into town, how Running Deer had left her lodge. There was significance in both of these truths, but so far the nature of it was not too clear.

He wished he could find something solid, something concrete; these Crows, though, were short of tongue. Even Broken Leg, hobbling into his cell with the death penalty on him, had no comment; he had shrugged off the judge's questions, maintaining he had not killed Charley Peterson, yet volunteering no additional information, even though Judge Bates and Tobacco had tried to trip him up with questions. He had knifed Peterson, sure; but he had not killed him. You cannot kill a man by stabbing him in the shoulder, can you?

"The knife, he hit bone—shoulder. He make small hole. I know; I heard blade hit bone."

"Then who killed him?"

"I no know."

"Do you have any idea who killed him, at all?"

About this time Broken Leg seemed to lose all ability to understand or to talk English. He would begin mumbling under his breath in a combination of Sioux and Crow, maybe throwing in a few words of Cheyenne to further mystify the partners.

But Judge Lemanuel Bates and Postmaster Tobacco Jones agreed on one thing: Broken Leg had some ideas of his own and intended to keep them.

Now, sitting in the Spotted Pony Cafe, Judge Bates realized that Broken Leg, despite his woe-begone, tattered appearance, was indeed a proud man.

Maybe he knew who had killed Charley Peterson; maybe he didn't—but chances were he knew, the partners had guessed. Anyway, he was saving that killer, or the killers—whichever the case might be—for none other than the Crow buck named Broken Leg.

Pride demanded that he revenge himself on the men or the man who put him behind bars under a death sentence. Though how he intended to do it was beyond Judge Lem Bates; Broken Leg was in the Cowtrail jail and the Cowtrail jail was hard to break out of. Better prisoners than Broken Leg had tried and failed. But still, even with this confronting him like a high stone wall, Broken Leg would not concede. Maybe it wasn't pride; maybe it was sheer bullheadedness and stupidity.

The entrance of Jack Frazier and Mike Perrine broke up the judge's train of thought. Both men, he noticed, were unshaven; Perrine's black whiskers were black wire on his jowls. Perrine's eyes were a little bloodshot, too; Judge Bates laid this to the night-ride and a little too much of John Barleycorn.

The two exchanged greetings with the Cowtrail partners, and then ordered. Judge Bates and Tobacco Jones finished, paid for their meal, and went out into the wind.

Tobacco said, "Winter's here, Bates. Today our rent is up on our rooms. Do we stay?"

"What is your opinion?"

"I'll—I'll stick aroun', if you do."

"Get the rooms on a day to day basis, then."

"Where you goin'?"

The judge was going to the livery-barn to check on their mules. Tobacco went with the wind; Judge Bates went into it. Their mules looked up as he came into the warmth of the barn, smelling the good odors of sweet Montana hay, the sharp odors of manure.

"How's our mounts, hostler?"

"Good, Your Honor. You want them right now?"

The judge inspected the hay in the manger. Good bluestem hay, and a mule could make muscles on himself with hay like that. He seemed satisfied, for a man was only as good on the prairie as his mount was strong, and he stood in the doorway and watched Agent John Miller coming toward him.

Miller ducked into the doorway with, "That wind sure is sharp, Judge Bates. Winter's right around the corner."

"So's prosperity," the jurist reminded. "Only nobody's ever found the corner yet. Do you think the advocates of free silver will win out, sir?"

Miller didn't know. He expressed the opinion that he didn't care much, just so he and his wife had a job and a roof over their heads. The judge paid little attention to the agent's monetary philosophy. He had his own ideas concerning free silver; he'd just mentioned the subject to Miller to have some core around which to wrap conversation.

Miller was the type of man who wanted nothing to come in and break into his routine. The hanging of the squaw, Hungry Dog, had shattered his routine in a dozen pieces. Because of this, his mind came back to the cell wherein he and Judge Bates had found the hanged squaw.

"Sir, I'm afraid that squaw hanged herself. She's had a rope somewhere on her person for just such a purpose."

"The hangman's knot," the judge murmured.

Miller had an evasion for this, also. He claimed he had talked with various Crows and two had admitted that Hungry Dog had been capable of making just such a knot.

The judge nodded, seemingly only mildly interested, but inwardly wondering just what had happened to a man to make him such a coward. Miller was deliberately making up pseudo-evidence in order to salve his conscience—if he had one—; to restore his routine, and to hang onto his measly little job.

Judge Bates felt the pull of anger, but kept it from showing on his massive, good-natured face.

"Your logic sounds well-based, sir."

Miller said, "These Crows are surly, Judge Bates. I wish that beef consignment would arrive. It should be here today, along with soldiers from the fort. They are only sending me ten soldiers, though."

"That should be enough."

"You think so."

Personally, the judge would not have called on the army at all; the Crows were peaceful, had long been peaceful, and soldiers in his estimation, were not necessary. Crows had even guided Custer against the Sioux.

"In fact, I hate to see soldiers come."

"Are you a pacifist, sir?"

"A realist."

The judge moved away, feeling a strong coating of distaste. Tobacco Jones came along and said, "I rented them for two days. Looks to me like maybe we might have snow, an' if we do the trail will be closed a day or so."

Leaves came from the cottonwoods—green and scarlet and gray—and swept with the wind. They swirled across the street and built a pyramid in the doorway of the store.

Jack Frazier and Mike Perrine came out of the Spotted Pony. Frazier said, "Well, how about a game today, Your Honor?"

"Later. In the pool hall."

The toothpick bobbed in Frazier's mouth. "See you there." He and Perrine went with the wind toward the pool-hall.

Tobacco said, "Where to, Bates?"

"Have you seen Red Beaver this morning?"

Tobacco gave his partner a slanted glance. "No, I ain't. Now what would you be seein' that ol' brave about? Don't git down wind on him."

"Just a hunch."

Tobacco shrugged and looked away. "I've seen your hunches get us knee-deep in trouble," he finally said.

They went back of the cafe and the judge called Jimmy Hungry Dog to the door. He asked where they could find Red Beaver. Jimmy said maybe Red Beaver was at his lodge. He came out in the alley and pointed out the lodge belonging to his grandfather.

"He's got red rocks on the ground to hol' down the hide," the boy said.

The cook stuck his head out. "Come on back here, you injun, an' git to work. You earn your keep here, believe you me."

"I believe you," Jimmy replied.

Eleven

Red Beaver was alone in his lodge. From what Judge Bates had heard, the old buck had worn out about five wives in his long lifetime. Red Beaver had a fire in the middle of the circle and the smoke was supposed to go out the top where the lodge-poles joined and were trussed with buffalo-hide thongs.

But despite the wind outside, the smoke did not rise—it hung in the tent, seeping out its seams. At first the partners had thought the wigwam on fire but a boy had told them, "All time, it smoke. He burn wet wood."

Judge Bates had hollered, "Two friends want to see you," but had got no response and Tobacco had said, "Mebbee the ol' skunk has smoked hisself to death."

"No such luck. Two friends want in, Red Beaver."

"Jus' go in," the boy said.

So they had just entered, letting the flap fall behind them. Inside it was a smoky-gray color and there was the stink of burning wood. Red Beaver sat cross-legged beside the fire and looked at them. His gnarled, walnut-colored hand held a huge pipe made of wood and encrusted with brown crust.

"What the heck's he puffin'?" Tobacco murmured.

The judge said, from the corner of his mouth, "Kinikinick, I'd say."

"I'd say it was buffaler droppin's in thet pipe."

Red Beaver took the pipe from his thin lips and made a gesture, flat and meaningful. Judge Bates and Tobacco Jones sat on the ground. Red Beaver put the pipe back between his scraggly teeth.

He sucked on it, bit it; he studied them. He had small eyes that peered from beneath hairless brows and they reminded the judge of a set of marbles placed far back in two holes burned in wood. The jurist found himself wishing he had seen as much life as those eyes had seen.

"We come as friends, Red Beaver."

Red Beaver grunted around the pipe.

Tobacco had decided to leave all the talking to the judge. The postmaster found himself glancing around the lodge. Yonder was Red Beaver's bed, a buffalo-robe thrown on the ground; there was no pillow. Here and there were sacks of supplies—some spuds and some coffee and some sugar and salt—and he judged they were government issue from the agency.

Beside having the stern smell of the smoke, the lodge also had the stink of a place long unaired—the smell of unwashed bodies and personal clothing, long dirty. He thought, I wouldn't be a bit su'prised to see a scalp hangin' from a lodge-pole, and then he stiffened visibly when he noticed the four scalps hanging from the far pole.

They were old, dried-up, and curled; still, hair hung from them. Red Beaver had watched the postmaster while he had been making his scrutiny. He took his pipe free and his few teeth clacked.

101

Tobacco jerked his gaze from the scalps. His eyes met Red Beaver's, and the old buck's eyes were suddenly hard and without give. Tobacco said to his partner, "Well, Bates, start."

But now and then, against his will, he had to glance up at the scalps.

Judge Bates went through the preliminaries. "You Broken Leg's father? You know Broken Leg fight white man, Peterson? You know I judge in Broken Leg's trial?"

Old Red Beaver did not speak, he merely nodded.

"Broken Leg, he kill Peterson?"

"No know."

"Broken Leg, he fight Peterson?"

"No know."

The judge asked, "Where daughter-in-law, Running Deer? Where she go?"

"No know."

Tobacco peeled the tinfoil off a new plug of Horseshoe he had bought at the agency store. He cut off a hunk without looking, balanced it on his knife, stored it in his cheek with the blade of the knife.

Red Beaver watched him.

"You want tobacco."

Red Beaver put out his hand. He did not bite a chew off, though; he lifted the edge of his bed-robe, put the entire plug under it. Evidently he considered it a gift. He made some signs, but said nothing.

Judge Bates interpreted with, "He says thanks, Jones."

Tobacco growled something, but held his temper. He knew darned well that Red Beaver had known all the time he was only lending him a chew. The old buck was taking advantage of the situation.

Judge Bates went back to his questioning: "Why Broken Leg fight Peterson? Why Peterson try to rob your son?"

"No know."

Tobacco murmured, "Interesting conversation, Bates."

But Judge Bates kept on trying. He knew full well that Red Beaver had some opinions, maybe even some evidence, pointing to the source of this trouble. He kept emphasizing he was a judge—a judge for the White Father in Washington—and he could help Broken Leg, if only Red Beaver would talk and tell him what he knew.

But it was like talking to a waterfall; the water still kept on falling. It was like hollering against rock; the rock returned the echo and made no answers. It was like spitting tobacco juice against a hard wind. It came back and sprinkled itself all over your own face.

"You tell us, Red Beaver; we help son, Broken Leg."

"No know."

Tobacco found himself thinking, "I don't blame the ol' buck too much. If the Injuns would have won an' have treated me like my race treated them I'd've gone tongue-tied on 'em too."

When they got a beef issue, it was always of the poorest beef. Old cows, too old to calf, being got rid of by some big cow-outfit. And many times it went down on government requisitions as A-1 top beef Anyway, that's what the agency officer drew pay for, and that's what the cow-outfits got for pay. Sometimes the agency officer kept the difference for himself; sometimes he cut in the cow-outfit. Usually he had to cut in the cow-outfit that furnished the old beef.

But the Indian got old meat, tough and stringy; ten years before and less he had dined on tender young buffalo calf. He had downed buffalos and used only livers, but that had been no waste compared with government hunters who had been hired by the White Father in Washington to wantonly kill millions of buffalo. Kill them in herds, and leave their flesh for the wolves and coyotes and buzzards, using not a pound of it.

For to the Indian, the buffalo was life. His flesh filled the redskin's belly, his hides made robes for sleep, pelts for lodges; his guts made lines to fish with, and his horns made decorations for medicine dances and war parties. But the Great White Father had ordered the buffalo killed.

Tobacco thought, not a nice deal for them, the poor devils.

Now every iota of hate, of fear, of loathing he held for the white man came into Red Beaver's face, giving the deep lines a greater depth, adding degree by degree to the stoniness. And all he could say was, "No know."

"You sit by jail yesterday?"

Red Beaver did not answer that. His small eyes were on Judge Bates; he nodded, and the pipe sent up more smoke.

"You figure Hungry Dog, she hang herself?"

"No know."

It seemed to Judge Bates that the old buck was more reluctant to say his two words this time. But afterwards the jurist wondered if he had heard correctly. Afterwards he was not sure.

But the judge was persistent. "Hungry Dog, hang herself?"

"No know."

The judge went into detail. He got on his knees and stood like a dog on all fours and scratched a map in the dust of the lodge. Red Beaver leaned forward and watched and Tobacco watched the old Crow. He saw not a looseness of a facial muscle, not a trace of interest; the old man watched like a man made of stone.

He made only one movement while the judge talked and sketched. And that was to take the pipe from his mouth and hold it in one hand the color of tanned buckskin, but without buckskin's suppleness.

"Now here is the jail, Red Beaver." Judge Bates' stubby forefinger sketched in the jail: four movements and the jail was there. "Now here is this building, right opposite the jail door. The front door, too. Remember, the back door was locked, then."

Red Beaver did not even look up. He kept staring at the drawing. His gaze slanted down and seemed to inspecting the drawing for flaws he never did find; if he did find them, he did not voice his decisions.

"Whoever hanged Hungry Dog went in this front door and came out the back door. You were sitting here." The jurist's finger made a dent to show the location of Red Beaver. "By rights, you should have seen the men—or man—enter."

The judge rocked back on his thighs, still on his knees. Red Beaver's head came up. His head was but a short distance—maybe two feet—from the heavy jowls of Judge Bates.

They looked at each other—white man and red man—and Judge Bates could read not an iota of anything in Red Beaver's eyes. They looked at each other, eye to eye, for a long moment; they measured each other, trying to find the limits of the other's strength. They were bound into this, white man and red man, but the red man would not give.

"No know."

Judge Bates said, "Ah," and settled back, still on his knees. He reached down and took dust in his right hand and he pounded it savagely, making it geyser through his fist. It was the Crow way of saying one man had violated the friendship of the other.

"No."

Judge Bates got to his feet. He said, "Come, Tobacco, there's nothing here." And to Red Beaver, "So long."

Red Beaver had no answer.

The partners went outside. They had spent more time than they had figured in the lodge of Red Beaver. Tobacco Jones had a slight headache from the smoke and stink; he rubbed his forehead.

"Feel sick partner."

"That stink an' smoke."

Judge Bates pulled air into his lungs. "It feels good." He was feeling his defeat; he had played his cards. Yet each card he had had proved worthless. A man had looked at him—a red man—and he had only said, "No know."

"He's got a scheme," Tobacco said. "I know redskins. I know that. But what is it, Bates?"

The judge said, "Quite a conversation."

"Very enlightnin'," Tobacco said, smiling wryly. "Very touchin', an' straight to the point, huh?"

"No know," the judge said.

Twelve

They met Jimmy Hungry Dog coming toward the Crow encampment. He said, "You talk with him?"

"We talked with him," the judge said.

Jimmy said, "He know two words: No Know. He that way." His hands made motions: Red Beaver was an old man, stubborn. "Hungry Dog, he say she is loco."

"You get your pronouns mixed," the judge murmured.

Evidently Jimmy did not know what a pronoun was; if he did, he seemed not to understand the jurist's statement.

"Me get hair chop," the young buck said. "Like China boy, down the street. One braid, then."

Tobacco said, "Dang it, Bates, is we nuts, both of us? Here we stan' talkin' like two idiots to a young un who wants a 'hair chop.' This wind is col', friend, an' there's a hot fire in the lobby."

"Where's Running Deer's lodge?" the judge asked.

Jimmy made another motion. "Me, I through wash dishes, for today until tonight. Come, friends."

They went between lodges. Dogs barked and

one nipped at the judge but Jimmy got the cur and lifted him and flung him back. The judge was afraid the dog had bit the youth but he did not say anything. After a while, he got a good look at Jimmy's hand; it had not been bit.

The boy had acted so quickly the jurist had not even had time to start a kick at the dog. He realized he meant a lot to this boy. Well, at least one Crow trusted him. He was surprised how quickly Jimmy had seemingly forgotten the death of his mother. But he had been trained in a hard school, the judge realized; the boy was seemingly without grief, but the jurist was willing to wager there was plenty of grief inside the youth.

"Here, judge."

The boy lifted the flap to Running Deer's lodge and then followed Judge Bates and Tobacco Jones inside. The oldest girl, who turned out to be Broken Nose, was cooking something for her sisters; it had a sweet, good smell. At the entrance of Judge Bates and Tobacco Jones the youngest girl, Little Sister, began to cry. Broken Nose said something in Crow and a girl went to Little Sister and talked to her.

Jimmy introduced the judge and postmaster. Broken Nose did the talking for herself and her sisters. She was a small, pretty little girl, quick with her hands and her tongue; her dark eyes darted around the lodge—she could sparkle and glisten, she could show sincerity and puzzlement.

"They no talk much white man," Jimmy said, "You talk me, I tell them in Crow."

The judge had some candy and he gave it to the girls. Little Sister unwrapped her piece gleefully. Evidently a stick of candy in this lodge was a real treat. The other two girls—Owl's Hair and Long

Woman—also unwrapped their sweets. But Broken Nose, being the mistress of the lodge, was more reserved—she put hers under her sleeping robe.

But the ice had been broken by the gifts. While her three sisters sat and sucked their hard candies, Broken Nose and Jimmy kept up quite a conversation, with the judge stating his questions and with Jimmy reciting them in Crow to his cousin.

Where had Running Deer gone to? Broken Nose did not have to answer that; she shrugged in typical Indian fashion—she did not know. Why had she gone? That drew a quick, fast answer. Her mother was afraid she would be killed. It was common knowledge that her sister, Running Dog, had been killed.

Why would anybody want to kill your mother?

Jimmy put the question into Crow. Broken Nose gave it some thought, her small, dark face showing her sincerity. She talked in slow Crow, and Judge Bates caught some of it; he was not proficient at the tongue, though, and many words escaped him.

Running Deer had, for some reason, been afraid she'd suffer the same death as her sister had suffered. She had left for some unknown hiding place. She had not told her daughters where she would be hiding. She had packed supplies with her. Broken Nose did not know who had hanged Hungry Dog. She did not know who her mother was running from.

"But her father, he have something to do with it," Jimmy said. "She does not know."

"My father?" Broken Nose said in broken English. "He come back, sir?" She addressed her question to Judge Lemanuel Bates.

This was a question the jurist had dreaded. He

was sure Broken Leg would get an appeal and a new trial; but would he be acquitted at his second trial? He hated to lie to this earnest little girl. But he had to, for the same reason he had had to lie to her mother, Running Deer.

"Your father will come home again."

"That good. Hope he come soon."

Long Woman said, "My father already back, Broken Nose."

Broken Nose turned, face lighted. "Who tell you?"

"Big Foot, he tell me."

Broken Nose let the light die out of her face and eyes. "Big Foot, he big liar."

"He like Red Beaver," Owl's Hair said.

The judge could understand that much of their conversation. They jabbered on, and he lost meaning in the rapid shuffle of their words. He had asked his questions; he had found out nothing.

"Tell them they find out where their mother went, Jimmy, and I'll give them a sack of candy."

"What'd you want Runnin' Deer for?" the boy asked brazenly.

The judge growled, "None of your smart lip, young man. I gave you an order; now carry it out."

Jimmy did as ordered. Already Tobacco Jones had left the tepee. The judge slid from under the flap and straightened, Jimmy behind him.

Tobacco asked, "Where to now, Bates?"

"Hotel, I guess. As good as any place."

Tobacco chewed, and seams gathered around his eyes and built small dikes. "That squaw sure pulled her picket pins an' drifted. But what gits me, Bates, is this: What do you want her for?"

"She knows why Hungry Dog got hanged. She knows why Charley Peterson tried to rob her wig-

110

warm that night."

"How do you know she does?"

"I'm sure she does. That's why she fled for her life. She knows something and somebody here wants that information. They did not get it from Hungry Dog. They intend to get that information from Running Deer."

"What information?"

"You've got me there," the judge had to admit.

Tobacco chewed and spat, missing Jimmy's bare feet by a straw. Jimmy pulled back his foot and Tobacco winked at Judge Lemanuel Bates. Jimmy did not see the wink.

"Anyway," Tobacco said, "she lived up to her handle, Bates. She's run like a deer. But usually a deer don't run far." He added, "That one girl claimed her father was back on the reservation."

Judge Bates said, "Jimmy, run over town," and the boy left. Then to Tobacco, "Her father is in the Cowtrail jail."

"I hope so, Bates."

The postmaster went to their hotel room and Judge Lemanuel Bates went to the poolroom where he got into a card game with Jack Frazier and Mike Perrine. They played for small stakes, mostly to pass away the time, and the game was dealer's choice.

The jurist did not like poker any too well. But they were the only white men in this locality outside of the few townsmen and Tobacco Jones; he wondered why they were here in this reservation town, and he wondered what their purposes were here on this range soon to be covered with winter snow.

But he found out exactly nothing relating to these two questions. Both men were close-mouthed; when

111

they did talk, it was of irrelevant points. The judge tried to swing the conversation over to the killing of Charley Peterson and the supposedly mysterious death of Skunk Ferguson—he got only grunts and nothing in the way of comment.

He deliberately lost a few dollars, hoping good luck would help open the conversation; here he was wrong, too. Two Crows shot pool, hour after hour; the pool balls clicked, spun, found pockets and rails. Four other old bucks sat in a card-game, playing with hardly any talk.

There was a fire in the pot-bellied heater, and it felt good. Judge Bates experienced a feeling of futility. Here he wanted to get some information out of Mike Perrine and Jack Frazier and he didn't got an iota; instead, it seemed they were feeling him out for some reason.

And why?

He was convinced, by now, that these two were involved in this trouble, but still he did not know the core of this trouble. That was the damnable truth; and it didn't make sense. But so far he had got nothing out of Broken Leg, or out of Red Beaver; Running Deer had left, and where had she gone?

"Your play, sir," Mike Perrine said.

The judge lost another pot, not due to bad playing but due to lack of cards. Perrine pulled in the chips.

"Tough luck, Your Honor."

Tobacco came in about five and perched on the rim of a pooltable. Finally he said, "We'd best get on our way, Bates; it's that time."

The judge stood up and cashed in his chips. He had lost over five bucks. Jack Frazier looked up, one eyebrow higher than the other in interest. And the judge said, "Us for chuck with Agent John Miller."

"Gettin' up into high company, eh?"

"The top of the social ladder, Frazier."

They went outside and Tobacco said into the wind, "Bates, why does a man of your mental standin' argue an' gamble with men of such low standin'?"

"They're the only white men here that are strangers."

"We're strangers," Tobacco corrected.

"Yes, but everybody knows our backgrounds. The backgrounds of those two are unknown. Mind how Jimmy told how they had made a midnight ride?"

"Well, is there anythin' really suspicious in thet, Bates? Mebbe they was just down to Garryowen for some gamblin'?"

"Garryowen is not too far away. Jimmy said their cayuses were sweaty and tired."

"Jimmy might've been wrong."

They met Jimmy in back of the cafe, where the young Crow was emptying the garbage. He said to Judge Bates, "Tobacco's been in the cafe all afternoon, makin' eyes at Miss Emma."

Tobacco said, "I was drinkin' coffee, Bates."

"No excuses, Jones."

Jimmy pounded his pail against the garbage can. "Danged Crow dogs raid this can. They tip it over an' fight an' snarl. Hey, they tell me Red Beaver has pulled his tepee pins."

"You mean," Judge Bates asked, "that he has left his lodge?"

"Red Beaver's gone."

Jimmy rattled the pail again, mostly for the cook's benefit, and then returned to his job. The partners went down the alley toward the home of John Miller.

113

"Red Beaver—gone?" Tobacco grunted. "I don't savvy that, Bates. With gover'ment issue comin' in, he run out; he won't git no beef unless he butchers it hisself, an' where did he go an' why? He's an ol' man?"

"Maybe somebody killed him."

"Kilt him? Why?"

"He sat there and watched that jail door and I still believe the ol' fool saw who entered an' if he did he knows who hanged Hungry Dog. An' knowing that, his life would be in danger."

"So's he's left, huh? For the same reason Runnin' Deer pulled out, you figger?"

"I do."

"But who hung Hungry Dog?"

"Now," said the judge, "we're going around the same old racetrack. Well, here's Agent Miller's home, an' we're in what I hope is not an unpleasant evening."

"Bates, you're an optimist."

Thirteen

Mrs. Miller was the lioness of the evening. She was the type of woman, who, because of a few more years of schooling than her husband, never let him forget this fact, and she impressed her company with the fact, too.

Tobacco Jones, his supper over, chewed tobacco and spat covertly in his bandanna, wishing the clock would move faster, yet too polite to run out on their host and hostess. When questioned too closely, he answered; when the question was not too pressing, he merely nodded.

Once he caught Mrs. Miller slanting a glance at him, but when he detected her scrutiny she continued her rapid conversation with Judge Bates. Tobacco realized that, for the first time, she had caught him chewing tobacco. Mrs. Miller, he had heard, was an ardent foe to the weed.

I oughta spit on her rug, the postmaster thought in malicious glee. But he didn't.

Tobacco leaned back in the rocking-chair. The meal had been excellent; he had to give the devil—or the lioness—her dues. Mrs. Miller was a good cook and knew what constituted a good meal. Out in the kitchen they could hear the scrape of a knife against plates as the Crow girl washed dishes.

John Miller sat opposite Tobacco, also reclining in his chair; they let Judge Bates and Mrs. Miller carry the conversation. Tobacco fought off lassitude by thinking of Red Beaver. Now where had that old fool gone?

The postmaster gave this earnest thought, bringing in Broken Leg, Hungry Dog, and Running Deer. But, as usual, he added the digits, and got no answer; the bottom line was all zeroes. He decided maybe Judge Bates could think this through. But still his mind grappled with its problem.

"Looks like an early winter, Mr. Jones."

Tobacco realized that Agent John Miller was addressing him. He agreed, listening to the sounds of the wind in the eaves; it sounded awesome and cold and snowy. He and Miller talked about winters for a while: which was the hardest one, which winter was an easy one, and Tobacco came out with one conclusion: everybody had different evaluations of winters. To one man a winter would be hard; to another the same winter would seem an easy one.

He heard Judge Bates say, "Madam, as a president, may I be permitted to say General Grant was of small moment, but as a general he was a fine officer. He could give instant decisions on the battlefield but in presidential office he wavered badly."

"I think he was too consistent with his friends," Mrs. Miller maintained. "He was an army man and he gathered only army men around him in important posts. Now I think—"

"Politics," Miller said.

Tobacco said, "Politics."

Miller said, "You might just as well try to argue about religion or philosophy. The only thing I'm sure of is that this country is getting too much from its people through taxations. Taxes are robbing us blind, Mr. Jones."

Tobacco was not in an argumentive mood, he was in a sleepy frame of body. "You are right, sir. One hundred per cent right."

Miller beamed, and talked some more. Tobacco listened with one ear on Miller, the other on the wind; he nodded occasionally. The talk switched to Sitting Bull, then to General Nelson A. Miles, then back to Washington. Finally the big hall clock tolled ten.

"Time we was headin' home, judge."

The judge consulted his pocket-watch in a surprise that Tobacco, because he knew the man so well, knew was feigned.

"Why, so it is, ten o'clock! My, we must again thank you folks for a wonderful dinner and wonderful conversation."

Miller stood up, rather sleepily, and they shook hands. Mrs. Miller was liquid softness.

"Indeed, Your Honor, it was delightful to talk to you. It is not often that one gets to converse with a person of your great mental stature."

Miller shook hands again.

"Do come again, gentlemen."

They accompanied the judge and postmaster out to the porch. Judge Bates said, "You'd best stay in the house, madam; this wind is cold."

"How I hate to see winter come."

"I hate it, too," Tobacco said.

The stars were windswept and high, now and then hidden by scurrying clouds. Judge Bates

117

pulled his collar up.

"That gal sure was ready to cry on your shoulder," Tobacco said. "She sure can lard on the act, huh?"

"She should be on the stage."

"Yeah," Tobacco said. "A Concord Stage."

They took the short-cut. By this hour Spotted Pony had no lights on its mainstreet. One or two tepees of the Crows' showed a faint tinge of candle-glow through the lodge skins.

Tobacco murmured, "A wasted evenin'."

To this summation, the judge had no answer. The wind held the same chill, but so far it had spit no snow. The judge found himself hoping this matter would be solved soon, so he could head back for his home in Cowtrail.

"Let's go in the back door," Tobacco said. "We kin head through this alley, Bates. Wonder if Jimmy's in your bed? Tough on a kid to be out on a night like this."

"He knows where my room is."

The alley was very dark. It had the smell of garbage from the Spotted Pony Cafe, and a pile of tin-cans were across the alley from the restaurant. A dog yelped and ran away. He was a Crow cur and he was afraid of a white man.

"Guess he can tell a white man from an Injun by his smell," Tobacco said. "Wonder which one—"

He never got to finish the sentence. They were walking past a building, dark and almost invisible in the night; something hit him across the back, right across the shoulders. The blow finished his sentence and knocked him ahead at a lurching gait, his breath smashed out of him and wonder inside of him. His first thought was, Did a hoss run into me? Then he thought, But I'd've heard him runnin' an'

118

I'd've got outa his way.

He found himself on his knees. He grunted, "Bates, what the—!" and he felt the blow again, this time across an outflung arm. He realized a club had hit him. A man had clubbed him, knocked him down, and had swung again. Only he had missed his body and hit him on the left arm.

He plunged ahead, seeing the outline of a man. Somehow he got his arms around the man's knees and the tackle downed his assailant. By this time he had his wind back partially; still, his lungs ached and his back was very sore. He and his assailant went down.

He didn't know whom he was fighting. But he realized he had to whip the man, or the man would whip him; this was part of this trouble, he thought. He fought as if his life depended on his whipping his foe.

Then fear ran through him. He called, "Bates," and he heard the judge grunt, "I got my hands full." There were two of them then; each of them had been jumped. Now who was he fighting?

Because of the darkness, he could not clearly see his opponent. They were down, and he was on the bottom. The man had lost his club and Tobacco could feel it under his back. The man was clubbing him with both fists.

Tobacco got his knees up, put them against the man's belly; he lifted and kicked. The man hung on momentarily and the postmaster heard his shirt rip. This angered him more, for it was a new dress shirt he had just bought for the dinner at Agent John Miller's. His kick ripped the man back; he took a part of the shirt with him.

The shirt was white, and it made a patch in the man's hand. He threw it from him and hollered,

"Run, pard, run." He spoke broken English. This registered immediately on Tobacco Jones.

The words were not spoken with the broken tongue of a Sioux. They were broken, yes; they sounded as though they had been spoken by somebody who usually spoke a Latin tongue.

The man lit out on the run down the alley. Tobacco followed him, wishing he had his pistol: but who packs a gun to a dinner at a friendly house? The postmaster gained on the man. Suddenly, for the second time, Tobacco Jones fell. This time, though, he fell over a wheelbarrow somebody had placed in the alley way.

His shins hollering, the postmaster plunged ahead, skidding on his chest and belly. When he got up he was as badly shaken as when he'd been slugged He hobbled, then stopped; he returned to the scene up the alley.

"Bates?"

"I got him, Tobacco."

Hobbling painfully, Tobacco went toward the jurist's voice. "My man got away, Bates. He shoved out a wheelbarrow in front of me. I'm danged sure he did that, or else some iggnerant son left the wheelbarrow there. You got the hellion what jumped you, huh?"

"I sure have."

Judge Bates was sitting on the man. The fellow lay on his back, either groaning from the jurist's tremendous weight or the weight of the judge's fists. Tobacco could not make out the man's face. He kept making sounds like a whipped puppy, whining and sharp.

"Light a match, Jones."

Tobacco knelt and said, "You got hold of his fists? I

don't want the son to belt me in the mug." He was stiff and sick inside from his fall and the fight. A man gets the wind knocked out of him and it takes some time to get it back. Until he does he's plenty sick in the stomach.

"I got his fists."

Tobacco found a match in his pocket. He lit it and the wind snuffed it out before it had a start. He got around, still on his knees, and put his back to the wind.

Judge Bates panted, "Hurry up."

Tobacco Jones lit another match. This flared, flickered, almost died, and then it caught. He shielded it between his bony palms. The light showed into eerie, terrified dark eyes. The man was not much more than five feet and six inches, if any over that mark; hard to tell a man's height with the jurist astraddle him.

The match lasted only a second or two, then the wind killed it. But it showed a swarthy, long face, and hair that, in the midst of its dark hue, had a big white spot in it. The mouth formed curses.

"Well," said Tobacco, standing up, "who is he?"

"I don't know. Do you?"

"If I knowed him, would I jaw you as to who he is?"

"Easy, pard," Judge Lemanuel Bates said quietly. "I got bunged up, too. I caught a glimpse of him an' his club missed. But as he went down, he belted me across my left shoulder."

"My shins," Tobacco mourned.

Judge Bates hammered a fist down at the man. The man moved his head; some of the blows missed, others connected. The judge stopped.

"Who are you, fellow?"

"None of your bizness."

121

"I'll make it my business," the jurist prophesied grimly. "What do you mean by jumping two law-abiding citizens under cover of night? You could have killed one of us, or both."

"T'hell with you."

Judge Bates said, "Too bad you didn't get the other one, Jones. Between the two of them, we'd have a better chance to find out what's behind all this, and who they are, and why they jumped us—strangers."

"Ever try runnin' with both legs busted?"

The judge overlooked that and said, "Well, let's tie this gent's hands, then take him over to Miller's and the agency jail."

"What'll we tie him with? You got a hundred feet of spotcord rope on you, Bates?" Tobacco was cynical. His shins hurt.

Judge Bates reminded the postmaster that he had on suspenders. Tobacco jerked them off and handed them to the judge.

"We got to get him on his belly, so I can truss his hands behind him. You hang onto his feet while I turn him."

Tobacco sat down and anchored himself to the man's ankles. "He's a-wearin' ridin' boots, Bates. Must be a hossman."

Despite the wiry man's protests, the thick judge got him on his belly.

Tobacco kept his grip on the man's boots. Judge Bates knotted the suspenders around the man's thin wrists, puffing and grunting as he tied the secure knots. He said, "There, that's done, Jones. Now get me a rope, please."

"Shore, I'll git you one. Pick it right off yonder star. What do you crave, judge: a maguey, a spotcord, or us' plain Manila?"

"There's a barn behind you. Get a rope off a saddle in it."

Tobacco went to the barn, lit a match, saw a saddle hanging from its right stirrup from a spike in a log. He untied the catch-rope at its fork and took it back to the judge who tied one end of it to the man's wrists over the knotted suspenders.

"Them braces sure are goners now," Tobacco mourned. "An' they cost me twenty-three cents at his highway-robbery store here."

"You'll live to buy another set."

Tobacco felt of his shins, then jerked his hands back; his shins were as sore as boils. They started up the alley, back toward the Agency buildings, the gent ahead. Once he started to run but the judge braced himself, like a cowpony braced to throw a calf.

And throw the fellow he did. The man hit the ground with, "Come an' help me, pard!" Then dirt finished whatever more he had hoped to say, if anything. The night was late and the merchant opened his window in his quarters over his store.

"Get outa that alley, you danged drunks!"

"Come down an' make us," Tobacco challenged.

"I'll come down with my scattergun." The window made a bang as it closed. But already the judge and postmaster and their captive were around the corner.

"He'll search that alley," the judge said, smiling.

"Do him good. Only work he'll have done for months. He sets by that cracker barrel an' doles out hot air."

The judge spoke almost shyly. "He's postmaster, too. And that's a hard job—you've told me that a

123

dozen times."

"Ever watch him, Bates? He's some postmaster. He doesn't even know Regulation 8 in Book 3."

The judge didn't know the regulation either; nor did he care to learn. His bottom lip was swelling from the impact of his assailant's fist. He had no interest in postal regulations. He was interested in one thing only: Why had these two tried to beat him and Tobacco?

At first, he could see no rhyme or reason for the attack. Then he realized that possibly two motivations had made the men jump them. One, they wanted to rob them; two, they didn't want them in Spotted Pony and were trying to scare them off this wind-crazy range.

The first summation seemed the more logical, His Honor decided. He mentioned this to Tobacco Jones.

"They'd never git away with their loot," the postmaster said. "We'd've had riders out an' by mornin' these two would have been picked up. Crows would track them down on solid rock. Only a crazy man would try such a thing."

"Maybe these two are crazy."

Their prisoner made the wrong turn. Tobacco pushed him, almost knocked him down; the man was spent. Judge Lemanuel Bates offered his second solution. Tobacco was in accordance with this immediately.

"Yep, Bates, you got a idea there, pard. But I don't figger they aimed to kill us. That'd been risky for them. 'Cause I'm a federal worker—the postmaster general'd've stepped into the case hisself had I been kilt—and you're a judge, and that would bring the governor an' militia into the search. Our

124

killers wouldn't have lasted long."

The judge admitted his partner spoke logic. "But I'm not sure, myself. Still, I figure somebody doesn't want us on this grass, Jones."

"For once, Bates, you figure rightly."

Fourteen

Agent John Miller came to the door wearing a long red nightgown and with a blue nightcap on his head. He held a lighted lamp but he did not get to speak first, for his wife's voice, squeaking with excitement, said, "Well, Judge Bates and Mr. Jones! What in heaven's name happened?"

The judge disregarded the domineering female and asked, "Mr. Miller, do you know this fellow?"

Miller peered at the man. Finally he said, "No, I don't. He's a stranger to me."

"What happened?" Mrs. Miller was adamant.

The judge gave a sketchy account of the fight, and this seemed to satisfy the woman, who said ah and oh and gaped. She did not know the prisoner, either. "And I'm sure, if I'd seen him before, I'd have known him."

"I'm sure of that," the judge said.

They got the prisoner to the jail after Miller had slipped into house-slippers and had donned an overcoat. Hungry Woman had been the only prisoner—and now she was dead—and the place was dark. Miller found the lamp and lit it and the feeble rays showed up the gloomy interior. Miller

126

kept repeating, "More trouble, more trouble," and occasionally he broke in with, "But why would they try to waylay you two?" He did not wait for an answer but continued with, "And how I do wish you had captured the other man."

"Where's your jailer?" the judge asked.

"He's in his tepee. No use having him here when we had no prisoners. The keys are on yonder hook. I'll go awaken him."

Miller hustled out and Tobacco unlocked a cell and the judge gave the silent prisoner a push that propelled him into the cell. The jurist went in with him, threw him down, and searched him. He found a short pistol and a knife and he handed these back to Tobacco.

"Nice friendly chap, Bates."

"Slam shut the door."

The cell-door clanged. Tobacco knelt and pulled up his right pant's leg, for that shin hurt the most, and he inspected his leg. The skin was only broken a little, and the shin looked not too bad; it sure hurt, though. Just about that time the prisoner, hands untied, smacked the floor.

Tobacco watched, grinning.

The prisoner got up, wiping blood from his mouth. The judge stood in a stance, fists up. The prisoner moved back; the judge followed. The prisoner squealed, "You want a fight?"

The question was sort of ludicrous, for it was plain the judge was going to do some fighting The prisoner ducked, came up; he put both fists into Judge Bates' ample paunch. Then he was flying back, and he hit the wall. He was stunned, not so much from the single blow, but because he had not seen it coming.

127

"He hurt your belly, Bates?"

Judge Lemanuel Bates had no answer to Tobacco's question. He was shuffling in a circle, following his opponent who circled him. Judge Bates grunted, "Why did you try to slug me, you devil?"

"No tell."

"Then I'll make you tell!"

This time, though, the judge was the one to backstep. Tobacco saw that this lithe man with the pinto spot in his hair was a tough hombre. They fought in the middle of the cell, and the judge finally knocked the man down.

"Get up and fight, man!"

"I got—enough."

"If you have, why did you try to slug me back in that alley? Hurry up, now, and talk!"

"You go—"

Tobacco watched, mouth opened slightly. He saw that the match was fair enough, at that; what the judge had in weight was offset by the youth and greater agility of the younger man.

But the thing that really surprised him was to see Judge Lemanuel Bates so angry. He had seen the judge work over prisoners before and he had seen the judge pound them into confession. But usually the judge worked with a sort of mechanical efficiency, entirely untouched by anger. But this time Judge Bates was angry, and Tobacco did not blame his partner.

It was one thing to hold back a confession from the law. It was entirely another item when a thug knocked down a judge in an alley.

"Come on, fellow; fight!"

The gent had made his fourth trip to the floor. The

bed, a steel cot, was on its side, bedding on the floor. Judge Bates, shirt out, a little blood around his mouth, breathed a trifle heavy, but his eyes were slitted and ready, and his huge fists were up in defense.

"Come on, fellow——"

The man made a sprawling tackle, hitting the judge below the knees. Tobacco unwittingly winced, remembering the wheelbarrow and his sore shins. The pair went down, the judge on the bottom.

A wild sort of ambition seemed to be firing the man with the white splotch in his hair. He sat on the jurist, beating him in the face, and Tobacco, for the first time, felt the strong pull of uncertainty. Maybe the judge had spotted the younger man too many days.

But then the man was flying backwards against the far wall, propelled there by the judge's boots. He looked like he was trying to grab air to steady himself. His mouth was open, his arms flailed, and he gasped something. He hit the wall, cracked his head against the partition, and when the judge lumbered over the man had slid down the wall to sit in a stupid-looking position.

His legs were out in front of him, his arms hung limply at his sides, his head lay on his chest. Tobacco moved close to the bars to watch as the jurist lifted the man's head by his hair.

The man's ox-like eyes rolled, settled. His mouth flapped at the jaw-pins and the man's tongue eased out.

"Knocked him cold, Bates."

That presented a new problem. "Unconscious is right. He must've hit his skull hard against that wall."

"Well, hades, Bates. He hit his jaw hard ag'in your fist!"

"We'll wait until he comes to."

Tobacco said, "Hades with that, Bates, I'm tired, I need some iodine on my leg, an' he'll keep to mornin'. Besides, let him think it over a spell, an' maybe you won't have to persuade him come daylight."

"Here comes Agent Miller."

Miller was puffing like a U.P. wood-burner on a steep grade. His Crow jailer had got drunk and he couldn't wake him up. "Now where do you suppose he got the whiskey, Bates? No whiskey on this reservation."

"Maybe he's got a coil, a mash-kettle, an' some mash."

"I'll have to investigate," Miller puffed. He looked at the prisoner. "What happened to him?"

"Fell down an' cracked his head on the wall," the judge intoned seriously. "Well, what's going to happen, sir?"

Miller said he would sit as jailer. The partners read his open distaste for the job and realized the agent did not want the job, but was just doing it to make it look good to a federal judge. For, after all, Miller held a federal job, and he had to please a federal judge.

Judge Bates said, "If you want to, Mr. Miller, you can hang him for me. He's treated me kind of rough."

The joke was wasted on John Miller. Life to him was a serious business that did not end in a useless grave.

"I'll watch him closely, gentlemen. Will one of you stop by and tell Mrs. Miller where I am for the rest of the night?"

The partners promised and left. Time had gone by rapidly and it was almost two o'clock after they had doctored Tobacco's skinned shins. The postmaster had winced when the iodine hit the raw flash. He hopped on one skinny leg, then transferred to the other.

Jimmy Hungry Dog blinked in the lamp-light. "What—what happened?"

"We were out bear-hunting," the judge said solemnly. "We found a bear and a cougar fighting and we separated them."

"What with?"

"Our hands."

Jimmy said, "Blahhh . . ." and watched. The postmaster then doctored the judge's cuts. Iodine on his lip, on his skinned knuckles. Now it was Judge Lemanuel Bates' turn to wince.

"We sure found out a lot," Tobacco admitted grudgingly.

The judge had to concur with his partner. Jimmy watched, deep in the covers, and was silent. Finally, he said, "Red Beaver, he gone."

"You told us that before," the judge reminded.

"Nobody knew where he go, either."

"Forget him," the judge murmured. He was stiff, sore; he'd gone through two fights—one in the alley and the other in the cell. Tobacco went to his room and the judge heard the key turn. He blew out the light and the springs sagged as the mattress settled.

Sleep did not come quickly, but it came. Jimmy awoke the jurist as the Crow boy dressed to go to work at the Spotted Pony Cafe.

"Late," Jimmy grunted, pulling on his moccasins.

The judge asked him to hand him his watch from

his pants. Jimmy held it up and the jurist saw it was six o'clock and swung gingerly out of bed. Even at that, he wasn't as stiff as he had expected; his lip, though, was swollen rather bad. But it would eventually go down.

"I wake Jones."

"Do that, Jimmy."

Jimmy pounded and finally got response from Tobacco's room. The judge dressed and went into the hall and said, "Ready, Tobacco."

He got a sleepy, "In a minute, Bates."

He was in the lobby when his partner came down the hall, grumbling as he pulled tight his belt. "I sure wish I had some new suspenders. This belt is like a cinch, Bates, it like to cut me in two."

The judge assured him the store would open at eight and he had seen a display of suspenders in the showcase. They headed for the Spotted Pony Cafe. The wind had died before the dawn, and the sun was just tipping the far hills. The air had a spicy chill.

"Bet the trout are rising," the jurist said. "So far, no fishing, and the Little Big Horn has fine rainbows."

"Yeah, an' I've caught cut-throats there, too."

The judge said, "Before we eat, let's check on our prisoner."

Tobacco wrestled with his appetite against his curiosity, and the latter won. They went into the jail without knocking and they found Miller sitting in the chair. He was sound asleep. He did not awaken.

They looked at him, listening to his snores. The judge said, "Somebody could pry off the jail-doors and tote them past him and auction them off outside, and he'd never know the difference."

"Maybe it's the only chance he's had to sleep for

some time, Bates. Who knows? Maybe his wife even keeps her jaw workin' in her sleep an' keeps him awake?"

Judge Bates shook Miller. He came awake with a jerk, reaching for the gun that had lain in his lap— but Tobacco had the gun a few inches away from the agent's whiskery face.

"Jones, please—put that down!"

Judge Bates said, "See how easy it would be to make a jailbreak with you as guard, Miller? That man who jumped Tobacco could have come back and got the keys and let his partner out and you'd never have known the difference."

"But he didn't come back," Miller said, awake now.

Tobacco said, "Are you sure?" and alarm sent him scurrying down the cell-corridor, Miller's six-shooter in his hand. Judge Bates saw his partner come to a sudden stop, and then Tobacco stood there, gazing into the cell.

"Tobacco, anything wrong?"

"Bates, come here!"

The postmaster's voice was high-pitched, little more than a croak. The squeakiness of it brought the judge down the corridor, with Miller tramping on his heels.

"What is it, Jones?"

"Look!"

The judge stopped. Miller stopped, too. The judge's eyes turned tight and hard, black as obsidian, and his mouth came shut. But Miller's eyes were loose and his jaw open, showing his teeth.

"How did that—happen?"

"When you slept," Tobacco growled.

The judge didn't say anything for some time. The

prisoner hung from a beam, the suspenders around his neck. His face was bloated and already blue.

Tobacco said, "We forgot them suspenders in his cell, Bates."

"Sure looks like it, partner."

Fifteen

There was an occasional snowflake, driving with the wind from the northwest. The two riders were small ants moving across the vastness of this land wherein General George Armstrong Custer and his men had fought and died. They came closer, moving slant-wise with the wind, and finally they came to the old cabin.

Jack Frazier said, "Winter's close."

"Too danged close for comfort." Mike Perrine blew on his numbed hands. "Summer's a short affair."

"Like life."

But Mike Perrine had no desire to delve into philosophy. Years before his limited intelligence had put a strict fence around his philosophy. You were born, you went through life doing as little work as possible—even if it meant lifting the other fellow's gold—you loved, lived, and some day you died. Beyond that, no man alive could tell you what awaited you, if anything.

"I can't git over it, Jack. Pinto done hung hisself."

Jack Frazier's smile was abrupt. "One less to divide this gold among. He sure must've been scairt

135

of us an' what we'd do with him for bunglin' this beatin' up of Jones an' Bates."

Mike Perrine agreed with that logic. For neither he nor his partner had hanged Pinto in the agency jail. That task had been performed exclusively by Pinto. But there was one point that did bother Mike Perrine.

"Wonder if he done tol' Jones an' Bates he was workin' for us, an' that we hired him an' Hermando to jump on them?"

Frazier shook his head.

"How do you know?"

"Have Bates or Jones said anything about it?" He answered his own question. "No, they haven't. Yesterday, after they'd found Pinto hung, Bates played a afternoon of poker with us, didn't he?"

"Yeah, but—"

"Lemme finish, fella. I talked with Miller, too. He claims that Pinto held a tight set of lips, an' Pinto tol' the judge an' Tobacco exactly nothin'. But he sure must've bin afraid we'd come in thet jail an' kill him for bunglin' that set-to with Bates in that alley."

"You figure Hermando'll be at the Cabin?"

"I figure so."

"He might run out, too. He might figure like Pinto did—thet we'd be mad at him—an' he might've lit out."

"I doubt that."

"What meks you say that?"

"Well, Hermando knows they got Pinto. But he'll figure we got Pinto free an' Pinto'll ride out with us today."

"Maybe. . . ."

Jack Frazier turned in saddle, weight on his near stirrup, and looked at the dark Mike Perrine.

"Mike, use your brains, fella. Put yourself in Hermando's boots for a minute. Hermando's no fool; he knows we're after big stakes. He still remembers that poke of nuggets that Broken Leg lugged into Spotted Pony. He wants to find out where them nuggets come from, an' he wants some of them."

Mike Perrine showed a slow smile. "So do I. I wonder where thet map is, Jack. If we could only git that map—"

"I think Red Beaver's got that map. That's why the ol' buck lit out without even gittin' his gover'ment issue beef for this winter. He was afraid you an' me'd call on him next, jes' like we called on Hungry Dog."

"Wonder where he is?"

"I got a hunch, Mike, that Hermando knows where he is. Wait till we talk with him."

Mike Perrine spoke so quietly he might have been talking to himself. "Onct there was six of us—there was you an' me an' Pinto an' Hermando an' Peterson an' Ferguson. We come together by accident—all lured by gold. Broken Leg hid them nuggets, us six was headin' through to the Black Hills for the winter—an' from a butte we watched Broken Leg make his cache. We lifted it, then decided to stick around, an' then Runnin' Deer mentioned somethin' about a map, how she had made a copy for Hungry Dog."

"Why rehash that?"

"I'm jes' thinkin'. We stuck aroun' because of gol', with Pinto an' Hermando in the hills. Heck, Skunk even hooked up with a squaw, tryin' to git that map. Well, they was six; jus' one-half of us are dead."

"We all have to die."

"But we don't have to die in violence. We had to kill Peterson—we had to get him out of the way—an'

137

that got Broken Leg out. One gone."

"For hell's sake, close your mug!"

Perrine gave no evidence he had heard. "Then Bates an' Jones came in with Skunk dead, shot to death. Heck, they kilt him, before he could get to them. Two gone."

"Perrine, shut up!"

Mike Perrine sent Jack Frazier a slow, slanting glance. "Am I hurting your ear-drums, my purty friend?" He got no answer and he continued with, "Now Pinto's gone. Three gone. One-half of us."

Jack Frazier had his pistol out, the barrel across his saddle and on Mike Perrine.

"Mike," he said.

Perrine looked at the gun. "Your nerves are touchy." He shrugged and looked ahead, seemingly interested in the sweep of the distance. Frazier finally holstered his gun. Frazier's hands trembled and he thought, My hands are cold.

They got their broncs in the high brush and went down. Here they were out of the wind and the sun was almost warm. Frazier said, "Look for his bronc," and Perrine went into the brush. Frazier waited, rubbing his hands together to warm them; Perrine came back.

"No horse tied in the brush, Jack."

Frazier jerked his head toward the cabin. "We'll wait inside. He'll come along. There's a deck of cards in there."

But when they came into the warm cabin, the deck of cards was already in use. Hermando had a game of solitaire going. He had a cut across his right cheek, and his eye was very black.

Perrine said, "I looked for your bronc, but couldn't find him in the brush."

138

Hermando jerked a thumb over his shoulder. "I tied him up on the ridge, in the rocks. Where's Pinto?"

Jack Frazier said, "Pinto's dead," and he told about it, watching Hermando. He saw the man's dark eyes mirror something: was it fear, or was it disbelief? Frazier did not know.

"Pinto, he hang himself?"

"He did," Perrine stated.

Hermando looked from Frazier to Perrine. Then he lowered his eyes to his cards. "He would do that," he finally said slowly. "In his heart—" he pointed to his chest "—he was the coward."

"He had guts enough to hang himself," Frazier reminded.

Hermando swept a dark, skinned hand out and collected the cards. He riffled them into the desk. Jack Frazier noticed the slight unsteadiness of Hermando's hand and Hermando did not see the look he sent Mike Perrine.

"Well," Frazier said grimly, "you bungled it."

Hermando looked up, eyes savage. "Don't rub me wrong, Frazier. We did our best. How could Pinto know he was going to be caught?"

Mike Perrine watched, holding his tongue. Although Hermando seemed simple, Perrine did not underestimate the dark man one bit; he had seen Hermando handle a gun.

Frazier said, soothingly, "Let's forget all about Pinto, huh? He's dead, he told nothing to Bates an' Jones, and it's best we don't mention him, eh?"

Hermando said, "He was my partner. For many years, he ride by me."

Frazier snagged a chair and settled down. Perrine moved over to the corner and licked a cigaret into shape, never taking his eyes from the others. He lit his sulphur and looked over the cone of red as he lit his smoke.

Perrine said, "Let's get down to brass tacks. There's gold in Big Horn Canyon. We've got some of it when we robbed Broken Leg. We want more of it. Those Crows know where it is. We get that gold, and then we leave this section. We know it's pocket-gold. We sluice it out and leave."

"How we find it?" Hermando asked sarcastically. "Pinto an' me, we watch. We watch good. We no see Crow come to gold, wherever it is. We no find gold. We know where gold can be found, too." He looked back at Jack Frazier. "Red Beaver, he know."

"Red Beaver is gone."

"No? Him dead, too?"

Frazier smiled unpleasantly. He told about Red Beaver leaving the Crow camp. "We was goin' to call on the ol' devil, too. But he left afore we could pay him a visit. Runnin' Deer is gone, too."

Hermando gave himself to thought. "That was him I see yesterday," he said. "I see Red Beaver yesterday."

He had seen a rider over at the mouth of Big Horn Canyon. His glasses had identified the rider as a redskin; but distance had not allowed identification concise enough to recognize who the rider was.

"He meet man, back in rocks, men. That man, I see clearer; I think he was Broken Leg."

Jack Frazier spat in disgust. Mike Perrine's eyes showed nothing. Frazier said, "It couldn't be Broken Leg. He's in jail down in Cowtrail."

"You sure of that?"

"He might've busted out," Perrine put in.

"I could be wrong," Hermando said.

140

Frazier put his head down and stroked his whiskery jaw, eyes hidden from Perrine and Hermando. He seemed to be talking to himself. "Runnin' Deer is in hidin'; so is Red Beaver. One of them has that map. One thing is certain: they ain't far from that gold. They'll stick around its vicinity to make sure none of us find it."

Perrine nodded.

Hermando was silent.

Frazier continued with, "We tried to scare Judge Bates an' Tobacco Jones out of this country. You tried, Hermando; so did Skunk Ferguson. None of the tries worked."

Perrine ground his cigaret dead on the dirty floor. "You cain't scare them two, Frazier. I said it then an' I say it now. If you'd've listened to me, you'd've killed them afore they reached Spotted Pony. Shot them down from the brush."

"There'd been a hell of a stink," Frazier said. "They both hold federal jobs." He was silent, and the wind spoke through the eaves. "Wonder how much them two know?"

Hermando shrugged, seemingly without tongue.

"I don't know how much they know," Mike Perrine said, "but I do know they are suspicious of us. We're the only whites on this reservation that are strangers. Them two is bound to suspicion us."

"That right," Hermando agreed.

Frazier stood up. He had the expression of a man who had weighed circumstances, had matched one item against another, and had thereby come to his decision. And now, that decision made, he would fight to attain it.

Mike Perrine and Hermando watched him. Perrine's dark, ugly eyes were sharp, and Hermando

141

watched with a wary dullness.

Frazier said, "You an' me is done in Spotted Pony, Perrine."

"I've known that for some time," Perrine murmured.

Frazier sent him that hard, piercing look. "Wait until I get done talking. We stuck around there trying to git thet map. We didn't git it. Now we pack a pack-horse, get our critters, an' head into the Canyon. We watch there. Red Beaver is in these rocks; so is Runnin' Deer. Somewhere they've got a camp. We get them an' we fin' out where that free gold is."

Perrine said, "Good plan."

Hermando got to his feet and crossed the room and put the deck of cards on the shelf. He turned, back to the wall, hands on the wall behind him, and he looked from one to the other; they waited for him to speak.

All he said was, "Good."

Frazier continued with, "Hermando, make camp in the Canyon. Mind them red standstones on the right flank? We'll meet you there with grub an' bullets."

"When we meet?"

"Tomorrow."

"I be there."

"Meanwhile, you watch. Get on a crag with your glasses an' watch. We'll be out there sometime in the afternoon."

"I watch."

They went outside, and the wind reached with cold fingers. Hermando said, "I go now," and he climbed to his horse. Perrine and Frazier found saddles. Perrine said, "Snow might catch us. Then what good would a gold mine be? You can't work gold in the winter."

"Anyway, we'll know where the pocket is."

Mike Perrine tasted that and found it sweet. "Then we can work the pocket when spring comes." Something bitter came in. "But what if it's a small pocket, and it's worked out already?"

"We'll have to chance that."

Sixteen

Agent John Miller said, "I can't understand it. Beef issue finally comes, an' ol' Red Beaver is gone. Usually he hollers for the fattest steers and usually he gets what he wants."

"There are no fat steers in this bunch," Judge Bates said dryly.

They were standing outside the agency corral and looking at the cattle being driven in by the cowboys. Dust rose and the cold wind broke it and took it away; through dust they could see the cattle comprising the beef issue. And the sight was not a cheering one.

For the cows were poor. And cows they were, not steers. They were old cows, unable to throw calves because of their age; they were poor and they would make stringy beef.

"No wonder Sittin' Bull led his warriors on the warpath," Tobacco grunted.

Miller asked, "What was that?"

Tobacco looked at Judge Bates, who shook his head. Tobacco said, "Nothin' much, just a remark about these cows."

Miller looked from the postmaster to the judge,

then looked back at the cows in the corral. The Crows were lined along the corral, the bucks sitting on the top rail, the squaws and children on the ground. They were deriding the cowboys who were putting the cows into the corral.

The cowboys didn't know it, though, for the Crows did not use English. Jimmy translated for the judge and postmaster.

"Crow ask how they can drive a cow that is dyin' so far. Crow say cowboy is Manitou to keep cow alive when she should be dead. Another Crow say he can chew rock as well as jerky from these cows."

"I agree with him," Judge Bates said. Miller had gone away to talk with the boss of the cowboys and to compare tallies with him, for the last cow was in the corral.

The squaws were grumbling, some screeching, some just mumbling. Occasionally a dirty glance was sent toward Judge Lemanuel Bates and Tobacco Jones. The judge seemed not to notice them, but Tobacco was none too easy. For some reason he kept remembering those dried-up scalps in Red Beaver's lodge.

"Heck, we ain't to blame for these skinny ol' cows, Bates."

"They don't know that," the judge said. "We're white men, we're here, an' this is a dirty deal."

Miller came back, a man on horseback beside him. The partners recognized him as the trail-boss. Miller introduced him as Joe Carson, and introduced the partners as Lemanuel Bates and Tobacco Jones, not using the judge in front of Bates' name. And evidently Carson had never heard of Judge Bates.

"Sir," the judge asked, "are those the worst beef

you had on your range?"

You could see Joe Carson stiffen. He had the habit of rubbing his long nose and he did this now.

"I don't follow you, fella."

The judge pointed out that usually a beef contract called for fat steers. And a man could hang his Stetson on the hips of any of these old cows. Carson kept getting stiffer and stiffer.

"And what bizness is it of yours, fellow?"

Miller was silent, face slightly pale, and not from the wind. Tobacco chewed and grinned, anticipating agreeably what was ahead.

"When Mr. Miller introduced me, Mr. Carson, he forgot to point out that I am **Judge** Lemanuel Bates, presiding judge of Cowtrail, Wyoming, district, also a federal judge. I just presided at the trial of a Crow Indian, one Broken Leg. Now, I hope, you understand my qualifications?"

Carson mumbled something, the starch out of his spine. "Best beef we had," he said. He sent a glance at Miller and it was not pleasant. "Fattest beef we had." He turned his horse and rode away.

Miller sent a desperate glance at Carson's back, then said, "I'm sorry you do not approve of these cows, Your Honor."

"Best beef he had," Tobacco repeated cynically.

"Sure," the judge said. "Best beef he had **after** he'd shipped out his top stuff from the closest Northern Pacific corral."

Miller said, "I'll argue him down on the price per pound," and walked away, thoroughly miserable.

Jimmy had gleefully listened to the conversation. Now he interpreted it to another Crow boy.

Judge Bates snapped, "None of that, Jimmy."

Jimmy stopped in the middle of a sentence. He

looked at the judge. "All right, Mr. Bates. You go away, Charley."

The whole town, such as it was, had turned out to see the beef issue. Jack Frazier and Mike Perrine came up and Frazier said, "Sure, poor cows, Mr. Bates. Not much meat on them."

The judge agreed with them. The pair talked a while, then went around to the other side of the corral. Carson and his cowboys left in a cloud of dust, hats up and yipping. The Crows hurled curses at them, according to Jimmy; the cowboys thought the redskins were cheering them, and their hats went higher, their yips sharper. They headed toward their mess-wagon, which had stopped a few miles out of town; they were heading north again.

Jimmy said, "Them two, they leave soon, Bates."

"What two?"

"Frazier an' Perrine."

"How do you know?"

Jimmy said he had been in the general store and the pair had come in and he had heard them order grub. "They bought some bullets, too."

The judge had seen the pair in the store, but of course he had not gone in, for he had not wanted them to get suspicious of him.

"They buy a pan, too."

"A pan?"

"Yes, a pan. What they do with it?"

That seemed odd. A pan? Now what could a man do with a pan? Boil coffee in it? Yes. Maybe that's why they had purchased a pan.

"A flat pan," Jimmy said.

The judge said, "Jimmy, watch their barn. Get in the haymow. Watch it, savvy?"

But Jimmy protested. He wanted to see the bucks

kill the meat issue. The judge realized this was always a big event in an agency. The bucks selected the beef they wanted. That beef was then run out of the corral and the buck, mounted on his top horse, would then ride in close and send an arrow through the beef.

His job was then through. He, the boss of the tepee, had killed his winter's meat; his squaw would then bleed the beef, skin it, and quarter it. The buck was through. The squaw and his children would lug the beef to his tepee while he sat and smoked and made talk with his masculine neighbors.

"I want to see them down beef, judge."

The judge and Jimmy made an agreement. Jimmy would keep his eye on Frazier and Perrine, and he would trail them when they left. That suited both parties, and Jimmy moved away.

"You put a lot of faith in that young one," Tobacco said.

"You're wrong there," the judge corrected. "He puts a lot of faith in me, Tobacco."

Tobacco stayed there and the judge moved away, intending to listen to the reactions of the Crows to these skinny cows. But whenever he came close to a group of bucks talking, they immediately stopped talking. He circled the big corral and stopped beside Frazier and Perrine.

"They don't cotton to these skinny cows," Frazier said.

The judge nodded. He didn't tell the pair, but there'd be an investigation into this, and his influence would bear heavily against Miller. Miller was getting a good salary from the government: he didn't need another by buying poor beef. "They aren't too fat," he admitted.

Perrine looked at the sky, his face dark and thoughtful. "Looks like snow. It'll come any day now. I reckon it's me for Deadwood and a hotel for the winter. Sit in the lobby, roast my shins, and spread the hot air with the other boys who get snowed-in."

"Good idea," Frazier said.

Judge Lemanuel Bates got the impression, from somewhere, that they were feeling him out. They were discussing their future plans in an attempt to get him to disclose his.

"Well, our fishin' trip is over," he said. "Come tomorrow, Jones and I are heading back for Cowtrail, and a warm stove."

"Any luck?" Frazier asked.

The judge said, "Had some luck. Got some nice rainbows in the Little Big Horn. Never got to fish the Big Horn, though. Maybe next time when we come up we'll fish the Canyon."

"I've fished it," Frazier said. "Never got a rise. Water too fast, Mr. Bates. Muddy most of the time, too."

"Well, thanks. That'll save me and Tobacco a useless trip, I reckon." The judge went back to where Tobacco stood. "Those two are talking about heading out, Jones."

"Good riddance of bad rubbish. Where do they aim to go to put their curse on another area?"

Judge Bates smiled thinly. Apparently Tobacco did not hold Jack Frazier and Mike Perrine in high esteem.

"Deadwood, Perrine said."

"An' Frazier?"

"He didn't say."

"Good riddance," Tobacco repeated.

All of a sudden, the Crows sent up a wild shout.

Squaws hollered, kids screeched; even old blanket bucks let smiles break their wrinkled, cold faces. They had all converged around the gate of the corral.

"Must've turned loose a beef," Tobacco said, and climbed the corral to the top rail, the jurist climbing beside him. Dust was thick for a moment, and then the wind ran it away with a silent club.

Two Crow bucks were in the corral. They had cut out a cow and had hazed her into the open area. A rail fence ran along here—really wings of the corral used to make it easier to drive cattle into it—and back of this and along the top perched the Crows. They were gaudy in blankets and some of the bucks wore head-dresses.

Then they saw the cow. She was wild with fury and she charged the fence, smashing into it, but was repelled. Tobacco scowled and admitted the cow should not have been that wild. Hadn't she just finished a long, tiresome trek from the northernmost edge of Montana Territory?

"They've doctored her," the judge said.

"Wonder what with?"

"Some Crow hocus-pocus, I guess. They cut them a little on the belly, pour some of this solution on them, and then run like hades. Look at her charge that rider!"

Head down, the cow charged, digging in. She was a roan beast, bony and quick, and she intended to make short work of a certain Crow buck and his pony. But both the Crow and his mount had different ideas.

The pony turned sharply, the buck low on him. Judge Bates saw the tip of one sharp horn miss the pony's shoulder by mere inches. The cow turned, too, but too late; she slammed into the wing of the corral, and knocked herself down, and she landed sprawling in the dust.

The Crow was crowding his horse on her, riding her to her feet. He was grinning and shouting, brandishing his bow high. The cow charged again, and this time the pony was not quick enough; the cow upset him.

It was a tricky moment. There was dust, and through this the partners saw the shadowy outlines of the bronc on the ground, the Crow on his feet. Then, out of this dust came the wild cow on the run. She had an arrow in her back, slantwise through her high ribs; the Crow had put it there. The Crow ran out of the dust and up came his bow. But, before he sent in another arrow, the cow had gone down.

She went down suddenly, rolling in the dust. One moment she had been running, the arrow bobbing; the next her four legs had run out, letting momentum make her roll. And she didn't move.

"One cow gone," Judge Bates murmured.

By now the wind had moved the dust. The pony was on his feet, his right front leg limp. The Crow came back to him, grinning to the hollering of the crowd; he looked quickly at his horse's shoulder, then mounted and rode away. One buck called something in a loud voice.

"Wonder what he said?" Tobacco pondered.

Jimmy had climbed up beside them. "He say, Go get a jackrabbit to ride," the boy reported.

The buck's squaw had cut the dead cow's throat. The buck, despite the fact his bronc limped, threw down a rope and the squaw tied it around the cow's hind legs.

The buck, of course, rode bareback. He made a

signal with his arm and an agency worker, a white man, came out driving two work-horses, one of them dragging a double-tree from one tug. The horses snorted, afraid of the smell of blood, but he got them close and hitched them to the double-tree.

The Crows were hollering for them to get out of the way, for already another cow had been hocus-pocused in the corral, and already a buck waited outside the gate, mounted and with his bow and arrow ready.

But the squaw and the agency worker took their time. Finally the end of the rope had been tied to the clevis-pin. The worker clucked to his team and they dragged the dead cow away, hind feet first. They dragged her into another corral and got her carcass under a tripod made of green cottonwood poles.

"Good," the squaw grunted.

From now on, it was all up to the squaw to hang up the animal, peel the hide from it, gut it and quarter it. Tobacco noticed that the buck's bronc had been cut rather severely on the shoulder.

"Thet cow sure had sharp horns, Bates."

The judge and postmaster watched the butchering all afternoon. Agent John Miller flitted around like a fly, travelling from one carcass to the other as they dragged off the recently-killed cattle for quartering. Buck after buck rode out, dust boiling between him and his beef, and a brown arm would come back, the arrow between thumb and forefinger.

There would be a dull **whang**, many times audible above the cries and pounding of hoofs. One buck shot an arrow right through the deep chest of a big, bony cow. Evidently it had pierced the heart. The cow came to a crumpled, headlong stop.

"Sure hate to have them send one of them things into me, Bates."

"I've seen them shoot one through a bull buffalo. That was over in Custer, over in the Black Hills."

Tobacco was looking toward the butchering-corral. "Them squaws sure don't seem to cotton to them skinny beeves."

The squaws were gabbling and hissing, sounding like a bunch of mad geese that could talk. One buck sat and ate the raw liver of a beef. Knives flashed, dust rose, and there was the smell of fresh manure.

"They'll git thet beef all dirty, Bates."

"They aren't hollering about that," the judge corrected. "A little dirt means nothing to a redskin, as well you know. They're belly-achin' about the quality of the meat, not the dirt."

"Make good pemmican an' jerky."

The judge agreed with that. The meat would make tough pemmican, at that. Jimmy Hungry Horse had slipped off the corral and had gone somewhere. The judge looked for Jack Frazier and Mike Perrine, who had been perched across the corral. They were both nowhere in sight.

For the hundredth time, he added up all he knew, and it added up mostly to conjecture, nothing more. Broken Leg was in jail awaiting a new trial, they had had to kill Skunk Ferguson, and somebody had hanged Hungry Dog, right in front of Red Beaver's seamed, weather-marked eyes. Yes, and now a gent with a splotch in his hair was also dead; had he hanged himself, or had somebody sneaked past the sleeping Miller and hanged this stranger?

If so, who had hanged him, and why?

Experience had taught Judge Lemanuel Bates not to deal too much in the area of conjecture. A legal man, trained to the law, his mind wanted concrete evidence; it discarded evidence based on conjecture. And to whom did all this point?

He didn't know, for sure. He had his suspicions, true, but many of the loose ends would not weave into the cloth; at this stage, they were off-color and did not fit the over-all pattern.

But he realized this matter had to come to a head soon. He and Tobacco had been in this town a week—in fact, some days past one week. Common sense told him Mike Perrine and Jack Frazier were involved in this. Discreet questioning had confirmed the fact that Charley Peterson—yes, and even Skunk Ferguson—had been chummy with Perrine and Frazier.

Jimmy Hungry Dog had confirmed this, too. By now the jurist was very glad he and Tobacco had met the Crow youth. Jimmy had good ears, a close mouth, and his skull encased a sharp brain.

Then, too, there was another finger that pointed to Jack Frazier and Mike Perrine. They were the only outsiders—white strangers—in Spotted Pony. And Judge Bates, just by looking at them, could almost tell you their past lives. He had sat on a county and federal judgeship for years. And during those years he had seen criminals parade before him. And, into this lineup, a man could insert Perrine and Frazier: they would fit, too. Fit perfectly.

But you cannot convict a man just because of his looks. And one thing was seriously missing, the jurist realized. What had caused all this trouble? Broken Leg had said, "Peterson, he try to steal my moccasins." Hungry Dog had said exactly nothing of value when they had questioned her.

And Red Beaver? What had he said?

"No know."

Two words, that was all.

Running Deer, Broken Leg's squaw, had also given them nothing of any value. This thing was a puzzle, and big, too. The judge felt a thrust of exasperation. Just to see justice done, he and Tobacco Jones had ridden miles, and then had run into this mysterious, blank wall of silence and enigma.

The day's celebration was just about over with, for darkness was encroaching on the dim, uncertain twilight. And the wind, which had been chilly all day, was even gathering more coldness to it.

About one-half of the beef issue had been butchered. Enough cattle remained in the corral for another day's kill. Squaws lumbered by, carrying quarters of beef; there would be no rest for them until the meat had been cut up for jerky, and strung in trees. There, dangling in the breeze, it would dry, for Indian summer was still ahead—there might be many warm dry days. Or, for that matter, it might freeze any night, and stay below freezing. Then, of course, the beef would keep, using the great outdoors as a refrigerator.

Squaws used skinning knives. Papooses bawled, children ran and cried and played, and the judge caught the slow, almost nauseating odor of blood. Braves thundered by on ponies, quirts working as they showed off. One almost rode Tobacco down as they went toward the hotel.

"Danged redskin. He git off that hoss an'—"

"An' he'd beat the tar out of you," Judge Bates finished.

They ate supper at the Spotted Pony Cafe. Emma asked, "Did you see the beef slaughter?" and they replied they had.

"Did you see it?" the judge asked.

She shuddered, which made her even prettier. " couldn't look at it. I think I'll become a vegetarian."

They ordered.

"Jimmy was in here looking for you," Emma tol them.

"Where is he now?"

"I don't know. I sent him to the hotel, thinking you were there."

"How long ago?" the judge asked.

She puckered her lips, and frowned a little. "Oh about five minutes. Maybe not that long, even."

"We'll see him," the judge promised.

Seventeen

Jimmy Hungry Dog said, "Yep, they leave town, men," and then he looked at Judge Lemanuel Bates and Tobacco Jones, his importance weighing heavily across his youthful shoulders. "They headed down the trail to the south, toward Wyomin'."

They were in Judge Bates' room. The partners had met the young Crow just as he came into the lobby, coming from looking into Judge Bates' room for him. Dusk had fallen before night, and the lamp on the dresser showed a weak, almost sickly glow.

"You follow them any distance?" the judge wanted to know.

"I did."

Tobacco, who sat on the bed, made a Deadeye Dick shot into the spittoon. He shifted his cud. "Wahl, that means they ain't in on nothing', don't it? Perrine said they'd head for the Black Hills. They git to Fort MacKenzie, then swing east an' cross Clear Crick an' the Powder, an' first thing they'll be in Sundance, an' it ain't much more'n a jump an' a holler from Sundance to Deadwood."

Judge Bates nodded. "Looks like they're headin' for Deadwood, sure as heck. Wish I had some good evidence and I'd get them jailed in Fort MacKenzie."

"But we ain't got it," Tobacco supplied.

Jimmy said, "You mens, you done talkin'?"

The judge cast the youth an inquisitive glance. This young buck needed a little of discipline; he was pretty cock-sure and ornery.

"What do you mean, Jimmy?"

Jimmy's hands helped out his English by making gestures as he talked. "They go down trail south for six, seven miles." His hands waved and helped. "They leave trail there."

"What are you saying?" the judge demanded.

Jimmy sent a glance at Tobacco. "The judge, he always wanta talk."

Judge Bates had had enough. He grabbed the youth by the shoulder and shook him. "Don't sass me, young man. You might be eleven years old but I sure can lay you over me knee mighty fast!"

The importance left Jimmy Hungry Dog. He became just a Crow youth with a message to tell.

"They leave trail, turn to that direction." He gestured to the west. "They cross Little Big Horn, go still west."

The judge released the youth. He and Tobacco studied each other. This point put a new angle on this situation. Deadwood, South Dakota, certainly wasn't west, it was southeast by east.

"How far did you follow them?" the judge wanted to know.

Jimmy held up three fingers. "No further, judge. Got dark an' I come back an' look for you. No see you at corral."

"We were there," the judge said. "You just didn't find us in the crowd. Jimmy, you got a fresh bronc?"

"Get one."

158

"Go get him."

"Why?"

The judge dug and came up with two silver dollars. They made him remember Mrs. Miller and her argument about free silver. Why he thought of her, he did not know; maybe it was with a sense of relief, for now he knew he and Tobacco would soon leave this agency town of Spotted Pony.

"See those two dollars?"

Jimmy eyed the money like a sinner looking across the boundaries into heaven and wondering about his possible entrance.

"Me see. Why?"

"You can earn those two dollars."

"How earn?"

"You get fresh horse. Then you ride out and follow those two. Later on there will be a moon."

"I follow them in dark." Jimmy's dark eyes were riveted on the two dollars. His gaze followed them down until they disappeared with a clink into Judge Bates' pocket. "I go get horse. When I get money?"

"One dollar when you leave. One when I meet you in the morning, if you have faithfully discharged your duties."

"What that last mean, Bates—I mean, sir?"

The judge did not take the time to explain. He and Tobacco would meet Jimmy in the morning at a place the youth would pick. Jimmy scowled, scratched his head, and thought real hard. He was important again. Two men—white men, too—were asking him to set a meeting place.

Judge Bates realized the youth knew this Little Big Horn country very well. Come summer the Crows drifted from Pryor Mountains to the Rosebud Mountains, south down to the Big Horn Mountains, and north to the Yellowstone River. And Jimmy, being a Crow, knew this territory very well, the judge was sure.

"They go for Big Horn Canyon," Jimmy said. "I see that. End of canyon is old building."

"Ol' Fort Smith," Tobacco murmured.

"Yes, that name." Jimmy was beaming. "This way is big black rocks. You remember them?"

"Black Crown," the judge said.

"That it," Jimmy said. "Meet you there. Where's dollar?"

"You get your pony and pick it up on your way out."

Jimmy's face suddenly looked mournful. "No trust me?"

"I trust you," Judge Bates was quick to say. He handed the youth one of the dollars. "Ride past here on your horse. I want to look over your outfit. You need grub, remember."

"I get grub. Red Beaver's lodge."

The youth left by the back door. Tobacco sat on the bed and chewed and the judge got out a flask and took a long, rumbling drink that brought Tobacco's eyes up and brought disgust into them.

"Hittin' the bottle ag'in, eh, Bates?"

"A nip, my friend."

"Ain't you runnin' kinda low?"

The judge thought he detected a gleeful note in his gaunt partner's voice. He had, truthfully, been allotting himself just so much whiskey per day; his cache was running out, much as he hated to admit it. He had scouted for possible reinforcements but the Crows were afraid to let him have any of the whiskey they had concocted.

He knew there was whiskey—and plenty of it—

among the lodges. The Crows made some, some was smuggled in by traders, and some was bought by the Crows themselves from unscrupulous saloons off the reservation's limits. But none of it seemed to be for him.

He had even offered one Crow, Wicked Eye, twice the usual price, but Wicked Eye had fastened his single eye on him, given him a long surveying look, and then had shrugged, saying he had no whiskey, had never had any, and did not know where any was.

In other words, the judge's calling as a federal judge had gone before him, and whiskey was not for him from the Crows. So he had rationed his own, and now he was getting close to the bottom of his last flask.

"I got lots left, Jones."

Tobacco smiled. Then seriousness again enveloped the lanky man with the big adam's apple.

"You really goin' send that kid trailing' them two?" He did not wait for an answer. "What we goin' do tonight?"

"Get a good night of sleep."

Tobacco studied him with a half-smile. "Bates, I do believe man, you're gittin' old."

"I am, of course. All living things must grow old."

Tobacco waved a tobacco-stained hand impatiently. "Always some evasive answer . . . But there was a time when you'd jump up, grab your mule, an' ride out, night or no night."

"Them days," intoned the jurist, "are gone forever."

Jimmy came in, after being gone half an hour or so. He said, "Got my hoss out behind, men," and they followed him outside. He had a ewe-necked, spavined old mare of unknown vintage. The horse

161

stood on her sprung legs and seemed asleep.

"Don't git too close to her, Mr. Tobacco."

"That ol' plug—"

The mare came suddenly to life. Her teeth clicked, but Tobacco had jumped back in time; her teeth did not close on his arm, but missed by inches. Then, apparently discouraged, she hung her head again.

"She'll do," the judge said.

"One of Red Beaver's hosses," Jimmy said. "I cleaned out his tepee, too; got grub in sack."

"You got a gun?" the judge wanted to know.

"Got this."

The boy dug into his pocket, twisted his hand, and tried to get something free. Finally he came out with an old derringer and handed it to the judge who inspected it in the lamplight that came from his hotel-room window. He handed it back. "It's not loaded."

"Me throw 'im," Jimmy said. "Throw 'em good, too."

"Do a good job of trailing them," the judge said. "And we meet you about noon."

"I wait on rocks."

The boy rode away, high in the stirrups of his old saddle, the silver dollar warm in his pocket. The judge and Tobacco went to their rooms but there was little sleep for the jurist, who awoke Tobacco at dawn. And a leaden, gray dawn it was—no wind, but chill hung to the northern earth.

"The kid said they took a pan with them, a flat pan, Tobacco."

Tobacco was sarcastic, as was his habit early in the morning. "Maybe they intend to milk a wild goat an' set the milk in the pan to cool an' rise cream, huh?"

"You're far from funny, Jones. I take it they intend to use the pan to pan gold. I lay awake last night and gave it deep thought."

"What a wonderful conclusion." Tobacco pulled on his shirt. He sat and stared at his boots. "Maybe you got somethin' at that, Bates."

"Wonderful conclusion."

They were the first customers at the Spotted Pony Cafe. Emma had that rare gift that few women have: she looked good early in the morning. The cook asked, "Where's that Injun kid? I got work for him."

"I don't know," the judge said.

The cook pulled back his ugly head, mumbling as he cooked their hotcakes and boiled coffee. The judge told Emma they were leaving town. She said she'd be leaving, just as soon as she sold her cafe; she had a buyer lined up, too. And the judge asked, "Where to, young lady?"

She blushed a little, and said she was going to be married in Minneapolis, and her husband-to-be was a young lieutenant whom she had met at Fort MacKenzie. "General Terry is going to stand-up with him."

"A fine man, General Terry. When you see him, give him my compliments. He will remember me, lady." The judge chuckled as his memory swept back to the Civil War, but he did not mention his war days.

"Terry sure didn't look good when the Sioux knocked out Reno an' Custer," Tobacco grumbled. "Why didn't he take up the chase, 'stead of lettin' them git away?"

General Terry's actions after the Custer Massacre had long been a bone of contention between the partners. Tobacco always maintained Terry should have hit the Sioux, and the judge maintained that Terry could not have done that—when Custer and Reno had failed, Terry had thereby lost at least one-half of his command. Had Crooke come up from the Powder, Terry could have had a chance, but Crazy Horse and his warriors had put the fear into Crooke, who sat and hollered for help with a command as great as Terry's had originally been.

Now the judge, not wanting to argue the matter further, joked with Emma, wishing her luck. By this time the general store was open. The partners, breakfast finished, paid.

Judge Bates said, "Miss Emma—"

She looked up from her cash-box, where she was putting their money, and the judge kissed her on the lips.

She said, "Oh, thanks."

She kissed the judge again, her lips girlish and warm. Tobacco said, "My turn, Miss Emma, and may God bless you and keep you," and he kissed her. They all wished each other luck again and the partners went toward the livery-barn for their mules.

Tobacco said, "Some young man is sure lucky."

"Anybody who is young is lucky. They're lucky because they are young."

"He sure is lucky," Tobacco said.

Their mules were rested and frisky, ready for the trail. They paid their livery-bill and saddled. Because of his bulk, the judge used a crouper and martingale on his mule. The crouper kept the saddle from sliding ahead on a slant, the martingale kept it from sliding back when his mule climbed a hill. But Tobacco, being of lighter weight, did not need these two additions.

They led their pack-mule to the general store and got supplies. Mrs. Miller came in the store, expressed surprise that they were leaving, and the judge knew that within five minutes, at the most, everybody in Spotted Pony would know that Judge Lemanuel Bates and Postmaster Tobacco Jones had left the reservation.

They lashed their supplies on to the pack-mule and Tobacco made the diamond-hitch, saying, "Well, we're all set, Bates."

"We got rid of Mrs. Miller easier than I thought possible."

Tobacco squinted and spat. "Her husband had done tol' her about you protestin' ag'in them skinny cows, an' she was as cold as the weather."

"Hit a man in the pocketbook an' you knock him out faster than a blow to his belly." The judge shook his head in feigned sympathy for Agent John Miller. "You got plenty of eating tobacco, Jones?"

"Jus' bought five new plugs. Wish you could buy some hard stuff, don't you?"

"I got plenty," the judge fibbed.

They found their saddles, the judge took the lead-rope of the pack-mule and twisted it around the horn of his saddle. When they rode past the Spotted Pony Cafe, Emma Dalberg waved at them through the window. The wind had come up again, and an occasional snowflake hurried by to hit the ground and melt.

They rode past the Crow camp. Bucks and squaws were up, ready to renew the ceremony marking the beef-butcher. Old Wicked Eye came hobbling over to the trail, stopped them with a up-raised palm.

"You no fish no more?"

The judge admitted that their fishing-trip was

over. Now they were going back to Cowtrail and winter there.

"You see poor cows?" A ragged, unkempt claw gestured toward the corral. Judge Bates nodded. "You do somethin'?"

The judge shrugged. He wasn't tipping his hand to this old buck. Wicked Eye's single eye was a gimlet boring into him.

"Maybe," the judge murmured.

"Oh."

They left the one-eyed old Crow buck standing there and rode on, pointing their mounts south. This way the wind was behind them. They rode past the last of the tepees, dogs barking at them; the pack-mule kicked a cur and knocked him yipping and sprawling. The dog, tail down, scurried into a lodge. A young squaw came out, saw them, and spat in their direction, her hatred plain toward a white man.

A boy of about two stood in the open wind in front of his lodge, wearing only his skin. How he stood the cold wind, the judge did not understand. Then the lodges and their gabbing and hissing were behind, and to the south the valley ran, heading for Fort MacKenzie in Wyoming Territory.

"Wonder if we're bein' trailed, Bates?"

They rode for a few miles, and here the edge of the eastern hills swung in and touched the trail. From the crown of a hill they watched their back-trail for an hour, but apparently they were not going to be followed. They watched another hour, with the judge stretched out on the sandy soil, protected by an igneous boulder, and with Tobacco squatted in the windbreak, holding the glasses.

The judge went to sleep, and the next thing he

knew Tobacco was shaking him. "Nobody follerin' us, Bates."

The judge asked for the time and Tobacco said it was a few minutes after nine.

"Well," Judge Bates said, "we head for Black Crown."

They cut across the Little Big Horn Basin, which was narrow at this point, and soon they were in the eastern hills, heading across the hilly country that separated the Big Horn from the Little Big Horn. This was a benchland country, marked by dried buffalo-grass, spotted occasionally by sagebrush and buck-brush. Coulees held choke-cherry trees and cotton-woods and boxelders.

"No game," Tobacco said. "Not an antelope or deer or buffalo."

The judge reminded that they were still on Spotted Pony Reservation, and the Crows had killed all the game for grub.

"Don't blame 'em, Bates. Them cows the government sends them ain't no 'count."

But to this the jurist had no answer; that problem had been discussed sufficiently. Although the wind held no warmth, the obese man felt a strange form of satisfaction, almost of contentment. His mule was fresh and strong for the trail, his pack-mule held bedding and grub.

To the north, the hills ran on to level off at the junction of the Little Big Horn and the Big Horn, some twenty odd miles distant as the wild goose flew. Southward, the hills ran on, and far south could be seen the Big Horn Mountains, defying the Wyoming clouds, with Fisher Mountain prodding its height upward.

To the straight east were the Rosebud Mountains,

out of which Custer had come for his annihilation, and south of the Rosebuds, set eastward a pace, were the dark slopes of the Wolf Mountains.

But the jurist, never one to look much to the back, either through retrospect or through geographical space, kept his eyes on the mountains ahead, ignoring what lay behind.

Straight west were the mountains that closed in and made Big Horn Canyon. At their northern base was old Fort Smith, now abandoned. Beyond the Canyon lifted other mountains, snow-tipped and cold and aloof; these were the Pryor Mountains.

Ahead, too, Black Crown rose, topped by dark rocks, its sides spiked by lodge-pole pine and spruce. Black Crown sat at a strategic spot: here a man could be hidden and yet watch the Big Horn Canyon.

They pointed their mules toward the mountain. But, although they made good time, the distance did not seem to diminish. Always the mountain seemed the same distance away.

Here in this high northern air, distance was very deceptive. They were ants, crawling across space, moving with an ant's slowness. Then, without warning, the mountain seemed suddenly to move on them, another trick of the thin air in this high altitude.

Eighteen

Jimmy Hungry Dog lost the trail of Jack Frazier and Mike Perrine close to the mouth of Big Horn Canyon. The moon fell at about two that morning, and the youth could not track in the darkness that settled like a black tarp across the hills and coulees.

Therefore he headed for Black Crown. He could not see the jagged upthrust of rock, but he headed the old ewe-necked horse toward its general direction. The horse travelled at the same gait—an unhurried trot unbroken by the uneven terrain, a gait that consumed miles with a bouncing monotony.

His plan was simple: dawn would find him on the top of Black Crown. From that high vantage point the country would lie clearly below him, and because of height he could watch into coulees and gullies, marking them for the movements of man or beast.

He did not know why Judge Lemanuel Bates had commissioned him to follow Mike Perrine and Jack Frazier. He only knew that he was performing this errand for the judge and Postmaster Tobacco Jones. The judge had cautioned him against danger, and although he did not know why he should be in danger, he was careful because the jurist had so ordered.

The wind had died down in the lull before dawn. Still, there was cold: a cutting, penetrating, icy cold—the cold of the high mountain regions. Down in a gully, a tree cracked suddenly, the noise sharp and strong, cutting through the monotonous sound of the old mare's trot.

He knew that the cold had made the crackle. His hands were icy and he blew on them, but this did little, if any, good. He put his hands under his thighs, sticking them between himself and the seat of his old saddle, an old army saddle the agency had given him because its army life was through.

He hoped dawn would bring a warm sun. He hated to see winter come, for a lodge got terribly cold in the winter, what with snow packed high around it. He hated winter, for then you huddled around the lodge-fires; you couldn't fish, for the streams were ice-covered. Of course, you could slide down hills on a bull-hide toboggan, and that was fun.

His brow clouded. There was one disturbing element in his thoughts, a thought that really scared him. And it did not concern Jack Frazier or Mike Perrine. It was a rumor that had almost all the young Crows excited. And the rumor was that the Great White Father was going to start a school in Spotted Pony, a school for the Crow children, all from the age of six winters up.

Jimmy had heard about schools, although in a round-about way. One thing seemed certain—they were no good and were places of torture. At the Rosebud pow-wow, early in the last spring, he had talked with a Sioux boy his age, who had come to the pow-wow from Fort Lincoln, which was somewhere to the east on the Big Muddy. And the Sioux youth had told him about the school the Great White Father had forced him to attend the winter before.

Jimmy hadn't understood all the conversation, for he did not know much Sioux, but he had found out something about papers called books. The Sioux said you had to learn to read and write. What good, Jimmy asked himself, was that ability? Only foolish white people could use such habits.

He didn't need to know how to read and write. He knew sign-language fairly well; his grandfather had taught him some signs, and he could read the track of deer, telling whether the track were made by a white-tail or a mule-deer, a buck or a doe. He knew a cougar track and a lynx track, and he could tell where a beaver den was just by looking at the bank above a beaver dam.

He was really worried about this thing called school. Already he had decided not to go to it. But the Sioux boy had said that the agency had made him go. He had hid out, but the man had found him. Jimmy resolved that he'd find a hiding-place where nobody would find him, not even Red Beaver.

Red Beaver had good eyes and a good nose, though. He was like a wolf, when it came to seeing or scenting. Jimmy found himself wondering where Red Beaver and Running Deer had gone. But there was no use wondering about this, he reasoned, and he switched his mind back to school.

Funny, how a person always seemed to think of unpleasant things.

Suddenly he pulled the old mare to a willing stop. He slid off her and stood at her nose, hand across her nostrils. She was scenting the air, nostrils distended; she made no effort to whinny.

He listened. He was silent, graven; the mare, too, stood still. Somewhere he heard a sound that sounded like a hoof hitting against rock. But it must have been very distant, for he did not hear the regular sounds of hooves; there was just this one sound, now dead against the distance and time.

He stood there for twenty minutes, listening, his hand on the old mare's nose. Finally she lowered her head and cropped idly at some bunch-grass. Jimmy heard no more sounds, save those of the night-wind, now lifting a little in sing-song through the rocks.

He thought, I hear a deer run, and he let it go at that. He squatted on the ground, sitting squatted like a brave sits, and the mare tried to graze, but she had hard going with the rope tied around her bottom jaw. Finally she gave up and stood with her head low and waited.

When the first streaks of dawn came, he was in the old McClellan saddle again. Now the wind was icy, for it came from the glaciers; it was not fast, but it was sharp. It brought cold to his high cheekbones, made him sit again on his hands, the mare walking toward Black Crown, seeming to understand he wanted to go to the butte.

When he reached the scattered, dark boulders dotting the talus cone that surrounded Black Crown, dawn was a reality, not a promise. The clouds were low, and the sun could not penetrate them; this would be another raw, cold fall day. The wind would hurry the clouds across the sky the way an old squaw hurries her grandchildren about their errands.

172

He got some pemmican from his pocket and chewed on it. The meat swelled when saliva hit it and he gulped it down. Pemmican had strength and braves had made wars with it in their bellies for courage and stamina.

He led the mare up the slope, tackling it from its south side, for the wind was not as strong there, for the crested butte turned it. Puffing, sliding now and then in shale, he led the wise old mare upward. He could not take the mare to the top, for it was too steep.

"You stay here, Wolf Meat," he said.

He got his rope and picketed her among the rocks. She could crop a little bunch-grass, for occasional clumps of the wiry grass stuck out between rocks. Besides, Judge Bates had said he would be along about noon, and then he could water the horse.

He climbed upward, scaling rocks, creeping between boulders. His breath came quickly, and the climb drove the stiffness out of him that the cold night had planted. It was good to be warm again, but the crest of the butte would be cold, for there the wind would blow savagely.

Below him, boulders became specks, and coulees and draws fanned out, running into the distance, but their bottoms discernible because of his rising height. He had to stop and rest twice. Had anybody been around to see him, he would have kept on climbing, but nobody was around. Finally, he reached the top.

His guess had been right: the wind blew with tornado force. It whipped across the flat, black top of the butte. It had whipped away all loose soil and small rocks; the top was about as flat as a lodge's floor, and about ten horse-lengths across, and about that wide, too. He crept toward the north rim, crawling on his belly, the wind bringing tears to his eyes.

Finally, he reached the lip of the butte.

Although high clouds hid the sun, daylight had become strong, and the scene below him lay clear. Yonder was the Big Horn River, still frothy from its mad run through the Canyon, its bed marked by huge boulders and ripples and whirlpools. Mountains grew clearer and took on their properties. The wind sang in the pine and spruce, making a perpetual lullaby.

His eyes came to the edge of the butte below him. He wasn't sure, but he thought he had seen a movement down there. Had he seen a deer? He watched the clump of rocks, and finally he made out the figure of a man, seated back against a boulder.

He watched, waiting for daylight to make identification positive. So far, because of the dawn's low light, he could not clearly see the man. So he lay there and waited with a Crow's patience; that patience was finally rewarded.

He saw the man was old Red Beaver. He went over the side of the butte and, unknown to the old man, he crept through rocks and brush, and finally arrived in some brush about a hundred feet from the oldster. He lay on his belly and watched the old brave.

Red Beaver sat crosslegged, chewing on something Jimmy decided was pemmican. He chewed with the diligence and slowness of a man who lacks all his teeth. Finally, his meal finished, he dug into the soil at the base of one rock. He came out with a stick of something, and Jimmy decided it was dynamite. He remembered that old Red Beaver had watched the white men—when they had dynamited out a foundation for the agency house. He realized old Red Beaver had stolen a stick of the dynamite.

He didn't like dynamite. It exploded and if you were too close, the explosion would kill you. He found himself backing away and circling the butte, heading for his old mare on yonder side. By the time he had reached the top of the butte again, old Red Beaver had his horse and was riding to the northwest, heading toward the mouth of Big Horn Canyon.

The old man rode at a walk, and Jimmy noticed he kept close to brush and convenient cut-coulees down which he could duck at a moment's notice. Red Beaver rode bareback, a sack thrown across his horse's shoulders. That would be his grub-sack. The stock of a rifle protruded from the end of the sack.

He saw Red Beaver wheel his bronc and ride into some thick buckbrush, and he had not much time to spare, for two men had come out of a coulee. Their hiding-place had been so complete that, even from the top of Black Crown, Jimmy Hungry Dog had not seen them until his eyes caught the flash of their movements.

He knew who they were. The two white men who had hung around Spotted Pony, and their names were Mike Perrine and Jack Frazier. The two rode toward the mouth of Big Horn Canyon; they had made a camp in the brush. Jimmy knew they had not lit a fire to cook breakfast; had they had a fire, he would have seen the smoke. They had eaten pemmican, if anything.

But Judge Bates had ordered him to watch these two, and so he did. It was like being high in the air over a big checkerboard—the kind Henry Owl's Nest had—and watching the move of players. They didn't know he was up here, and he was watching them; this gave him a sudden feeling of mystery, and his boyish mind took up from there, giving his job a sudden spicy taste.

Mike Perrine and Jack Frazier rode towards the Canyon's mouth, some five miles away, maybe less. Now old Red Beaver, coming in like an old shaggy prairie wolf aiming to cut down a bull buffalo, left his bronc in the buckbrush; he followed them on foot, moving from boulder to boulder, from one clump of brush to another, and he toted his rifle now. Once he had been a dead rifle-shot, so Jimmy's mother had said, but time had dulled the old man's eyes.

Now why was he following these two? Jimmy Hungry Dog felt the pangs of professional jealousy. Judge Bates had commissioned him to follow these two, and now Red Beaver was cutting in on the deal.

Finally he saw a man ride out of the river's bend, and this man met Jack Frazier and Mike Perrine. Their horses hidden, the trio went to the sod, where they squatted and evidently talked. They were talking for quite a time, and Jimmy was glad the sun was showing a little, for he was finally getting warm.

Jimmy swung his gaze back to old Red Beaver. The old man was in the brush, a half-mile or thereabouts behind the three who hunkered along the edge of the river.

What was this, anyway?

The trio kept in a bunch for a couple of hours. Jimmy looked toward Spotted Pony, somewhere out there in the hazy distance. He crept back so the wind did not hit him. He found a sheltered place behind a rock. Here the sun was warm; the air was good.

Sleepiness hit him. He had spent the night in the saddle, and his eyes would not stay open. He thought, I have to stay awake, and he caught himself falling into sleep.

He looked across the basin, hoping Judge Bates and Tobacco Jones would soon be on the horizon. He did not know when he went to sleep, but when he awoke the sun was close to the zenith.

He thought, I slept for about three hours. He started to cross the top of the butte, aiming to again spy on the white men and old Red Beaver, but he saw the judge and Tobacco Jones were below him.

Evidently he had awakened at the right time, for the pair were dismounting from their mules, their pack-mule standing with his head down. They had found Jimmy's old mare and they were close to her.

Jimmy came down the slope, right hand raised in the Crow sign of friendship. The judge asked, "And so you got here, son?"

Jimmy told them about seeing Mike Perrine and Jack Frazier and how the pair had met another man, one he could not identify. He also told them about seeing Red Beaver.

Judge Bates murmured, "So that's where the old begger went, huh? What else did you see?"

Tobacco Jones had, so far, said not a word. He chewed tobacco and studied the Crow with sharp eyes. Before Jimmy could speak he said, "They's hell ahead, men."

177

Jimmy had seen another man, over behind Red Beaver. He was not sure, but the man had looked like an Indian; he seemed very hesitant. The judge noticed this and pressed him to the wall with, "Who was he, Jimmy?"

"Me no know."

"You sure?"

Jimmy spoke slowly. "He look to me like he is Broken Leg. He limp like Broken Leg."

The judge's gaze met that of Tobacco Jones. Tobacco had ceased chewing, his cud jammed into his cheek.

"They's hell ahead, Bates."

"You've said that before," the jurist reminded. "Well, Broken Leg might've jumped jail. That Sheriff Whiting ain't got too much savvy. I don't figure it would be too hard for a smart Indian to trick his way out of the Cowtrail jail, using Whiting or one of his stupid deputies."

Jimmy had not told them about the dynamite old Red Beaver had stuck into the belt of his buckskins.

The judge squatted, summed it up. "Mike Perrine and Jack Frazier have another man with him. That'll be the fellow that jumped you down in Spotted Pony maybe, Tobacco. They're in here for a showdown. Red Beaver is here, maybe also Broken Leg; that means that somewhere is Running Deer, too. Maybe Broken Leg sneaked in and got his squaw to hide out with him."

"Wonder what it's all over?"

"That's beyond me," the judge said.

"They ain't out here to play checkers, Bates."

178

Nineteen

With Jimmy Hungry Dog as a guide, the partners rode toward the mouth of Big Horn Canyon. They did not ride openly; they kept to buckbrush and to coulees. A rosebush slapped back and hit Tobacco Jones across the mouth, its thorny spines bringing a drop of blood on his cheek. He rubbed it away, looked at his hand, and growled, "Bates, you let that rosebush snap back a-purpose. Be more careful, man."

Judge Bates showed a tight smile, unnoticed by his partner who rode behind him. Tobacco was in a belligerent frame of mind, and that was good. Tension had borne against him and turned his nerves to steadiness. What little irritation he possessed had been spilled in this tirade against his partner.

"That's the talk, Jones."

They followed a sinuous gulch, and it lifted out onto a flat that was covered with pine and cottonwoods and with dense buckbrush. Jimmy found a trail made by deer and bear and this led toward the river. He said, "Wait here, huh?" and rode ahead.

They reined in, heard his bronc move away; these sounds died against distance. Judge Bates took a long pull, studied his almost empty flask, an almost pathetic look on his thick-jowled face.

"Almost outa hard drink, Bates?"

The judge pocketed the flask. "It seems to me," he said dryly, "that your voice held a somewhat gleeful note, Tobacco."

"Why not quit the habit, Bates?"

"Why not drop chewing, friend?"

Tobacco swung his leg around his saddle-horn and rested. "This young un's a good hand in the brush. He knows his way. But what can we do, Bates?"

"I don't follow you."

Tobacco spat in exasperation. His gnarled hands made gestures of impatience. His nostrils flared, and his eyes seemed smaller.

"You know full well what I'm drivin' at, Bates. They's three white men out here in this brush an' wilderness. Why they're here, we don't know, but we do know Red Beaver ain't out here for a good cause, or is Broken Leg—if that is him the button saw."

"Yes?"

"We cain't ride up to Frazier an' Perrine an' arrest them, with you actin' as a police-officer because of your judgeship. We ain't got nothin' ag'in them in a legal sense."

"That's right."

"Well?" Tobacco chewed, studied him.

He was telling Judge Bates nothing new. This whole thing was based on conjecture of the most uncertain type. With Red Beaver and Broken Leg on this range, with Mike Perrine and Jack Frazier here—well, something was bound to happen. And when it did happen, the judge figured he and Tobacco would end it; in ending it, they would get the evidence they needed.

"Your guess." The judge shrugged.

Tobacco said, "Bates, we're a couple—" He did not finish. His mouth went shut, hard and tight, and his eyes pulled down. He looked at Judge Bates and his sunken eyes showed a thoughtful watchfulness.

"Three times I counted them reports, Bates. An' them came from rifles, didn't they?"

The judge did not answer immediately. By now the report of firing had died against the barrier of timber and brush and rock and hill. Another report came, alone and harsh; the snarl of a rifle.

"The fight," said Judge Bates, "has started."

"An' what is it over." Tobacco did not make it a question. The question could not be answered; it was merely a statement.

There came the crash of brush and Jimmy Hungry Dog loped in, his face wild with excitement. He reined his old ewe-necked horse around, waving his fist over his head.

"The fight, she is start, mens!"

The judge snapped, "Where at?"

"Ahead, by reever."

The judge was already on the ground, pulling his rifle from its boot. Tobacco swung down and his Winchester came free. Jimmy Hungry Dog left his old nag; he stood wide-legged, his mouth open.

"Somebody—might get killed!"

The boy's suddenly-awed tone made the judge smile a little. For the first time the significance of this seemed to hit Jimmy.

"Somebody always gits kilt in a war," Tobacco

181

philosophied. He winked at the jurist. "You cain't live forever no way, fella."

"Gimme a short gun?" Jimmy asked.

But Judge Bates told him he was not going to get into this mess. He knew that Jimmy had no desire to get into this fight. While the young Crow acted brave, he was only a boy at heart; he acted like he wanted to get into the fight—for he wanted to save face. And face was an important thing to a Crow, even if he was only a youngster.

"You stay with our mules and hold them," the judge ordered. "We need somebody to hold them so they won't stampede and leave us on foot if the fight gets too close to them."

"They won't run, Your Honor."

Tobacco said, "We need you more to hold mules than to fight, Jimmy. Your job here is just as important as if you were out there shootin'."

That was all the logic Jimmy needed. He wanted to be assigned to an important job, and Judge Bates—and Tobacco, too—had said his job here was important. So he appeared to give in reluctantly.

"Well . . . all right, but . . ."

The judge broke his Winchester, slid a cartridge into the barrel, and put it on safety. The sliding of the breech on Tobacco's rifle made a sharp click in the mountain air.

"Ca'tridge, Bates?"

"Got some on my mules." Judge Bates untied a sack and took out shells. "Take this box."

Tobacco took the cartridges from the box, dumped them in his pocket, and tossed the empty box away. They were bulky in his pocket but, for some reason, the bulk seemed very assuring.

"Not much shootin' goin' on now," the postmaster murmured. "Kid, for hades' sake, don't lose these mules; perfect them with your life, savvy."

"Me savvy."

Judge Bates said, "Well, here goes." He patted his mule on her skinny nose. "Be waitin' for me, Betsy."

Betsy nibbled at him, got ready to strike with her forefeet, but the judge, knowing her from long acquaintance and bruises, moved to one side. Betsy lowered her head and stood silent without a worldly care.

Tobacco trailing, the jurist went into the brush. Now and then, ahead of them a rifle talked, and occasionally a short-gun barked. Bluejays talked angrily, evidently ired because of the invasion of their bailiwick. A grouse came out of the buckbrush, making its whirring noise, and the judge settled down as if expecting a bullet to come.

But no bullet came and Tobacco grunted, "They didn't hear that grouse rise, I reckon. Figger they shot too steady along that time, an' what if it did rise with such a noise—they'll figger the gunfire scairt it. They sure don't know we're on this range."

"How do you know?"

The judge had Tobacco stumped, and therefore got no answer. To be safe and sure, they squatted for a full minute, and then rose to go forward again. And the judge tried to work out some plan of procedure.

He knew one thing for certain: Jack Frazier and his two men outnumbered old Red Beaver, for Red Beaver had only Broken Leg, and Judge Bates wasn't even sure of this. Of course, Running Deer would be somewhere around, and she would be another hand, but she was just a squaw. The jurist thought, I wonder if she can handle a rifle.

They came to a rise, the top of it dotted with boulders, and the judge said, "Watch behind us, Tobacco." Tobacco squatted, rifle across his thighs as he watched the brush through which they had just come. This was brush warfare, and therefore it was liquid and moving; a man might have cut their back-trail sign and be moving in.

The judge crawled forward on his belly, creeping toward the top of the rise. Tobacco lost sight of him in the rocks. The judge came to the top and lay and watched, the country below him rather clear. It was a rocky flat, and it looked to him as though old Red Beaver had penned in the white men among the rocks. If so, that was good for the old Crow; he was a good hand in rough country, and his buckskins fitted in good with the terrain, making him camouflaged.

He saw a puff of rifle smoke from behind a rock on the outer rim of the flat. From the heavy blackness of it he figured it was army ammunition, for the army had been getting a bad grade of powder for years. Possibly, then, the rifleman was Red Beaver, for he, like most of the Crows, had somewhere managed to steal an army rifle and army ammunition.

He maneuvred around and from here he could see a bit of the rifleman's leg, and he saw he was wearing buckskins. He knew then the rifleman was either Red Beaver or Broken Leg.

He went back to Tobacco who said, "Not a man in sight, Bates. See anythin', pard?"

The judge sat down and drew a map in the dirt. "Here's the circumference of the flat, Tobacco." His forefinger dug out a circle. "It's all dotted with boulders. Yonder's the river." His forefinger made a line. "Now old Red Beaver's right here."

Tobacco studied the drawing and nodded. "So they got Jack Frazier an' Mike Perrine in the center, huh?"

"That's right."

Tobacco's eyes grew thoughtful. "Reg'lar Injun style of fightin'. Surround your enemy, keep moving, cut them down as you come in. Jus' what Crazy Horse did to Crooke down on the Powder almost ten years back."

Judge Bates nodded.

Tobacco continued with, "Well, Red Beaver's outnumbered, even if Broken Leg is sidin' him. Me, I figure that third gent with Perrine an' Jack Frazier is the gent what waylaid me down in that alley." He felt of his back. "Got some pain back there yit, Bates."

"They're murderers," the judge agreed.

"What'll we do, Bates?"

The judge outlined a plan. They would sneak down and talk with Red Beaver, and then see what he had to say. Then they might try to call to Jack Frazier, tell him Judge Bates was on the scene, and get him and his men to surrender. And at this logic, Postmaster Tobacco Jones vigorously shook his whiskery head.

"Them hellions won't guv up, Bates. They're fightin' for somethin' they want, an' they aim to git it."

"I agree with you. But the try would not hurt."

"Let's talk it over with Red Beaver."

Now they crawled on their bellies, looking like giant crabs that moved from rock to rock. Old Red Beaver heard them and the judge said, "Judge Bates and Tobacco Jones, friend."

Red Beaver sat cross-legged, watching them. If

he had any emotion his face did not show it.

"You come to help?"

The judge nodded.

"Me no need help," Red Beaver said stolidly. He swiveled his eyes from one to the other. "Me an' my son, we enough."

The judge shot a glance at Tobacco. Now they both knew for sure that Broken Leg had broken out of the Cowtrail jail.

"What's the fight about?" Tobacco wanted to know.

"Red man's bizness. Not white man's bizness."

Tobacco murmured, "Well, we got more out of him than we got the other day, Bates."

"Fight end soon." Red Beaver's old eyes were deep and mysterious. "Fight end in little while."

The judge said, "Nothing we can do here, Jones." Red Beaver went down on his belly and inched forward, putting his rifle ahead of him. He came to his natural fortress of rock and some part of him must have showed, for a bullet whammed into the flint, driving out splinters. Old Red Beaver went down, grinning at the closeness of the bullet. He dug into his pocket and came out with a handful of matches and these he lay beside him.

"Must be figgerin' on doin' some heavy smokin'," Tobacco said, "if he aims to use up all them fire-sticks."

The judge said, "We sneak over and see Broken Leg."

"No use." Tobacco shrugged. "He won't tell nothin', Bates. Why not try to call this off by talkin' to Jack Frazier?"

"We'll try that. Hide down good, pard, for my words might bring a burst of rifle-fire."

186

By this time the first wild edge of the fighting had become dulled as men's nerves steadied. There was very little firing. Each side was waiting for a member of the opposing forces to show himself for an open shot. It had settled down to a game of watch, get aim, shoot.

Tobacco lay on his belly, boulders shielding him, and he said, "Shoot, Bates; do your talkin'."

The judge called out, "Jack Frazier." There was a silence and finally Frazier answered, "Who's that?"

"Judge Lemanuel Bates, sir, and his partner, Tobacco Jones."

A man cursed suddenly, from surprise. Tobacco listened, said, "That's the voice of the man who jumped me in the alley, Bates." Suddenly Jack Frazier's strident voice halted the man.

"What d'you want, Bates?"

The judge outlined his plan. If they surrendered they would not be harmed by the two braves; he'd guarantee that. If they were guilty of any crime, he would see they had an honest trial; in fact, he placed them under arrest, and he placed Broken Leg and Red Beaver under arrest, too.

"You cain't arrest us, Bates."

The jurist reminded that he was a federal judge and he was on a federal Indian Reservation and that therefore he had the power of a peace-officer. Again he ensured them safe delivery to jail and a quick hearing. He knew that both Red Beaver and Broken Leg were listening, and they could understand every word he said. He spoke slowly and now he did not have to speak so loudly, for the rifle-fire had ceased entirely as men lay and listened.

Tobacco grumbled, "I doubt it, Bates."

The judge made no reply to this pessimism. The silence lengthened, and he heard the broken-voiced man—the one Tobacco claimed had jumped him back in that alley in Spotted Pony—say, "For murder, they hangs men."

That was the judge's answer. Again the gunfire started, and he heard not another word from Jack Frazier. He and Tobacco squatted, protected by the boulder, and Tobacco said, "Best let them fight, Bates. There is some matters that cain't be settled by nothin' but war."

"How can I stop them?" the judge asked sarcastically.

Tobacco asked, "What'll we do?"

"Pull back, Jones, and get altitude. From there we can peg down at all of them, not aiming to hit them, but to drive them into surrender." Suddenly the jurist halted his speech, looking toward the south. "I thought I saw a man run by yonder opening, back in those rocks!"

"Bates, you're seein' things—"

The judge had moved forward, getting a clear view of the terrain ahead. "I've seen only the old Indian," he grunted. "There he goes, running toward those white men. Tobacco, they'll kill him!"

Tobacco said, "He wants to commit suicide, mebbe, Bates. He's an ol' Injun, Red Beaver is—"

The old man was hurrying forward, keeping protected by boulders. Evidently he did not see them or if he did, he paid them no attention. He was trotting, head down, rifle in his hand. He was about an eighth of a mile away and he was heading straight for the hide-out rocks of Jack Frazier and his gang.

Judge Bates hollared, "Red Beaver."

The old man looked at him, but kept his pace. He cried something in Crow, but the partners did not understand his words. He disappeared behind some rocks.

Tobacco said, "He lit a match, didn't he?"

Judge Bates scowled. "Sure looked that way to me. And he had no pipe in his mouth. I don't get it. He's risking it all on an attempt to smoke those rats out. He's going in there alone, hoping to kill them and save his son."

"That takes bravery, Bates."

Suddenly the world seemed smashed apart. Ahead of them—where Jack Frazier and his men hunkered—was a wall of roaring fire. Self preservation made the partners hug the ground, the rock protecting them. The world seemed to have gone crazy. The roar died and rocks fell, thrown upward by the giant explosion.

"Bates—"

"Yes?"

"I don't git this, Bates. That was dynamite, weren't it?"

"What else could it be?"

Judge Bates was on his knees, peering over his boulder. Ahead of him dust hung in the air and he smelled the sharp odor of exploded powder. The explosion had occurred on the spot where Jack Frazier and his men had been hidden.

"That killed them," the jurist said. "It had to. No human or animal could live through that blaze."

Broken Leg screamed, "Red Beaver!" and got no answer. It was a bleating, lingering cry.

Judge Bates grunted, "Somebody's comin' on the run."

"Sombody's lived through it," Tobacco said.

The man was short and swarthy. His hair, dark and long, was singed, and he ran limpingly. He did not see the partners until Tobacco hit him. Then he rolled like a cat, lashed out with his rifle, and Tobacco went back. The judge closed in on the man.

The jurist's thick arms went out, grappled the slender man. The man seemed stunned but he fought with a wildness. The judge bent him back, and they went to the ground, the man screaming curses, the judge grunting and breathing heavily. Judge Bates was on top.

Two fists came in, found the man's jaw, and he lay still.

Tobacco panted, "He was like a bull, he was. He threw me to one side. Bates, who is he?"

But Judge Bates had gotten to his feet, and had his rifle. Then the Winchester lowered as Jimmy Hungry Dog, face showing excitement, came running.

"Blow-up," Jimmy panted.

"Sure, it was a 'blow-up,'" Judge Bates panted. "You know this gent?"

"I see him, Spotted Pony. Name Hermando, or somethin'. Red Beaver, he cause blow-up?"

"Why say that?"

"He have dynamite, judge." He said, "Red Beaver, he dead. Blow up."

Today the old Crow buck, Jimmy Hungry Dog, is the only person alive who saw the gunfight on the mouth of Big Horn Canyon. He is a blanket-buck and you'll find him on the Crow Reservation in southern Montana. You could question him, but he'd not tell you about the fight on the Big Horn. He'd look at you, and you could almost read his thoughts, "White Man, I tell you nothin'." But he'd say, "No know."

The rest is recorded either in the annals of the War Department or the court-books left by Judge Lemanuel Bates. The man known as Hermando confessed, and the men known as Jack Frazier and Mike Perrine died in the dynamite blast, along with the man who sacrificed his life to bring peace, the old buck called Red Beaver.

The irony of it all lay in the fact that a map had never been made showing the gold pockets on the Big Horn River in that deep canyon through which the river runs wild and foamy. When Charley Peterson had raided Broken Leg's lodge, he had heard the map was hidden in the lining of one of Broken Leg's moccasins; actually, no map had ever been drawn.

Therefore, after the battle was over, only two people knew the location of the gold-pocket, and these two were Broken Leg and his squaw, Running Deer, who was watching the battle from a butte. They never went back to the gold. White men, hearing about it, sneaked into the Reservation, prospected for the gold, but it was never found.

And Judge Bates used to say, "They might have worked the pocket dry, Tobacco. Or there might still be gold in it. Anyway, those two have seen the misery gold brings, and if there is more gold they'll leave it forever buried."

And, if there was more gold, it is in the Canyon of the Big Horn River, even today. It lies there, and the Crow who knew its location is dead, and dead men have no tongues.

The man called Hermando drew life in the

federal penitentiary in Atlanta, sentenced there by Judge Lemanuel Bates, who sat as a federal judge on the case. He died within three years, knifed by a fellow prisoner.

Broken Leg had said, "Come here, an' I tell you confession," and Sheriff Whiting had come close. Broken Leg had grabbed him through the bar pulled him in, got his gun and keys, and so had escaped the Cowtrail jail. Judge Lemanuel Bates had talked Sheriff Whiting into dropping the charge, thereby freeing Broken Leg, for the confession of Hermando had cleared the Crow of the death of Charley Peterson.

Now the blanket buck, Jimmy Hungry Dog, knows all this, but he does not know where the gold is located. If he did know, he would not go after it—the gold had brought only death and greed and hate and fear. And Jimmy Hungry Dog is an old man. Even when a young man he had no desire to get the gold, even if Broken Leg would have disclosed its position, which he would not have done.

For Jimmy did not want strife, he wanted peace.

CALLAHAN RIDES ALONE

Chapter One

Red-headed Al Callahan stood trail-weary and unshaven under the boiling July sun and gazed happily at a dark green shirt hanging in silken splendor in the fly-specked window of the Mercantile in Mill Iron, Territory of Montana.

Al Callahan wanted that magnificent green shirt. For six long years he'd kept his blue eyes hopefully peeled for just a shirt and now, at long last, he'd found one.

He bowlegged through the open door, the good aroma of dried apples, gingham and leather meeting his nostrils. He remembered the first—and only—green shirt he'd ever had.

His now-dead mother had given it to him on his sixteenth birthday, down on the home ranch in Texas. Two years later he and Ronny James had gone on a spree down in San Marcos.

"Ten bucks against two, Ronny, that I can hoolihan that ol' bull."

"Called, Al."

Yeah, he'd hoolihanned the mossyhorn, all right. Driven his cayuse close, piled off on the dead run, anchored his wiry weight behind the lumbering longhorn's massive horns.

When you hoolihanned you didn't drag bootheels to pull your beast to a halt. You landed hell-bent on the brute's neck. Your weight took his head down. His horns caught in the sod.

And over you went, you and the bull.

And during the melee, the mixup of cowboy and longhorn. That beautiful green shirt.

It hung in shreds.

And Al Callahan—a man by all standards at eighteen—had sat unashamedly in Texas' red dust and bawled like a baby.

"He's got a cryin' jag," Ronny James said.

Now Callahan stopped just inside the Merc's door, keenly aware of the ten thousand in Uncle Sam's gold certificates riding in his money belt under his broad cartridge-filled gunbelt.

Three months back he'd read the ad in the Lubbock, Texas, *Journal*.

For Sale: Circle Cross ranch. Mill Iron, Custer County, Montana. 10,000 down, rest on time.

Max Heywood, Mill Iron,
Custer County, Territory
of Montana.

Two others occupied the Merc. One was a sawed-off skinny oldster with bald pate. This stood on the

6

clerk's side of the long counter.

The other stood on the customer's side, and Al Callahan momentarily forgot even the green shirt.

One word—and one alone—fitted her. *Beautiful.* Callahan catalogued her vital statistics.

As high as his shoulder, the right height. Thin waist, womanly behind—just right there, too.

Her buckskin half-skirt showed dimpled knees. Her Justin half-boots were highly polished. Black. Spurs? Garcia spurs, he'd bet—the expensive ones. And her hair—her wealth of glistening hair.

Brilliant red, natural red.

She heard him enter. She turned. She looked at him. Her eyes were the color he'd expected. Green. Glistening green. As green as the green silk shirt.

And Callahan liked green.

Callahan said, "Good afternoon."

She didn't answer. Her green eyes looked beyond him. They held no interest.

He was just another drifter. A no-good cowboy, worthless—nothing more, nothing less.

She looked back at the clerk. "Put these on my bill, please."

"With pleasure."

She picked up two small parcels. Callahan moved courteously to one side so she could pass.

"I'm Al Callahan."

"You could be Jesus Christ," she said, "and I wouldn't give a damn." And she stepped into the street.

Callahan watched her pass the window. He looked at the bald-headed clerk. "Who?"

7

"Ann Scott."

"She own the world?"

"Not all. Just a part. Rockin' U. Big local spread."

"She hate the world?"

"Not all. Just Max Heywood."

Max Heywood? Max was to be his partner. Circle Cross. What was he buying into? Trouble? The usual Callahan luck?

Would Ann Scott be his enemy? Callahan didn't like that idea. He wanted Ann as a friend. A close friend. Well, maybe more than a friend—

The clerk brought him down to earth. "Somethin', Callahan?"

"That green shirt, sir. In the window."

"Oh, that green shirt. Wonderful silk. Just have had it two days. Bought it off a drummer last Tuesday. He went through on a mule. Only green silk he had. Only one I got, too."

Callahan's heart plummeted. He wanted to cross himself, but you don't do such things in public—not over a shirt, anyway.

Maybe it wouldn't fit?

Carefully, reverently, Shorty leaned over the wooden partition, gnarled hands reaching into the display window. Reverently, carefully, he removed the dazzling shirt from its hanger.

He held it at arm's length. Green danced, green shimmered, green blessed. Callahan's mouth was dry.

"Try it—for width, please."

Callahan had difficulty speaking. He turned his back. He felt Shorty's claws pull the shirt tight across

8

his shoulders.

Good lord, the shirt was too narrow!

Shorty fumbled. Shorty pulled. Finally Shorty said, "Just right. In fact, a slight too wide."

Callahan breathed again.

Shorty planted a thumb on Callahan's neck. He pulled down on the shirt. He pulled harder. The shirt was too short!

"Just right," Shorty finally said. "Mite too long, in fact."

Again breath returned.

"The neck," Callahan said.

Shorty pulled a tape from his belt. He measured Callahan's thick neck. He measured the shirt-collar. He pursed his lips. He clucked. Then he said, "Mite bigger than your neck, Callahan."

Callahan said, "I breathe normally again. What's the tariff?"

"Twenty dollars."

"No, No."

"What's your bid?"

"Twelve."

"Eighteen, Callahan."

Callahan said, "Those two ginks acrost the street? Under the awning. Trail Weary Saloon?"

"Len Rourke. Bud Harding."

Callahan nodded. Rourke and Harding had trailed him into Mill Iron. He'd seen them clearly in his field glasses.

"Which is Len Rourke?"

"Tall hairpin."

Len Rourke appeared in his middle thirties. Tall,

gangling, spare—like Callahan. Hawked nose, whiskered mouth. Gun tied low, right hip.

Callahan looked at Bud Harding.

Early twenties. Short. Ornery-looking. Shotgun chaps. Harding's .45 rode in a halfbreed holster, right thigh.

With a halfbreed, you didn't draw. You just slapped down, leveled, fired—gun in holster, for the gun-barrel stuck out an inch from leather.

"Local boys?" Callahan asked.

"They punch for Ann Scott. Eighteen bucks?"

"Sixteen, Shorty."

Shorty pursed his lips. Evidently he did fast mental arithmetic. "Sixteen it is. Wanna change? Go behin' in the storeroom."

Callahan paid. He and the green splendor went into the storeroom. He returned in a few moments, but he wasn't all smiles.

Harding and Rourke still loafed across the street.

"Looks wonderful," Shorty said. "Here's the sack with your old shirt. Goin' be aroun' long, Callahan?"

"Dunno for sure."

Callahan flexed his arms. The shirt didn't bind. Through the fly-specked window he saw lovely Ann Scott leave the Buffalo Head Cafe.

Ann Scott saw him. She looked away. Callahan grinned. Suddenly, his grin died. Ann Scott walked in front of Harding and Rourke.

Callahan saw her lift her little finger on her right hand slightly. He knew a signal when he saw one.

Ann Scott had signaled to Harding and Rourke.

Callahan's blood raced. He thought of two things:

10

His ten thousand bucks and his letters to Max Heywood. He'd mentioned in one letter he would be carrying ten thousand.

You damned fool, Callahan.

You could have put the money in the Malta bank. Got a certified check. Too late now, Callahan.

And you forgot. And you mentioned it in a letter. Didn't being a Texas Ranger teach you anything, Callahan.

Callahan stepped outside.

Dazzling sunlight reflected from green silk. Traildust clogged his throat. He looked up and down Mill Iron's main street, all two blocks of it. The Trail Weary was the closest saloon.

Harding and Rourke stood in front of the Trail Weary. That cut no ice with Callahan. Callahan never believed in wasting steps. When born God had given him a certain quota of steps to use.

When that quota was gone, Callahan was dead.

Callahan started across the street. His runover boots stirred Montana dust. His boots found the plank walk in front of the Trail Weary. There, they stopped. Rourke's harsh words stopped them.

"Jus' a minute, Callahan."

Callahan spread wide his strong legs. Automatically, his right thumb hooked his broad gunbelt just ahead of his tied-down .45.

"Odd," Callahan said. "An' me a stranger here— an' you know my name."

"We want a word with you," Rourke said.

Callahan's blue eyes studied the tall Rourke. "You could have talked to me out south on the trail.

11

You trailed me in, remember."

"We trailed you?" Harding said.

"You trailed me, Harding. An' you, too, Rourke."

Rourke said, "That Shorty—That clerk—He talks too much."

"Nice chap, boys," Callahan said. "Congenial, friendly. But, sooner or later, we'd know the other's name."

"True," Len Rourke said.

"You came to sling a gun for Circle Cross," Bud Harding accused. "Hired gunman, huh?"

"No hired gun," Callahan said.

Callahan was keenly aware of his money-belt hugging his muscular middle. If that ten thousand left him it would do so in three manners: by his own volition, by brute force, or ripped from his dead body.

Rourke said, "You're buying' into Circle Cross. Ten thousand bucks worth, Callahan."

Callahan forced a laugh. "My ten thousand, gentleman, lies safe and sound in the Malta bank. I don't have it on me."

Harding's brows rose. "You hint we're out to rob you, Callahan?"

Callahan's blue eyes narrowed. He had at first figured this pair fired by booze—false courage. But he could smell no whiskey on them, even though the wind came from their direction.

"Rob you?" Rourke asked. "A crazy idea, Callahan."

Callahan said, "Many a corpse has been robbed in public or when the stiff lay stiff in the morgue."

Harding said, "Sonofabitch."

Callahan looked at Harding. He judged Harding the more dangerous. Surely and slowly, Harding seemed to be working himself up to a blind, killing rage.

Len Rourke was the more settled type, the experienced gunslinger. He would take no chances. He would await the right, the correct, moment.

Callahan judged Bud Harding to be the faster.

Now Len Rourke came slowly toward Callahan. He was lanky, tough—an alley fighter. He stopped ten feet from the Texan.

Slowly, carefully, eyes riveted on Callahan, Bud Harding moved ten feet away from Len Rourke's right.

Mill Iron watched. Mill Iron held its breath.

Ann Scott watched from safety on the plank sidewalk. Her red hair glistened but her mouth was not sweet, feminine. Her red lips were peeled back. Her white teeth glistened. Ann Scott was all feline.

Callahan said to Harding, "That's far enough."

Harding stopped. He went into a crouch, fingers splayed ten inches above his gun in its halfbreed holster.

Len Rourke also came to a jerky halt. He also now crouched, fingers spread above his holster.

There was a moment of hanging silence.

Then Rourke said, "That time, Bud!"

Len Rourke's palm slapped his gun's handle. Callahan thought, Rourke is fast but he needs to draw.

Harding would shoot first, Callahan reasoned.

Harding didn't have to draw. All Harding had to do was tip the halfbreed holster on its rivet-pivot, and let go.

Callahan's gun rose. Heat shot through Callahan as his gun lifted. For Callahan knew one thing—he was ahead!

Chapter Two

Callahan's Ranger training came in. He leaped to his right as he drew. His gun's barrel hacked down savagely. It smashed down on bone. The bone was in Len Rourke's gun-arm.

Rourke howled in pain, gun falling to the dust. His fingers hung limply from a numbed wrist. Within a few seconds, Rourke had been eliminated.

Callahan whirled toward Bud Harding, who had fallen to one knee. Harding had already got in one shot, smoke trailing from the end of the tipped-up halfbreed holster.

Again, Callahan's Ranger training roared in. You laid your forefinger along your gun's barrel. You pointed at your opponent, the barrel following your finger.

Callahan pointed at Harding's heart.

Callahan's .45 kicked back. His soft-nosed bullet hit Bud Harding squarely.

The shock lifted Bud Harding slightly and, as it lifted, it bent him forward. Harding fell wordlessly. He lay on his belly, nose deep in the street dust.

Harding didn't breathe. If he had been breathing, dust would have risen around his mouth and nose.

Len Rourke massaged his wrist. He stared at Harding. One moment Harding had been alive, lips snarling, face filled with hate. The next, he lay motionless in the dust.

"He's dead," Len Rourke gasped.

"You'll be dead, too, if you make a bad move, Rourke."

Rourke stared at Callahan. Fear ran into Rourke's eyes. Callahan meant what he'd said, and Rourke didn't doubt a word.

Rourke trembling raised his left hand shoulder-high, his right hand shivering and useless at his side. "Don't—don't kill me, Callahan."

A terrible thought hit Callahan, freezing his blood, chilling his marrow. Bud Harding had got in one shot. Had Harding shot a hole in his new shirt.

Hurriedly, Callahan pulled his shirt around, studying it. Then, his heart began beating again.

No hole.

He picked up Rourke's pistol. He kicked the cartridges out of it, jammed it back into Rourke's holster. Then, he turned and looked toward Ann Scott.

But Ann Scott had moved. And Callahan soon learned where she'd gone. A round hard steel thing—plainly a gun-barrel—was jammed hard into his back.

Ann Scott hissed, "You Texas bastard!"

"Be careful! Don't shoot a hole in my new shirt!"

The words rang across Mill Iron. Crazy words, loco words. Mill Iron heard. Mill Iron broke out laughing. Mill Iron talked about it later on in saloons.

"Scott came in behind, you say? I don't savvy how-come a ex-Ranger could let his guard down an' be caught that way—by a woman, too."

"Easy. He was worried about his new shirt. An' who'd expect a woman to come in behin' with a gun? A man, yes—a woman, no."

"You got a strong point, Sam. How'd this Callahan bucko get out of it?"

"Easy. Ol' Ranger trick. Never poke a gun ag'in a body. Always stan' back beyon' his reach, your weapon on his middle."

"Yeah?"

"'Cause if your weapon is next to him, he can jump to one side, bat the barrel away—an' that's jes' what Callahan did. Scott pushed hard. When he moved, she fell ahead. He grabbed her wrist. An' boom—he had her pistol!"

"She get to fire?"

"Once."

"Bullet burn Callahan's back?"

"Nope. Never even put a hole in his shirt."

"Then what?"

"He puts Ann Scott over his knee, right there in the street. He aims to paddle her purty ass, see."

17

"He did!"

"But he never tetched her. Guess his Texas trainin' came in. Be polite to females, even dance-hall sluts—that's the Texas way."

"He let her up, huh?"

"Nary a spank. She's hoppin' mad. Damn' near jumpin' up an' down."

"She wanted to get pounded?"

"Hell, I dunno. What man knows a woman? Max Heywood an' her brother—thet Roger—was in town."

"You don't say."

"An' Max butts in. An' Max don't love Ann, you know."

"I'm new here on this grass. Who all is this Max Heywood gent?"

"Max ain't no man. Max is a female—an' as purty as Ann Scott, too. Real name is Maxine, they tell me. Max is for short. All call her Max. Well, it looks like fireworks between the two heifers."

"They fight?"

"Never had time, 'cause then them damned timber wolves come roarin' in fangs clickin'."

"Timber wolves?"

When Max Heywood came into the dusty street, Al Callahan was in the act of kicking Len Rourke in the pants as Rourke ran for safety in the watching townspeople.

Callahan stopped.

Max Heywood stopped. She looked at Callahan. Callahan looked at her. And once again Callahan admired a lovely young female.

18

"This town is lucky," he said.

"Why?"

"Two beautiful women. You're almost as beautiful as Ann Scott."

"Ann Scott? That bitch? I'm prettier, Callahan."

"You know my name," Callahan said, "but I don't know yours."

"Max Heywood."

Callahan swallowed. "Max is a man's name." His voice was weak. He forgot Len Rourke, who glared at him.

"Short for Maxine, Callahan."

"I come to buy into your Circle Cross." Callahan's voice was normal, now. "I wrote you."

"I know, Callahan. I told nobody you were coming to buy. Ann Scott heard someway, but I never told her. I'm going out and beat the hell out of her for jumping you."

Max Heywood also came to his shoulder. Right height, also. But where Ann Scott was red-headed, Max had raven-black hair. Ann's eyes were green. Max's, sparkling black.

She stepped around Callahan. Callahan grabbed her. "Women don't fight. Not where I come from, anyway."

"This isn't Texas. This is Montana."

Callahan didn't release her shoulder. She had a nice, rounded shoulder. He saw Ann Scott bearing down. His heart plummeted. One damned thing after another. One devil chasing the other?

Ann Scott stopped. Ann's gun was back in leather. Max Heywood also carried a .32 popgun on

19

her hip. Callahan moved between them. H
appealed to the crowd.

"Ain't there no law in this burg? If there is, get it—
and fast!"

"I'll git Mike Jones," Rourke hastily said. "Jone
is deputy sheriff."

"Mike's home eatin'," a townswoman said.

Rourke scurried away. Callahan frowned. Ha
Rourke reformed? Did he want to become a usefu
member of society?

Callahan grinned. Callahan had a funny thought
totally incongruous to the demands of the moment
A woman named Max.

Only girls in red-light districts adopted men'.
names. Billy, Billy Jo, Hank, Jackie. Yes, Jackie
Jackie was very popular in the whorehouses at thi
time, he'd learned on his long trail up.

Ann Scott's angry words recalled him to th
present. He stood dusty and dirty on a Montan
cowtown's main drag, standing between two armed
irate, spitting females. He decided to take command
Or, at least try.

"I should have paddled you, Miss Scott."

"You can say that again," Max Heywood said.

"You shut up," Al Callahan told Max Heywood
"You tricked me. I thought Max Heywood was a
man."

"I'll meet you folks in the livery. If I'm not in sigh
I'm in the hay, sleepin'. My honor, Callahan."

"My honor, Roger."

Roger clumped out, rowels clanging. Deput
Jones said, "I'm goin' to the Trail Weary. Talk with

20

Miss Scott. Come along, Len."

He and Rourke left.

Max Heywood made circles with her shot glass. Callahan sent a covert glance. Her face was troubled. Callahan killed his beer. He remembered forgetting to offer Roger Heywood a drink.

Max Heywood said, "Ready to ride, Callahan?"

"As ready as I'll ever be."

They went outside, Callahan's hand lightly on her elbow. Len Rourke crossed the street. "Mr. Callahan?"

Callahan stopped. "Yes?"

Rourke said, "I got off on the wrong foot, sir."

"Maybe we all did," Callahan said.

He and Max Heywood walked on. The town livery was at the street's end. When they entered the barn, Callahan looked back.

Rourke had left the street.

Callahan shrugged.

"What'd you think now, Callahan?"

Callahan's green shirt played with the Montana wind. He looked down at Max Heywood's burgeoning blouse.

"You're definitely a woman," Callahan said.

Ann Scott said, "Two loco fools."

Callahan looked at Ann Scott's out-bulging blouse. "The same goes for you, Miss Scott. How'd you know I was coming into Mill Iron?"

"Ask and be damned, Callahan."

"A sweet answer," Callahan said. "One a loving wife would give her loving husband. But we aren't married, Miss Scott."

21

"And never will be!"

"Never use the word never," Callahan said.

Max Heywood said, "Let me hit her, Callahan."

Callahan stalled. He needed help. Wouldn't somebody step from the crowd and help him?

Callahan spoke to Ann Scott. "How come you know I aimed to buy into Circle Cross?"

"You guess, Callahan."

"Another answer a loving wife would give," Callahan said.

Max Heywood said, "Callahan, let go of my wrist. I want to beat this red-headed bitch to the ground!"

Callahan was sweating. He was in a bad predicament, and Callahan knew it. Women didn't fight with fists. They used fingernails. He'd seen plenty of red-light girls fighting. When the battle had been over, fingernails had marked some with lifetime scars.

If these two fell to fisticuffs, he'd have to protect his face. The shirt clung to his back with sweat.

Then, he heard people screaming.

Townspeople were running into stores, up the street, behind buildings. Women grabbed children. Children and women screamed. Men pushed women and kids into stores.

Callahan stared in amazement. The tension had been broken. The two female combatants had forgotten their contemplated conflict.

He released two female wrists. The women just stood there, staring, also surprised.

And then the pack came. They ran forward in deadly silence, paws padding silently on dust. They headed straight for Callahan and the women. They came at a smart gallop. They ran in liquid ease, long tongues out, eyes on the three standing in the street. And Callahan's blood turned to ice water.

He faced a pack of wolves.

Chapter Three

Callahan's .45 swished upward. Max Heywood fastened both hands around his wrist. She pulled his gun down.

"Don't shoot, Callahan."

Callahan stared at the oncoming pack, pistol pointing down. Behind the wolves rode an old man, beard flying, astraddle a blue-roan mule.

"They'll kill," Callahan said.

"No, just stand still," Max Heywood said. "They're tamed."

"Tamed?"

"Yes, they're tamed—and trained."

Ann Scott said, "The damned things. A rangeland nuisance. Somebody should kill all of them. And kill their boss, old Wolf Zukerman, too."

"They smell Harding's blood," Max Heywood said.

She was right. The wolves had swerved right. They were around Bud Harding's body.

Callahan said, "They'll tear him to pieces." He struggled to lift his gun, but Max Heywood's smallness contained strength. And he didn't struggle too hard, either. Curiosity had him.

Timber wolves. Trained, tamed? It wasn't possible. You couldn't tame—or train—a wolf or coyote. Everybody said that. Many had tried. None had succeeded.

Old Wolf Zukerman put his mule on haunches. He raised a tin whistle to cracked lips. He blew.

Callahan heard nothing. Evidently the whistle didn't work? Then, he stared. For the wolves had pulled back. They lined up in a row. They sat on haunches, tongues out, huge fangs showing.

Callahan could only stare.

Wolf Zukerman dismounted. He rode bareback with a half-breed rope hackamore around the blue roan mule's jaws. He was stiff, bowlegged, ugly, whiskered, unwashed.

He stood upwind. Callahan got a stinking odor, and it was not from the wolves.

Wolf Zukerman grinned. "Scared the spit out of you, eh, Callahan?"

Callahan said, "Everybody knows my name." He still eyed the wolves closely. "Even the wolves proba'ly know. You're Wolf Zukerman?"

A low chuckle. "Only man in existence—in history, in fact—who has trained wolves. They ain't all timber, Callahan. Three are lobos. Dan there, an' Muggins, an' Killer."

25

"Lobos, huh?"

Max Heywood said, "I've told you time and time again, Zukerman, to never—yes, never—take those damned wolves into town. One bite, and a child is in two parts."

"I'm sorry, boss."

"Why did you bring them in?"

Wolf Zukerman reached upward, as though to doff his hat. But he wore no hat. He folded his gnarled hands in a respectful attitude.

"Like this, boss. I heard Callahan was in town. I wanted them to all meet Callahan cause if he buys into the Circle Cross—well, he'll be my half-boss, won't he?"

Callahan surrendered. Who on this range *didn't* know he had been riding in? Max Heywood's next words again froze his blood.

"Well, introduce them to Callahan, and then make tracks for Circle Cross. You understand?"

"I sure do, boss."

"Me, I don't hanker to meet any wolves." Callahan spoke quickly.

The old wolfer laughed, toothless gums red. "But they aim to meet you, Hannigan."

"Not Hannigan," Callahan corrected. "Callahan. Al Callahan."

"Good name, Mattigan."

Callahan gave up.

Ann Scott said, "You people are crazy." She walked toward the Trail Weary. Callahan admired her hips. She disappeared behind the batwing doors.

"Somebody should get Harding out of the street,"

Max Heywood said, "but nobody will come for him as long as these wolves are around."

"Do you blame them?" Callahan asked.

Wolf Zukerman said, "The introductions begin, Mannigan." He bowed extravagently the ring master of a five ring circus. "First, Oliver. Oliver, meet Mr. Jonnigan."

Oliver came to Callahan. He raised his right paw, a wild dog wanting to shake hands.

Callahan hesitated.

Oliver looked at Callahan. Callahan saw an enormous canine head. Long white fangs glistened. Oliver's eyes were a good four inches apart. Callahan figured Oliver would weight at least a hundred odd pounds.

"He wants to shake your acquaintance, Mister Monaghan," Wolf Zukerman said. "Shake with him, please. Oliver is very touchy."

"Shake his paw," Max Heywood said.

"You've shaken hands with him?" Callahan asked her.

"With the whole damn' bunch. Every time I do something at the ranch that Zukerman doesn't approve of I have to shake hands with every damned wolf the old fool has."

Callahan counted wolves. "An even dozen. Lots of paws to shake, Miss Maxine."

Townspeople stared from store windows. So far Len Rourke and Deputy Sheriff Jones had not made their appearance.

"Oliver's awaitin'," Wolf Zukerman said.

Callahan settled on his haunches. His right hand

went out. The wolf's right paw rose. Man and wild canine solemnly shook hands.

Callahan's eyes were inches from Oliver's. He had an eerie feeling. Oliver eyed him like a potential porkchop.

"Okay, Oliver," Zukerman said. "Maizie, you're next."

Callahan thought, Is this a dream? A cockeyed, crazy dream? Me and wolves, shaking hands?

What if my old pals, the Rangers, saw me doing this? When and if I get back on the Panhandle—and I tell them this—they'll send me over to Doc Stone to have my head examined!

"How are you, Smitty?" Callahan told a gray wolf.

Smitty didn't answer. Smitty pulled back and sat in a line with the others, huge paw well shaken.

Martha was the last wolf. She yawned as she shook hands.

Max Heywood said sternly, "Get those damn' things out of Mill Iron. Head back to Circle Cross—and fast, Zukerman!"

Zukerman cackled. "Look at me, folks. Eighty-nine years of age last August twenty-second. Born and raised around Hinsdale down east on the Milk. My folks were tough stock. My ol' man lived to one hundred an' sixty three years old."

The old man ran, braced his dirty hands on the mule's rump and vaulted onto the critter's back, despite the mule kicking with both hind hooves. Zukerman grinned down at Callahan. "See you aroun', Milligan."

The mule, ears back, leaped into a dead run.

"Ride 'em, Cowboy!"

Zukerman beat the mule with the hackamore rope's free end. The mule kicked first, then broke out bucking, scattering the following wolves.

"Hook 'em, cow!"

Zukerman rode with a mane-and-tail hold. His spurs raked the mule high in front, then high behind. He held his left hand high in best stampede manner.

The mule quit bucking. It leveled out on a dead run, ears back, tail flying, the wolves running hard behind. The mule skidded around the corner. Zukerman's yell came back.

"Ninety-seven last July fourth."

Callahan grinned. "He got eight years older between here and the corner. He sure kicked out that ol' mule."

"No saddle, either," Maxine Heywood pointed out.

"I was scared," Callahan said. "My knees were knocking."

"I always feel scared around those wolves, too—although I know they won't jump me."

"They'd jump a human if he ordered them," Callahan said. "Is he loco, or is it an act?"

"I never could tell for sure, Callahan."

"That one wolf—that big gray dog-wolf—you see what he did? He come up, sniffed my leg—then he lifted his leg—hind leg, that is."

"But he didn't do it, Callahan."

"He thought I was a post," Callahan said. "And that whistle—You can't hear anything when he blows it. Anyway, I didn't hear anything. Did you, Miss Heywood?"

"You can't hear the whistle."

"Why not? I got good ears."

"Special kind of whistle. Wolf told me about it. Something about it making sounds the human ear can't pick up. But the wolf ear can."

"Where'd he get it?"

"He made it. Cut a tin can to pieces with tinsnips. Did some soldering. And thus, the whistle."

"Why don't you get shut of him?"

Max Heywood spread lovely hands. "At his age, where would he go? Who'd take him in?"

"You're almost human," Callahan said.

He'd said the wrong thing. He realized it instantly.

Max Heywood's lips tightened. "Callahan, my fur rubs but one way."

Callahan took her arm. "Look, I came up with a Texas trailherd to Miles City. Friend of mine trailin' in beef for the Crows there. My throat has the dust of North Texas, Colorado, Wyomin' and Montana cloggin' it."

"Long way."

"It was. What say we wash the dust down in some pleasant bar near at hand?"

She started off. Callahan caught her elbow. "Scott's in there. Once is enough, Max."

"Max?"

"Okay, Miss Heywood."

"We haven't known each other very long."

"I'm easy to get along with. All I need have is my own way."

Now that the wolves had gone, four townsmen

30

were taking away Bud Harding's corpse. They had a home-made stretcher with canvas suspended between two tough diamond willows.

They carried Harding down-street toward a small frame building. Callahan said softly, "I'm sorry about Harding, but if I hadn't killed him he'd have killed me."

"I know how you feel, Callahan."

"Have you had any other trouble with Rocking U?"

"Only small things. Insulting things between that damned Ann Scott and me."

"Somewhere there's a leak."

"Yes, but where?"

Callahan could only shrug.

The Barrel Stave started filling up after Maxine Heywood and Callahan entered, townsmen covertly studying the Texan. Callahan felt proud. He had a beautiful cattle-queen on his arm.

The saloon had the good smell of stale tobacco smoke, whiskey and beer. Callahan and the dark-haired beauty went to the bar.

Callahan said, "Down in Texas good girls don't go into saloons."

"Again, this isn't Texas."

White Aprons ambled up, smiling toothlessly. White Aprons had a huge belly that rumbled when he walked.

"Good day to you, Miss Heywood. And good day to you, too, Mister Callahan." He turned watery eyes on Maxine. "What's your choice, beautiful lady?"

"Hogwash, Smoky! Beautiful lady, bull! The

31

usual. Spring Valley, water chaser."

"Comin' up, beautiful lady. An' your desire, Mister Callahan?"

"Beer. Coldest you can get." Then, to Maxine, "You know your booze, Miss Heywood. Rourke, now? He went for the deputy, remember?"

"Jones probably was asleep. He's a lazy, good-for-nothing. Speak of the devil and he appears—here the two come now."

Deputy Jones was forty, short, bowlegged. The broken veins on his face showed his love for the bottle.

"Everything happens when I sneak off a few winks," he said. "Baby with the colic. Up most of the night. You're Callahan?"

"I am. And you're Jones?"

"Deputy Sheriff Mike Jones, Custer County, Territory of Montana. You killed Bud Harding?"

Jones' roughness antagonized Callahan. "I did. And I claim self defense."

"He's right," Len Rourke said. "Self defense, Mike. I was there."

Jones waved Rourke aside. "You were in the gunfight, they tell me," he told Rourke. "What do you say, Miss Heywood?"

"I saw it," Max Heywood said. "Mr. Callahan killed in defense of his life."

The deputy said, "All right, all right. Don't be so stern to me, Miss Heywood. I'm only doin' my sworn duty. There'll be no formal legal inquest. I'll register it as justifiable homicide in my books."

"Thanks," Callahan said.

"Harding have any relatives?" Len Rourke asked.

Nobody knew. A barhound said, "He was alone in the world. I knowed him purty well. He never mentioned nobody."

"He'll go into the boothill section," Mike Jones said. "Could I buy you a drink, Mr. Callahan?"

"My turn."

Mike Jones smiled widely. "Don't remember ever buyin' you one, but that's water under the bridge. Smoky boy, the Jones usual."

"Comin' up, Mike."

Smoky reached back. He snagged a quart of Old Horseshoe from the backbar rack.

"Two glasses, please," the deputy said.

Smoky shoved out two glasses. Jones poured for himself and Rourke. "My private bottle," he told Callahan.

Rourke raised his glass to Callahan. Callahan raised his beer bottle. They drank.

Callahan hid his grin. Len Rourke seemingly had suddenly become friendly. Callahan knew Rourke was afraid of him.

Rourke's eyes bulged too far out, Callahan thought. Also his hands trembled. Something was wrong with Rourke. Or was there?

Callahan realized he'd just met the man. And that meeting had been under somewhat unfavorable conditions. But just so Len Rourke stayed afraid of him Callahan would be happy.

"That dark green shirt is just the right size for you," Maxine Heywood told Callahan. "I saw it in the Merc. I almost bought it for my brother."

"Your brother?"

"Roger."

"Oh."

Maxine had downed her whisky. Callahan still had half a bottle of beer left. Callahan ordered another drink for her.

"Not me," he told Smoky. "Later, but not now."

Deputy Jones began talking about the trouble between Circle Cross and Rocking U. "You two should be like sisters," he told Maxine. "I refer to you an' Ann Scott."

"We are like sisters," Maxine assured. "We fight the minute we meet."

"That ain't the sisterly feelin' I mean," Jones said.

Callahan listened. He didn't like it. He'd expected peace.

He'd planned to become a respectable Montana citizen. A rancher, a land-holder. He'd planned eventually to marry. And raise a few children.

He looked forward to the day he'd boost his first-born—girl or boy—onto the back of a tame old cowpony.

But this!

This was warfare. Open, deadly warfare. Range-war, and threatening to become more deadly. Men got killed in range-wars.

He knew that from Texas. He'd gone through the Wire Cutter's War there on the Staked Plains.

Cowmen against farmers. Rifles against barbwire. And barbwire had won.

He decided to look Circle Cross over. Then, if it didn't please him—He hadn't signed any papers. Or paid any cash yet.

"Here comes Roger," Max Heywood said.

Max Heywood's brother had just come in. Callahan looked at him. And Al Callahan's lip curled in a sneer.

A range dandy.

Roger Heywood was almost his height. Callahan judged him to be twenty. He was plainly a show-off, a saloon cowboy.

Cheyenne-legged chaps, finest calfskin. Highly polished Hyer's half boots. Big, silver-roweled Miles City spurs.

Two bone-handled .45s, tied low. Best saloon gunfighter fashion, Callahan thought.

"Sister," Roger said.

Max Heywood said, "Roger, Mister Callahan. He might buy into Circle Cross."

"Was in the Trail Weary. Saw the gunfight through a window. Fast gun, Mr. Callahan. Deadly gun."

They shook hands. Roger put on the pressure. Callahan grinned inwardly. Callahan met the pressure. Roger pulled back. Callahan won.

Roger Heywood spoke to Callahan. "I must warn you. Scott's Rocking U outfit is rustling our Circle Cross cattle."

Deputy Jones cut in with, "Can you prove it, Heywood?"

Roger Heywood's gray eyes studied the lawman. "Did anybody ask you a question, law-badge?"

"You're making accusations," Jones pointed out.

"I'm a citizen. I help pay your wages. I can say

35

what I want as long as it hurts nobody. Free speech Jones."

"It hurts Ann Scott," the deputy said.

Roger Heywood yawned. "Time I head for home Sis. Five days buckin' the tiger in the Trail Weary."

Max Heywood scowled. Callahan had the impression she was displeased. Callahan was still trying to gauge Roger Heywood. Some of these dudes were just actors, nothing more.

Some were damned tough, underneath.

He gave up on Roger Heywood. Heywood would have to prove what he was.

"Dice?" Max Heywood asked.

"Poker. Dealer's choice. Draw or stud."

"Another, please," Max Heywood told Smoky.

Roger Heywood frowned. "Always the bellyache What if I won a big pile?"

"You didn't."

"She knows all, she knows all," Roger Heywood said. He again yawned. "You ridin' out to Circle Cross, Callahan?"

"I reckon so."

Chapter Four

Far ahead were the dim blue peaks of the Little Rockies. Callahan rode behind Max and Roger Heywood.

They followed a wagon-road. Brother and sister were not getting along too well. Callahan could not avoid overhearing their conversation.

"Maybe I said wrong. Maybe we aren't losing cattle," Roger Heywood said.

"You told Jones different." Max Heywood rode a silver-mounted, hand-carved Miles City saddle. "Why say this now?"

"Simple. Spring tally might've been short because our lazy cowpokes didn't run them out of the rough country."

"What rough country?"

"Wild Wolf Hills. Bitter Creek."

"The gather was complete. I rode most of that roundup. You didn't. You rode a chair in the Trail Weary, gambling. And losing, as always."

"You back on that again?"

"Don't get uppity, Roger. I've yet to see any money you've won gambling. This drouth has hit Circle Cross hard. Three years of it, now."

Callahan didn't like to hear brother and sister arguing. He and his only brother—four years his senior—had argued and fought all their youth.

He gingerly fingered scar-tissue over his eyes. Brother John's pounding fists had put those scars.

He learned certain things. Roger Heywood was a few days shy of being nineteen. The Heywoods' father had died the year before. Bad heart.

Roger was not in school this year because of money-shortage. He was in his second year of medical school at a high-toned eastern university. He wanted to finish medical training.

The Heywoods' mother had been six years dead. The father's will had given Maxine, his only daughter, control of Circle Cross until Roger, the only son, became twenty-one.

Roger received one hundred dollars a month from the ranch by his father's will. According to Max, he spent this money gambling, boozing, wenching in Mill Iron.

The day's heat was dying. The wind had gone down slightly. Mosquitoes were coming out.

Callahan learned other things, too.

Ann Scott was an only daughter, too. Her father, Matt Scott, now rode a wheelchair, a bronc having

38

gone over backwards with him three years before. According to Max Heywood, Matt Scott would never walk again.

Callahan looked about with a cattleman's eye. Although drouth rode this high range, it was still good cattle country—the second best he'd ever seen.

The first best?

The Big Bend country, down along the Rio Grande. In his home state, Texas.

But a man needed a fortune to buy into the high-grassed Big Bend. The Big Bend had been in the same hands for over a century, father handing down to son and daughter.

Circle Cross lay north of Mill Iron. Callahan had ridden into Mill Iron from the south. South the range had really been burned bare. Although this area could have stood more grass, it was still high with bluejoint in coulees where winter-snow ran off slowly.

They came to a good-sized stream. "Rock River, Callahan," Max Heywood said. "Circle Cross' south marker."

"North limit?"

"Sixty miles north. Doggone Creek. West we run to the Larb Hills. East, Boxelder creek. East and west is around eighty miles."

"Lots of grass," Callahan said. "Why are you selling?"

Max shrugged pretty shoulders. "Roger wants a medical career. He'll be gone soon. I'll be alone. I need a man who knows range and cattle. You're a Texan, born on a ranch."

Callahan nodded. A mosquito landed on his sleeve.

Callahan could have batted the mosquito, killed it. He didn't. He didn't want a blood-stain on the shirt.

He waved it away.

"How many head, Miss Heywood?"

"Max, please, Al. As I said in my letter, around twenty odd thousand, according to spring roundup's tally string."

"Little over twenty thousand," Roger Heywood said.

Callahan's ten thousand would buy him into twenty percent of the ranch, or four thousand head. What cattle they rode past had good blood, he noticed—mixture of Texas longhorn and Shorthorn and Hereford.

Heywood—their father—had trailed Texas longhorns in on this grass long before the Sioux and Assiniboine were forced on reservations. Then Heywood imported good bulls to breed up the Texas stock.

The elder Heywood and Matt Scott had driven cattle up from Texas together. Scott's rocking U lay south of Rock River and ran to the Missouri River brakes.

Rocking U was not as huge as the Circle Cross. It ran around eight thousand head, Roger Heywood explained. Callahan had a thought. Down in Mill Iron Max had demanded that he call her Maxine. Now Maxine wanted him to call her Max.

Women, Callahan thought, women!

Callahan said, "This will last but a few years, no more. Then rails will come in. With the rails come farmers. The days of free range will be gone."

"Bullets," Roger Heywood said.

Callahan shook his head. "Not if I'm part owner. They tried bullets down on the Panhandle. Bullets didn't win. Bullets buried farmers and cowmen, both."

"I've heard of the Wire Cutter's War," Max Heywood said. "Dad used to mention it. He came from around Uvalde. How did it turn out?"

Callahan shrugged. "Side with the most wins. All the time. More farmers than cowmen. Cowmen had to pull back onto patented land."

"What's the answer?" Max asked.

"Get cowpokes on homesteads. They can homestead up to a section of land—six hundred and forty acres. Original homestead of a hundred and sixty— Then, hill claims, grazing land claims, things like that."

"Where would you settle them?" Max asked.

"Water is the key. Whoever owns the water, owns the grazing area around. The other way is hay. Up to now, I understand you've not fed winters. Cattle rustled in snow."

"And winter-killed by the thousands," Max said.

"And there went your profit," Callahan said. "We need to build feed sheds for blizzard shelter. Cut hay in meadows and along rivers where there's water seepage."

"We'd be farmers," Max said.

Callahan said, "Part cowman, part sodbuster.

There's just no other out, Max."

"Dad spoke like you do, Callahan."

Roger Heywood made no effort to join the conversation. Callahan noticed he looked bored. Heywood evidently was through with ranching. His mind dwelled on a medical career ahead.

Callahan figured part of his ten thousand would return Roger to his studies. He hoped so. Roger didn't appeal to him.

He figured Circle Cross would be better off without Roger, for he'd definitely made up his mind to buy into the spread.

Roger Heywood turned. "You married, Callahan?"

"No."

"Your father? Mother? Brother? Sisters?"

Callahan said, "I'm only buying into Circle Cross, not giving my family history."

"All secret, huh?" Roger Heywood sneered.

Callahan said, "Watch your lip, buster!"

"Roger," Max Heywood said.

But Roger Heywood was on the trail and he wouldn't give up. "Okay, tell us the story, huh?"

Callahan shrugged.

"My father was killed in the Wire Cutter's War. He was a cowman. Bullet. Just one. Right between his eyes.

"Bad," Max said.

"Your mother?" Roger asked.

"Dead some six years. Natural death. Pneumonia. Never had a sister. Had one brother—four years older than me—John Callahan."

42

"What happened to him?" Roger Heywood asked.

"Killed one night. Same war. Two days after my father."

"You kill whoever killed them?"

Callahan summoned patience. What was this fool driving at? Was this fool baiting him? For what purpose?

Callahan said, "Around a thousand guns were in that trouble. Most fighting was done at night. A dark night doesn't let you see who killed, Heywood. Dark nights hide secrets."

"By God, I'd have found out!"

"How?"

"I'd have found out, somehow."

"Roger, you've gone far enough." Max Heywood spoke sternly. "If you must insult and devil somebody, do it to me. I've grown a thick skin around you."

"I'm not insulting Callahan. Nor am I deviling him, as you say. I'm merely reciting facts. You seem to forget one point, sister."

"And that?"

"Callahan's a Texan. And Texans brag about being the toughest around."

Callahan pulled his buckskin to a halt. He reached out, snagged Heywood's reins, stopped Heywood's horse.

Max Heywood reined in, too.

Callahan said, "Just what are you driving at, bucko?"

"Get your hands off my reins," Heywood said.

Callahan didn't release the reins. For one momen
his blue eyes clashed with Roger Heywood's angry
eyes. And then, without warning, Heywood struck

His right fist lashed out. Callahan had expected
this.

Callahan hit.

Callahan smashed in a savage left hook. His
knuckles landed on Roger Heywood's mouth,
splitting his bottom lip.

The blow loosened Heywood in his saddle. It
almost drove him from leather. The dandy caught
his balance on his stirrups.

He said, "Drop down, Callahan."

"With pleasure, Heywood."

Both dismounted. Callahan glanced at Max
Heywood. Nothing showed on her calm face.
Callahan thought, This is foolish. This punk and I
have no real reason for fighting.

Then, Roger Heywood was on him.

Texas Ranger training had taught Callahan how
to use a gun—and his fists. He was saddle-tough. He
had speed, power and hitting force. His fists had
subdued some tough men.

He soon learned Roger Heywood was tough.
Despite hanging around saloons and drinking, the
fool was still in excellent physical condition.

For a few moments, it was touch and go.
Heywood could take and hand out. Finally,
Callahan's better physical condition, his stronger
legs and better wind, began to tell.

And his fists started taking deadly toll. He saw his
opening. His left staggered Roger Heywood. A hard

uppercut—a right—dropped Heywood.

Callahan figured Heywood would stay down. Heywood didn't. Callahan almost got knocked down. Again, he dropped the younger man. Again, Roger Heywood, bleeding, snarling, got up.

The fifth time Callahan dropped Heywood, Heywood stayed down. He was knocked out.

Callahan breathed deeply and noisily, legs braced. He'd been through a rough, tough battle—and he knew it. Finally he looked up at Max Heywood. He brushed blood from his nose.

"He knows how," Callahan said.

"Light-heavyweight boxing champ in college."

Callahan raised his arm to sleeve blood from his nose.

The girl said, "Roger's gun fell from holster. It's there behind you, Callahan. He's coming to."

Callahan handed her the pistol. His own gun still rode in holster. "He going to stay on Circle Cross?"

"He'll go back to college this fall. Your ten thousand dollars."

Callahan looked at Heywood. Heywood was getting to his feet. His right eye was almost closed. His lips were battered.

"I understand," Max Heywood said.

Callahan nodded. He had small desire to buy into Circle Cross with this fool hanging around. He decided to let things ride for a while. There was no hurry.

Heywood was now on his boots. He went into a gunfighter's crouch, fingers stiff and erect over holster.

45

Max Heywood said, "Your gun fell. I have it, Roger."

Heywood's hand went down. It smacked only the leather rim. He said, "Give me my gun. I'm going to kill me a Texan."

Max Heywood looked inquiringly at Al Callahan. Callahan said, "What ever you want to do. But I'll kill him."

"You don't get it," the sister said to her brother.

Heywood had a Winchester .30-30 in saddle-boot. Bloody face enraged, he reached to pull the weapon free.

Callahan's .45 leaped up, leveled. "Don't do it, please," Callahan said.

Heywood looked at the pistol. Common sense came to him. He could never pull the rifle free in time.

Heywood's hands dropped.

Callahan stepped forward. He snaked the rifle from the boot. He handed it to Max Heywood. Roger Heywood was now completely disarmed.

Roger Heywood glared at his sister. "Whose side you on?"

"My own," his sister said shortly.

Roger Heywood swung into saddle, boots anchored deep in oxbows. "To hell with both of you." He spurred forward, bronc lunging.

Within a minute he was over the ridge, heading for Circle Cross. Al Callahan wet his lips. His bottom lip was cut.

He felt over his eyes. The scar tissue there hadn't been broken. He'd taken a few tough ones on cheekbones, though. His left eye would soon be closed. Within an hour it would be shiny black.

Max Heywood said, "I hope you two crazy roosters are happy now."

Callahan didn't like her tone. Too cynical. He was having a tough time on this Mill Iron range. Things weren't working out right. There was too much interference.

He almost said, "Hell, I'm riding out...and for good," and then he remembered her written description of Circle Cross. Just the spread he'd been searching for. High grass, water, fat beeves, a tough horse-remuda.

There was no rush. He'd have to ride Circle Cross grass from end to end. He bought no pig in a poke.

Then, if suited, there'd be the legal angle. Partnership agreement to be brought about. That would require a Malta lawyer.

He had time.

"Everybody's happy," he told Max Heywood.

They rode on.

Callahan said, "He deliberately picked a fight. I was a fool to oblige. But what is gone is gone. Why?"

"I don't know, Callahan."

Callahan thought of red-headed, beautiful Ann Scott. She'd sicced two gunmen on him. She'd put her gun in his back.

He thought of rustled cattle. Stolen cattle. You couldn't change a Circle Cross brand to Scott's Rocking U.

Besides, Circle Cross was on left ribs. Rocking U was burned into a critter's right ribs. He knew that.

If you stole cattle, you needed a market for them. Where was that market here?

Callahan knew the answer. Redskins, for one. No, they didn't rustle. Oh, maybe they run-off a beef, but only now and then. But they had mouths. Uncle Sam had corraled them on reservations.

The redskin mainstay—the shaggy buffalo—was practically extinct except for a few ranging higher in mountain foothills. The redskin needed raw red meat. One outlet for stolen cows.

Far south along the Milk River was a railroad. Cattle could be driven overland to cars. And shipped into Chicago or the Minneapolis slaughter pens.

The railroad was many miles south. And unscrupulous cowbuyers sometimes didn't care which brand a cow packed. Just so the critter sold at a low enough price.

Callahan washed his bloody face at Dahl Springs. Here a freshet of clear water seeped from a hillside. Spore of cattle and cattle-dung showed cows drank here although Max Heywood reported the spring at a low ebb due to the long drouth.

Callahan saw boot prints. He judged Roger Heywood had washed here, too. He and the girl rode on.

The further Callahan rode, the more he liked this grass. A man could stay here and work and—he was falling in love with this high northern range.

The wagon trail twisted up a high hill. They reached the summit, horses breathing. Max Heywood reached down. She pulled Callahan's buckskin to a halt.

"Circle Cross buildings below, Callahan."

Callahan looked. And what he saw made his Irish heart leap in pure joy.

Chapter Five

They rode across a plank bridge, hoofs clattering.
Below danced a creek, water mountain-clear.

"Buffalo Creek," Max said.

"Trout?"

"Full of trout. And pike, too."

Callahan's blue eyes danced. "Fishing," he said.

A covey of northern grouse lifted with sharp
wings from the willows to zoom out of sight beyond
the timber.

They rode into Circle Cross' yard. They drew
horses to a halt.

"All these buildings are on homesteaded land,
Callahan. My father had the foresight. Uncle Sam
can never touch them."

"Smart."

"The title to this land is good forever. A hundred

and sixty acres, Callahan. But the range outside—it's unpatented."

Callahan saw two huge barns, complete with haymows. Five big corrals stretched out on the flat. A long log cookshack, a blacksmith ship, a two-story bunkhouse of rock that Callahan judged could sleep at least thirty cowpokes.

And a small foreman's shack, too.

All buildings were freshly painted. This was a spread—a real cow-spread.

Callahan asked, "You get any response to your ad—that is, except mine?"

Max Heywood hesitated. Her dark eyes looked at the tumbling creek. Finally she slowly said, "A few, Callahan. But none of them showed up, for some reason."

Callahan scratched his red head. He knew men in Texas who'd buy this complete ranch at almost any price at the drop of their Stetson.

A graybeard hobbled out of the closest barn, plainly the hostler.

He peered up at Callahan, faded eyes probing.

"Al Callahan, Jim."

Callahan and the hostler shook hands. "Irish, heh? Ain't got no come-on for the Irish."

They laughed. He led their broncs away. Callahan and Max walked toward the house—long and made of native stone with a porch its north length. A substantial, tough house. One that could and had stood blizzard, hail, storm, rain.

Montana morning-glories climbed the porch's pillars. Wild roses grew in profusion from beds.

51

"My flowers," Max said.

"Nice."

Max swung open the heavy oak door. Callahan stepped into a living room. Heavy and bright Navajo rugs covered a sandstone tiled floor. Furniture was of handhewn Montana pine.

A huge soot-blackened rock fireplace occupied the complete far wall, its mantel holding various bric-a-brac.

"Nice home," Callahan said.

Max stood in thought. "Not a home, Callahan, since my mother and father died. A place to stay, no more."

"I understand."

He remembered standing in the living-room of the home-ranch down on the Panhandle, saying goodby to his birthplace, the money resting in his money-belt—where it still rested.

The big stone house was built in a U. Two wings ran off opposite the other. Max led him down the west wing.

They passed three closed doors. Al Callahan judged them to be bedrooms. The girl opened the fourth door. Callahan looked into a room containing a double bed with bright colored spread.

All the furniture looked hand-made. It was sturdy. A desk, a bureau, more Navajo rugs on a sandstone-tiled floor.

"This will be your room."

Callahan said, "I haven't bought yet, Max."

"I know. But it's yours if you want it. It's dad's room."

Callahan said, "I thank you. Where's Roger?"

"I don't know. His room is the first. I'll look in."

"It isn't that important to me," Callahan said.

They returned to the living-room. Roger's room was empty. Suddenly, a wolf howled.

"How long's Zukerman been with you?"

"Let me see. . . . Roger came home a year ago last June. Zukerman turned up about the same time with his damned wolves."

"Turned up?"

"Just came in one day. Riding his mule, wolves around him. I had two watchdogs. They saw the wolves and took to the hills."

"They ever come back?"

"Never. And the wolves never killed them. Not in the yard, anyway. They started after the dogs but Zukerman called them back."

"I don't blame them. I felt like running off when they swarmed around me down in Mill Iron. I'd have run if I hadn't been afraid they'd have jumped me."

"They'd not jumped you unless Zukerman had ordered them to."

"Ever think of shooting them?"

"Many a time. But each time, Roger's against it. I don't know why, but he is."

Callahan felt his left eye, now almost closed. "Roger sure as hell wasn't that considerate around me," he said. "These wolves, now? They howl much come night?"

"Very seldom. Odd, too. They live in a steel corral beyond the haystacks. Zukerman sleeps with them."

"Nice," Callahan said. "A bunch of stinkin'

wolves sleeping with a stinking' old man, and the old man stinks the most. I got down-wind on Zukerman in Malta. He not only smells rotten. He smells putrid. The last bath he had his mother must have given him."

"He isn't attar of roses, for sure. But here we stand blah-blahing, and you must be hungry. When did you last eat?"

"A bit with a cowboy in a line-camp way down south, daybreak this morning. That buckskin of mine is tough—a real trail-horse. He can carry you a long ways in a day. That line-camp must be sixty miles from here, I'd say."

"Sit down in that big chair. No, the other. That's my father's favorite chair. I'll rustle a little grub."

Callahan sat.

Maxine Heywood hurried from the room. Callahan admired her. She looked just as good going as coming, he decided. He had thoughts—male thoughts.

Well, time'll tell, Callahan, he told himself.

Callahan looked at his boots. He thought of Ann Scott. She also looked attractive headed either direction.

He heard a tinkle. Like glass hitting ice and vice-versa. Max entered with a tall glass on a tray.

"Ice?"

"Cut it winter time on Buffalo. Thought you'd like a refresher, Callahan."

"Where's yours?"

"In the kitchen."

Callahan sipped. Whiskey and water. He got to

his boots. "I'm lonesome. I'll talk to you as you cook."

"Come with me."

They went to the kitchen, at the far end. A Kalamazoo wood stove, a heavy hand-made table, blue tablecloth, lots of wall shelves, all hand-made of native lumber.

Callahan sat at the table. He raised his glass. "To Circle Cross."

"To Circle Cross, Callahan."

Callahan drank. Max Heywood drank. Max turned her attention to her stove. Callahan smelled frying venison. And frying spuds, too. Coffee sent out its magic.

"You really losing cattle, Max?"

"The tally shows so, Callahan. And quite a few head, too."

"You mentioned Bitter Creek. And that that area maybe hadn't been combed of cows during roundup this spring?"

"That's right."

"Where's Bitter Creek?"

"North of here. Almost due north. Around twenty-five, thirty miles. Close to where they're taking out the copper ore."

Callahan's battered eyebrows rose. "Copper ore?"

"My spuds! They're burning!"

She grabbed the skillet's handle. It was hot. Callahan handed her the cloth pot-holder. "I hope they're not ruined," Maxine said.

The copper ore was forgotten momentarily. Callahan asked, "Don't you have a cook?"

"My cook got word her father was sick. Assiniboine reservation, on the east—oh, about thirty miles. Said she'd be back as soon as possible, but I have my doubts."

"Other reservations close?"

"Gros Ventres, west. Oh, another thirty miles or so. Reservation limits are flexible. Most redskins come and go as they please, just so they don't gather in big bands."

Callahan nodded.

"They start banding, and Uncle Sam's troops step in. Usually from Fort Assiniboine, south of Pacific Junction west of here near Havre."

The meal was good. Homemade bread, butter. Callahan raised his brows at the butter.

"We have a couple of range cows we've broke to milk. I guess most ranchers have lots of cows but no milk."

"Few in Texas have a milk cow."

"Zukerman does the milking. I tried to make him wash his hands first but it's a chore. I strain the milk and boil it."

"Zukerman isn't the world's cleanest human."

Meal finished, Callahan offered to help wash dishes. She said that could come later. "Still daylight enough to inspect the ranch, Callahan."

"Okay."

They went outside. Twilight was inching in. With the wind down, there were mosquitoes.

Callahan batted.

"They here all the time?"

Max Heywood laughed. "Not during winter. Too cold, then."

Circle Cross had but seven hands, counting Zukerman, for it was between roundups—and few riders were needed. It had no fences to patrol.

Three were out on line-camps. They turned back Circle Cross cattle who wanted to stray. Three ate supper in the cookshack.

Zukerman was the cook. Zukerman was the jack-of-all-trades on Circle Cross.

"Good evenin', Mr. Bookerman," Callahan said. Callahan grinned.

He and Maxine Heywood continued on. Callahan got the smell of canines. They were close to the wolfpack?

Zukerman's wolves were behind heavy meshed wire in a large, circular corral. They rushed toward Callahan and the girl, then skidded to a halt to sit on haunches, watching.

Occasionally one lifted his great snout. A blood-curdling howl came from his throat.

"You told me Zukerman sleeps with them," Callahan said.

"Yeah. In that little house, over there."

"Just big enough for him to crawl into," Callahan said.

"Wolves surround it during the night. Sometimes his feet stick out. I've seen them lick his bare feet."

"They won't lick mine," Callahan said.

The wolves gave Callahan an eerie feeling. One wolf sat and gave the Texan that porkchop look.

57

"What does he feed them?" Callahan asked.

"They run down jackrabbits. My cowboys say there are darned few jackrabbits within miles of the ranch. They kill coyotes and that's good. Coyotes kill freshly-dropped calves, as you're bound to know."

"Wolves can kill calves, too. And colts and old cows."

"Zukerman watches them. Him and that whistle."

They climbed a high western hill. Al Callahan saw tumbling rangelands for miles despite the encroaching darkness.

Callahan saw a dust cloud, far to the west. "Somebody movin' cattle?" he asked.

"Ore wagons."

"You mentioned copper ore," Callahan reminded.

"Yes, I did. Those are ore wagons heading for the railroad. The ore then goes on gondolas and is shipped west to the refinery in Butte."

"The mines, are they on Circle Cross grass?"

"Just beyond our limit, Roger says. They've got quite a town there. Sageville, they call it. Lots of saloons, I hear—and women, too."

Callahan listened.

"I've never been there. Long ways off. About thirty miles, I'd say. I trade mostly in Mill Iron. Sometimes I make the long trip into Malta, but not often."

Miners need beef, Callahan thought.

"Look at our buffalo, Callahan. Down along the draw below us. Can you see them?"

58

Callahan could scarcely see them because of the deepening dust. He counted eight head. "Never saw a buffalo on the way up from Texas," he said. "Gover'ment hunters sure killed them off in a whale of a hurry."

"Roger found them in the foothills of the mountains. They'd run there to escape the hunters. He's interested in preserving things."

"Where is Roger now?"

"I don't know. He might have come home, changed to a fresh horse, and then hit back for Mill Iron, circlin' so he'd not meet us."

Callahan nodded.

"Or he might have ridden west to Sageville to gamble. Or down into Malta. He's really got the gambling fever. Sometimes I think it's worse than being a drunk and having to have booze."

Callahan was silent.

They went down the hill.

"I hope you like Circle Cross, Callahan. The ranch needs a good manager. And I think, being a Texan, you know grass and cattle and how to handle cowboys."

"Outside of being a Ranger, cattle have been my life."

"Goodnight, Callahan."

"Goodnight, Max."

The woman moved off into the dusk. Callahan walked about. He looked at this building, than that one.

He liked what he saw.

He'd ride range at a later date. He'd comb Circle

Cross grass acre by acre, noting the length of grass, the amount of water.

The wind had again risen. The sun had set. The wind blew the mosquitos away, lifted heat from the parched land.

Callahan decided to turn in. He was in front of the big stone ranch-house when the wolves swarmed in.

They came in a black, running stream of death. And again they came directly at him.

And again, Callahan's blood chilled.

They didn't yip. They didn't howl. They just ran in silence. They split when they came to him. They rushed on like a stream of wild air. One brushed his leg slightly.

Callahan's .45 leaped into his hand.

Then, the wolves were gone. And then came Zukerman. He rode his mule. He quirted the beast for more speed. The mule ran with plunging hoofs, ears back, grass-stained jaws open.

Then, Zukerman saw Callahan.

The half-breed hackamore set the mule on his haunches. Dust rose. Wind whipped it away.

"Killingan, by gosh."

Callahan said, "Where do you go, old man?"

"Where do I ride?" Zukerman was bareheaded. He threw back his bald head. A deep cackle broke from his tobacco-stained teeth. "I ride where Satan rides. I ride to death."

"Death?"

"Death to all I tell my wolves to kill, Mattigan."

Callahan said, "I'm buying into Circle Cross.

You'll work for me, then. And if one of those wolves so much as nips a cow—drags down a calf—"

"They run by night, Milligan. They die by night, too!"

Callahan stared up at the loony. Was this man drunk? He could smell no alcohol and he was close enough.

"Who? What runs by night? Who dies by night?"

"Five graves, Willigan."

"Graves?"

Old Zukerman rocked bareback on the mule. His dirty forefinger went out, pointing at the wolves. Callahan turned, pouching his gun; he looked at the wild canines.

The wolves sat in a row thirty feet away. They wagged tails, making halfmoons in the dust. Tongues lolled. They waited.

"My friends," Zukerman said. "My only friends."

Callahan looked back at the oldster. "Five graves?" he prompted.

"On the prairie, Callahan. Someday, maybe, there'll be six?" He leaned forward, face a few inches from Callahan's, his beady eyes boring into Callahan's. Again, no liquor smell.

"Why six?" Callahan asked.

For some reason, he was chilly. His belly was ice. The whiskered face moved back.

The mouth opened. "Look, Callahan, the moon comes. The moon is mad. My wolves await. Jack rabbits run. Hunger tears their vitals. Goodnight, Callahan."

The quirt rose. Its shot-loaded length smashed down on bony ribs. The mule leaped from its tracks, ears back.

It took a bite at Callahan. Callahan leaped back. Teeth clicked. And then the mule—and the wolves—skidded around the bunkhouse corner and out of sight.

Leaving Al Callahan staring.

Chapter Six

Callahan should have been tired. He wasn't. He went to the horse-barn. He saddled a black Circle Cross gelding. He rode west.

He reined the black into the cottonwood trees on the hill. For thirty minutes he sat a silent saddle, watching. Nobody trailed him.

His money-belt bothered him.

Common sense told him that as long as this range knew he had ten thousand dollars on him his life was in danger. The money-belt had worried him on his long ride north.

Lone men were robbed and killed on trails, in saloons, boarding houses, hotels. Some cowpunchers split their saddle-skirt sewing. They inserted their bills in this opening, then had the skirt sewed shut.

He'd discarded that plan. Saddles could be stolen.

He remembered Zukerman's cacklings. Zukerman was a loony? Or was he? Callahan reined in, looking back down on Circle Cross.

Zukerman and wolves were returning. They'd headed out west; then returned from the south. Evidently they'd made a quarter circle while hunting.

Circle Cross' dark buildings absorbed the loony and wolves. Callahan rode west in the direction of the dust he'd seen raised by ore wagons.

The black sought a trail lope. He was well-gaited. He had good blood. Callahan reached down. He petted the horse.

A good bronc was a valuable thing. He'd heard that a good wife also was valuable. Because of this he thought of Max Heywood and Ann Scott.

He grinned. Both females had to prove themselves.

He rode and rode. The wagon-trail was further away than he'd figured. Distance in this high clean air was deceptive. Finally he found the wagon-ruts. By pure coincidence a wagon-train happened along that time of the night.

Mounted armed guards accompanied the oxen- and mule-pulled high wagons, rifles across saddles. Starlight offered enough illumination to show them that Callahan sat saddle with empty hands shoulder-high.

"Where to, cowboy?"

"North. To the mining town."

"Sageville it's called, cowboy."

Four mounted men surrounded him, rifles in hand. Callahan said, "Work for a man there?"

"For a miner, yes. Cowpunch, no."

"I can trade my saddle for a pick," Callahan assured. "Why the artillery? I thought this was only rock-ore."

"Free gold, too," a husky man said shortly. "Move off the trail to the east about a hundred feet and let the wagons go by. And when you move, keep riding north. Hank, ride with him."

The guards rode on. Hank and Callahan swung wide and turned broncs north, Hank riding close. Callahan said, "How big's this Sageville?"

"About three thousand, they tell me. Big if not bigger than the county seat, Malta."

The heavily-laden wagons lumbered through starlight, wheels creaking wagons rocking over bumps. It was eerie, there in the soft Montana night. Ghost wagons, lumbering.

Callahan counted eighteen.

"Reach Halfway House twelve miles or so down," Hank said. "Grub there, women, booze—and fresh mules an' cows."

The last wagon passed.

Hank drew rein. "All right, cowboy. On your own now. Hope you hit it good in Sageville."

"I need it."

Hank rode south. Soon he was hidden by night. The last sounds died. Stillness held the night.

A wolf howled east. Again, Callahan thought of

Zukerman. Callahan turned the black beast toward Circle Cross.

He'd learned much. He knew where Sageville was located. He knew its approximate population. Three thousand people needed much beef.

He knew that Montana Territory had no brand registrations. Cattlemen had not yet organized as they had in Texas. A beef-buyer need not report to the sheriff the brands his purchased cows bore.

Circle Cross could sell Rocking U cows. No questions would be asked by the buyer. By the same token Rocking U could sell Circle Cross beef. And no questions, either.

Cricle Cross lay in darkness. He unsaddled the black, rubbed him down with a gunnysack, and entered the big ranch house. He went down the long hall carrying his boots to make no noise. He entered his bedroom.

He pulled shut the heavy window-drapes before lighting the kerosene lamp. With the drapes closed, there was no air; the room soon became unbearably warm.

He kept remembering Bud Harding and Len Rourke. Had they killed him they could have easily covertly lifted his money belt while his body was being carried to the morgue. Or they could have sneaked into the morgue later and stolen.

Bud Harding no longer was a danger. But Len Rourke still lived. Callahan looked about. An old newspaper lay on the trunk. A pair of scissors were on the bureau.

He cut the newspaper into shreds. These he packed in his money-belt after taking out the ten one-thousand buck notes which he put in his socks—five thousand to each foot.

He found a loaded gunbelt and pistol in a drawer. These he hung over a bed-post. He then put the money-belt hanging over these things.

He rolled up a rug. He put it in the bed under a sheet. He then hung his hat over the head of the bed. It threw a shadow where his head would naturally be.

He stepped back. An old trick with moss on it, but better than nothing. He then went out the window. He restored the screen to the window and went to the foreman's shack, thirty feet away.

Max had told him her foreman was visiting back east. The shack was empty. Inside was a bed and some old furniture. A window looked out at the bedroom window with its parted drapes.

Callahan pulled the bed close to the window. Thus he could lie and watch the bedroom window.

He had little worry about a midnight robber hitting him at Circle Cross, but it was best to take precautions. He trusted nobody on this grass. He pulled off his boots, aware of the five thousand dollars in each sock.

He did not intend to sleep, but sleep overtook him. He came awake hurriedly, hand grabbing his sixgun beside him. He looked out at the bedroom window.

The window was open. The screen had been

removed. It rested against the side of the house.

The drapes swung in the wind.

Gun in hand, lying on his belly, Callahan waited, eyes riveted on that window. The night was very still. Only a slight wind sang in the eaves. Callahan waited, heart pounding.

The drapes parted. A figure put a leg over the window-sill, came out of the bedroom. Male? Female? The starlight was deceptive, but Callahan glimpsed his money-belt the robber's shoulder.

The shadow pointed its handgun at the bed. He shot three times, gun-roar smashing across sleeping Circle Cross.

The robber wheeled. He ran for the corner of the house, money-belt still across his shoulder. He disappeared around the house.

Callahan got in but one shot.

He was sure he had missed. He'd dropped trigger just as the would-be murderer slid around the corner.

He heard his lead wham off stone.

He ran into the open. He sprinted for the house-corner. As he got there, he heard the drum-drum of fastly-departing hoofs.

Gun smoking, he listened.

The sound of hoofs died against distance. Callahan figured the shadow rode northeast. It was hard to tell for the wolves were howling. And cowpunchers came running, also adding to the din.

When Max Heywood arrived, Callahan stood outside the bedroom window. "Callahan, what happened?"

Max wore a red dressing robe. It accentuated her small waist and flaring hips. Her raven-black hair hung almost to her waist.

Callahan gave details. Zukerman listened, the cowpokes listened. "He got off with your money-belt?" Max asked.

"Had it hanging over the bed post."

They entered the bedroom. Callahan lit the kerosene light. The pistol and gunbelt lay on the floor. "Those are father's," Max Heywood said. "They were in the drawer."

"Drawer's open," Callahan said.

"He must've been going to steal it, too, but decided against it," the girl said. "He sure shot into that rug you rolled up, Callahan."

Old Zukerman cackled, "Heh, heh, heh! If'n Milligan had been in bed, Killigan'd now be dead." He looked about, eyes wild. "Hell, it rhymes, men."

He began a war dance, knees lifting high, a sharp keening whine cutting his adam's apple.

Max spoke to a cowboy. "Get rid of him, Clarence."

"With pleasure, boss."

Clarence picked up the old man by the nape of the neck and the seat of the pants. He threw him out the window. Zukerman cursed as he landed on the gravel outside.

Clarence followed him out. He carried the screaming, kicking oldster toward the wolf pen. The other cowboys returned to bed. Max Heywood and Callahan stood alone outside the window, Callahan still carrying the lighted lamp.

"I can't see a track," Max said.

Callahan said, "All gravel and hard pan." Suddenly, he stiffened, head cocked, keening the starlight. "Rider coming."

Roger Heywood rode a black and gray pinto. He reined in and said, "It's four in the morning. False dawn is practically here. And I find my sister in her dressing robe and Al Callahan out with a lamp."

Callahan said nothing. Max Heywood said, "You're not funny, Roger. You're half drunk."

"Not half, sister. I must correct you. Roger Heywood is completely drunk, soppingly drunk—and he won three hundred and six dollars and fifty-four cents this night in the Trail Weary."

"I'll have to see it," Max said.

"I need a cup of coffee. I need a gallon of coffee. I'll show you the money in the house while I brew the coffee. And to get back to this lamp—usually a lantern, not a lamp, is used on a snipe-hunt."

"Somebody tried to kill Callahan," Max Heywood said. She gave details. Roger rocked in saddle, hands clutching the fork. When his sister had finished he said, "Too bad the bastards failed."

"Thanks," Callahan said.

"Should of at least shot a hole in that damned green shirt," Roger Heywood said. "Hey, Zukerman! Zukerman, make tracks, you old bastard!"

Callahan walked over to lay a palm on the pinto's shoulder. The horse was not sweaty. Evidently Heywood had ridden at a slow gait out from Mill Iron. Callahan's hand dropped.

The would-be assassin had headed out fast. Had he been Heywood, the pinto would have been sweating.

Zukerman showed up. "What is it, Roger?"

"Put Patches in the barn. Oats him and hay him good. Then fall into the creek."

"Fall into the crick?"

"With a bar of soap. Good lye laundry soap. I'm downwind on you. You do more than smell. You stink."

"Heh, heh, heh. I'll get on your other side."

"You'll get Patches into the barn, or I'll boot your rump up to your shoulders. Move, and fast!"

"Goin', Roger."

Zukerman and his stink and the pinto moved into the starlight. Roger Heywood balanced himself on drunken boots.

"So some bastard got off with your ten thousand bucks, eh, Callahan? Damn, I wish I'd been the man. At least I could finish school without a worry. Some guys have all the luck."

"You never got a good look at the person?" Max Heywood asked.

"Only a shadow," Callahan said. "Sounded as though the horse went northeast. You just came from that direction, Heywood. See any riders?"

"You go out and look," Roger Heywood said.

Heywood went to the house, staggering slightly. Dawn was inching in. Callahan said, "Well, I can't buy into Circle Cross now, Miss Heywood."

Max Heywood hesitated, said, "I guess not.

71

Maybe you could get money sent up from Texas?"

Callahan laughed. "Fat chance. Anyway, now nobody'll want to kill me for my money."

"I reckon not."

Callahan looked at her. She looked at Callahan. "Could have been a number of people. First, Len Rourke."

"Even Ann Scott," Max said. "Rocking U is northeast. I wouldn't put it beyond her. Did it look like a woman?"

"Could have been. I can't say either way. Could have even been Deputy Jones."

"Jones?"

"He knew I had the money on me. Just because a man packs a star is no sign that man is honest."

"I agree. Who else?"

"Your brother."

Max Heywood shook her head. "I doubt that. Roger's father was a Texan. My dad had a strong sense of honor. I hope he handed it down to both of us."

Callahan nodded.

"Roger may gamble and drink, but he's okay underneath. Some day he'll make a good medical doctor, I'm sure. No, it wasn't my brother, Callahan."

"Sorry I said that, Max."

"You leaving the country?"

Callahan hesitated. His plan was working. He wanted to buy into Circle Cross—or Rocking U— but he wanted to investigate thoroughly and fully

72

first. And if all thought him broke, his investigation would be easier to accomplish.

"Not until I get my ten thousand back."

"What're you going to do first?"

Was her voice cold? Without money, was he no longer welcome on Circle Cross? Or was her tone normal?

"See Deputy Jones," Callahan said.

Chapter Seven

Deputy Mike Jones slept head-down on his battered desk. Callahan unceremoniously pushed the deputy's face down hard. Jones awakened with a curse.

He stared up. "Callahan."

"In person, deputy."

Jones said, "Somebody's goin' kill you, Callahan. I was kept awake most of last night by a howlin' kid. Colic. Didn't get much sleep."

"This office is no hotel."

Jones' eyes narrowed. "You go out lookin' for trouble, Callahan. You don't wait till trouble comes to you. What's on your mind?"

"I was robbed last night."

Jones sat up, now awake. "Tell me?"

Callahan gave all details. Jones said, "Ten thousand dollars in federal notes. Ten bills. You got their numbers?"

"Here it is."

Jones studied the list in Callahan's small book. He copied them down on a slip of paper. He handed the book back to Callahan. "You sure you couldn't identify?"

"Just a shadow," Callahan said.

Jones leaned back, eyes lidded. "Nobody could cash a bill that big around here. He'd have to go to the bank. Nearest bank is in Malta. I'll send a rider in with this list."

"I found my money-belt," Callahan said.

"Yeah, where?"

"Laying in the sagebrush a mile or so out of Circle Cross. Robber'd stripped it and tossed it away."

"I'll be damned," Jones said.

Callahan said, "I didn't last long."

Jones got to his boots. "This ain't over yet. I'll get word to the sheriff in Malta. You ain't pullin' out, are you?"

"Not for some time, deputy."

Jones went to the open door and spat out into the dust. "Another scorcher of a day comin'. You goin' to Bud Harding's funeral? Goin' be held this mornin' at ten."

Callahan shook his head.

"Buryin' him from the school house. School house is our church an' town meetin' hall. Body don't keep long in this heat. Nobody around to embalm. He's already bloated in the morgue."

Callahan didn't want to talk about Harding. "I'll drop in once in a while, deputy."

"Where'll you stay?"

"Wherever I hang my hat."

"Where to now, Callahan?"

Callahan eyed the man. "You ask questions, Jones—too damned many questions."

Jones' face reddened. Under the red lurked hardness, Callahan read. "Part of the duties of my office, Callahan. By law I got the right to know where every human in my bailiwick should be at such a given time—and what that person should be doing."

Callahan nodded.

"I hear tell you used to ride Texas law, Callahan. What I've said, then, shouldn't be news to you."

"It isn't, Jones. I'm riding to Rocking U."

"You'll like ol' man Scott. He was rough and tough in his day, but his day is gone."

"Comes to all of us in time." Callahan left.

He grubbed at the Mill Iron Cafe. Ham and eggs and a stack of wheats. Town kids peered through the greasy windows at him. The owner was a broken-down waddy.

"Damn' nice green shirt. Had my eye on it in the Merc, but you beat me to it. Fits good."

"Fits just right. Like tailor-made."

"How goes things?"

Callahan told about his being robbed. He wanted to spread the word out as far and fast as possible. Those who had wanted to rob him—and didn't—would wonder who robbed him.

Everybody would suspect everybody else.

"Goin' to leave now, Callahan?"

Callahan got off the stool, inner man now silent.

He took out his wallet. "Damages?"

"Thirty cents."

Callahan dug through loose change. He counted out three dimes. He looked in his wallet. "Not much cash, man. Might have to sell my buckskin."

"Good lookin' cayuse. Come to me first?"

"I'll do that, friend. Which way to Rocking U?"

He got necessary directions. Outside the kids followed him wide-eyed to his buckskin. One boy said, "Man, you sure are a gunfighter."

Callahan leaned down. "Just do one thing for me, boy. Never follow in my footsteps."

"My daddy tells me the same. Hey, where you goin'?"

"Back to Texas."

Callahan loped out of town, buckskin's shod hoofs kicking up dust, the endless Montana wind whipping it away. He had a hunch he might meet the Scott rig coming into Mill Iron for Bud Harding's funeral.

The sun rose higher in a cloudless sky. Callahan remembered finding his money-belt. Shreds of newspaper had been hanging from sagebrush and greasewood. The robber must have really been surprised, Callahan thought.

His buckskin hit a trail lope. He was very easy riding. You just sat and fixed your body in time with his. Callahan had had many saddlers in his day, but never one as tough as this lineback.

He reviewed his relationship with Ann Scott, brief and hectic and filled with gunpowder and death as it had been.

He grinned. He'd put her over his knee. He'd been ready to paddle her attractive behind, and then had changed his mind.

Her sea-green eyes had flashed hate and anger. She'd tossed her brilliant red hair in disgust.

He pushed on, occasionally pulling the buckskin down to a fast running-walk. He felt better. His breakfast had been a good one, although his lip was still rather big from Roger Heywood's fists.

He healed quickly, though. He had good strong blood. He met not a rig coming from Rocking U, headed for Mill Iron. He knew the Scotts had not been in town. Jones had told him that.

He topped a high hill. Surrounded by buckbrush and scrub cedar, he drew rein to breathe his buckskin. He took his field-glasses from case behind saddle. He swept the range to the southwest, the direction of Circle Cross.

Circle Cross was a goodly distance away. He judged over twenty miles, cross country. The range had changed. Evidently this area had less rain than Circle Cross.

For grass was burned brown. Cattle he'd ridden past had not been fat. Most grazed in coulees and draws where there was still a bit of green bluejoint. Sidehills were brown, barren.

Four miles away a rider angled northwest toward Mill Iron. He apparently followed no trail for his horse zigzagged through high sagebrush. Apparently he headed for Bud Harding's funeral?

Callahan had a wry smile. A man gained stature by dying. He'd seen it before when a ranger, a confirmed and deadly killer, fell before a ranger's gun.

The town didn't honor the ranger who'd staked his life on his gun-ability. Hell, no! The town honored its enemy, the dead killer. The town turned out enmasse for the killer's funeral.

Callahan focused his glasses carefully but the distance was too far. He lowered them. Evidently a cowpunch from some line-camp. Callahan rode on.

Rocking U lay on a flat along Wisdom Creek, a scatteration of log buildings. Callahan's heart rose at the sight of a Texas dog-run connecting the two sections of the long ranch-house.

Chickens scratched in the yard. Horses grazed in a pasture along the creek which appeared to have little water. Three Holstein milk cows grazed with the saddlers.

Callahan was surprised. He'd not seen a Holstein since leaving the Panhandle. Holsteins had to be imported. They were wonderful milkers. One Holstein gave as much milk as three range cows.

And besides, they were not so ornery.

Dogs barked as he rode in—three golden collies. Ann Scott was on her knees in the shade of the porch digging in a flower bed. She stood up hurriedly as Callahan rode in, the collies leaping, running.

"What're you doing here, Callahan?"

Callahan leaned on saddle-fork. "You're real purty this morning, Miss Scott. Beyond purty. Beautiful."

And she was just that. Skin-tight wash-faded Levis hugged her hips. Worn black boots covered her small feet. Her blue blouse swelled under her womanhood.

Her green eyes flashed. "Did you buy into Circle Cross?"

Callahan slowly shook his head.

"Why didn't you?"

Callahan told about being robbed. She watched his face, eyes losing their harshness. "And you couldn't see for sure who shot and robbed?"

"It could have been you."

Again, the green eyes showed fire. "Callahan, if you were on the ground, I'd slap your face!"

Callahan got off his horse. "I'm afoot now, Miss Scott."

She slapped his face. Ringing, loud slap. Callahan grabbed her wrists. He pulled her close. She bit his knuckles. He released her. He rubbed his right hand. Her teeth had cut in.

"What's goin' on out here?" a man's voice asked.

Callahan turned. Unconsciously, his hand dipped, then held. He'd have to get rid of that habit. No longer was he a Ranger. When with the law, your life was forever in the balance.

The man in the wheelchair was grizzled, gray. He wore old Levis, worn boots, a blue chambray shirt, an old Tom Watson Stetson. His eyes were green, like those of his daughter, but time had faded them, giving them a thoughtfulness the daughter's eyes did not possess—but someday might as time progressed.

"Matt Scott is my name," the man said. "And I'd say you've already met my daughter, Ann."

Callahan was not in a favored spot and Callahan

knew it so he fell back on an old prop—a wide, boyish Irish grin. "Your lovely daughter and me were practicin', Mister Scott."

"Practicin' for what?"

"For matrimony, maybe? I'm Al Callahan."

The seamed face went blank. The mouth opened slightly. The green eyes probed, tested, felt.

Callahan glanced at Ann Scott. He saw another pair of green and lifeless eyes. Yes, and slack, emotionless lips, also.

Finally Matt Scott said slowly, "I've heard of you, Mister Callahan."

"And all bad, I bet." Callahan grinned. "Some days a man shouldn't crawl out of his sougans."

"Your hand. It went down fast."

"Bad habit, sir. Former Texas Ranger, sir. I quit a year ago and went out looking for a ranch."

"My daughter says you intend to buy into Circle Cross."

"Not now, sir. No money." Callahan told of his robbery.

"And you have no idea who robbed you?" Ann Scott asked. She looked at her father. "He says I could have been the robber. That's why I slapped his face."

"Where's Len Rourke?" Callahan asked.

Ann Scott answered. "Rourke is stationed at one of our southern linecamps, Louse Creek."

"Twenty odd miles away," Matt Scott said.

"He might be riding for Mill Iron now," Ann Scott said. "Naturally, he'd go to Bud Harding's funeral.

81

Callahan remembered the rider zigzagging through sagebrush. That could have been Rourke heading for Mill Iron.

"Do you think Len Rourke robbed you?" Matt Scott asked.

Callahan shrugged. "Maybe yes. Maybe no. Starlight. Hard to see in. Now if there'd been a good moon. This grass is troubled, Mr. Scott."

"In what way?"

"Circle Cross says it's losing cattle. And not in small bunches, either."

Matt Scott winced. Evidently pain momentarily held him. He closed his eyes, gnarled hands clenched on the wheelchair arms.

Callahan waited.

Finally, the eyes opened. "Maybe Rocking U can say the same, Callahan. Damn that bronc! Went over backwards, caught me off-guard. Jus' a damn' jackrabbit jumpin' out from under a greasewood!"

"Some broncs are shy," Callahan said.

Scott's eyes swept Callahan's face. "You care to buy into Rockin' U?"

"No money now."

"You can raise another ten thousand, I feel sure. I'll sell one third of Rockin' U at that price. My daughter isn't happy here since her mother died four years ago."

"Father, please," Ann Scott said.

Callahan looked at the red-head. She did not meet his eyes. He knew that ranch-life was indeed lonely for a young woman. It was bound to be. He cocked his head. Wind sang in the eaves. Wind always sang here on the high northern plains, he'd heard.

The wind alone was enough to drive a woman crazy, not to mention the mosquitoes and flies and various other household bugs.

"You've been asking me to go," Matt Scott told his daughter.

Ann came behind the wheelchair. She put her hands on her father's shoulder. "That's because of you, darling. I want you close to a doctor and a hospital all the time. And there isn't even a doctor in Mill Iron."

"There's Roger Heywood."

"He's not a full-fledged doctor of medicine. He hasn't a license."

Callahan listened. Roger Heywood, then, practiced medicine? That was new to him. He was learning.

"There's Doctor Yeager."

Ann Scott laughed sourly. "That old drunk! Never a sober breath. And he's a horse doctor, not a human doctor."

"Who's Doctor Yeager?" Callahan asked.

"An old drunk living alone on Willow Creek, two miles south of Mill Iron. He used to treat humans but since Roger Heywood got home from school all Yeager does is consort with the bottle."

"He's a good doctor, though," Matt Scott said. "Drunk or sober."

"That's your opinion," Ann said.

Callahan decided to pay Dr. Yeager a visit. There was an outside chance that his bullet might have hit the robber. Dr. Yeager might have treated a bullet wound lately.

Ann leaned over. She kissed her father's forehead. Callahan had a feeling her affection was forced, for his benefit.

Her blouse-sleeve slid up. Callahan saw a small red mark near her elbow. Catclaw spine had pricked her? He then remembered there was no catclaw on this range.

Bullberry bushes, though, had sharp spines.

Ann Scott's red head rose. The sleeve slid down. Callahan wanted more information. "I got fooled on Circle Cross."

"How?" Ann Scott asked.

"The name Max. The Texas ad had Max, not Maxine. I thought all the time I was dealing with a man, not a woman."

Old Matt Cross said nothing. He folded his rope-gnarled hands. He closed his eyes.

"Not a nice trick," Ann Scott said.

"She ever do that before?"

Ann Scott's brows rose. "I'm afraid I don't understand, Callahan."

"She ever have others ride in to look over Circle Cross?" Callahan asked.

"I don't know for sure, but I think so."

Matt Cross spoke without opening his eyes. "You'll have to overlook what my daughter says about Maxine Heywood. The father Heywood and me drove our herds up—one combined herd—from Texas."

Ann Scott bit her bottom lip.

Matt Scott continued, "Heywood and me and our

84

wives were friends to the end, but Ann and Maxine—"

"I've hated her from the first time I met her," Ann Scott said.

"Too bad, too bad," the old cowman murmured. "Life is so short and hate so unnecessary."

Callahan said, "I leave now. I bid you both goodby. And good health to you, Mister Cross."

"I thank you, Callahan." Matt Cross kept his eyes closed.

Callahan and Ann walked to Callahan's buckskin. The collies lay in the shade, tongues extended against the heat.

"What's next, Callahan?"

Callahan swung into leather. "I really don't know. A smart man would pull out. Odds against my recovering my money are so high the task seems impossible. But maybe I'm not a smart man?"

"Those serial numbers, though?"

"In one sense, they mean nothing. The bills could be cashed miles away. Chicago, San Francisco, anywhere. They won't be cashed—or tried to be turned in—close to Mill Iron, if I'm a judge."

"I guess you're right."

Callahan rode out. Plainly, Rocking U was running down. Buildings needed fresh paint. Here and there, a broken window. The windmill fan lacked three blades.

Rocking U needed a rancher's hand.

This ranch had potentialities. It needed supervision and hard work—the work of a man who knew cattle, not of a cattle-queen.

Matt Scott had not asked why Len Rourke and Bud Harding had jumped him. Callahan was glad for that. He might have told the rancher that Ann Scott had sicced the two on him.

Then he realized he'd not done this. Matt Scott had enough trouble now. Better that he never know of his daughter's actions. Plainly, Ann Scott was all the maimed cowman now had.

His daughter and memories.

Callahan headed northwest at a running walk. He saw Rocking U cattle; they needed grass. He saw no cowpunchers riding range. He remembered seeing nobody but Matt Scott and his daughter on Rocking U.

Rocking U punchers undoubtedly had been out on riding chores. Or stationed—as Len Rourke was—on linecamps. And this was also the slack season between calf- and beef-gather. During that time a ranch laid off many punchers to rehire them again when fall roundup came.

Callahan pushed on. Overhead the cloudless sky. Overhead, the blazing sun. Under hoof, parched and bitter earth suffering—crying—for water.

For rain.

Chapter Eight

Callahan's fingers dug into the scraggly hair. He got a handhold. He raised the man's head from the table.

Dr. Yeager did not object. He did not open his eyes. His mouth hung open, spittle hanging.

Callahan held the head. He studied it. Sunken cheeks, slack thin lips, unshaven jowls.

"Dr. Yeager?"

"Go 'way, you sonofabitch!"

Callahan grinned. "At least, you show life," he said. "I'm Al Callahan."

"I'm Ghengis Khan."

"Your eyes aren't slanted right," Callahan said. "Who've you treated for gunshot wounds lately?"

The left eye slowly opened. It was bloodshot and sunken. The right eyelid quivered but did not open. It seemed stuck.

Callahan reached down. He took hold of the eyelid. He suddenly pulled upward. The eye flew open. It hung open momentarily, then dropped closed again. It stayed closed. Callahan thought, Hell, one eye is enough. This man is dead drunk.

He lowered his head close to the veterinarian's. No smell of booze. Callahan's eyes narrowed.

"I'm drunk," Dr. Yeager mumbled.

Callahan had no answer.

"I know you," the veterinarian said. "You're Calligan."

"Callahan, not Calligan."

"You killed Bud Harding. I signed Harding's death certificate yesterday. Harding was no good."

The right eye fluttered open. This time it stayed open.

"Harding and Rourke? Why'd they move against me?"

"To kill you."

"Why'd they want to kill me?"

"How would I know. What'd you want?"

"You treat Rourke for a gunshot wound?"

The heavy brows lifted. The right eye opened halfway. "You never shot Len Rourke yesterday. You shot Bud Harding."

"Since yesterday?"

"Who'd shoot Rourke? No, I haven't treated him. He'd gone to Roger Heywood, anyway." A short, snorty laugh. "He's the range medico now. Comical, huh?"

"What's comical?"

"The whole damn' mess. Are you done with your questions?"

"Go back to sleep," Callahan said.

The right eye closed. The left eye was closing as the shaggy head went again on its owner's forearms.

Doctor Yeager had hairy forearms. On them Callahan saw pustules that looked like mosquito bites.

Callahan thought of Ann Scott's arm. It had shown similar markings. She'd worn long sleeves. He judged her sleeves had been long for protection against mosquitoes.

Montana raised big, healthy mosquitoes. Callahan's face and hands had been bitten. They had stingers like ice-picks.

Were it not for the continious wind, the mosquitoes would drive stock skin-poor, he knew. When the wind died at sundown and sunup, range horses ran berserk in attempts to escape clouds of the stinging insects.

Callahan walked out, star-rowel spurs clanging. He was getting nowhere in a hell of a hurry, he realized. The day was growing even hotter. He swung into saddle.

He'd ride into the country seat, Malta. But first, he'd see Len Rourke. Rourke had once tried to kill him. Rourke might have been the dark-night ambusher.

Rourke should be in Mill Iron. Callahan turned his buckskin north. The lineback was leg-tired. He'd traveled many miles since sunup. He needed a roll in dust, water, oats and hay. And a night in a manger eating his head off.

He rode out of the timber. He caught the wagon-road leading north to Mill Iron. And then, he heard the wolves.

He drew rein, blood chilling despite the cloyish heat. He sat saddle on a mesa high with greasewood and buckbrush. Sagebrush scent was in the wind. He looked west.

The wolves poured over a western hill. They ran spread out, a coyote running ahead for dear life. But the wolves were the faster. They drew up on the coyote.

The lead wolf hit the coyote on the dead run. Fangs fastened in the coyote's rump, the huge wolf did a complete roll, taking the yipping coyote with him.

The coyote flew into the air. He came down amidst the snarling, tearing wolves. He was instantly in shreds. The wolves then played, throwing up bits of coyote fur, entrails. Suddenly, they stopped gamboling. They sat as one and raised their huge black nostrils and scented the air.

Then, they started for Callahan.

They spread out as they ran, using the pincher movement. They thus entrapped their prey as they had done the coyote. And in the closing jaws would be Callahan and his buckskin.

The buckskin scented them. He then saw them. He fought the curb bit, wanting to flee. He reared; he snorted. Callahan held him. Callahan snaked his .30-30 carbine from saddle-boot.

He knew better than to run. Fangs would rip in, hamstring the buckskin, send him—and rider—down in the brush. Where was old Zukerman? He did not trail his wildings?

Had the wolves broken free? Did they now run without human commands, a pack of crazed canine killers?

The buckskin pawed, fighting reins. The wolves ran nearer, and Callahan raised his rifle. He knew he and the horse were doomed. But he'd take some of the brutes with him.

Now the wolves were only a hundred yards away. They ran directly toward him and the buckskin. Then Callahan saw Zukerman suddenly appear on a hill two hundred feet to the north.

"Call them off!"

Zukerman rode a dun mule. He reined in. He now rode a saddle, Callahan quickly noticed. "Heh, heh, heh, Milligan!"

"Call them off! Or I'll start shooting!"

"Heh, heh, heh, Killigan!"

Callahan shot the saddle-fork under the wolfer. The blow sent the mule on his haunches. The saddle-form exploded. Zukerman fell from leather. He landed on his feet.

His whistle went to his lips.

The wolves stopped. They looked at Callahan and the horse, then at their boss. They seemed undecided.

Callahan had the sights on Zukerman's heart. "Blow again or I'll kill you, you old bastard!"

"Heh, heh, heh, Mattigan. No sense of humor."

"Blow!"

The whistle rose again. This time the wolves obeyed. They wheeled and trotted to Zukerman where they sat around the mule, tongues out.

Callahan rode up the hill. His buckskin shied at wolf-smell, and would not get close.

"You pull that trick again," Callahan said, "and I kill you first and your wolves second."

Zukerman rubbed his thighs. "You damned near druv that saddle-tree through my pins. My kak is plumb ruined. Max will give me hell. Saddle belongs to Circle Cross."

"Ride bareback. But don't ride around me, understand?"

"You sound mad, Hannigan."

"I'm not happy," Callahan assured. "What you doing over here miles from Circle Cross?"

"Killin' coyotes. I gotta hunch coyotes kill Circle Cross cattle. No rustlers."

"How's Maxine?"

Zukerman blinked. "Why interested in her? You aim to marry her?"

"How is she? And where?"

"She's all right. Mad as usual, but did you ever see a female who wasn't?"

Callahan said, "Some aren't ever angry."

"She's at Circle Cross," the wolfer said. "Roger is there, too. You got robbed, huh?"

Callahan thought, Completely loco. Memory gone. And then he thought, Or is this just an act?

Hard to tell.

"Robbed," Callahan said. "You were there. Remember?"

Again, that high-pitched cackle. The tin whistle lifted; gaunt cheeks blew. Huge wolves leaped to their paws.

Zukerman ran toward the mule, vaulted into saddle without touching the horn. His boots hit stirrups. The stirrups—and boots—swung ahead. Spurs landed in the mule's shoulders.

The surprised mule broke wind loudly, then started bucking. He bucked down-hill. Zukerman rode a tough, hard saddle. Not a bit of daylight showed between him and saddle-seat.

He hooked high on the shoulders. His spurs then ran high behind. The wolves roared after him, snarling and growling.

Callahan watched, grinning.

The mule quit bucking. He leveled out on a dead run across the basin, ears laid flatly back, dust kicking behind, the wolves around him. The mule raced across the flat, dodging brush.

He flashed over the low southern hill, then dipped behind out of sight. The wolves also disappeared.

Callahan heard only the fading whoops of the old wolfer. Mingled with these yips were the deeper yips of the wild canines. Then distance took command and all sounds died.

Callahan realized his shirt was wet. And not sweat from the heat, he thought. He mopped his sweaty forehead. He'd never been so ascared in his life.

He rode toward Mill Iron.

Mill Iron held more than its usual occupants. Cowpunchers had ridden in for Harding's funeral. Callahan went to the bars, looking for Rourke. Rourke was not in evidence. Callahan met Deputy Sheriff Jones in the Trail Weary.

"Rourke left town right after the funeral," the deputy informed. "Headed back for his line-camp. Said Rockin' U cows got stuck in Sunken Springs. Water low, boggy."

Callahan understood. Cattle waded out through mud to get to water. They bogged down.

"Beer, Callahan?"

"One."

"Not a drinkin' man?"

"Now and then," Callahan said. "I early learned from booze the truth of an old Irish saying."

"Yeah?"

"My best friend and my worst enemy come out of the neck of the same bottle," Callahan said.

Jones laughed. Callahan judged him half-drunk. Most of the saloons' occupants had been drinking all day. A funeral was an excuse to get outside of alcohol, he knew.

He noticed hard looks sent his direction. He was an outsider, and he had killed a local boy. Also, he was Texan. And he well knew that Texans were not too welcome on Montana grass.

Too overbearing, too bossy.

He ate at the Lone Stirrup Cafe. He did not sit at the counter. He sat in a booth alone. He had learned that if a man stood at a bar, or sat at a bar, he was more prone to get into trouble. He was in open view.

94

He was thus brought to mind.

While at a bar, trouble could easily move in on either side, but trouble was not apt to slide into a booth-seat beside you.

After eating, he went to the hotel. He got an upstairs room. The one window looked into the alley. A man would need a long ladder to get up to it. He jacked the back of a chair under the doorknob.

He undressed and went to bed. His money was now in his money-belt. He slept wearing the belt. His unholstered .45 lay on the chair beside his pillow. His .30-30 carbine stood stock-down at the bed's head.

He was tired. His thoughts before sleep were few. One thought stood out. Logic told him only two people on Mill Iron range knew he had not been robbed. He was one. The other was the marauder, whoever he was.

The night-killer had missed his first time. Would he hit again? He might and he might not. Callahan went to sleep.

He awakened at dawn, very hungry. The hotel's cook was just starting his morning. Callahan waited in the small dining room. Finally hotcakes, three fried eggs, two toasted biscuits, and coffee arrived.

Thirty minutes later, he rode out of Mill Iron, heading toward Sunken Springs. Deputy Jones had given him instructions.

"About twenty mile out, Callahan. Can't miss it. Right west of the wagon-trail runnin' into Malta."

The night of oats and hay had rested the buckskin. He fiddlefooted, dancing sidewise, chewing his bit, playing with Callahan. Callahan patted the arched neck. The lineback responded, dancing, pulling—and Callahan let him have his run. Then, the bronc settled down.

Callahan knew the buckskin. The lineback buckskin knew Callahan. They'd spent hours together. Each appreciated the other.

Callahan scouted the range. Well did he know that within ten years or so this great expanse would be broken by fences of the farmers, the land within that barbwire would be plowed—the native grass forever gone.

He did not like that thought. But it was true and it would come, he knew—after that, no more free range. And cattlemen, operating against drouth and hard winters, needed free range to keep operating.

Had they to pay taxes on their range, they'd have gone bankrupt—they worked on such a close margin, Callahan knew.

What, then, was the answer?

Callahan had seen the answer down on the Panhandle. You cut down on the head-count of your herd. You raised better beef. Shorthorns. Herefords. Angus. Cattle beef to the hock.

One well-bred beef ate no more grass than a scraggly longhorn. The grass he ate made more beef—and you grew cattle for beef, not for long horns.

So you shipped in good bulls. And you seeded the land to different grass. Grass that grew thicker and was richer. You cut hay in the summer. Even in this country of short summers and long winters you could cut two cuttings of alfalfa a year.

Sometimes, he had learned, with longer summer you could cut even three cuttings.

With hay in stacks, you built shelters for your cattle for wintertime. No more cattle standing freezing on hoofs, rumps pointed toward the below-zero blizzard.

Cattle stood in timber grooves that cut the wind. Cattle stood behind snow-fences or in feed-lots, out of the thirty-below gale.

And water? What did a cow do for water under the new conditions, during the terrible winter?

No longer did a cow lick snowdrifts for water. Or get on her front knees to stick her head into a waterhole chopped into a stream frozen two or three feet deep.

You had a watertank. Under it you threw worthless hay or chips to heat the water. Vapor arose from the lukewarm water. And bossy buried her nose in the water and drank to her heart's content.

Water—and hay—made beef.

The buckskin sought a trail-lope. Callahan rode deep in stirrups, body fitted to the cadence, momentarily thinking of his bunk last night in the Mill Iron hotel.

Had somebody tried his doorknob during the night? He remembered coming awake, hand on his pistol. He'd lain tense, listening, gun-grip hot against his palm.

But he'd heard nothing alien. His muscles had relaxed. He'd gone back asleep, the .45 in bed with him.

Had he imagined things?

He brushed such thoughts aside. This was a new day. He was very, very much alive. He rode across a range that held great promise. He wanted this range.

The sun was halfway to noon when he rode down on Sunken Springs. The Springs were in a small coulee. He drew rein on the northern hill. A man on horseback was below him.

The man was Len Rourke.

Chapter Nine

Len Rourke was angry. This pulling damned Rocking U cows from this damned bog was a dirty job. The dirtiest job cowpunching had.

You stripped off your shirt. You waded out through blue ooze to the damned cow stuck until her belly rested on the mud.

The cow bawled, tried to pull out, couldn't. Then she just lay there, unable to move, chewing her cud. Content to eventually starve to death. Or get killed by hungry coyotes.

Or get pulled out by a stout saddle-horse—or a team—and with the help of a muddy, cursing human.

Len Rourke had kicked off his boots, spurs and socks. He wore only an old pair of faded Levis. He kept remembering Bud Harding lying stiff and dead in that makeshift pine coffin.

Except for luck, he'd been there, not Harding. The thought still chilled his blood. That damned Texas gent! That fast-gun Al Callahan!

He wanted no more of Callahan. Under no circumstances—He cursed himself for listening to Ann Scott.

Scott had said that with Callahan dead, they'd cut the ten thousand three ways. Three thousand, three hundred and thirty three bucks and thirty three cents.

Never in his life had Len Rourke that much money. Never before the coming of Callahan had he had any prospects of attaining that much. But Callahan had proven to be a tough one—a tough gunslinging son of Texas.

Now Callahan had been robbed, eh?

Len Rourke reached the cow. A brockle-faced brute, four-year-old, mother of two calves. Her second calf hung along the edge of the hills, bawling occasionally for his mother.

The bull-calf was hungry.

Rourke's short-handled spade rose and fell as he dug a trench under the cow's belly in the muck. A long one-inch manila rope extended from the cowboy to the team of work horses hooked to a double-tree, on dry ground.

Muck flew from the shovel. Rourke shoved the rope under the cow, pulled it around her, and tied it on her back. Then he waded back to the team, Levis blue with muck, socks dripping water.

He tied the rope's end to the double-tree's clevis.

He then picked up the team's lines.

He slapped the off-horse on the rump with the reins. "Get into that collar, Dan! Hit the tugs, Flip!"

The horses lazily responded. The rope became taut between double-tree and cow. As it tightened around her barrel, the cow bawled in anger and pain—but her bawl was wasted.

The team put its weight against collars. The rope became very taut. Slowly, the critter began to leave the sucking mud. Finally, her four legs were free. She slid in the ooze on her side.

She bawled angrily. Her off-horn plowed mud. The team kept pulling, Len Rourke handling the ribbons.

The cow got on dry ground. Rourke stopped the team. Tugs fell slack. The cow lunged to her feet. She was blue with mud. She charged the cowboy. Rourke leaped nimble to one side.

The cow plunged on. She hit the end of the rope. She threw herself and her horns plowed dried ground. She got to her feet. Her nigh-horn pointed down, not up.

She'd broke the horn loose in her fall. When she charged the second time, the horn fell free. This time the noose was slack. She ran out of it and headed toward her calf, shaking her one-horned head.

Blood ran down her muddy face.

Len Rourke picked up the discarded horn. "Well, I'll be damned," he said. He looked up and repeated, "Well, I'll be damned," and added, "If it isn't Callahan."

Callahan walked out of the brush. He carried his

.30-30 rifle. "No more to pull out, Rourke."

"More'll bog down later. What'd you want?"

"Take off your pants, Rourke."

Rourke stared. "Take off my pants. Did I hear you rightly, Callahan?"

"You heard right."

"Why do you want me to take off my Levis?"

"I was robbed night before last on Circle Cross. I got in one shot at the robber. He might have been you. I might have hit him."

"I ain't got no bullet marks. It weren't me, Callahan."

"Get out of your pants."

Anger rimmed Len Rourke's mouth. He looked at the rifle. Then he looked at his own rifle, on his saddle-horse tied to a diamond willow fifty feet away, his gun-belt and pistol hung over the saddle horn.

"You're the boss, Callahan."

He kicked off his muddy trousers. He wore blue b.v.d.s. underneath. He quit those, too. Callahan walked around the nude man. He saw no bullet-marks. He moved to a respective distance.

"You're okay, Rourke. Dress."

Rourke sat on a boulder pulling on his wet pants. "I wish to hell you'd quit poundin' me, Callahan." His skin was blue with thin mud.

"You should've thought of that two days ago. You and Harding, both. Harding'd still be alive, then."

Len Rourke's lips twisted. "One thing for sure—Harding never robbed you."

"He tried," Callahan said.

102

Callahan pulled Rourke's rifle from saddle-holster. He picked up the cowpuncher's gunbelt and handgun.

"You stealin' weapons now?" Rourke's voice held cynicism.

"The next hill south," Callahan said.

He rode south. He dropped the weapons on the next hill. Then he pushed the lineback the rest of the day. It was getting dark when he rode into the county seat, Malta.

A wide red cloth was suspended across the cowtown's main street that said:

RETAIN MALTA AS COUNTY SEAT!
SAGEVILLE WILL SOON BE GONE FOR GOOD!
THANK GOD FOR THAT!

Evidently Sageville and Malta were in a political fight?

Malta's two block long main stem was lined with empty ore wagons, oxen loafing at yokes, mules hip-humped with sagging tugs. Cowponies lazed at hitching posts.

The street consisted of saloons and cafes and hotels. The brick court house sat at the street's end. Callahan dismounted before it. A galvanized steel water-tank stood flush with the street, a pipe running water into it, another leading it out.

Evidently a spring back in the hill fed the tank. The buckskin buried his soft nose in the clear water. Callahan saw a few trout finning lazily about in the tank.

He remembered the creek running through Circle

Cross. Trout had leaped in it, picking off mosquitoes and flies.

What had Maxine Heywood called the stream? Oh, yes, Buffalo Creek. The buckskin's thirst quenched, Callahan tied the animal to the hitchrack and went up the stone path to the sheriff's office.

The wide door was open. A young deputy sat at the desk. "Somethin' I can do for you, cowboy?"

"Sheriff Dunlap?"

"The sheriff left about three hours ago for Mill Iron. Word came of a shootin' out there."

Callahan scowled. "Odd I didn't meet him on the wagon-trail. I jus' rode in from Mill Iron."

"Probably missed him when he swung off-trail to visit the Heywood Circle Cross ranch. Trouble out there, too, he heard."

"I see," Callahan said.

"What happened in Mill Iron?"

Callahan said, "I don't know. I just rode through. I'm trailboss on a herd coming up from Texas. The dogies are down on the Missouri now. Waiting for me to come back with a cow-buyer."

"Doubt if there's a cow-buyer in Malta, cowboy. Too early in the season. You must've headed north outa Texas danged early in the spring."

"Snow still on the ground in many places. Somebody told me the sheriff used to buy cattle before he got elected a few years back."

"You were told right, Texan. But no more. He's got cattle on his ranch but he's breedin' them up to better stock. Not many buyers come in since the railroad built in rails."

Callahan understood. Now cattle were not driven overland to market. They were loaded here in Malta in cattle-cars. Buyers awaited in Chicago or East St. Paul or some such slaughter-yard district. No need for them to journey all the long way west anymore.

They didn't now go to the cattle. The cattle now went to them.

"The federal Indian agent might be lookin' for beef," the deputy said. "He buys for the two Injun reservations handy. Assinboine and Gros Ventres."

"Where's his office?"

"South side of town. Bunch of green buildings. Can't miss them, cowboy. Good luck."

"I'll need it," Callahan said. "Thanks."

He rode to the government agency. The heavy-set supervisor was just locking his door for the night.

"No beef bought, cowboy."

"You read my mind," Callahan said.

"You got the look. Uncle Sam buys in the early spring each year. Advertises for bids. This year a Judith Gap cowman quoted the lowest price."

The door locked and tested, the man said, "Bronc with Circle Diamond iron. Lubbock, Texas."

"You know brands. And their locations."

"My job. Sorry, cowboy."

The man walked the block to Malta's main drag. Callahan decided to spend the night in Malta. He stabled his horse and went to the Malta House. There he got a room.

"Last one I got, sir," the bald-head said. "Twelve bucks, cash in advance."

"Kind of steep."

"Big boom on. Lotsa money floatin' aroun'. Tak
it or leave it."

Callahan dug out twelve silver dollars. He carrie
his pack upstairs where he bathed in a big porcelia
washbasin. He changed clothes. He needed som
clothes washed.

He shaved. He went downstairs, gun on hij
clean-shaven and bathed. He ate in the hotel dinin
room, back to the wall as usual, looking at peopl
and rigs move out on the street.

Malta was coming to life. Night was pushing bac
heat. An oldster carrying a long pole with a kerosen
flare on it began lighting the street lights.

Flies and mosquitoes instantly began attackin
the lights.

After eating, Callahan returned to his room. H
peeled down to his b.v.d.s. and lay on the bed. ₄
breeze came through the second-story window. H
dozed off.

Outside, noise increased in direct ratio to nigh
At ten he dressed and went into the street. Cool nigh
air arose from Milk River and its many cottor
woods.

The tempo had picked up. Ore wagons—loade
and empty—toiled up and down the main sten
Skinners lashed out with popping whips at errar
mules. Oxen-drivers prodded charges with shar
barbs.

Callahan soon discovered two of the man
saloons had most of the customers. Dad Jones' Joir
catered to local citizens. The Milk River Valle

louse was patronized by mule- and oxen-skinners
nd cowboys.

He entered the Milk River Valley House. The din
vas ear-splitting. A harpy floated up and took his
rm.

"Upstairs, cowboy. Best you've ever had."

"Later."

"Buy me a drink, then."

"Later."

Her hand fell. "Cheapskate."

"Born that way," Callahan went to the bar. It
tretched the length of the long saloon. Booted men
oafed, boots on the brass rail. The cook at the bar's
nd had his fires going.

"All you want to eat. Free on the house, stranger."

Callahan thought, And I paid for a meal. Two
kinners broke out fighting down bar.

They were both big, brawny men. They fought
vithout science. They slugged and slugged. Space
vas given them but only a few watched. One was
nocked down.

His opponent staggered with fatigue. He ex-
ended a hand. He helped his opponent to his boots.

They both bled and were raw in spots. They put
heir arms around each other. They turned to the
•ar. They resumed their drinking.

Callahan grinned. He cupped a cold, foaming
nug of Great Falls beer. The beer hit the spot. He
elt of his lips. His face had healed fast. It held few
narks of combat.

He looked around. Card tables. Faro. Poker,

Blackjack. A red-headed woman stood at on
blackjack table. The dealer was dealing around.

She wore a white blouse, blue Levis and boot
with star-roweled spurs. Her back was straight. Sh
was about five feet one, Callahan judged. And sh
looked familiar.

Beer mug in hand, Callahan moved to his righ
He wanted to see her profile. He finally saw her fac
And surprise touched him.

Ann Scott!

Chapter Ten

Callahan considered factors. Many miles lay between Malta and Rocking U. A damn long horseback ride in such hot weather.

Then he realized he'd seen her last yesterday afternoon. She'd had ample time to ride—or drive—the distance.

He touched the bare shoulder of a passing prostitute. She stopped immediately, eyes glowing. "My room with me, sir?"

Callahan shook his head. "Just information, miss. That red-headed woman—At yonder blackjack table."

"I see her. What about her?"

"She hustle customers here?"

"Two bucks, mister. I'm not free. My time's worth money."

Callahan fished out two silver dollars.

"She doesn't hustle. Anyway, I've never seen her do that. She comes here quite often. She's always gambling. If it isn't poker or faro or chuckaluck, it's blackjack. Blackjack, mostly."

"Know her name?"

"I don't. An' I don't care to. I'm Jennie. I can give you the best time you've ever had. Twenty minutes, too—long time. Twenty bucks, cowboy."

"Some other time."

"Crib Nine. Upstairs. On the left."

"Thanks. I'll remember."

Jennie went on. Callahan, mug in hand, neared Ann Scott's table. Finally, he stood behind her three feet.

The dealer asked, "Hit, Miss Scott?"

"Hit me, Mac."

Mac dealt her a trey. "I stand, Mac."

The dealer continued on down the line. He knew Ann Scott. Ann knew him by his given name. That spoke of long acquaintance.

The dealer showed eighteen. Ann Scott showed twenty. Ann Scott had won at least a hundred bucks.

Callahan left. He'd no desire to meet the red-headed cattle queen. Dust shuffled around his boots as he crossed the street to Dad Jones' Joint. Again, din met his ears.

He bought his beer. He looked about. Onlookers were converging on a poker table. A back facing him there looked familiar. Mug in hand, he moved forward.

He was so tall he could see over the heads.

110

Roger Heywood's cream-colored Stetson was pushed back in best devil-be-damned manner. A blue silk shirt covered wide shoulders. His pants were California grey; his boots, black and polished.

He was a range-dandy.

And he sat in a big game. Stakes were high. Piled in the table's center were gold coins, gold certificates. Callahan could only guess at how many thousand lay there.

Callahan looked at the other three gamblers. He recognized housemen when he saw them. Heywood bucked three Dad Jones' Joint's pro cardmen. Three, playing together against one.

Betting went around. It came back to Heywood. He raised five hundred. He put the eagles on the table. There was hedging, hawing—the three mules traded glances.

Then, all tossed into discard.

Heywood had won. Callahan saw not a trace of emotion on the young face. At this rate, Heywood could return to medical school. If he had sense enough to quit when ahead, of course.

But few had, Callahan knew.

He'd seen Heywood's hole card, a mere trey. Heywood had run a bluff. And Heywood had won *this* time.

Callahan went to the livery-barn. His buckskin had cleaned out his oat-bucket but the manger was full of good bluejoint hay. Callahan patted the sleek neck.

The buckskin nuzzled Callahan's sleeve. Callahan drew back. He wore his green silk shirt. He didn't want it marked with grass-stains.

The buckskin's head went again into the manger. Callahan looked at his saddle. It hung on a saddle-rack with about a hundred other kaks. Overhead the kerosene lantern showed the saddles clearly.

His saddle's skirts had been slit open. Tough, tall, gun-hung—Callahan stood there, a bell ringing. The would-be thief had not given up.

The midnight-marauder was in Malta. He still wanted that ten thousand dollars.

He'd split Callahan's saddle skirts open in an attempt to get what he'd failed to get at Circle Cross. Was he still in Malta?

Two Mill Iron residents were in this county seat. Ann Scott and Roger Heywood. Either could have cut the saddle open.

Callahan decided to look in other saloons. Somebody might have trailed him down from Mill Iron. Somebody but Scott and Heywood, of course.

He started for the big front door. The hostler's cubicle was to his right, a small room set against the wall.

He heard a commotion in it. The door was closed. Somebody hollered in pain; a boyish yelp.

But this was no business of his. He was near the door when the cubicle's door burst open and the old hostler came out. "Hey, mister, a moment, please!"

Callahan stopped.

"Your saddle's skirts cut open, cowboy?"

"They are."

The old man sweated profusely. "That kid—that damned Sonny Westrab—he cut them open—

112

almost thirty saddles."

Callahan hadn't looked at other saddles. He'd figured only his skirts had been cut open.

"Thirty saddles?"

"Sneaked in while I dozed. Damn kids been readin' them stupid Western stories. Written by ginks east of the Hudson. And he read where sometimes cowboys carried money sewed in their saddles' skirts."

Callahan's bell stopped ringing.

"What's the noise in your office, hostler?"

"I got the little bastard locked in there. Waitin' for the town marshal. I'll make good, mister."

Callahan nodded.

"I'll get over Hank an' his Myers sewing-awl. When you ride out come mornin' your saddle'll be sewed back together."

"Thanks."

"You have any money in your skirts?"

"Not a cent."

"No cowboy had a penny there. The kid never got a nickle."

Callahan dug in his change. He took out a dime. "He's got two nickles now," he said.

He had a sour taste. He'd hoped he'd run onto a clue. What had had that promise had turned out false. He was back where he started.

Callahan went to his hotel. He'd picked a second story room with a high window only a long ladder could reach. He sat on the lumpy bed pulling off a sock when somebody knocked on the door.

"Who?"

113

"You Al Callahan?"

A man's voice. "Who's there?"

"Sheriff Ike Dunlap."

Callahan went to the door. "Just a minute, sheriff." He removed the chair from under the doorknob. He swung the door open. And as it opened he leaped to his left, flattened against the wall—his .45 covering the door.

A short, thin man entered. Lamplight glistened on the polished silver star pinned to his vest. He saw Callahan. He saw Callahan's .45.

"You take no chances," he said.

Callahan holstered his weapon. He shook hands. "Sit down, sheriff." Sheriff Dunlap took the only chair. Callahan sat on the bed, one foot bare. "Something I can do for you, sheriff?"

"You were at my office? This afternoon?"

Callahan nodded. "I don't remember leaving my name."

"You didn't need to. My deputy made a few inquiries."

"Roger Heywood, huh? And Ann Scott?"

"Right, Callahan."

"You were riding toward Mill Iron, your deputy said."

"I rode no further than Circle Cross. Maxine Heywood told me all I wanted to know."

"I'm thankful to her," Callahan said.

Sheriff Ike Dunlap smiled softly. "I have a feeling that Miss Heywood likes you, but that's beside the point. My deputy in Mill Iron—Jones—cleared you of Harding's death. Justifiable homicide. That stands with me. And Miss Heywood told me of your being robbed."

"That's why I'm in Malta," Callahan fabricated.

Sheriff Ike Dunlap's wheat-colored brows rose questioningly. "I don't quite follow, Callahan."

Callahan gave the little lawman a second scrutiny. This man, he figured, was tough—small but all rawhide, no give. He'd met similar small men before as a Ranger.

Sheriff Ike Dunlap was the head lawman on this grass, Callahan felt sure. He liked the man.

"First, Malta has the only bank in miles. Those certificates each bore a number. I have the numbers in my little black book."

"Could I make a copy of them?"

Callahan dug the book from his saddle bags, hung over the bed post. Dunlap found a stub of pencil in his shirt-pocket. He had no paper. He looked up questioningly.

"Tear loose a sheet," Callahan said.

Dunlap ripped. He began copying numbers. "Harding and Rourke wanted to kill you and rob you?"

"That's how I figure, sheriff."

"It's possible. It's been done. If you swear out a warrant, I'll arrest Rourke."

"What charge?"

"Attempted homicide."

Callahan shook his head. He thought of an old gnarled cowman condemned for life to a wheelchair. If an arrest were made Ann Scott would be involved. "I'll let it ride, sheriff." Ann Scott had given the signal.

Sheriff Dunlap got to his feet. He folded the paper and put it and the pencil in his shirt pocket. "Could I ask you what are your future plans, Mister Callahan?"

"I kinda like this range. Good grass if it had more rain, and that'll come, Matt Scott said. I might want to run cattle here until the farmers and plows move in."

"They're bound to come."

"I figure there'll be maybe ten years of open range left, sheriff. I might be able to get more money out of Texas. I might buy into trouble, though."

"How come?"

"Maxine Heywood says Circle Cross is losing stock. Matt Scott told me Rockin' U is being rustled, too."

Sheriff Ike Dunlap's sandy brows rose. "Miss Heywood didn't mention a word of that to me today.

"Maybe she didn't think of it."

Dunlap paused, hand on doorknob. "This is a damned big country, Callahan. Montana is divided into only four counties and Custer is the biggest."

Callahan nodded.

"I've not been around Mill Iron for six months or so. I've left that area to Mike Jones."

"You figure stolen stock is shipped out of Malta?"

Dunlap shook his head. "Not a hoof, Callahan. I've watched that angle close."

Callahan again nodded.

"Me or one of my deputies has checked every beef shipped out, Callahan. Sageville, up north—wide

116

open. Once Custer county was peaceful, but no more."

"Then Malta, no?"

"Right, Callahan."

"Indian reservations?"

Dunlap shrugged. "Could be a band of bucks. God almighty, some parts of this county are godforsaken and big. A lawman can't be an eagle."

"Well do I know that, sheriff. From Ranger days."

"Ex-Texas Ranger, huh?"

Callahan had no desire to talk of the past. "Ann Scott's gambling in the Milk River Valley."

"She breaks even, no more. Wins a little one time, loese the next. Diversion for her, I reckon. One way to keep from going completely crazy on that hardscrabble."

"Roger Heywood's gambling in Dad Jones'."

"Not now he isn't. Never had sense enough to move out when ahead. Those housemen cleaned him to his last cent, my deputy told me."

Callahan said, "Too bad."

"Medical school will have to wait."

"He couldn't go until next fall, anyway," Callahan pointed out. "No school during summer."

"I don't know. I got enough to worry about without taking in account young Heywood. His father was a wonderful man. Close friend of mine although some years separated us."

"So I've heard."

"Good night, Callahan."

"Good night, sheriff."

Chapter Eleven

Next morning some ten miles north Al Callahan jumped a buck deer that leaped out in majestic glory, Montana's warming sun reflecting from his red coat.

Callahan rode a short cut to Sageville. He'd jumped the buck drinking in a coulee spring. He'd been down-wind from the mule deer. Had he been up-wind the deer would have caught his scent long ago and would have sneaked out of sight in the down-coulee buckbrush.

As it was, Callahan surprised him.

The three-year-old buck bounded north, tail upraised. Callahan reined in to watch such wilderness beauty. When the buck was a half-mile away, a strange thing happened.

Callahan saw a band of wolves come swarming

out of a draw. They spread out and took after the buck.

This surprised Callahan. Wolves never hunted in broad daylight, he had heard. During daylight wolves hid in their caves or in brush and came out to hunt when night fell.

He then realized these were Zukerman's wolves.

This was logical. He rode Circle Cross' far western limits. From here to the Buffalo Creek ranch-house was at least thirty miles, he figured. As the crow flies. Across country.

Then a mule leaped from a coulee, a monkey-like thing hanging to its bareback. Callahan moved his buckskin forward. This moment saw the wolves up-end the buck.

They had taken advantage of the buck. He'd run fast a distance; they'd come in fresh. They spread out and built their deadly net and sucked the mule-deer into it.

Fangs tore hot flesh from bones as Callahan rode close, his bronc smelling blood and skittish. By now, Wolfer Zukerman sat his mule watching the slaughter, an insane giggle breaking his whiskery lips.

"The law of the wild, heh, heh, heh. All meat lives to be et by other meat. Now who'll eat my carcass?"

"I will," Callahan joked.

Zukerman then saw him. "Good mornin', Mattigan. Quite a kill, eh? Oliver downed him. For once, he got there ahead of Genevieve."

"Nice of Oliver. You're a long way from home."

"Started out early. Robbery at the ranch. Gink from Texas—this morning—he got shot at, robbed."

"That was three days ago."

"Hell, no! I know what I say! Was this mornin', Killigan!"

"This morning, Callahan corrected. "Who got robbed?"

"A gink named Mattigan. Hell, you know him, Rannigan."

Callahan had to smile. "I reckon I do. How's Miss Max?"

"Look at the stars, man!" The old wolfer waved his arm skyward. "Sure bright tonight."

"This is day, not night."

"Well, I swan. You're right. Hey, you sonsofbitchin' dogs! I want a little red meat, too."

Zukerman waded into the wolves, kicking left and right. They pulled back, snarling. He cut a hunk of the deer's haunch free with his sharp hunting knife. He returned eating raw meat.

"Any more graves?" Callahan asked.

"Graves?"

"Five graves. Remember?"

Zukerman blinked. "Graves? Can't place any graves. Oh, yeah—I know now. Buried six dead wolf pups. Long, long ago. But six ain't five, Flannigan."

Callahan shook his head.

Zukerman said, "Sioux war dance!" He threw back his grizzled head. His adam's apple bobbed under his wild chant. His knees lifted. His boots smashed sod.

He danced in a small circle, whooping like Sitting Bull. And between yelps he chanted, "Look at ol' Oliver! He's sure unstrippin' that buck! Pull, Oliver, pull!"

Oliver pulled on an entrail. Huge paws braced, Oliver pulled harder. He shook his head, emitting savage growls. Finally the entrail broke loose. It began disappearing down Oliver's gullet.

Zukerman stopped his war-dance. "Some sonofabitch stole my whistle."

"Who?"

"Damned if I'd know. But I fooled them. I made a new one." He dragged the whistle from a short pocket. "Look at me, Martingan." He blew on the whistle.

The wolves instantly stopped eating and snarling. They looked at their master, eyes evil and wicked. Callahan felt his guts crawl. The eyes of the wolves were blank, mad.

He looked at Zukerman. Zukerman stood wide-legged, smiling down at his wildings, whistle in hand. Zukerman's eyes were blank, too. They were also mad.

"Go back eatin', boys."

The wolves fell to again. Zukerman looked up at Callahan. "Now who the hell are you? Where'd you come from? Ain't never seen you before. You must be new on this grass."

Callahan rode away.

He nooned on a small creek running southeast. He snared a cottontail with a horsehair snare, his

121

buckskin's tail donating material. The broiled rabbit inside, the buckskin on picket, he dozed with his back against a cottonwood's thick bole.

He summed things up. The answer was a nice big round zero. He was no further along than when Harding and Rourke had lifted guns against him four days past in Mill Iron.

He still wanted to buy into Circle Cross. Or even Rocking U, for that matter. He did not like the idea of partnership. He liked the idea of his owning completely. But beggars, he told himself, cannot be choosers?

Or can they? Each ranch belonged to a lovely young Montana cattle-queen. Cattle-queens married, didn't they?

Callahan grinned.

But he wasn't buying into a cow-ranch being rustled. Being slowly but surely bled to death. Matt Cross was a cowman—dyed in the wool, an old Texan cowpoke.

He claimed Rocking U lost stock. Maxine Heywood had told him that Matt Cross rode range in a buggy.

Callahan decided to give himself—and his buckskin—an afternoon of rest. This camp was as good as any. From the brush a man could see the skyline on all four sides.

And the buckskin was a good watch-horse. The slightest foreign scent, or sight, immediately raised his ears and brought a soft, warning nicker. Callahan dozed, sombrero over his eyes.

The day was blistering hot. He went for a swim in the creek but never at any time was very far from his weapons on the bank beside his clothes.

He washed his green silk shirt. He handled it with the care a mother uses on a new-born. He had a bar of soap in his kit. He rinsed it and hung it on a cottonwood's low branch, making sure no snags touched it.

He watched it dry.

It dried perfectly. An iron would have helped, here or there, but it held no creases. Finest Jap silk, he told himself.

Supper consisted of a young grouse the horsetail snare also captured. Its flesh was white and tender. Chokecherries grew in profusion; so did currants and gooseberries. They made his dessert.

Daylight found him scouring his frying pan clean with creek sand. He felt rested. He'd had a good night. Never once had the buckskin awakened him. The buckskin danced under saddle.

His pack tied over the back of his saddle, Callahan rode toward Sageville, his inner man fed with the remains of the grouse, the Arbuckle comforting in his belly.

He reached back. His hands felt along the new stitching on the saddle-skirt. Good job. He looked southwest. You could just make out the purple cones of the Little Rockies.

South were the Milk River breaks. East was the limitless sweep of the Montana prairie stretching toward the Dakotas. North fifty miles or so was

Canada.

He patted the buckskin's glossy neck. Five graves, old Wolf Zukerman had chanted; then, he'd reneged. Was the old hellion as mad as he portrayed? Or was it all an act?

Naturally other men had ridden in to buy into Circle Cross. Where were they now? Why had none bought?

Callahan said, You're running on guesses, Callahan. You've got no proof. All you need to do is ride a tight saddle with your .30-30 close, your handgun tied down, Callahan.

At noon Callahan hit the wagon-trail running southeast to Mill Iron. He took it, buckskin at a long lope. Fifteen miles out of Sageville he came upon a buckboard.

The team of bays had been worn by the trail and sun to a trot. A lone man rode the high seat. Callahan went to lope past, lifting his hand in rangeland greetings; then, he recognized Matt Scott.

Scott pulled his team to a halt. "Hot day, Mr. Callahan."

"Real hot, Mr. Scott."

Callahan noticed the buckboard seat had been built up as a back support. Scott said, "They said you'd left the country."

Callahan smiled. He liked this pioneer. "I'm still here. I'm a hard man to scare. Heading for Sageville?"

"I am. Scouting range, as I go."

"But this isn't Rocking U. This is Circle Cross grass."

124

"Well I know, Callahan. And for the life of me, I can't see where the Heywoods have lost the cattle they claim."

"You think not?"

"I'm rather sure, Callahan. You headin' for Sageville?"

"I am, sir. Would you like me to drive for you?"

Matt Scott's white teeth showed in a soft smile. "I'm thankful to you, sir. But I mosey along, my team an' me. I'll meet you in Sageville. A man gets tired of the same walls. I'll bet a little and look at a new set of human fools."

"I'll mosey along, then."

Callahan reached Sageville at dusk. The town boiled with miners, prostitutes, housewives, children. Streets were rutted deeply by ore-wagons. Dust hung over the dirty sea of tents, log cabins, frame shacks.

You could see it for miles before you entered it because all was surface-mining and fresnos and scrapers tore at the earth, sending dust spiraling high against the Montana sky.

Drifters elbowed their way along the plank sidewalks. Roar came from saloons, and along the main go every other building seemed to house a saloon and red-light house.

A small boy directed him to the slaughter-house east of town in a coulee. As he neared, stink increased. Stink of rotten meat, decaying hides, discarded entrails.

Cattle bawled in the chutes. They'd soon not bawl, though—soon they'd be beef, hung on hooks

125

in the ice-house.

Callahan rode close. He looked at brands. Skinners and killers, bloody and gory, looked at him, then continued their work. Callahan saw not a Rocking U or Circle Cross brand.

"What're you doin' here, Callahan?"

The words came from a short, middle-aged man. Callahan was surprised. He'd never seen this man before.

"How come you know my name?"

"Come over to the office. Less stink an' bustle."

The man walked to a small building set a hundred yards away next to the bluff, Callahan and buckskin following. Callahan dismounted at the hitchrack, twisted reins, followed the man inside, where the man gestured to a chair, which Callahan took.

The man took the swivel chair behind the desk. "My name's Decker," he said. "I own this yard. Now what can I do for you, Callahan?"

"First, tell me how you know my name. I've never been in Sageville before, Mr. Decker."

Decker laughed. He laughed easily. "I was in Mill Iron when you shot down Bud Harding and ran Len Rourke out of town. You're a tough man with a gun, Callahan."

"Thanks." Dryly.

"You lookin' for rustled Circle Cross beef?"

Callahan studied the man. "Why say that?"

Decker spread his fingers. "I heard you aimed to maybe buy into Circle Cross. They say in Mill Iron that Harding an' Rourke tried to kill you for your money in your money-belt."

126

Callahan nodded.

"And young Roger Heywood claims Circle Cross is bein' rustled, but he lays it on Rockin' U."

"And Rocking U lays it on Circle Cross," Callahan said.

Decker got to his feet. "You'll find no hides here bearin' either Circle Cross or Rockin' U. You'll find no critter in the pens either wearin' either brand."

"I looked over the stuff in chutes. All brands but not Circle Cross. Nor Rocking U."

"You want to look at my books?"

Callahan shook his head. "Your word's good with me, Decker. Then where could rustled cattle go?"

Decker rubbed his whiskery jaw. He seemed in deep thought. "Where you been lookin'?"

"Malta. Stockyard there. Slaughter house. Even went to the Indian Agency. I wore out my boots, that's all."

"I see. That leaves only Wood Mountain?"

Callahan's brows rose. "I've heard of Wood Mountain. Across the Line in Canada. Gold rush there, I've heard. Tent town, lots of activity—like Sageville."

"They ain't shippin' outa Malta? Or any town along the new railroad? You ask?"

"Checked with the railroad bigwigs in Malta. Saw freight and cattle manifests. All brands registered, inspected by territorial agents. Sure, Rocking U and Circle Cross shipped out—but last fall, at the right time. Nothing there, Decker."

"That leaves only Wood Mountain."

Callahan said, "The Mounties. Royal Canadian

Mounted Police. I've heard they're tough."

"Maybe so, but toughness sometimes doesn't count. Not when you got a few thousand miles of border to patrol—you an' three or four others. An' no bobwire fence to mark the line, an' things like that."

Callahan swung into saddle. "I thank you, Mister Decker." He went to turn the buckskin. Decker's next words stopped him.

"Lem Rourke came into town a couple of days ago. You heard about him, didn't you?"

"No. What happened?"

"Rourke's dead."

Chapter Twelve

Callahan studied the rugged face. "Who killed him?"

"Did somebody have to kill him?" Decker smiled up. "Did he have to die under somebody else's hand?"

"Men like Rourke die by the gun."

Decker nodded. "He'd died that way, Callahan. But by his own gun, not somebody else's."

"Suicide?"

Decker nodded. "Damnedest thing I ever seed. Last night, in the High Saddle. That's a gambling—whorehouse joint on Montana Avenue, the main street."

"I rode past it. I saw the sign."

"I was at the same poker table. Just small stake stuff for cowboys an' bums like me. There was three others—the dealer, Hank Snow an' Jim Jergens. Jus' a peaceful, time-passing game."

Callahan waited.

"Rourke wins some, loses some. Nothin' big, nothin' small—just a few bucks, now an' then. All of a sudden he does the damnedest, craziest thing I've ever seen a man do."

"And that, Decker?"

"He swung back his chair. Between deals, it was. He pulls off his right boot. He pulls up his pants. Never wore his chaps. Hung 'em up by the door. Well, here's his leg bare."

Callahan gritted his teeth.

"He's got some marks below his knee. Above, too. Look like mosquito bites. An' he looks at me an' says, 'Decker, I'm goin' kill this sonofabitchin' thing afore it kills me.'"

"Then what?"

"He snakes out his .45. He jams it against the roof of his mouth. He pulls the trigger. Swamper had to get a high ladder to clean a part of his brains off the saloon ceiling."

Callahan remembered Len Rourke standing covered from ears to toes with heavy blue mud. He'd never seen the marks because of the mud, he figured.

He remembered two others mosquitoes had chewed. Lovely Ann Scott. Yes, and the veterinarian, in the cabin below Mill Iron. Dr. Yeager.

"Why you suppose he killed himself, Callahan?"

"I don't know. I guess only he'd know, maybe?"

"He talked about you before he kilt hisself, Callahan. Said he figgered you a right good sort. Odd, he said that. An' him, he'd pulled against you. I

130

still can't read sign right."

Callahan remembered Mill Iron's dusty main street. He remembered the glassy look in Rourke's eyes. Callahan had his thoughts.

"He mumbled on about you. He weren't drunk but he didn't sound right, an' he had no booze on his breath. I smelt hard to make sure."

"What more did he say about me?"

"Claimed he'd wrote you a letter. Said he'd addressed it to the deputy in Mill Iron. Care of Jones, that is."

Callahan looked away. The hills were a wavering line in the intense heat.

"I'll pick it up in Mill Iron."

"What'd you suppose he'd wrote in it?"

"I don't know. Maybe an apology?"

"Must've been that. Jus' thought you'd like to know from an eye-witness, Callahan."

"I thank you, Mister Decker."

Callahan rode back toward Sageville.

Callahan found Sageville's deputy-sheriff taking two drunks to the lockup. A great barrel of a man, he lumbered with a drunk suspended on each arm, the drunks bloody and stumbling.

"Damn fools got in a knife fight. Who are you?"

Callahan told him. "I'd like to see Jim Rourke's body, wherever it is. We were old friends."

The body was in a shed behind the deputy's log office. A local man was fitting Rourke to a coffin, taking measurements. The deputy deposited his drunks behind bars and lumbered behind to the shed.

"Rourke pulled a gun against you in Mill Iron, they've told me. Now why would you want to see his carcass?"

"He's supposed to have written me a letter before he killed himself. I thought maybe he hadn't had time to mail it yet."

"There's his clothes," the deputy said.

Evidently they were going to bury Rourke in Sageville and bury him nude. While he went through Rourke's pockets, Callahan eyed the corpse which already was becoming bloated.

Rourke's arms also had the red marks. Callahan found only an old jackknife, a blue bandana and a bent nail in Rourke's pockets.

"Got his wallet in my office," the deputy said. "A few cents over twenty bucks in. Just pay for Joe' lumber an' work. My missus will wash the clothes. Give them to a poor family here. No use buryin' good clothes."

Callahan nodded. He didn't feel so good. Rourke was beginning to stink. The deputy sniffed. "Get him in that box, Joe, an' out to boothill. He's beginnin' to stink up the joint."

"He'll be down for good inside of an hour."

The air outside was clean and fresh. "Who said Rourke'd writ you a letter?" the deputy asked.

"Decker. Out at the slaughter-house." Callahan gave details.

"Decker's an honest man," the deputy said. "If Decker said that Rourke said he'd writ you, Decker spoke truth."

"Rourke worked for Rocking U. Rocking U's owner—Matt Scott—is in town, deputy."

Callahan told about meeting the maimed rancher.

"Scott might want Rourke buried in Mill Iron or on Rocking U," Callahan said.

The deputy grinned. "If he does, he'd best hurry. Heat's got the body. Long way to Rockin' U. Or Mill Iron, either. Rourke would be right ripe by the time he got there. I'll continue on with plans to bury the stiff here unless you or Scott say different."

"I'll talk to Scott."

Callahan and the deputy parted in front of the Sageville Saloon, with Callahan ducking inside for a cold beer. He didn't know just what to think. Rourke's suicide signified something, he felt sure— but what was that something?

His beer downed, he looked for Matt Scott. He went from saloon to saloon, looking for a man on crutches or in a wheelchair. He'd been told that sometimes the rancher could use crutches.

Scott had not used good sense, in Callahan's judgment, in making the long drive alone. How he got alone in and out of the buckboard was beyond Callahan's comprehension.

Callahan remembered that no wheelchair had been behind in the buckboard. He didn't even remember seeing a pair of crutches. Crutches, though, could have been under the tarp he remembered seeing thrown across the buckboard's rear box.

He searched stores. He couldn't find Matt Scott.

He checked the livery-stables. He found the Rocking U team in the Town Stable. The owner had no idea where Scott was.

Callahan then circled the boomtown on horseback. He rode in a circle with Sageville the pivot point looking for clandestine butchering operations. He found none.

He then tried to sell beef on the hoof—or dressed—to the butcher shops and stores. None would buy. All bought from Decker. He became convinced that all meat in Sageville came from Decker's slaughter-pens.

Boothill was north of town. He sat his buckskin along the barbwire fence watching them bury Len Rourke. Two other bodies went into the earth before Rourke.

When you have many people, there are bound to be many deaths, Callahan thought. At last came Len Rourke's burial. Callahan recognized the coffin. He put his hat over his heart until the box was lowered.

He rode into Sageville—brawling, fighting, breeding boomtown that it was. He stabled his horse at the Town Stable. Matt Cross' team was still in its stall.

Evidently Cross had not heard of Rourke's death? He'd not been at Rourke's burial. Or if he had heard, he'd not wanted to attend. Callahan walked out into the setting sun.

He was tall, rangy. His rugged face, seamed by weather, was handsome in a masculine manner. His gun was tied down. The mark of the long trails, of the law, was on him.

He stood there, and had thoughts. This thing was adding up. He could not lay a thumb on all the parts, though—but they were gathering, like pieces of a deep and tragic puzzle.

You kept looking. You talked here and there. Finally you were bound to learn what you wanted to know.

Malta was eliminated. The Indian agent was out. Sageville was clean. What remained?

Wood Mountain, Canada?

He'd heard of Wood Mountain's gold rush. He knew the area was about a hundred miles to the northeast, give or take a few miles.

He had made up his mind to buy into Circle Cross. Or even into Rocking U, if Matt Cross would sell. But first you had to stop this cow-thievery. You can't run a ranch at a profit with rustlers stealing you blind.

He walked down the plank walk, a tall cowboy among shorter miners. A train of ore-wagons pulled downhill south, heading for the rail-point. Oxen lumbered with yokes bobbing.

Skinners prodded with sharp prods. Luck was on the side of the oxen, Callahan reasoned. Geography was in their favor for it was downhill to the town on the Milk River.

Suddenly, Al Callahan stopped, stared. Among the jostlers he had glimpsed a woman walking the same direction he walked—and she looked from behind like Maxine Heywood.

He hurried, aware of his heart beating faster than normal. He came in behind and his heart beat even more rapidly. He touched her gently on the shoulder.

"Maxine."

She whirled. She raised her heavy cowhide purse as though to hit, and then she recognized him. The purse lowered.

"Callahan."

Callahan noticed onlookers watching. "That purse," he said. "You were going to slug me. People will think we're married."

"Would that be too bad?"

Callahan took her elbow. "Be rough on you, Miss Max. I'm a heller with my women. What brought you to this den of inquity?"

"Tired of the old ranch. Tired of being alone. Wanted to see how the bustling half lived."

Callahan looked over the mob's head. "And it's bustling. Have you seen Matt Scott in town?"

"No. Should I have?"

Callahan briefed her. She also had not heard of Len Rourke's suicide. He mentioned the red spots on Rourke's body. She became serious and she looked away.

"Poor misguided man. And he wrote you a letter?"

"So Decker told me. No, let's back up. He told Decker he wrote me a letter in care of Jones, in Mill Iron. But Decker never saw the letter. And people say things sometimes that do not ring true."

136

"How true that is!"

Callahan said, "Here's a nice little cafe. I could use a cold beer. And I'd like to feed my best girl."

"Callahan!"

But she liked the banter, Callahan felt sure. He was very, very aware of her—and the envious glances passing males bestowed. Aware of her raven-haired beauty, her splendid body, her dark mysterious eyes, her faint but pleasing perfume.

"And my only girl," Callahan added. Then, he caught himself. He'd promised he'd not marry until thirty, at least. And here he was thinking seriously of a prospective wife. And he was only twenty-four.

They took a booth. "You asked me, now I'll ask you," Maxine Heywood said. "What brought you to Sageville?"

"Trying to raise money to buy into Circle Cross."

Two cold beers arrived along with sandwiches. "You still like this range, I take it, Callahan?"

"Good range."

"Are you having any luck?"

"Oh, maybe yes, maybe no. If nothing else, I'll get ten thousand out of Texas, in time."

"Circle Cross needs a man. Roger is no cowman. He never did care for the ranch. To him it's always been a prison. He never had the slightest desire to learn ranching. He was a disappointment to my father in that respect."

"And you? Do you like ranch life?"

"I learned one thing early, Callahan. Life can be miserable or tolerable, and much depends on who is

137

around a person. It depends upon person-to-person relationship."

Callahan lifted his mug.

"Now my mother and father. They were always content when with each other. They could have been poor in a hovel as long as each had the other. Oh, what makes me talk like this?"

"Maybe because it's true," Callahan gently said.

She lowered her beer mug. "You have no idea who robbed you?"

Callahan shrugged. "Rourke's letter might tell me something. I checked at the post office. It went out early this morning on the stage to Malta. From Malta it goes by stage to Mill Iron."

"Take about five days, at the least," Maxine said. "Callahan, what's going on outside?"

Outside, the din was greater than usual. Callahan heard *runaway*. "Ore-wagon teams on the prod," Callahan said.

"Let's go see!"

They hurried to the door, others following. People fled from the street. A buckboard rocked closer, team running madly, ears back.

"Matt Scott's rig," Cailahan said.

Callahan ran into the street. He grabbed at the off-horse's bridle, but missed. A buggy wheel barely missed him. He leaped back, the buckboard rocking away.

The team had swallowed their snaffle-bits, going cold-jawed. Crippled Matt Scott was alone on the street. He'd given Callahan a terrified look as the rig had careened past.

Matt Scott see-sawed on the ribbons. The buggy swung around an ore-wagon, wheels skidding. The corner was just ahead. The team—and buckboard—skidded around it.

The buckboard's tongue broke. Its sharp end became embedded in the earth. The plunging team hit collars hard. The broken tongue acted as a fulcrum. The buggy lifted, suspended on the tongue.

The double-trees snapped. Coupled by the neckyoke, the wild horses plunged on, the double-tree beating their hind legs, the reins dragging.

Matt Scott was thrown free. He landed on his belly. The buggy came down on top of him.

The team plunged onward. Another corner, and the horses were out of sight. Callahan ran to the buggy, Maxine following. The buggy's wheels spun uselessly.

Matt Scott was pinned under the seat. The sharp rim of the seat rested across his ribs.

He didn't move.

"Oh, God in heaven," Maxine said. "Help us, God."

Callahan and five others lifted the buggy. They carried it to one side and set it down, still upside down.

"Get a doctor," Callahan told a boy.

The boy scurried away. Scott didn't move. Callahan knelt beside the old cowman.

Callahan put his ear to Scott's ribs. He listened carefully. He heard no heart-beat but his own.

Maxine knelt beside him. He raised his head. His eyes met hers. Callahan said, "I'm not sure. My own heart is beating so hard."

Callahan stood up. He helped Maxine to her feet. She put her head against his shoulder. "He and my father, Callahan—such close friends."

Her Stetson had fallen back. Her chin-strap held it. Callahan stroked her dark, smooth hair. A husky young man pushed through the crowd. His small black bag identified him.

The doctor knelt. He took Matt Scott's limp arm. His forefinger found. He knelt, head down. Then he dropped the arm. He stood up.

He shook his head.

Chapter Thirteen

Silver starlight lay across Montana rangelands. Scraggly greasewood stood on in eerie silence. Ann Scott and a Rocking U rider met the buckboard at Willow Springs.

Ann Scott was brazen, cold. "I'll take over, Callahan. He was a fool for going alone. I wasn't home when he left. If I'd been home I'd not have allowed him to go alone."

Callahan and Max Heywood had rented the buckboard in Sageville. Matt Scott's body rode behind in a fresh pine box. Callahan's buckskin and Max's sorrel were tied behind.

Ann Scott paid no attention to Max Heywood who returned the compliment. Callahan judged they were some twenty miles east of Rocking U. He'd sent a man ahead on horseback from Sageville to tell Ann of her father's death.

Callahan assisted Maxine Heywood down. He spoke to Ann Scott. "I told the fellow in Sageville—the one we rented the team and rig from—that this outfit would be turned over to Deputy Jones in Mill Iron."

"I'll see Jones gets the team and rig," Ann Scott said.

She climbed onto the high seat and took the reins. Her cowboy tied his horse and hers behind.

Callahan held the buckskin's reins. Max held her horse's lines. Callahan said, "Your team is in the Sageville livery-barn, Miss Scott. The rig was completely ruined."

"Your runner told me that, too, Callahan. I thank you, sir."

"Glad to be of service, Miss Scott."

The team had been driven hard. Sweat covered shoulders. Slobber hung from bits. The Rocking U cowpuncher climbed up and sat down.

"I'll see you, Callahan," Ann Scott said.

She jigged the lines. The team trotted away. She did not look back. The rig disappeared in a draw. Moonlight again held sway.

"She didn't even look at me," Maxine Heywood said.

Callahan glanced at her. "Did it break your heart?"

Her laugh was mechanical. "Not one bit, Callahan. But it was rather embarrassing."

"Not for Ann," Callahan said.

"She might have been drunk. Stiff with drink."

Callahan had thought the same, but had smelled no alcohol on her breath. He held Maxine's stirrup while the cattle-queen mounted, then swung up on his own buckskin.

"I smelled no alcohol," he said.

They loped southeast across country toward Circle Cross. Dawn colored the east when they arrived at the ranch on Buffalo Creek. Once again the primitive beauty of the ranch buildings stirred Callahan's cowman-blood.

No dogs came out barking, like in most ranches. Callahan knew that Zukerman's wolves made the keeping of dogs impossible. The wolves would kill the dogs immediately.

Were he to buy into Circle Cross, he'd not do so until Zukerman and the wolves were gone—forever.

"I'm tired," Maxine Heywood said. "A long night, Callahan. Listen to those wolves."

The wolves made a howling din in their steel cage. Callahan led their horses to the water tank, the windmill lazily lifting water. He tied his buckskin to the hitchrack, led her horse to the barn, stripped him of saddle, bridle and blanket, then turned him into the horse pasture.

Callahan was in a solemn mood.

He walked slowly to the house. He had this puzzle almost solved. He had only to find where the rustled cattle went, and then the sack would be drawn shut.

And where would Maxine be? Would she be

143

caught in the sack or would she be outside? Callahan
did not know. He wished he knew. For he knew now
that of all the women he'd met, Maxine Heywood
could easily be the one. And this bothered him more
than he cared to admit.

For circumstances might force him to kill Roger
Heywood. And Roger was Maxine's brother. And
you can't marry the sister of a man you have killed. It
just wasn't being done. No man and woman could
live as husband and wife with such tragedy between
them.

Five graves, Callahan, five graves.

Max had coffee and hotcakes and ham awaiting.
They ate in the kitchen. Callahan had little to say.
His tenure as a Texas Ranger had taught him how to
play his cards close.

"Serious, Callahan."

Callahan cut his hotcakes. "Thinking of poor old
Matt Scott. Where will Ann bury him?"

"Her mother's buried on Rocking U, so I suppose
her father will be buried there, too. This may be
wrong to say, but I think that if Mr. Scott were here,
he'd be happy he went as rapidly as he did."

"Now he isn't suffering," Callahan said.

Callahan finished eating. He got to his feet and
thanked his hostess. "I'm tired, Max. I'm going to
Mill Iron. I'll report Mr. Scott's death to Deputy
Jones and given him the death certificate the doctor
in Sageville made."

"Then what, Callahan?"

"I'll stick around Mill Iron. See if that Rourke

144

letter comes in, if there ever was such."

"You're welcome to stay in the foreman's house."

Callahan shook his head. "Your brother and me, Max. No, best I stay away. I'll send a letter down to Amarillo. I can borrow another ten thousand, but it'll take time."

"Who in the name of heaven robbed you?"

"I don't know. I wish I did."

"I'll see you in Mill Iron?"

Callahan took her hand. She looked up at him, eyes dark, mysterious. He almost put his arms around her. He held himself in time. He would have to avoid situations such as this until everything was worked out—that is, if that day would ever come.

He drew rein on the crest of the hill. He looked south down on Circle Cross ranch-buildings. He breathed deeply. Maxine came into the back yard. He could see her just beyond the magnificent house.

She scattered scraps for her chickens. He heard her clear voice call, "Come, chick, chick."

Then he thought of five graves. And he was again aware of deception and greed and he rode on, buckskin at running walk.

Deputy Jones sat behind his desk, eyes closed. Callahan rapped the butt of his .45 hard against the wall. Jones came instantly awake and he said, "Callahan, by golly. In the flesh, Callahan."

Callahan said, "I got Matt Scott's death certificate." He told about the Sageville runaway.

"What were you doin' in Sageville, Callahan?"

"Girl friend there. Only female in town with two

ears."

"You got two here."

"One quit me. The red-head."

Jones sighed. "I see I lose a friend. When a man marries, he loses all his male *amigos*. This range has been awful quiet with you gone. I've had reports."

"Any of them good?"

"My boss likes you. Said if you wanted a job, he'd pin a star on you. Ramrod Sageville with the boy there."

"I thank him," Callahan said, and meant it, "but not at the present." He told about Len Rourke's suicide and the letter Rourke was supposed to have posted to Mill Iron in Jones' care.

Deputy Jones rubbed his jaw thoughtfully. "Mail's snail-slow. All we can do is wait. Where'll you be if the letter does come in?"

"Around."

The deputy grinned. "Not much of a location," he said. "You still figure Circle Cross is losin' heads?"

Callahan shrugged. "No never-mind to me, deputy."

"Got any idea who robbed you?"

"Not a line. You know anything?"

"Not a thing. All we can do is wait on that, too. Sooner or later the serial numbers will show up, the banker in Malta told my boss. Boss got word out to me on the last stagecoach. Yesterday, it came."

Callahan knew that Mill Iron got a stage from Malta but once a week. This Concord carried mail and small freight and passengers. The arrival of the four horse stage was a big event in the lonely town.

146

Callahan got to his boots. "I guess that's all, deputy. Keep your eyes peeled and your ears pinned back."

"Same to you, Callahan."

Callahan looked back as he left the door. Jones' boots were again on the desk. Jones' head rested on his chest.

Callahan walked the two blocks, feeling out the town. Rigs and horsebackers were moving southeast toward Rocking U and Matt Scott's funeral. Noon came and Callahan ate at the Steerhead. He was the only customer. All potential customers were at Rocking U.

The heat was terrible. It clung to the earth, sucking up what little moisture there was. Callahan dozed on the bench in the shade of the Mercantile's awning. When dusk came, he rode out.

He headed southeast. Two miles out, he cut at an angle northeast. He rode all night. He rested the next afternoon in the shade of cottonwoods along a creek bank.

The creek was almost dry. It consisted of only potholes. Bony cattle stood around in the shade. They were Rocking U cows. Callahan thought, With a little work, a check-dam could be built back in that coulee. It would hold water—plenty of water—all the year around.

Snow runoff-water would fill the area behind such a dam. A spillway could be built at one end out of rock and concrete. If there was too much water the spillway would relieve pressure on the earth dam.

Rocking U could be turned into a wonderful
spread with a little work and intelligent thinking,
Callahan knew. Matt Scott had been a cowman of
the old school. He had clung to old methods. He had
not known of the newer points or, if he had known,
he'd scorned them.

North Texas ranchers—and hoemen—had
learned. Now they fought drouth with check-dams
and small artificial lakes behind those dams. These
also made for good fishing, Callahan knew.

He remembered trout leaping for flies in Buffalo
Creek.

That late afternoon he rode off Rocking U range.
Cattle on this grass bore the Circle Y on the right
ribs. He changed horses at a line-camp, leaving his
buckskin behind.

"Be back in a few days," he said. "Use a port bit on
the buckskin. No spade, savvy?"

"A cricket and a roller, no more," the lanky
cowpoke said. "That roan's got bottom and wind."

"Thanks. See you."

"Luck, cowboy."

The cowpuncher had erred. The roan didn't have
bottom. Nor did he have the wind. He'd make no
mount for a man whose life depended on the speed
and toughness of his bronc.

That night Callahan traded the roan for a bay
gelding. The ranch was the R Bar N iron. This
trading broncs was nothing new. When a cowboy
returned, he just traded back.

The bay carried him to Wood Mountain,

Territory of Saskatchewan, another booming gold town.

Placer gold here, not gold-ore. Here grass grew higher than in Montana. Plainly, this area had more rain.

Conversations with various citizens taught him that the Royal Canadian Mounted Police had recently installed an office here, for the Mounties were establishing posts across western Canada.

There was still some Indian trouble but it was being settled, an old cowpuncher told him in a small bar. With Canadian Pacific Railroad now at hand, products such as cattle—and wheat—could be shipped east to the Canadian markets.

Next morning he went to the headquarters of the Mounted Police where he showed his old Texas Ranger credentials. He said he was looking for a Texas outlaw reportedly selling stolen cattle in Canada.

Then, he carefully described an imaginary cow-thief to the rangy Mountie behind the desk, who listened carefully.

"I haven't seen such a man, Mr. Callahan. Of course, with this gold rush on—these thousands of strangers coming in."

Callahan had crossed the border of Montana Territory and Canada without seeing a sign or an immigration post. There had to be many people in Wood Mountain who were in Canada illegally.

"Where does Wood Mountain get its beef?" he asked.

149

"Various local ranches, Mr. Callahan."

Callahan had learned nothing. The Mounties plainly had enough trouble with the rough element in Wood Mountain without their going out looking for cow-thieves.

"We've had no complaints from any Canadian rancher of his losing cattle to rustlers, Mr. Callahan."

"Any from Montana cowmen?"

"Not that I know of. Good day, sir."

That night Callahan went from saloon to saloon. He ordered a beer in each and barely tasted it before going to look in another saloon. He'd made a long, long ride—and maybe for nothing.

He entered the Canada House, a big ornate gambling den and house of prostitution. He went up to the bar. He studied drinkers in the backbar mirror. Across the room were the gambling tables.

The players were shown clearly in the backbar mirrors. His blood quickened. One back at a poker table held his attention. It appeared familiar.

He breathed rapidly. His heart beat in his ears. He might have found something and, by the same token, he might not have.

Beer mug in hand, he pulled away from the bar. He wanted a profile look at the poker player. He kept hidden as much as possible in the crowd of cowmen, miners and townsmen.

This was hard to do because of his height. Finally he saw the man from the side. He breathed deeply.

Then, he ducked out a side door. Din of the

150

mining town smashed his ears. Stars twinkled. He then remembered he had taken his mug of beer with him.

He grinned. He killed the cold beer. He put the mug beside the door. He went to the livery-stable and his horse.

He'd seen Roger Heywood.

Chapter Fourteen

Five days later Roger Heywood was on a high butte three miles west of the Scott Rocking U, his trail-weary horse cropping short bunchgrass while hidden back in boulders. Heywood had a small heap of green sagebrush sending up smoke into the blue Montana sky.

Three times he drew his saddle-blanket across the thin blue plume, eyes on Rocking U. Wasn't that damned woman ever home?

Then, he saw black smoke arise from the ranch-house's chimney. Three belches, no more. He threw his saddle-blanket aside.

Ann Scott arrived thirty minutes later, saddler breathing hard from the steep climb.

She hurried into Heywood's arms. They kissed long, passionately, her splendid body pressed against his hard muscles.

Finally, they broke. Setting sunlight glistened on her red hair.

"You were gone nine days, Roger. Did you get it?"

"Yes, on my saddle. Plenty. Where's Callahan?"

"I don't know. Nobody seems to know. He left about the same time you headed out for Wood Mountain. My father, he's dead."

"Dead?"

She gave him details. "I haven't seen Callahan since Jack Jones and I met him and your sister at Willow Springs, taking dad's body home from Sageville."

Roger Heywood stroked his jaw. He needed a shave.

"Rourke's dead, too."

"Come now, honey—no jokes, please."

She told him of Len Rourke's suicide. Roger Heywood listened, gazing across thousands of miles of wilderness spread out below. Night shadows were creeping in.

"Len knew too much," Heywood finally said. "Good riddance."

"Why would he kill himself?"

Heywood shrugged silk-clad shoulders. "Why does the sun rise, the moon set? Who knows. Maybe it got too heavy for him. Only Rourke would know, Ann. And he can't tell."

She said, simply, "I killed Doc Yeager."

Roger Heywood studied her. "Why?"

"He knew too much, too. He was getting loose in the head. I was afraid he might talk."

"How?"

"Simple. I talked him into going down to the creek for a swim. Promised him I'd go in naked with him if he went naked."

"He took you up?"

"His mouth watered. I merely held him under water long enough. He was so rundown he had little resistance."

"And Jones, the deputy? What'd he say?"

"A Circle Cross man—Shorty Jenkins—found Yeager's body. He rode to the creek to water his horse. Jones decided Yeager had gone swimming, had a fainting spell—and drowned."

Heywood laughed shortly. "There's only you and I left, Ann."

"What more are needed, darling?"

She cocked her red head. Her green eyes glowed. They became dark as he said, "You only missed on one assignment. You never killed that damned Callahan his first night when he slept at Circle Cross."

"He out-tricked me."

Again, the sardonic, tight laugh. "And he out-fooled you, too, by stuffing his money-belt with strips of newspaper."

"Let's talk of something else, please. That's old saw. When more cattle across the Line?"

Heywood hesitated, handsome face showing

154

indecision. Quickly, she read the signs. "Something bad happen up in Canada?"

"Mounties."

He explained. More Royal Canadian Mounted police had been moved into the Wood Mountain area.

"What does Sig Nelson say?" she asked.

"Sig says to make one more drive out of here. Then, to lay off a while. We move west and work north of Cut Bank and that region. He can ship out from there just as well as from Wood Mountain."

"But there's no mining camp there, is there?"

"No, but his outlet in Montreal will take all cows he can furnish, so the money will be about the same—minus a little for that long frieght haul."

"Oh, that's better."

Heywood teased. "I think you're money-mad, Ann."

She laughed softly. "How about yourself, darling? Stay with me tonight on the ranch. We'll be there alone, Roger."

"Okay."

Anger touched her lips. "You don't sound very enthusiastic. You don't have to sleep with me, you know."

He grabbed her roughly. He put his hand under her chin. He forced her chin up. He kissed her hard and convincingly but inside he knew he was just putting on an act, and he hoped she'd not read it.

He'd kissed his last whore in Wood Mountain just as strongly.

She evidently had no misgivings. Her warm lips opened, her tongue explored. Her arms went around his neck. When their lips parted, her eyes glowed in the dusk.

Then she said, "Where in the hell is that damn' Callahan? The other five—we intercepted them before they reached Mill Iron. But Callahan, damn him, got through."

"That's past history. Forget those damned fools!" His voice was harsh. "There's Zukerman. He might know too much."

"He should be eliminated."

"He will be, after this gather. We need him and his wolves to gather fast and quick. Then, down he goes."

"And after that?"

"My sister—damn her—can handle Circle Cross. Damned fool, thinks I'm yearnin' to return to that medical school. She don't know I was booted out—and for good."

"Maxine is still your sister."

"Well do I know that. Let's head for your spread, Ann. Then we start the last gather—for some time—tomorrow."

"You're the boss, Rog." They rode down, horses braced against gravity. "But I still don't believe Callahan has left."

Callahan indeed was still on Mill Iron range. Ten o'clock that same night he entered the sheriff's office down in Malta by its back door, hoping nobody had seen him.

156

Sheriff Ike Dunlap was down along Milk River, the deputy said, tending a trot-line. Callahan waited. Ten minutes later the sheriff came carrying a three-foot catfish.

"I'll skin him out back, Callahan. We can talk while I skin."

The lawman nailed the catfish belly-down to a post with a twenty-penny nail through the fish's head. He then cut long downward slashes through the skin.

"What've you found out, Callahan?"

Callahan told of his Wood Mountain ride. "The town has one slaughter-house. I sneaked into it one night. Some cowhides had just been thrown into a tanning tub."

"Yeah?"

"They hadn't been in the solution long. Some hair had slipped but I could read brands."

"These were what?"

"Circle Cross. Rocking U."

Dunlap sighed. He pulled down on a strip of skin. His pinchers slipped. "Look at the muscles on this cat? He'll be tough chewin'. Wonder how ol' the sonofabitch is? About thirty years, maybe? Then what, Callahan?"

"I turned my information over to the Mounties. The big boss there then started talking. They'd gathered quite a bit of information."

"In what form?"

"There's an ex-Texan outlaw working the Wood Mountain area. Name of Sig Nelson. I remember him from Ranger want-placards."

Sheriff Dunlap pulled the nail loose. He reversed the catfish so his belly showed. Then he drove the nail in again.

"I get it, now. Circle Cross an' Rockin' U dogies go north to this Sig Nelson? He then peddles to the Wood Mountain slaughter?"

"That's it, sheriff."

"But who drives those brands north, Callahan?"

Callahan said, "I saw Roger Heywood in Wood Mountain. Gambling in the highest-priced joint in town. He never saw me, I'm sure."

"Why would he steal—and sell—his own cattle?"

"Rourke wrote me a letter before he killed himself. I got it from the post office as I rode through Mill Iron. It will explain a lot that I suspected, sheriff."

"Can't read it in this starlight. Hey, Watson. Come out an' finish this fish. Come into the office, Callahan."

With Watson out back, Callahan and the sheriff were alone in the office, with Sheriff Dunlap holding Rourke's letter close to the kerosene lamp.

"Hard to read," the sheriff said.

Callahan smiled. "He won no prizes in penmanship."

The lawman read slowly. Then he just as slowly re-read. Finally he folded the letter and returned it to Callahan.

Dunlap scowled. "Who in the world would think it? And a woman, too. Somebody once wrote that the female was the more deadly of the species. He never missed it far."

"It wouldn't hold up in court," Callahan said. "Rourke is dead. We have no proof he wrote it."

"Why did he write it? And to you? He pulled a gun against you, tried to kill you?"

Callahan told about disrobing Rourke at the water-hole. "He had that against me, too."

"Conscience, I guess."

"Five would-be buyers killed and robbed before getting to Mill Iron or Circle Cross." Suddenly he remembered Wolf Zukerman's mumblings. "Zukerman knows. Zukerman's in on it."

"Why do you say that?"

Callahan explained.

"What does he do with those damned wolves?"

Callahan said, "I won't say for sure, but I think he herds cattle with them."

Sheriff Ike Dunlap studied him. "Come again, Texan. Me, I never knew a wolf could be trained. I've been told for years it's impossible to train one. And here you say they're used gathering stolen beef."

"I've seen Circle Cross and Rocking U beef with what look like fang-cuts on them. Only on steers, though. Three- and four-year-olds, big enough for market."

"Never a cow?"

"No cows. I ran a tally. Nine steers, sheriff."

Sheriff Dunlap slowly nodded. "A cow has little market value. She's fed a calf all summer and is skinny. What is your opinion, Callahan?"

159

"I really don't know."

"With what we got, could we convince a jury?"

"I doubt it, sheriff."

"What's the answer?"

"Catch them gathering."

Dunlap walked to the window. A hard man, a tough man—an honest lawman. Callahan knew what thoughts tormented Dunlap. He also had once carried a star. He remained silent.

Dunlap spoke over a shoulder. "Maxine Heywood? She's his sister. Does she know?"

"She knows," Callahan said.

Dunlap faced Callahan. "You told her?"

"I had to, sheriff. I asked her point blank, if she'd been in on this. She said she hadn't."

"I believe her. She came from honest parents."

"I told her that if she wanted me to, I'd ride south and do nothing. She told me to go ahead as I wished."

"Even if it meant her brother's death? Or a jail sentence?"

"Even if, sheriff."

"Those five graves? Five murders? She know of them?"

"She says no."

"Where is she now?"

"Here in Malta. Waiting for me in the Down Trail. Says you can put her behind bars until this is over so you'll make sure she'll not tell Roger. Or anybody."

"What do you say, Callahan?"

"I say send her back to Circle Cross. Have her stay

there as usual. Her being away might arouse suspicion. And throw a monkey-wrench into this whole operation."

"Send her home."

Chapter Fifteen

For five days Zukerman's wolves gathered cattle. Al Callahan watched through field-glasses, hidden on high buttes, the immense rangeland spreading out below.

Never had he seen cattle bunched so rapidly.

The reason was simple: beef had mortal terror of the huge wolves. And always Zukerman and the wolves worked by moonlight.

Daytime the wolves loafed in their Circle Cross pen with their master dozing in the hut within the steel corral. When night came—and the yellow moon rode the western sky—the wild dogs came out to work.

Buckskin hidden back in high sandstones, Callahan had a complete view of the range for miles and miles. South lay Circle Cross, buildings hidden by the north rise of hills beyond Buffalo Creek.

He clearly saw Rocking U. Each morning Ann Scott rode from the ranch to meet Roger Heywood at a given spot. Sometimes Roger passed the night at Rocking U.

Roger and Ann then rode out together to haze cattle from the breaks. The woman's cowpunching-skill brought admiration to Callahan. Ann knew how to work stock.

She and Roger Heywood cut the market-steers from the cows, bulls and calves. Ann rode good cowhorses. They knew how to cut, which steer to cut out of the herd, to follow that steer's tail until free of the herd—then to drive him down coulee to where his other unfortunate fellows awaited.

Then at night, the wolves bunched these steers into the main herd, which grew then rather rapidly. Callahan guessed it held over a thousand head in those five days.

The third day two riders came out of the northeast. They helped Roger and Ann cut steers. Callahan's powerful glasses showed them clearly. They were not local cowboys.

He had seen both in Wood Mountain. A mountie had pointed them out as riders in the Sig Nelson gang.

Sheriff Dunlap and a deputy—a tough, string-bean man with a low-tied old Colts .45—rode out from Malta the midnight of the third night. They met Al Callahan on Smokestack Mesa, the appointed meeting-area.

"Bring me up to date," the sheriff said.

163

Callahan did.

The deputy—MacDonald—chewed tobacco, saying nothing. That night the three of them watched the wolves work cattle.

It was eerie, uncanny. Wolves were dark, evil forces in the brilliant Montana moonlight. Shifting shapes, snarling lines of midnight, leaping, fangs clipping.

Steers were terrified. They ran the moment the wolves showed. They kicked, bawled, horned the wolves, twisted, then ran. Both then became hurrying forms darting, twisting, galloping in terror.

Dust rose. Wolf Zukerman raised his whistle. The wolves stopped as though shot, pivoted, trotted back. They grouped around the bearded man on the mule. They sat, tongues lolling. He dismounted. They scrambled to receive his petting.

"He's feeding them bits of raw beef," Callahan said.

"Their rewards," MacDonald said.

Sheriff Dunlap said, "It's unbelievable. If I hadn't seen it, I'd not believe it. That old man knows all there is to know about this, but no court in the world would believe this."

"Where's the main herd being held?" MacDonald asked.

"Down Creek," Callahan said. "About five miles northeast, closer to Rocking U's home ranch."

MacDonald said, "I was raised in this section."

Sheriff Dunlap watched the wolves work. "Odd, Callahan, odd. They don't make a sound. They work in silence. Have they had their voice boxes taken out, or something?"

Callahan smiled. "They can howl like wolves, sheriff—if they are allowed to. They're really trained."

"I wonder if anybody else could handle them?" the sheriff asked.

"I don't know," Callahan said. "Old Zukerman told me somebody had stolen his whistle—the one that only a wolf can hear. He told me he'd made a new one."

"What does that signify?" MacDonald asked.

Callahan shrugged. "Maybe nothing. Maybe something. Maybe somebody else has tried to work the wolves with the stolen whistle."

"That's a good point," Sheriff Dunlap said.

Callahan asked, "Anybody see you two leave Malta?"

"We sneaked out in the dark," Dunlap said. "I told my old lady that Mac and me were goin' fishing back in the Little Rockies on Beaver Creek."

"I told my boss the same," MacDonald said.

Sheriff Dunlap spoke to Al Callahan. "Seen any sign of Maxine?"

"Yesterday she drove the buggy to Mill Iron. She wasn't there long. She had boxes in the back when she returned. Evidently bought some grub and things for the ranch."

Dunlap shook his head. "Tough tittie," he said.

"Roger been at Circle Cross lately, Callahan?" MacDonald asked.

"Yeah, he's spent a night there."

"Wonder if his sister told him you're wise,

165

Callahan?" MacDonald asked.

Sheriff Dunlap said, "If he knew that, him an' Ann wouldn't be gathering stock. They'd be long gone. Both are guilty of murder and they hang murderers."

"That's right," MacDonald said.

The moonlight was bright. Zukerman finally quit working cattle. His whistle brought his wolves gathered around the mule. Then the group started for Circle Cross, wolves running ahead.

They flushed a coyote. A bitch hit him first, throwing the yipping coyote into the air. The coyote landed among the wolves. His yipping stopped.

The wolves next jumped a passel of jackrabbits. Only one jack escaped. He ran with long hind legs kicking his laid-back black-tipped ears.

He fell into a coulee and out of sight. The wolves trotted back, tongues lolling, jaws bloody.

That same day the three watched Ann Scott, Roger Heywood and the two Nelson outlaws work cattle. Sheriff Dunlap spoke around a hunk of pemmican. "How would you work it, Callahan?"

"You're the sheriff, not me," Callahan reminded, grinning.

MacDonald said, "Ike's tryin' to pass the buck!" They laughed. But their laughter was false, weighted by the danger all knew lay ahead.

"You've probably had more experience with cow-thieves than I've had," the sheriff told Callahan.

Callahan scratched his red head. "I'd like to take Heywood and the girl alive but I doubt if it can be done. People doomed for the gallows will fight until

166

dead, usually."

MacDonald and the sheriff nodded.

"Those two Nelson outlaws. Down in Texas they got criminal records as long as my arm. They're wanted for murder and other charges. The world'd be better off with them dead."

MacDonald said, "Some things here aren't clear to me."

"Drugs," Callahan said.

"Elaborate, please," MacDonald asked.

"Morphine, needle stuff. I saw plenty of it along the Texas—Mexico border. I figure Roger Heywood got the habit in medical school. Drugs handy there, and I've heard quite a few medicos jab."

MacDonald nodded.

"Well, he comes home. Frankly, I think he was kicked out because of drugs. That could be."

"Very likely," the sheriff said.

"So he has only the dope he brought with him. It doesn't last long. He goes to this vet, Doc Yeager. Yeager's a dope hound. Yeager can get the stuff because of his vet degree. From wholesale houses, back east."

"They'd only send him so much," Dunlap said. "Laws are rather strict on that point all over."

"That's what I figure," Callahan said. "I doubt if Yeager drowned himself by accident. He could have had somebody holding his head under. But that's beside the point. Heywood has made an addict of Ann Scott. Rourke and Harding find courage in the needle."

"Zukerman?" Sheriff Dunlap asked.

"His arms have the scars," Callahan said. "Dope costs money. So Scott and Heywood start stealing their own cattle and selling and buying dope up in Canada."

"I get it now," MacDonald said.

Sheriff Dunlap said, "I fear for Zukerman's life. He knows too much, Callahan."

"I've been thinking the same," Callahan said. "But if we arrest him—sneak him to Malta."

"Heywood would be suspicious," the sheriff said. "Zukerman's disappearance might tip him off—and he might pull out without a cow."

"We can't afford that," MacDonald said. "We need help."

Dunlap shook his head. "We get more men in and they might be seen, and then the jig would be up."

"I'm still thinking of Zukerman," Callahan said.

That night Roger Heywood murdered Zukerman.

Chapter Sixteen

That same night Roger Heywood rode away from Circle Cross on a midnight black four-year-old stud, the stallion fighting the stern restraints of the savage spade bit.

He drew rein before the ranch house. Maxine Heywood was on her knees, working in one of her flower-beds by the yellow light of a kerosene lantern.

"Mill Iron," Roger Heywood said. "Little poker. Be back early."

Max looked up. "You've ridden all day. You just rode in an hour or so ago."

"Checking the south line camps. Water holes are down and cows bog."

"Did you eat?"

"Cook shack, sis."

Max brushed back a stray lock of hair. "All right." She resumed her poking the ground with a trowel.

Roger rode past the wolf-pen. It was empty of wolves and Zukerman. Zukerman had already taken his canine charges out on range to work cattle. The stud's shod hoofs thundered across Buffalo Creek's plank bridge.

Heywood reached the summit of the northern hill. He glanced back down on Circle Cross. Maxine was entering the house. He turned and loped on, letting the stud run, taking the edge off him.

The black was not a good cowpony. He was hard-mouthed, bull-headed, and had little service as a cowpony. Still, he had bottom and he was fast, and sometimes bottom and speed counted more in this game than cutting-ability, Roger Heywood thought.

He had smuggled blankets and a sack of canned goods out of the house and cached it in the brush along a hill. Now he went down, tied this behind his hand-stamped Hamley rig, and rode on, heading northeast toward the rustled herd.

The cattle had been gradually inched toward Down Creek, some twenty miles northeast. There they grazed along the stream.

They'd be started toward Wood Mountain tonight. By morning they'd be another twenty miles away from Circle Cross.

He met Zukerman—and Zukerman's wolves—on Jackrabbit Flats. He pulled in his stud. "No chasing tonight, Zukerman. We're going to move north.

We've got enough."

"Then I go back to the house?"

"No, you go with me. With your wolves."

"Why, boss?"

The stud pawed. He snorted. His eyes were wide and wild. He smelled wolves, he saw wolves, he feared wolves.

The wolves sat and watched him, tongues out.

"We need to scare the crap out of those steers. Get them moving northeast, and fast—and your wolves will do it."

"How far will I go with you?"

"Maybe ten miles or so, no more."

"I could stand the needle."

Roger Heywood grinned. He opened his bedroll. He took out a small box. It contained the needle and syringe. Zukerman rode close. He pulled up his left sleeve. His mule stood solid and lazy against the black.

Heywood smiled. He'd not sterilized the needle but what the hell dif did it make with an old stiff such as this stinking wolfer? If Zukerman fell dead off his mule at this moment, the world would have lost nothing, Roger Heywood thought satanically.

He pushed down on the plunger.

"Not so fast," Zukerman said.

"We haven't got all night."

Heywood pulled the needle out of the tough skin. He threw the needle away and restored the syringe to the case, then to the bedroll.

"How long you goin' be gone?" Zukerman asked.

171

"A couple of days. Don't worry, I got some cached for you under the south end of the haystack behind the bar. Usual place."

"Good, boss."

They loped northeast, the mule running hard to keep up with the long strides of the black stud. A wolf came in. He playfully nipped at the stud's left hind leg.

The stud nickered. He kicked. The wolf dodged, lying flat. The stud caught his stride.

Anger touched Heywood. "Which damn wolf was that?"

"Oliver."

"Get the bastard back where he belongs with the others."

Zukerman had his whistle hanging from his neck with a cord. He blew into the whistle. Oliver moved back with the other wolves. They loped ten feet behind, jumping over sagebrush, leaping boulders.

"Wonder what the hell ever become of my other whistle," Zukerman said.

Heywood hid his smile. The whistle rode in his shirt pocket. He'd been practicing, on the side, with it. He prided himself on learning Zukerman's system of signalling.

He had the wolves obeying rather well, now.

Ann Scott met them in five miles. She rode out of the buckbrush growing tall along the base of a high hill. She rode in with her right hand high in the Blackfoot peace-signal.

The night had thickened. Without being aware of

it, Roger Heywood had pulled his .45 from holster—
the big handgun pointing at the lovely redhead.

Ann Scott said shortly, "You won't need that. Not
with it pointing at my guts, anyway, Roger!"

"He's rimmy!" Zukerman cackled.

The red-head looked at Zukerman. "What's he
doing with us?"

"His wolves," Roger Heywood explained.
"They'll give the herd a damn fast start. Come
daylight we'll be closer to Wood Mountain with the
wolves putting the fear into those beasts."

"Then I rides back?" Zukerman asked.

Heywood hid his smile. "You ride back."

"I don't like long trails," Zukerman told Ann
Scott, who scowled and put her black horse into step
on Heywood's right, Wolf Zukerman and his wolves
trailing two rods behind.

They put saddlers to a long lope, the mule taking
three strides to the stud's two. Heywood glanced
sidewise at Ann Scott. A .30-30's stock protruded
from her saddle scabbard. A eight inch long knife,
resting in leather scabbard, was tied to her back nigh
saddle-string.

A wide, cartridge loaded gunbelt circled her small
waist, the .38 Smith and Wesson tied to her right
thigh. Heywood looked away. He did not smile. He
knew Ann Scott. And he'd seen her handle every
weapon but the knife. And she seldom missed with
either rifle or handgun.

Ann Scott leaned closer to Heywood. "Anybody
seen Callahan around?"

"Not me," Heywood hollered back.

Old Zukerman cackled. "I've seen him."

"Where?" demanded Heywood.

"In my dreams. This mornin', I seed him."

Heywood scowled. He'd used Zukerman—and his wolves—long enough. He'd run into the wolfer on his way home from college. Met him a hundred miles east on the Milk River.

Zukerman had served his purpose. Heywood had carefully watched the wolfer's cheeks go in and out as he had handled the silent whistle. He had imitated on his whistle, experimenting on the wolves in their big cage when Zukerman had not been present.

It hadn't been difficult to make Zukerman an addict. And once on the needle, the wolfer—and his wolves—had been subservient and docile and obedient. Dope did that to a person, if indeed Zukerman could be classified as such, Heywood thought.

He'd murder Zukerman soon. He'd have the wolves gather the herd along Down Creek into a compact mass of bovine backs. Then he'd have the sport of shooting the wolves. For a long time he'd wanted to plant a .30-30 slug in Oliver's head, right between the wide-spaced eyes.

"Callahan's gone," Zukerman said. "Headed back to Texas. Robbed in Montana."

"Wonder who robbed him?" Heywood winked at Ann Scott.

"I did," Zukerman said.

Heywood turned in saddle. "You robbed him,

Wolf?" The old loony was getting even crazier.

"Yeah, I got his ten thousan'. Bought ice-cream with it, I did. Ten thousand bucks worth of ice-cream in the Mint down in Malta."

"Wonder a man could eat that much," Ann Scott said.

"I did," Zukerman said.

Heywood said, "Enough of this bull. We got cattle to move. The moon's coming up. Be light until about three."

"Sure was bright last night," Zukerman said. "I held up my palm. I could see my life-line."

"Even through the dirt?" Ann Scott asked.

"You insult me," Zukerman said. He went into a deep pout, which suited the red-head and Heywood.

They pushed on, hard riders streaking across sagebrush flats, rounding toes of hills, the wolves trailing. They came through the narrow defile leading to the prairie-banks of Down Creek. There they drew rein and Heywood loafed in leather, the black stud's ribs falling and rising under stirrup leathers, the good smell of cattle and sweaty horseflesh in his nostrils.

Heywood did not know that Callahan and Sheriff Dunlap watched from high brush on the northern hill. MacDonald had ridden into Mill Iron that dusk. He'd returned with ten sticks of dynamite.

Callahan had three sticks under his gunbelt, the sheriff had four. They had watched the two Nelson outlaws guarding the stolen herd. Callahan had said, "The tall jigger, there. He's Frank Blanton. The

175

short one, he's Olaf Rodin."

Dunlap and MacDonald had nodded.

"Both got nice reward money on their heads. Rangers still have an eye peeled for either in Texas. Disappeared about three years ago. Texas Law still wonders where they went."

"We know now," the sheriff said.

Al Callahan looked at Roger Heywood and Ann Scott and Wolf Zukerman, a quarter mile away and riding closer. "Tough to fight a woman."

MacDonald's thin brows rose. "Women don't ride with rustlers," he pointed out. "When they do, they cease being classified as females. They slip into another classification."

"Still tough," the sheriff said.

Suddenly Al Callahan said, "Look!"

Wolf Zukerman's mule was even with Roger Heywood's black stud. Heywood pointed to the right. Zukerman looked that direction, the back of his head facing Heywood.

Heywood's .45 left holster. It leveled just back of the unsuspecting wolfer's head. The .45 belched smoke.

It had taken only a second. Roar moved across the silent valley. Cattle jumped, looked, settled down. Zukerman fell from the saddle. The terrified mule ran to one side a hundred yards, stepped on trailing reins, then stopped.

Even the wolves moved back. They eyed their dead master. Callahan saw Heywood reach into his breast-pocket. Moonlight was brilliant now, as only a Montana moon can be.

"Cold blood," Sheriff Dunlap murmured.

MacDonald said, "The sonofabitch has ice-water in his veins, not blood. Man, deliberately and coldly."

Callahan had no reply. He watched. Heywood raised his hand to his lips. Callahan said, "He's got one of those wolf-whistles."

Heywood blew. The wolves hesitated, then suddenly swarmed in on the prone Zukerman. What followed froze the Texan's blood.

The wolves hurriedly took Zukerman's body apart, fangs tearing. They worked in deadly silence, tails wagging. Arms flew into the air, followed by legs and entrails.

Heywood and his woman moved horses to one side and watched in silence. Finally Heywood raised the whistle.

The wolves pulled back. They sat and looked at the dismembered Zukerman. Heywood said, "Good work, boys."

His words moved easily across the stillness, for the wind had, for once, gone down. Mosquitoes droned.

Callahan heard Heywood say, "Now, boys, we work cattle and then, damn you, it's bullets through your damned heads!"

He rode across Down Creek, wolves following, with Ann Scott trailing the wolves. The wolves began moving cattle. Steers ran in terror before them, tails up, bawling in fear.

177

The wolves had no need to nip the steers' legs. The moment a wolf trotted into view, the bovines started running down-creek toward Boxelder Canyon, the narrow outlet that they'd pass through to get to wide and grassy Wide Woman's Flat.

Screened by high buckbrush, MacDonald and Sheriff Dunlap started west around the toe of the hill toward their mounts, tied in a cottonwood grove out of sight, but Callahan stayed behind an extra minute to watch Roger Heywood command the wolves.

Heywood blew. Wolves wheeled, stood still, moved, herded cattle, worked with deadly precision. Zukerman had trained them well.

Callahan went to his buckskin, aware of the dynamite under his gunbelt. Sheriff Dunlap and Deputy MacDonald's horses were gone. Each knew his station, each his job.

Callahan swung into leather. From a western hill, a shadow in high sandstone boulders, he gave the scene below final scrutiny.

Cattle were moving toward the black maw of Boxelder Canyon, a narrow lane, some two hundred feet wide—where Down Creek tumbled forward more rapidly, and through which the steers had to pass.

The two Texas outlaws—Blanton and Rodin—choused steers in from side-coulees, pointing them toward the main herd moving northeast along Down Creek. Even as Callahan watched, tall Frank Blanton, mounted on a blood-bay gelding, loped toward Boxelder Canyon's dark mouth.

Blanton would lead the steers through the canyon. Al Callahan had seen enough. He'd be stationed in that canyon when the first steer entered, following Frank Blanton.

He'd circle and come in the Canyon's lower exit. The Canyon was not more than a quarter mile long.

He'd be waiting.

Chapter Seventeen

Satisfaction filled Roger Heywood. He knew how to control Zukerman's wolves. He sent them here, there—then back again. His whistle-control was perfect.

Steers were pouring down into Down Creek's brush. They ran, they jostled, they bawled, as they moved forward, cloven hoofs raising yellow dust, the wolves trotting lazily behind, their job of gathering over.

Ann Scott worked cattle across the creek. Her cutting-horse turned, pivoted, chased this steer, then that—putting the critters into the herd. Then, that beast in the bunch, she put the horse after another bunch-quitter, repeating the process.

Her bullwhip's chaser popped; she swung the

eight-foot braided leather lash like an expert—
which she was. The dust grew thicker. She tied her
blue silk bandana over her nostrils, only her sea-
green eyes visible.

A pack of grub rode the back of her saddle, tied to
the skirts. She had given her foreman power-of-
attorney. He could run Rocking U. She figured she'd
be gone some time.

Six months, at least. Reports said lots of cattle ran
north of the Milk River around the Cut Bank area.
Yes, and south of the river, too, on the wide, grassy
plains.

Her blood was warm. She had used the needle not
more than an hour ago. This was the life. She was
happy Roger Heywood had returned. They'd been
friends from school days in Mill Iron.

Roger had seduced her when she'd been thirteen.
From then on she and he had had a sexual
relationship when possible—except, of course, when
he had that crazy idea he'd wanted to become a
medical doctor.

She'd been happy when he'd been kicked out of
school because of the needle. He had then showed
her the joy of heroin. She had no regrets. She and
Roger would die addicts. Maybe they'd die young
but they'd die happy. And they'd die together.

Squat Olaf Rodin rode in from the west. She
scowled. She did not like him. In fact, she hated him.
He'd asked her a number of times to have sex with
him. She'd pointed out she was Roger's woman.

Rodin had thrown back his huge, ugly head. He'd

181

laughed. Now he reined close, bandana covering the lower half of his ugliness.

"Last drive outa here, honey?"

"Ask Roger. He's the boss."

"When you gonna get wise to that big fake an' bunk up with a real man?"

"Real man? Where is he?"

Rodin's bandana muffled his sardonic laugh. He rode left, bullwhip beating. The steer bawled in pain, ran to catch up. Rodin laughed sardonically. "Look around a bit," he said, and rode to his right.

Ann Scott said to herself, "The stupid sonofabitch."

She looked ahead over the bovine backs. The mouth of Boxelder Canyon was a quarter-mile north. The cattle were heading that direction, trampling down the brush and undergrowth along Down Creek.

Some waded in water, muddying it. Even as she watched, Frank Blanton angled in and moved to the head of the herd to pilot it through the Canyon. Ann Scott felt relief surge.

Once out of the Canyon, the wide area of Wide Woman's Flat would be rapidly crossed, for there was no creek there. Down Creek turned due south directly out of the Canyon. Without creek-brush to hinder the steers, the herd could be moved faster.

She thought of Zukerman. Those damn wolves had really made mincemeat of him. She thought of Zukerman in a detached way, in the past tense. Zukerman had never really counted.

The damn wolves had been more important than Zukerman. Roger sure knew how to whistle them down. Roger was a great guy. Roger loved her. She loved Roger.

She looked at the moon. The moon was dazzling yellow despite the dust. She threw a kiss at the moon.

She looked ahead, standing on stirrups. Cattle were a tight, compact group of backs swaying. Frank Blanton was just riding into Boxelder Canyon. She settled back, whip working.

All were converging in on Boxelder Canyon. Cattle, Roger, Rodin, herself—yes, and the wolves. She shuddered unconsciously. She loathed those wolves; she hated them. They scared her to death, although she refused to show her terror.

She breathed deeply. Once the cattle were—Then, it happened.

The world went mad—roaring, hoof-pounding mad. For up in the Canyon red flame lanced sky high. The roar was deafening. It almost knocked her from saddle.

Dismembered steers flew skyhigh in the red glare. They reached a zenith, swung there idly, legs going this way, then that, entrails dragging, and then they fell, shooting down like falling meteors.

For one long moment, the world stood still. Then, another roar, another catastrophe.

Roger's stud was terrified. He cold-jawed and bolted, but Roger got him around in time, she hurriedly noticed.

"Dynamite!" she screamed.

183

The wolves had hurriedly stopped. Roger Heywood hollered, "They've trapped us! Get out! And fast!"

"They'll stampede!" Olaf Rodin screamed.

For a long moment, the herd was suspended between motion and stillness, the cattle stunned, frightened. Then, cattle whirled as one, heading away from the Canyon—and the stampede was on.

Tons and tons of madly-running beef was on the move. It destroyed everything in its path. Small trees went down, uprooted; brush was instantly trampled flat.

Moonlight glistened on running bovine backs. Dust hung in yellow clouds.

And through the dust—and confusion—plunged Al Callahan's big buckskin, following the stampeding herd out of Boxelder Canyon. Dust choked him. The din of running hoofs—and bawling cattle— filled his ears.

He realized now he had thrown the first stick of dynamite too late. Or either the fuse didn't burn down as fast as he had expected, for he'd not intended to dynamite the herd.

His plan had been to merely scare the cattle into stampeding back onto their home range, not to kill and maim.

The blast had knocked down Frank Blanton's horse, sending Blanton toppling. Blanton had come up, gun in hand. Twice the pistol had belched flame in Al Callahan's direction.

But Blanton's hand was not steady. Shock and

the jarring fall had made him misjudge. Callahan had shot once. And Frank Blanton had staggered back, hit the Canyon's stone wall, and had fallen.

And Callahan spurred on, his horse leaping the fallen man. Now Callahan and buckskin were at the mouth of the canyon.

All was confusion.

Dust. Biting dust. Bawling steers, lunging steers. The ground shook. Hoofs hit the earth that hard.

Callahan used his rowels. He swung the tough buckskin west. His aim was to circle the herd. Ride down either Ann Scott. Or Roger Heywood. Or Olaf Rodin.

Then, he saw the wolves.

They had run to the west hills. Dark, killers all, they'd banded there, masterless. Callahan remembered Roger Heywood and the stolen silent-whistle. Without a master, the wolves apparently were confused, powerless?

Now a rider, bent over saddle-fork, roared across the valley, heading for the rough breaks. Callahan reined-in, buckskin cake-walking, fighting the stern port bit.

Then, Callahan recognized Roger Heywood.

Heywood lifted his hand to his mouth. Callahan realized he blew the silent wolf-whistle. Buckskin rearing in dust, Callahan saw the wolves suddenly bunch, then start in his direction.

Callahan's blood chilled. Evidently Heywood had ordered the wolves to attack him? Callahan wasted no time. He put the buckskin's front hoofs on the

185

ground. He spurred after Heywood's fleet black stallion.

The wolves wheeled, running across to intercept Callahan. Callahan bent low over saddle, six-shooter in one hand, reins in the other. From the corner of his eye he saw a rider angle in fast from the southeast.

He recognized Ann Scott.

Ann Scott, too, was heading for the breaks, the rough country. There she hoped to lose herself and horse in the badlands, Callahan knew—just as Roger Heywood also hoped to do.

Bent low over saddle-fork, Ann Scott's quirt rose and fell. Her horse ran in terrified rapidity, hoofs rising and falling.

Callahan saw Roger Heywood twist in leather and look back. Again, his hand rose to his lips.

The wolves, converging in on Callahan, suddenly paused, then, as one, swung south. They now chased Ann Scott, not Callahan.

Callahan's breath caught. Evidently Roger Heywood had blown the wrong signal?

Running low and hard, the wolf-pack sped toward the approaching Ann Scott, who saw them coming. The red-head reined in her plunging horse. Then, she turned him, and quirted him north.

A steer hooked out, caught the horse in the rump. The bronc lurched, caught his footing, then stumbled again, fell. Hundreds of mad steers converged on him.

Ann Scott screamed. She scrambled to her feet.

She began running. The herd absorbed her. The last Callahan saw of her was when a huge steer, head low, hooked her in his horns.

The steer threw her upward. She screamed again. Then, she fell among the stampeding cattle.

Callahan saw her—or her horse—no more.

Callahan's .45 spoke twice. He shot toward Roger Heywood, but the distance apparently was too far for Colt-work, for he saw Heywood twist on stirrups, shortgun belching flame three times Callahan's direction.

None of Heywood's bullets hit.

Callahan looked at the wolves. They seemed confused, lost. Their prey had disappeared under pounding bovine hoofs. They dared not run among the stampeding steers.

Callahan's buckskin was gaining on Heywood's black. Reins knotted at his mane, the buckskin ran free, Callahan cramming fresh cartridges into his pistol.

Again, Heywood raised the whistle. Callahan thought, He'll signal those wolves to run against me. Heywood's hand went down. The whistle had been blown.

But the wolves did not run Callahan's direction. Instead, they took out after Heywood. Heywood had evidently blown the wrong signal.

With great, huge leaps they jumped sagebrush and greasewood as they advanced—dark, somber, deadly. A black machine of death, the wolves sped in silence toward the fleeing Heywood.

No horse in the world could outrun them. Callahan reined in his buckskin, terror pulling his guts.

Flame ran from Heywood's pistol. Three times, he shot at the wolves, then no more.

Callahan thought, He ran out of cartridges.

The wolves caught the black stud. Long fangs tore into the running hind legs, severing the hamstrings. The black neighed in terror and then went down, throwing his rider forward to the earth.

Callahan heard Roger Heywood scream. Wolves instantly swarmed over the black stud. They roared in on Roger Heywood who had scrambled afoot and started to run.

Two wolves lunged through the moonlight. They knocked Heywood down, Callahan saw Heywood disappear beneath the rippling swarm of dark killers. Heywood's screams died.

Callahan saw Oliver throw one of Heywood's arms upward. Another big lobo ripped free one of Heywood's legs.

Callahan fired into the wolves. A big bitch rolled, biting where a bullet had landed. She died whining and kicking. The other wolves stopped their carnage. Jaws red, they stared at the bitch.

Callahan shot again. He missed.

The wolves wheeled, looked at Callahan. It was uncanny. It was unreal. Callahan stared at them. They stared at him. Then, Callahan shot again.

His bullet hit a big dog-wolf in the wide chest. The dog went down, kicking in death throes.

The wolves turned. They ran as a pack for the eastern brakes. Callahan shot again and again but the distance was too far. The wolves disappeared in a brush-filled coulee.

Callahan crammed cartridges into his hot pistol. The last of the steers were running by. They galloped slowly, slobber hanging. The stampede was over. The cattle would drift back to their home-range.

Rustling was through on Mill Iron grass.

Sheriff Ike Dunlap rode up, the tragedy of this night etched on his weather-beaten face. "I saw the wolves work," he said. "They're both dead. They have to be. God, it was terrible!"

"Blanton?"

"MacDonald went back to see. I got Rodin hogtied along yonder ridge. MacDonald shot him from leather. Looks to me like his collar-bone is busted, no more."

"I got a hunch he'll die at the end of a Texas noose," Callahan said. "Here comes Mac now."

Rodin's bullet had broken MacDonald's left wrist. He had it wrapped with his bandana, the blood already dried.

"Blanton?" Al Callahan asked.

MacDonald said, "Not much left of him, Callahan. Dead as he'll ever be." He looked at the dark forms lying on the prairie. "Terrible thing."

"But it had to be done," Sheriff Dunlap said.

The sound of the steers died. Silence held the valley. Slow wind moved yellow dust. "The wolves?" MacDonald asked Callahan.

189

"Back wild again. If *I'd* not seen it, I'd not believed it."

Sheriff Dunlap said, "We'd best get Rodin and Mac here into Mill Iron. There's no doctor there but my deputy can take over—even though Jones is the world's laziest man."

Callahan looked at the lawman. "You won't need me any more?"

"No, and I don't envy the job you got ahead, Callahan. My best goes with you, friend."

Callahan and the sheriff shook hands. Mac-Donald rode close to put his good arm around Callahan's shoulders. "That goes for me, too, Callahan."

Callahan's throat was tight. He rode around the two bloody bodies and pushed his buckskin southwest toward Circle Cross, his ten thousand secure in his money-belt.

Yes, he had a job ahead, he knew—but Maxine would understand. He was glad the blood of her brother was not on his hands. He came to Willow Springs where he took his green shirt from saddle-bag.

He shook it free of wrinkles. He put it on and buttoned it, then put his old shirt in the saddle-bag.

Only then did he head for Circle Cross.